My Ninian

Donna Brewster

GC Books Ltd
Unit10
Bladnoch Bridge Estate
Bladnoch
Wigtown
DG8 9AB

www.gcbooks.co.uk

First published by GC Books Ltd 2006

ISBN: 1872350046

MAP 1
BRITAIN AND ROME
The Journey Of Ninian

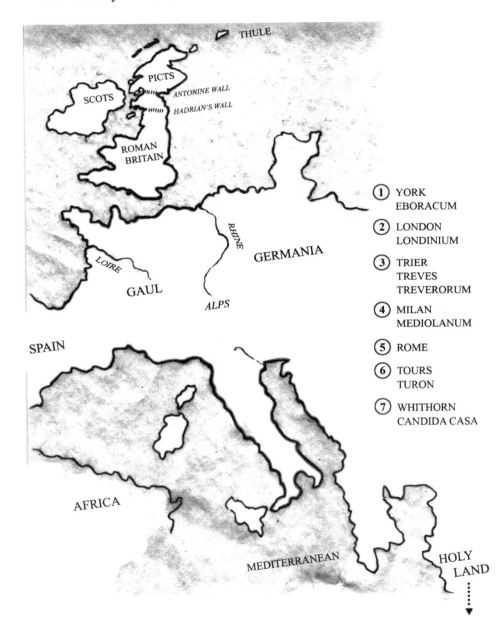

THULE

PICTS

SCOTS

ANTONINE WALL

HADRIAN'S WALL

ROMAN
BRITAIN

RHINE

GERMANIA

LOIRE

GAUL

ALPS

SPAIN

AFRICA

MEDITERRANEAN

HOLY
LAND

1. YORK
   EBORACUM

2. LONDON
   LONDINIUM

3. TRIER
   TREVES
   TREVERORUM

4. MILAN
   MEDIOLANUM

5. ROME

6. TOURS
   TURON

7. WHITHORN
   CANDIDA CASA

CONTENTS

FOURTH PART: TO THE ENDS OF THE EARTH.

FIFTH PART: GOOD AND FAITHFUL SERVANTS

MAP 2: NORTH BRITAIN - The Mission of Ninian

Author's Preface

The earliest surviving accounts of Scotland's first famous saint, Saint Ninian, date from the eighth century in the forms of a brief mention of him in the Venerable Bede's history of Britain and a poem about miracles associated with Ninian's work composed by Alcuin, a monk at Whithorn. A longer biography of Ninian's life is attributed to the twelfth century monk, Ailred of Rievaulx, who speaks of the existence of an earlier writing in another language, one that did not survive.

The universally accepted traditional understanding of a thousand years and more, that Ninian was born in the 4th century and that his work of mission through Scotland was accomplished during the first third of the fifth century, is easily entirely compatible with the brief reference to him in Bede's work, with the details in Alcuin's poem, and with Ailred's prose work. Until recently, it was always believed that Ninian lived from about 360 A.D. to about 431 A.D.

Modern scholarship now challenges this time-honoured tradition and much more. Because nothing speaking of Ninian that is contemporary with his time appears to have survived physically to substantiate the truths of the stories, either in written form or in the analysis of archaeological work, it is now contended that we cannot speak with confidence of very much about Saint Ninian at all.

Minimalists have stripped Ninian of almost all that was written about him, not only discarding the traditional time frame for his life but going on to dispute many of the previously accepted details of his life and work, even questioning his name. They declare that it is only safe to say that there was 'someone' who did 'something,' and that, whoever he was, he left 'a place' that commemorates him at Whithorn. Everything else is debatable, if not downright dismissable. They call him, "Shadowy Saint Ninian," if they dare to name him at all.

What is the story of Ninian that people of earlier generations understood to be true, based on the works of the earliest biographers combined with oral traditions? (Added to this question, how was this information interpreted by those who believed them?)

The biographers described a Romano-British prince, son of a king (or a chieftain), who was baptised as an infant and notably pious from the time of his childhood. They claim that he forsook his home and people to seek a theological education in Rome. He was guided in his studies by a Bishop or Bishops of Rome. (Some have named the Bishops of Rome as Damasus and Siricius, and in connection with Damasus have placed Ninian under the tutelage of Jerome himself. It has even been suggested that Ninian might have studied with the translator of the Vulgate version of the Bible in Bethlehem.) Consecrated as missionary bishop to his own land and people by another Bishop of Rome, Ninian was believed to have travelled back homeward through France where he was inspired by the devotion and working style of the famed Martin of Tours.

After a description of the public welcome he received upon his return to his land, it is said that he set about the task of correcting the doctrines of the church among his own people. When he had completed this to his satisfaction, he selected a site to begin a new work. He chose Whithorn in Galloway for a new establishment and, with the help of skilled masons he had brought with him from St. Martin's foundation, he built a stone church there in the style of Roman churches. Just at this time, it was said, he learned of the death of his mentor, and dedicated his church in honour of him. He encountered opposition as he worked in this area from local King Tudvallus, but that king, having been healed of a sudden painful blindness by the prayers of a forgiving Ninian, became a true supporter of his work.

Not content to have won much of the former Roman-occupied land of his nation to Christianity and established a solid work of ministry there, Ninian was challenged with the hope that the Picts, (the long-time despoilers of his peoples' peace at least temporarily driven back into their northern haunts by the efforts of Stillicho,) could also know the blessings of the faith. He set out, with a number of his own disciples, on a missionary journey (through the whole of the northern mainland and to the islands beyond it.) This journey resulted in many conversions to Christianity. Ninian baptised new believers and established churches in districts among them. He then returned to his Candida Casa with more students who could be trained to minister among their own peoples.   He is said to have died at Whithorn (on the 16th September, 431/2), much lamented.

'My Ninian' has been created by using the framework found within the fuller, somewhat poetical and rather heavily theologically phrased, accounts of Ninian's life that are now so widely dismissed. I have chosen to work on the assumption that those who wrote these biographical stories were not necessarily enlarging on core truths, or spinning tales with calculated political, doctrinal or personal motives. In our modern times, truth-telling seems to have gone so completely out of fashion that educated people expect lies and spin to have come from everyone, everywhere, in all ages. It has ceased to be considered as a possibility that historians of any age worked under a compulsion to write in as truthful a manner as they could understand, merely stating things they honestly believed to be fact as accurately, and yet as beautifully, as they felt the story deserved and their readers would expect.

I have taken all the phrases in the stories of the old lives of Ninian and, one by one, explored what 'could have been' if Ninian's biographers were truth tellers. It has been as easy a task for me as it could be for anyone to picture Ninian in this way. I live near Ninian's Candida Casa, and know his area well. I have travelled in 'the steps of Ninian' in this country, visiting sites marking his name from the north of England along the area south of the Antonine Wall, northwards and eastwards through the land mass of Scotland right to the Orkney and Shetland Isles. I have travelled, too, to Rome, overland via Trier and Milan, returning via Poitiers and Tours.

More often than not, fame is a very temporary fancy. Many well-known celebrities from all walks of life are forgotten before the time of their own deaths. The name of Ninian still lives, in many places, in many ways, after sixteen hundred years of history. I dare to believe that the 'could have been' of my admittedly fictional writing reflects to a considerable degree what really happened during his lifetime. I hope that this book does some justice to the memory of an obviously very great man. Scotland's Ninian changed the course of the nation that found its name long after it had first been won by the shining light of his life.

Donna Brewster
Wigtown 2006

The Story

Ninian has died.

The fame of this man had filled the kingdoms of the whole island to the very edges, drawing me to come to his Candida Casa to see him for myself. But I was too late. After a long, long journey, just as I finally approached the community of Whithorn, I heard the sounds of sorrowing and then I saw that all the people, everywhere, were weeping. I did not have to ask what had happened. No death but that of Ninian himself could have created this moment in this place.

There was something in their grief that sounded like bewilderment. When an old man who has been suffering for a long time dies, there is an acceptance in the eyes of those who have loved him, an understanding of the fact that death has come as a kindness. The people of this place, I thought, cannot be surprised that he has died, for Ninian was an old man, and even I, a stranger from a great distance, had heard that he was very ill. It isn't that he has died, I thought; it is that they must live without him. The central pillar of their existence was this one man. In his light was the certainty of their faith. They had pride in the fame he brought to their land. His presence even lent them courage to live without fear in our deeply troubled world. They had not imagined their future, any state of being, without him.

A funeral service was arranged quickly. The whitewashed stone church was as tightly packed as it could be, and people crowded the aisles, the doors, and the windows. They pressed against the outsides of the little building, filled the paths leading to it, thronged the enclosure around it, and still further, masses of them were standing in the village, between the homes of the people, spilling right out into the surrounding fields.

There was no end of it, because the crowd only grew as the hours went on. I was amazed at the sight! People could be seen rushing toward Whithorn across any open space in any direction I looked. Some said that people would come by land and sea. It would not matter that they arrived too late to be here for the laying to rest of Bishop Ninian. They would come anyway, and keep coming.

They must touch the place where his body was laid, press their faces to the stone, touch the marker with their hands, weep their tears. Here they would meet others who loved him, and together sing songs of thankful praise for his life. Those who came from greater distances were eager to tell the stories of Ninian's mission in their own home places, to witness to anyone who would listen about the effect of his life upon their lives. No one would be impatient with them if they spoke too many words, for all were full of such words.

It was apparent that Ninian was greatly, greatly loved. Love for him was in the very air. I wished with all my heart that I had come sooner. How could I not earlier have realised the importance of seeing this man, such a man, with my own eyes? I was sickened by my own stupidity, my tardiness, my failure, my loss.

I could only observe, as a complete outsider, what was happening around me. I felt that I was the only person in the world who had not known Ninian. Full of curiosity, I watched the mourners who had come immediately, and then the ones who still continued to come in increasing numbers from greater and greater distances.

There was great variety amongst the people. There were men and women, old and young, kings and paupers, rich and poor, Romans, Britons, Picts, and even Scots from Hibernia across the sea.

People naturally gravitated into groups according to their languages, but sometimes I found individuals speaking words across the linguistic barriers through the aid of willing interpreters. A Roman and a Pict exchanged their memories with the help of a multi-lingual priest. Scots and Picts, though both of Celtic tribes, could not understand each other; but there were some Britons who could provide a bridge of understanding between their tongues. In remembering Ninian, their common friend, there was no tribal enmity. Love for him and the need to remember, at least during the gentle mood of this mass mourning, fused different peoples into one family.

There was one woman, an older woman, who stood out from the rest.

She was almost always alone, but crowds parted for her, and voices quietened when she walked past. She was simply dressed, very plainly, with no indication of wealth or noble distinction about her. She did not appear in the company of any group, or seem to belong as wife or mother to anyone present.

Eventually I learned that she was Medana, a woman born in the lands just south of the wall of Hadrian, the closest and oldest friend of the Bishop. She had known him from her childhood, and had served his work all through her adult life. She had never married. I could not help but be curious about this solitary woman who had known so very well, and for so long, the man whose fame had drawn me to this place, the man who had died as I approached his home.

I decided that I must stay in Whithorn. I made myself useful to those who served the visitors and did all that I could to be accepted by the community of Candida Casa. I waited on until all the visiting mourners returned to their homes, until the landscape cleared of tents and roughly made shelters, until the street of the village was quiet again, until the monks returned to their routines of communal service, of solitary prayers, of teaching, of writing in their scriptorium, and of the tending of their gardens. Gradually, I learned to understand the workings of the place. I spent much time at the grave of the great Ninian, pondering, praying.

Medana lived in a simple community with several other women a little distance to the west of Whithorn. Without Bishop Ninian, the monks of Candida Casa turned increasingly to her, his closest surviving friend, as their senior advisor. She spent much time in council with them, and in prayer. She grew accustomed to my presence and began to speak quiet greetings whenever she passed me.

After some months a simple thought came to me, and it grew until it filled my heart and mind. I began to understand what I should do, the purpose for which I had been drawn to Whithorn. I prayed, and I prayed. I fasted. I struggled with the sense of urgent responsibility, and with the embarrassing realisation that I would have to make my plea for help to Medana, upon whom I would depend. There was in me a great fear of being rejected, for there could be nothing accomplished without her willing complicity.

When at last I approached her with my request, she sat listening, as still as a slender tree would stand on a day with no breath of wind, not a leaf quivering. She looked past me, beyond to some distant horizon, and I scarcely dared to breathe until she answered me.

"Of course you are right," she said calmly. "His story must be written down. I am the only one to tell it. You speak the simple truth. How kind of God to send you. I will tell you everything. All must know of the man who took Christ's message to the ends of the earth."

We talked together, day after day, as seasons came and went. Sometimes she spoke with the force of a stream in spate for long hours, and sometimes the words came haltingly, for only a little while. She told me the story of Ninian from an early beginning, from his youth, and on through the years to the last day of his life. I listened; how I listened. I listened because the story was truly wonderful; I listened also because I found that I was deeply moved by the tale, for Medana's love for the great man she called, "My Ninian" worked its way into my heart.

I am not a scholar; I am a simple travelling man who has learned to read and to write in a basic way for the purposes of doing my business. I am not a man ordained to teach the faith or administer the sacraments; I am a simple Christian, loving God, His Christ,and the Word that instructs me. I am not a saint; I am an ordinary sinner who asks God for His mercy and seeks to do His will as I understand it.

To listen faithfully to this story and to write it down as best I can is a great privilege, too great for someone like me, as many undoubtedly will say. This is the most important thing I have ever done, or ever will do. I am writing down the story of Ninian so that he will not be forgotten in the days of my grandchildren. It is the story is of a man who loved God, a man who proclaimed His glory until he reached the place where the world's peopled lands ended in the waters of an endless sea. This is the story as it was told to me by his closest friend. I, myself, arrived in Whithorn too late to meet him.

First Part: Leaving All

ONE: Rome in Britain
"...But when the fullness of the time was come,
God sent forth his Son......"
Galatians 4:4

Medana would come to a place beside the shore, to a curious large rock for a thousand years shaped by winds and rains into a natural seat. On clear days, and then only faintly, distant mountains would rise to horizon the eastern reach of the Solway's silver waters. These were the mountains of Medana's childhood homeland. Her hands folded in her lap, her eyes resting on the sea and the land outlined beyond it, she would sit in silence for a time. Perhaps she was praying; or maybe she was summoning memories from deep within her. Then she would speak to me.

Before she spoke of Ninian, she recited the tale of the coming of Rome to our country, long, long ago. Much of what she said was very familiar to me. During the years of my youth, the storytellers among my own people had repeated the same chronicle to all of us, the very same, over and over, until they were satisfied that we had all learned it.

~~~~~~~~~~

Almost eight hundred years after the founding of the city of Rome, after the city had grown into the greatest empire the world had ever known, our forefathers among the ancient Britons learned that the dreaded, all-conquering Roman forces were approaching the shores of our own island. Rome had determined to own Britain as she had possessed all other nations thus far.

The leaders among our people gathered to plan what defences they might make. They met in terror, admitting that they had no illusions about the inevitability of their defeat. No matter how much they schemed, or how desperately they might fight against the approaching invasion, they knew that they would be crushed one day. The power that was Rome devoured lands in the same way that fabled mountainous waves from the sea devoured fabled civilisations swiftly, mercilessly, and completely. The gods of Rome, as the gods of the sea, had an omnipotence about them, a force that could not be resisted.

Even so, from the southern to the northernmost parts of the island, British tribes returned from conference to prepare, at the very most, for an impeding resistance to the invasion. Some fused stone with fire into defensive towers; others secured themselves, as best they could, into defensible mid-lake dwellings; some abandoned vulnerable settlements and hid in caves. Spikes were buried to maim and kill advancing soldiers. All Britons, everywhere, gathered weapons, tempered and honed them, practised their use with grim determination.

When the conquerors first landed on Britannia's southern shores, tribes from the northern lands swarmed southwards to aid their cousins. The gathered fighting forces furiously defended the island as one. Sometimes they won; sometimes they were beaten back. For some years there were tides of advance by Rome and waves of counterattacks by the Britons. Even a British woman had held back the Empire's advance for a time. Her husband slain and her family cruelly abused by the Romans, she had risen to lead a rebellion against them herself.

Eventually Rome pushed right through the island to the far north. In this wild land, one of mountain and moorland, our most remote tribes valiantly resisted the invasion. It was there that the Romans decided that they had reached a limit. It was not that the land could not have been conquered and held, if they had wished to conquer and hold it, but they decided that the savage terrain and weather there, as fierce in character as the native inhabitants themselves, made it not worth their efforts. They concluded that no civilised society could thrive in such a world, so they withdrew to define their northern boundary further south, where land was more productive, where the climate was softer, and where the tribes seemed more manageable.

long-awaited Jewish Messiah and the widely anticipated Gentile Christ.

Those who followed him, Jews and Gentiles alike, blended themselves together into one faith and began to overturn the world. They claimed that there was, indeed, only one God, the Creator, and that God had visited the world so that all men and women everywhere could be reconciled to Him. Even more astonishing, they claimed that God, Himself, all-knowing, had allowed, even intended, that the death of His own Son would take place in order to effect this reconciliation.

This was a beautiful and powerful story. Henceforth, it was to be declared throughout the whole world, to all its peoples, that rocks, mountains, waters and winds, all of which were made by God, deserved no worship. Idols, made by men's own hands, were owed no adoration. Only God who was the Father of Yeshua the Jew, Jesus the Christ, was to be acknowledged and obeyed and His Son was to be adored and confessed by all mankind.

The new belief had burst upon the world like a new sun, blazing into the lives of the people of the Mediterranean with a light so bright that it penetrated even into far-off Britain. It spread as quickly as the storytellers could speed the message along the roads that Rome had made, right to the edges of the vast Roman Empire, even beyond its edges.

Believing and confessing this new faith were relatively simple accomplishments, but living it out was another matter. All that had been the natural, lauded pursuits of human endeavour, and material to the development of a newly-civilised world, the quests for pride, power, strength, wealth, learning, dignity and authority, were to be counted as nothing. Instead, the marks of being a follower of Christ must be truth, goodness, love for God, and even tender love toward one's enemies and other most unworthy examples of humanity. Further, even more impossibly, those seeking to attain these seemingly impossible standards, were to be characterised by an attitude of repentance toward God and humility toward all mankind. Men and women were to be equal. Slaves were to be regarded as brothers of their masters. No nation or tribe was to be preferred before another. This was the greatest challenge to face humanity, for it would cut across all that was most naturally human.

The Christian claims challenged minds and won hearts everywhere, but they were not universally accepted by any means. They unsettled the occupiers of positions of authority at every level within every kind of man-made institution. They deeply disturbed those who possessed power, and enjoyed wielding it over others. They pained those who lived lavishly and loved such living, those who had absolutely no intention of selling what they had so that they could share their wealth with the poor. Equally, the commands of Christ challenged people who suffered under cruel domination, writhed under unjust authority, or craved to have what others possessed. It was not always deemed desirable to relinquish the right to bear resentment, to forsake a pursuit of justice with vengeance, or to cease to covet what was covetable. Those who submitted to Christ found peace, and exhibited a new power within their lives; those who defied Him grew more and more agitated as the disturbing faith grew disconcertingly powerful.

Inevitably, the followers of Jesus the Christ began to suffer, just as their Master had been made to suffer, at the hands of those who feared that these teachings would imperil order. Rome led the way in devising mass execution programmes, and was inventive of terrible cruelties for the purpose. For nearly three hundred years after the death and resurrection of the Son of God in Judaea, the same three hundred years that Rome occupied our Britain, Christians were persecuted on, and off, and on again.

The faith did not die with the martyrs to it. The strange beauty of their lives, the steadfastness of their faith, the shining face of their glorious hopes that did not fade even while their blood was being spilt or their bodies were being burned, caused more to believe in their message. Christians were to be found everywhere. Sometimes secretly, sometimes openly, depending on the times and the places they inhabited, they gathered together in new, strangely assorted families of faith, comprised of governors, wives, soldiers, slaves, young women, old men, even children. The belief kept spreading. One British king named Lucius became a Christian. He travelled to the continent to seek baptism into the faith of the Christians, by proxy, for his entire kingdom.

In Britain, as in all the Empire and beyond its bounds where Christians were increasing in number, there were waves of persecutions. Here, too, the singing, peaceful acceptance of cruelty against them won the hearts of others who began to believe and filled the empty places of those who had died. Christians met together in churches they formed within devoted rooms in private homes or within public buildings.

One unforgettable day in Britain, Constantine was given the Emperor's title, a Romano Briton becoming the most important and powerful man in the world. The heart of this nation on the empire's edge swelled with pride. More astonishing and more wonderful was the news, when it came, that Constantine had declared himself to be a Christian. There would no longer be persecution of believers within the whole of the Roman Empire. Blessed Constantine! Thus he was named by overjoyed believers. Then there was more joy, to the point of delirium! The Empire itself was officially Christian. Surely, finally, the kingdoms of the world had become the Kingdom of God.

Not so, not yet. After his reign, Constantine was succeeded for a time by his co-reigning successor sons. Then, his nephew Julian succeeded to the Empire's throne. Julian apostatised from our faith, overturned the declaration of the late blessed ruler, and worked to re-establish pagan idolatry, outlawing Christianity — yet again. Our people were grateful to God that Julian's day ended quickly. His reign was over not long after it had begun, and Christians rejoiced in a freedom restored to them, for good and all. During his brief reign, pagan influences had returned to some measure of favour in Britain. The shrines and ceremonies had been renewed and, this time, they were not entirely relinquished. Britain was Christian again in name and rule, but not in reality in all places, amongst all our peoples.

~~~~~~~~~~

How strange it seemed that at this very time the empire itself should suddenly become endangered by outside forces. The power of Rome was the greatest that earth had ever experienced, reaching and holding control almost to the very edges of known civilisations. During the years since she had arrived at the zenith of her power, Rome had transformed the very spirit of all the nations held captive within her frame. They had become one under her influence. They walked on her roads, sailed on her seas, lived in houses of her designing, wallowed in her indulgences, dressed in her clothes, ate her food, drank her wine, and spoke to each other across their earlier national boundaries of language in her tongue. They even named themselves Latin names. Latin was learned from infancy, alongside the mother tongues of the land. Always there would be Rome. Rome, eternal Rome, could never die. Britain, long now Roman Britain, would always operate within her rule. So it had been believed.

The scene, though, was changing. Incursions by dangerous warlike tribes from the area lying to the east of the Rhenus River caused Rome to withdraw troops from the more secure island of Britain, reassigning them to the defence of stations in the more volatile Gaulish region. Rome's watchful eye being more occupied elsewhere, Britain was increasingly left to govern her own affairs.

The Britons did possess kings and queens of their own. Long before the coming of Rome, each tribe had owned its own rulers. Sometimes the tribal groups had joined in loose federations, one king over several lesser chieftains; others had kept themselves to themselves, within smaller, more separate identities under the sovereignty of their own kings. Rome had claimed sovereignty over all these lesser native rulers, whether of large, combined federations, or of smaller independent tribes. Those who had bowed their knees before the Empire's rule often willingly and ably served Rome's interests as client kings.

So very many generations had passed that there was no one left living who could remember the time when British royals did not bow before Rome. The pre-Roman period kings of Britain seemed more to our people like fabled beings than real men, but their descendants were still known, and the blood of these descendants was still considered as blue by the Britons. As the grip of Rome on Britain relaxed, when the troops withdrew to the guarding of Gaul, we began to rely more heavily again upon these people to take command once again. Robes, crowns, and titles of greater authority were gradually reassumed by them, with the nod of Rome, the delight of their own people, and in a renewed sense of destiny.

Among these ancient British royal families, marriages were contracted increasingly with a view to more powerful dynasty. Such marriages sealed federations between neighbouring tribes, consolidated their power, amassed lands in a strategic way. Daughters of kings brought wealth and territories to the sons of other kings. Their children were the foundation of powerful, newly merged royal lines.

The most influential of all the British kings was Eudaf, the elderly, famed, long-time over-king of the Britons whose base lay in the south and west of the island. Eudaf had served the purposes of Rome intermittently for decades, and cunning purposes of his own, when not of Rome's. Since he possessed only a single daughter, Elen, to inherit his title, it had been decided long before, that his heir must be his nephew Conan. A beautiful daughter could not be called on to lead the nation at such a time. The tribes that honoured Eudaf as high king had concurred with this declared intention, and Conan waited patiently to don purple robes upon the death of his uncle.

Eudaf, though, lived on and on, keeping his nephew waiting. An intriguing idea was born in the mind of his chief counsellor. If the beautiful Elen were joined in marriage to a powerful man who might not only command in Britain, but might also lay claim by some right to become the Roman Emperor one day, the most royal bloodline of Britain would merge with that of Rome. It was a certainty that any children born of such a union would eventually rule Britain unchallenged. The additional tantalising possibility that such progeny might also become a Roman Emperor, as Britain's Constantine had become Emperor, was not to be overlooked. Rome would never ignore or neglect Britain, if Britain were the homeland of her Emperor.

The plan was brought to fruition, and it would become legendary in its brilliance. Elen married the widowed Hispanic Roman Magnus Clemens Maximus, an experienced and acclaimed soldier who had campaigned for the empire from Africa to Britain alongside his famed contemporary and friend the Hispanic General Theodosius. A naturally charismatic leader, he was rumoured not to be Hispanic at all, but a mysterious claimant of descent from Constantine the Great, even of the gens Julia. The marriage was much more than a cold, dynastic union. Elen and Macsen loved deeply, honoured each other, and produced a family of sons and daughters. Britain rejoiced.

Conan alone was displeased. The ambitious nephew of old King Eudaf and cousin of Elen had been humiliated by his deposition as heir. Anger settled into an avowed determination to be revenged. He would wrench by force that which had long been promised to him. He, himself, was allied in marriage to the princess of the most distantly northern and western part of Roman Britain, the kingdom of the Cluith. In that far northern kingdom he began to work intrigues against Elen and her Roman husband with the neighbouring unromanised cousins of the British beyond the Antonine wall, those long since despised as being beyond the bounds of world civilisation. The barbarian former enemies were carefully courted by the bitter Conan.

More than a thousand years after the founding of Rome, exactly three hundred years after a British woman had raised her people against Rome's rule in Britain, the Picts from immediately beyond the Empire's northern edge and the fierce Scotti people from the Hibernian island to the west, joined together to do battle against Rome's Britain. These two peoples were from time to time natural enemies but, in other times, they made alliance in marriage, or in war. Aided, abetted, and encouraged by Conan, they joined together to lay waste the Empire's northern region, the area between the Antonine and Hadrianic walls. Roman troops were sent from Gaul to restore order. The peace they imposed did not last, for

Conan would not desist from his mischief making. Raids continued sporadically, each one quashed as it flared up, like the stamping out of tiny blazes around the edges of an advancing forest fire. A sense of uneasiness grew in the hearts of our people. Disorder developed everywhere, the disaffected of the whole land daring to initiate rebellions. There was an increasingly general breakdown in authority. The inhabitants of cities and the countryside villas of Britain were filled with a kind of fear unknown for a long time.

Less than a decade later, those same two nations joined with others, even more foreign than they were to each other, in a carefully calculated conspiracy, directed from afar again by Conan himself, an invasion that devastated understandings as much as the landscape. The combined force of Picts, Scotti, Atacotti, and even Angles from across the eastern sea, managed to storm over both northern Roman walls, pour in around the eastern and western coasts, and plummet like a waterfall over a cliff right down into the heart of Roman Britain. The attack was a terrible success. Rome's two chief military leaders on the island were ambushed, slain.

When news of the great invasion in Britain reached Rome, the efficient Spaniard Theodosius was sent to deliver our island. His coming relieved the besieged islanders who had been paralysed by the unexpected onslaught, cut off from each other and unable to respond. Theodosius and his four troops of professionals, together with Elen's husband and the reunited British armies swept the audacious savages back from all that they had captured within the Empire's boundaries, pounding and crushing those who had dared to challenge her authority.

The Hispanic General Theodosius returned to the continent where he had been summoned to fight more battles for the Empire, and it was then that Rome began to warn our people that they must cease depending on her might, must learn to defend themselves. Pax Romana was becoming a distant memory in the playing out of the final scene in long-running drama. It was nearly three hundred years since we Britons had ever needed to defend ourselves, had ever been allowed to defend ourselves, and our fathers were shaken by the reality that we had forgotten how to fight.

To a watcher on a shore, the tide may seem to come in very slowly. The waters rise, creeping forward, lap by lap, until they reach a furthest point, as high on a strand as they will go. The waters hold that mark, never passing it. For a while, they play there, toying with the sand, darkening pebbles, retreating in ebbings, lapping forward again, touching just that line, but moving no further. Suddenly, there comes an awareness that the rippling motion of the water is not touching the furthest edge any more, not at all. The waters do not cover the same ground, then less ground, and even less again, until the observer realises that the tide has truly turned. It has long since finished its advance; it is no longer holding its mark; it is retreating.

A long time before the personal memory of any living Briton, the Roman Empire had marked her farthest northern and western boundary on the earth with a doubled wall enclosing a part of northern Britain. The furthest reach, the outer wall, built in the time of the Antonine rule, had not always been securely held, and there had been periods when even the larger inner wall, the wall of Hadrian, had itself not been unchallenged. Until this time, though, Rome had, for fully two hundred years, always succeeded eventually in holding the ground defined by these walls as her northern limit. Rome might have reached her high tide line here, since the Empire had never permanently occupied the wilder territories lying further to the north of the area, but it had previously seemed inconceivable that the Empire would ever really abandon this particularly defined area. Yet, as tides do, even the Roman tide was turning, slowly. In stages it was retreating southwards and no guarantees were being given for the future.

This vulnerable boundary area lying between the walls of Antonius and Hadrian, an area before considered to be an integral part of the Empire, was now, in an increasingly troubled time, designated as a mere shield for the rest of the land. Client kings were empowered to represent Rome's authority there. They were charged with the responsibility, themselves, of holding their land; they were celebrated for doing so. They occupied what was acknowledged to be a dangerous situation, bearing the brunt of any attacks from the north. Their resistance on behalf of Rome would weaken any blows that might be intended to fall upon the Empire further south. This most northern area was newly named Valentia, for the Emperor Valentian. Magnus Clemens Maximus, anchored in his power base on the western side of the country, allied himself with the rising star Coel, king of the recently devastated British kingdoms on the eastern side of the land, and together these two formed the united kingdoms of Britain lying beneath, and guarded in some measure by, the willing protection of the client state of Valentia.

In fact, the Roman Empire had begun to die. Not, by any means, was she in the final throes of her death, but she had been discovered to be entirely mortal and all were aware that an end was possible — more than possible; it was coming. This was as certain as the certainty that death will come to even the greatest of men.

Britain would become British again, not Roman, but truly British. Not for hundreds of years had this been dreamt of. With the new situation came aspirations and ambitions never imagined for generations. Slowly, and in spite of the pressing reality of fearful times, our long-subdued British people began to lift their heads, to take pride in the voice of their own language again, to hear music of a national anthem.

~~~~~~~~~~~

"In the year when the barbarians began to invade," said Medana softly, "Ninian was born to a king of the Britons. The time was near to the year of one thousand, one hundred and ten years after the founding of Rome and past three hundred and sixty years after the birth of our Lord Jesus Christ."

TWO: A Prince Among Them
"Ninian's father was a king, a Christian by religion..."
"Vita Niniani" by Ailred of Rievaulx ,
trans. by Winifred MacQueen

She had learned of his early life from Ninian's own family. The stories of him were as familiar in their speech as the hills in the background of their lives, the windings of the river beside them, part of the very fabric of their lives. There were no mysteries about his beginnings.

~~~~~~~~~~

The Prince Ninian's first hungry cries mingled with the anxious voices of a threatened people; he toddled into walking during a time of terrorising raids and he was learning his letters during the period when the men of Britain were finally forced to engage in warfare, themselves and not Romans in defence of themselves, to ensure their own survival. Pride was born anew in them as they did so.

Ninian's father, among them, knew well that dangers were not completely, forever, eradicated by the seemingly successful actions. The possibility of the enemy returning another day remained, lurking within an unknown future. In the face of such harsh reality, there was gratitude to God for a present restored peace, at the very least, a peace that might in His providence endure long enough to allow new-born children to grow in safety.

The devoutly Christian royal father of Ninian chose to baptise his child in infancy, a choice that was not universal in practice in that time. Many people, kings and theologians among them, believed that it was better to wait until the wild surges of adolescence had passed, until a son or a daughter was of understanding and seemed set on a true course in life, perhaps even entering a settled middle age, before such a sacrament should be administered. By being baptised in later years, a Christian would perhaps sin fewer sins, requiring lesser need for repentances and harsh dealings with priests. In the minds of a few, it was yet better to risk leaving the matter until the very death bed. Then a person could die without a fear of post-baptismal sinning blotting his record at the gates of eternity. Tiny Ninian was dedicated by his father at the beginning of his life, perhaps because of the more terrible fear that barbarians would return to rob a precious son of any future at all, any opportunity to know the baptism before death. In his tiny white gown, the baby prince was proclaimed Christ's, body and soul.

Though Ninian could not have remembered his very young baptism, he behaved from the start as if he had. He proved to be a rather solemn child, with a hunger for learning and a tenderness of conscience marking him out as not quite normal. He loved to be in the church and he loved everything about the services there, the sweet mystery of the eucharist, the familiarity of liturgies, the intoned prayers, the psalms, the readings, even the exhortations. His soul fed on every Christian element offered to him.

While a priest might have regarded such a child as nothing less than a gift from heaven, Ninian's own people, even his devout father, came to regard him as distinctly odd. Boys should long to be running freely. They should disobey naturally. They should love to wrestle. They should be desperate to win. They should shoot bows, take pride in beautifully feathered arrows and what they shot with them, should crash about playing with swords, even to their own danger; they should shout often, eat vast quantities of food very noisily, and they most certainly should fidget throughout the services of the church.

Especially the son of a king, a young prince in this new world, should be driven by something deep inside him to strive until he could win, at anything! It was necessary that the nation produce leaders for the future. Imperiousness would be tolerated, even encouraged in a prince, while any meekness in his character would be regarded as a defect to be bullied out of him. Ambition was not only a prerogative for a prince; it was the responsibility to which he was born, for the sake of the prosperity of his tribe. Ninian's brothers were just such sons; he was not.

His character was entirely too meek, too deferential, to mark him out as a true prince. Respectful to parents, obliging to anyone in the community who approached him, he even seemed ridiculously courteous in his encounters with women, slaves and foreigners.

Put through his paces against his peers, the youth Ninian could run fast enough and shoot straight enough, but he annoyed those charged with his instruction in such practical skills by his disinterest in winning. He was appalled, whenever forced to practice his swordplay, if he thought he had wounded his set opponent.

He glowed, though, when he could be at his lessons, reading, writing, and questioning. He loved language, words, spoken or written. In matters of learning, he exceeded everyone around him. The only times he showed evidence of mettle was when he found some want in the progress or quality of his education. For that, he had no patience, no patience at all. Sometimes teachers whose logic proved faulty or whose grammar was incorrect were subjected to the sharpness of his tongue. He may have loathed the idea of wounding someone with a sword, or even of dirtying a friend by forcing him into the mud during a wrestling match, but he cared nothing at all about sparing the feelings of an ineffectual tutor. The burning red face of an embarrassed teacher caused the young prince not a moment of regret. His only concern was for accuracy in every detail. He assumed that all regarded effective education as more important than any individual's pride, just as he did.

When he mastered Latin letters well enough, he haunted the local priests and any learned visitors to his home for scraps of writing they carried, so that he might read. He particularly loved to borrow any portions of Scripture that people possessed. He would seek permission to copy these, whenever he could. He was teased about his 'library', something that no other child of his age would have been concerned to possess.

As he grew older, he discovered that his various copies of portions of some of the same Scriptures were not identical, and he was disturbed by his observation. Sometimes words varied slightly; in other instances, he found identical passages, but appearing in a different order. Most alarmingly, there was variation in quotations of the words of Jesus Himself in the different copies of the gospel of John he had gathered. Which was true? What had the Christ really said? Never able to tolerate error or falsehood in matters of learning, or of daily living, this was not a situation he could accept. It was utterly important to him that the beliefs on which his faith were based, out of which the behaviour of his life was formed, were true ones.

No one he encountered could answer these questions or explain the differences, and in fact most were embarrassed that he made such enquiries. They had not themselves gathered as much material as the young man had, and thus had never had the luxury of comparison. They had merely accepted their own precious scraps of Scripture to be the correct ones. He was desperate for answers, and answers were nowhere to be found.

Given the freedom to choose, he would spend his days and nights in prayer and worship, in copying and studying, in seeking truth, forevermore. However, a British prince, one born to be a king with a kingdom of his own, could not choose such a future. His birth rank and the political realities of the time dictated a different kind of future for him. A long-suppressed nation was rising again and it required competent leaders from among its native rulers.

~~~~~~~~~~

The northern Picts and Scotti from across the Hibernian Sea came again, raiding deeply into the lands south of Hadrian's Wall. Husband of high king Eudaf's heir Elena and father of her children, the Roman from Hispania, now known among the Britons as Macsen, would lead the tribes of the Britons against those who endangered them. During the previous invasion, he had ridden with his friend Theodosius against this enemy. In the changing times he would not be leading the Romans for Britons, but leading Britons, themselves, to defend their own land. With western-based King Macsen rode his own eager sons, the princes, and the youthful King Coel of the eastern Brigantes. Other British kings, with their sons, and the men of their various tribes rode together with the alliance of Macsen and Coel. With the fledgling warrior Britons rode experienced Romans who remained stationed, in lesser numbers, on the threatened island.

Like a summer storm gathering and rolling to cover the sky, increasing in number as they approached the broken wall of Hadrian, their sound was the approach of thunder. Ninian was there with his brothers, in the vanguard. The prince who would rather be reading and praying was riding, carrying his sword, in the midst of all his peers.

The Pictish and Scotti forces retreated before the advance of the army of Britons. Both groups moved northward beyond the wall, and then westward along the Solway's shore toward the place where its waters merged with the sea of the Hibernians. Centuries before, Agricola and other Roman conquerors had forged roadways some distance into this northern and western land, a fabled wilderness area termed by those who feared it as the 'otherworld', a kind of abode of spirits, not a suitable home for living men. In fact, among the sheltered glens and fertile river valleys of the area, there were many scattered settlements. Tribes of Britons occupied lands nearest the old Roman roads and a small separate but powerful group of Britons also held the furthest extremity of this land, a double-horned peninsula that looked across the stretch of water to the island from which the Scotti invaders had sailed. There were other settled pockets of people who seemed akin to the Picts more than to the British, and there were, here and there, small groups descended from the druids who had been banned from the rest of the Empire, further south, centuries before. None of these peoples joined in the flight of the northern Picts and western Scotti, or in the pursuit of them by the combined British forces. They merely observed, uneasily, as armed men passed in mighty waves of movement along the roads near their homes, some fleeing, others pursuing.

Eventually the British reached a place where the narrowing road plunged down a rocky hillside with views over the last broad, rolling sweep of grass and moorland that reached as far to the west as the land would go. Below that hill, in a beautiful sheltered valley enfolding the curves of the river called Icena, the Britons found and fell upon the retreating spoilers of their land in a screaming battle. Clubs, knives, and swords bashed, stabbed and sliced in a bloody confusion that looked, sounded and tasted like hell.

A drafted soldier prince, one who had not wanted to fight anyone, who was grieved to the depths of his soul at the very idea of causing anyone harm, found that his sword would kill as easily as anyone's. Nature's instinct for self-defence, and Christian instinct to protect an endangered brother were more powerful forces than Ninian had known they could be.

The roaring, clashing, clanging, pounding and smashing seemed to last forever but in reality occupied only a few minutes of time. When it was over, when rage born of fear subsided, a wave of revulsion filled the space it emptied. Ninian looked madly about him to see who had lived through the carnage. He saw that the kings had survived, that his brothers were still in the saddle. Anwn was rushing to confer with Coel. Peibio, a younger brother, was sitting off to the side of the battleground, staring at the scene, his bloodied sword still in a hand hanging limply at his side.

Then the sense of horror truly dawned, with scenes and sounds that would be seared into the memory forever. Bodies and bits of bodies, streams of blood, and mounds that were dead horses littered the sweet valley. Those severely wounded were in agony. Their groans were terrible. Some were so maimed that, if by some miracle they survived, they would be forever useless. There were anguished cries from fathers who found the lifeless bodies of beloved sons among the heaps of those who had fallen. There were truly pitiable cries for help from those for whom there would be no help. There were few cries from the fallen enemy who lay helplessly among their enemies, just terror mixed with the look of suffering in their eyes.

Perhaps most revolting of all were the grinning faces and

strutting strides of some who now, unaccountably, were blind to the tragedy of their surroundings. Considering themselves heroes, though they had looked as frightened as all those around them in the heat of the deadly battle, they were now eagerly shouting their boasts to anyone who would listen, boasts about their bravery and of how many men they had slain. They ignored the sounds of the cries of desperate men around them. They were drunk with blood.

~~~~~~~~~~

The homeward journey seemed twice the distance. Carrying the wounded, dragging the few reluctant captives who had been selected to live, the long train of exhausted men inched back across the landscape. Many were silent as they walked or rode; others talked quietly; a few continued to shout about their exploits; some would have prayed, if they could, but felt too stained by the bloodiness of their warfare to feel they dared look towards God.

There was no reason for shame, really. Innocents among their own people and the order of their civilisation had been threatened in unprovoked attacks. Defence was entirely honourable. It was right and natural for men to protect their families and lands, and noble sacrifices had been made for that purpose. Why, then, would the return from such a battle seem to be so difficult? Why were all the men not high-spirited, gladly triumphal, easily giving thanks for their victory?

For one whose heart would ask these questions, one whose hands were bloodied by battle for the first time, and whose ears were still ringing from the din of war sounds, there would come the answer that it was not that the cause was not just, for it was. It was plainly and simply the fact that war was a sickening, hideous thing. It was ugly beyond expectation, brutal in every way. Nothing could sweeten or soften it, not even the reality that peace was secured by it. One must either accept that the bloodshed of war, all the ghastly horror of it, was sometimes necessary, and somehow harden the heart to it, or one must find another way to stop an enemy, if there was one.

The gathered armies paused for rest and conference at a dividing of the ways, at the edge of the Solway's estuary near an ancient tribal meeting stone. Kings conferred with each other there for a time, while their sons cemented bonds of friendship forged in recent days, and weary soldiers relaxed. Some strayed down onto the peaceful tidal flats, one young man riding slowly out onto the seemingly endless dry shore. Those who knew the place noticed him and called out warnings. In the Solway, tides did not creep; they galloped. Apparently dry shorelines concealed dangerously deep mudpools.

Suddenly the distant waters surged forward and, as feared, the rider's horse stuck fast, the young man shouting in fear as he realised his danger. A single figure on horseback headed like a streak toward him, right into the advancing tide. His powerful horse carried him swiftly to the frightened man on the struggling, dying animal. The rescuer wrenched the terrified man from his saddle, flung him across his own horse's withers, and turned the doubly-laden mount toward shore, urging it on with all his might. The rising flood roared like a monster that would swallow everything in its path, but the labouring horse ploughed on through rapidly deepening water until it finally reached safe ground.

A huge cheer went up from those watching, and the ashen faced and shaking young man was deposited into the arms of waiting soldiers by his saviour, Ninian. The abandoned horse was already lost from sight beneath the merciless sea.

The entire incident had been witnessed by the kings who were gathered together on higher ground. Macsen thoughtfully considered Ninian, marking him as a future leader of the people. Courage was in him, and the young prince's actions had revealed that he had both the physical strength and the skill to enable him to accomplish what his great courage would dare. Such a man was a rarity. Ninian's father was proud. Coel and Anwn were among those who cheered. Peibio struggled to control an urge to weep.

When the returning army reached a settlement near Hadrian's Wall, the so- nearly drowned young man was delivered in safety to his home. His family eagerly, loudly hailed him as a returning hero, safely back from battle even though on foot. He hushed the cries of their welcome, insisting that they hear of the young prince who had risked his own life to save him when he had nearly perished, not during the heroics of battle, but through his own foolish actions.

~~~~~~~~~~

Medana looked into my eyes and smiled as she said, "That was the first time I heard of Ninian. It was my own brother whom he saved."

THREE: Turning Place
"Blessed Ninian left his native land and his father's home
and learned in a foreign land
what he would afterwards teach
in his own..."
"Vita Niniani" by Ailred of Rievaulx,
trans. by Winifred MacQueen

As a younger son of the royal family, Ninian's preferences for prayers over games, for church over casual society, and for learning over marriage had thus far been tolerated. Those who governed his future had not felt pressured to rush him into more serious involvements. He was able and fit enough, in spite of his disinterest in physical contests; society was entertained by others, not craving for his participation in particular; he was young enough, and marriage could wait yet longer. There was plenty of time for him to settle down, and any amount of learning he wished to acquire in the meantime would possibly one day prove to be an advantage to his kingdom.

The publicly witnessed act of heroism on the Solway shore instantly changed the course of his life. Once Macsen had marked him out, there would not be any more time for him to dally along his own chosen paths. Life must begin in earnest. To those around him, this seemed a truly golden moment in the life of the serious, abstemious scholar, one unexpectedly discovered to be a natural leader of men. His future now had a brightness that they might envy. Ninian, only Ninian, felt that walls had encircled him and a roof enclosed his sky.

Land. There must be territory assigned for him to rule. Where better for such a young man to exercise his abilities at such a dramatic time in the nation's history but in that very place where the battleground had been? The furthest western area between the two walls, within the buffer state of Valentia, a place made of fingers of land reaching out into a sea filled with the enemy's recurrent challenges, was an area never before more than loosely controlled. Bounded by wild mountains, encompassing high moorland, enriched by tracts of glorious woodland, watered by numerous rivers, and wonderfully fertile in its green valleys, it was a beautiful place and fit for a king of its own. It was inhabited by off-shoot bits of peoples speaking different languages, dotted with fortresses built and abandoned in different times by different forces, and featured several anciently noted towns lying in need of redevelopment. Brilliant young leadership, and probably only that, could assure the continued destiny of this remote Solway territory within the Roman frame. It was a place of continual danger. Ninian was suited for the task.

Marriage. He should marry the daughter of another king, an elder daughter who would bring with her marriage a strengthening confederation and increase in land holding. A marriage bonding with a kingdom straddling the Wall of Hadrian, at its western end or middle section, would reinforce the connection between the territory of the remoter western finger of land and that of one more securely resting within the protection of Rome. The influence of the Roman culture more deeply established within the bounds of Hadrian's Wall would also provide a reliable support for development within the new territory.

These matters were negotiated in council, and decisions were made. Ninian was not part of the discussions or of the arrangements. He was merely informed, and taken to meet those involved after agreements had been authorised. An official visit to a tribal fortress near the Wall of Hadrian sealed the bond of his planned marriage. There he saw his intended bride, still a child, not yet ready to be claimed as his. She looked at him frankly, and with admiration. He smiled at her, so kindly. Tenderness was born between them, and he had no regret at the plans for him.

~~~~~~~~~~

Almost simultaneously, two things happened to bring the forward momentum of his life to a sudden, shocking halt.

War. It would not seem to be enough that Ninian must neglect his studies, his copying, even his praying, in order to be part of the arrangements for his future in matters of estate and marriage. Those things he accepted. They seemed natural and right, part of the life he had expected from his earliest youth. With them, though, came a new challenge, and immediate pressure to accept it. He was to assume command of troops, his own men. He must oversee their training and be prepared to do battle at their head, at any time, going any place, whenever he was summoned.

Not again could he do this gladly or lightly, he realised. He wondered if he could do it at all. It was then that he began to question this future. It would be a terrible thing for any man to refuse to ride with his men in defence of his people and theirs, especially if the vulnerable, helpless ones among them, those whom they were honour bound to protect, were threatened by an enemy. As he wrestled with his thoughts, he conjured up the face of his own mother, a noble woman, worthy of his reverence, reverence that would be due to such a woman by any cherished son. He saw also the sweet face of his tiny future wife, one he would naturally long to protect. He considered the lives of his younger siblings, sisters, brother. How could he not be willing, even eager and proudly so, to prepare for war on their behalf? What was wrong with him?

Still, he remembered, without consciously bidding the memory to come, the valley that was drenched in blood. He heard the cries of the wounded, the sorrow of the bereaved. He had longed then, in that green place and on the long road home after the blackened day, to find another way, any other way, in which honour could be preserved, peace and safety secured, but by which this dreadful horror of war could be avoided.

He fled to the little church within the fortress community of his own home and there he poured out before the altar his pleas for wisdom, for strength to do whatever was right in the sight of his God. The longer he prayed, the more time he spent within the walls of that sanctuary, the less he found of an answer, for there was a great problem developing there, too, right before the altar. If anything, this difficulty unsettled him even more deeply than his struggle over the summons to prepare for war.

As he confided his problem to the old man who had long been priest in that place, he learned that changes were taking place. This priest was his long-time spiritual mentor, his best teacher, his trusted advisor in all the important matters of his life, the wise man who had watched him grow from the time of his baptism and who had guarded his soul. The priest had come to this place with a Roman governor as a young man, long ago. That governor had served his appointed time and quickly returned to Rome for another, even better, position but the priest had remained in the place where people were hungry to learn. Without him there, the sacraments would have been abandoned, for there had been no one to replace him. He had watched as Britain changed around him and, at last, in this changed place, he had grown old. He was now too aged to carry on any longer, too faltering, too weary in spirit as well as in body. He was terribly aware that the military was folding up tents and moving to Gaul, needing to protect Rome from greater danger nearer her own borders. He would lose all that remained to remind him of Rome when the soldiers and their accompanying hosts left the northern lands.

He longed for home. He longed to see the faces of his nephews and nieces whom he had never seen, now parents themselves as he would never be. He yearned to feel the sun on his old bones, to hear his familiar language in its familiar accent of childhood. He was leaving, he told Ninian.

In his place there would be only the layman who had come recently to the north and had already betrayed himself as a lesser shepherd.

The older priest had discoursed less about the details of his doctrines, more about God. He had seemed to walk with God and spoke of Him as one to be revered and feared, but one whom he truly loved and honoured. He had read to the people from all the Scriptures he possessed and any he could borrow. They knew from him of the writings of Moses about the beginnings of their world with paradise and the coming of sin to spoil it, of Noah and his boat, of the promises to Abraham, and of the deliverance of the people Israel out of slavery. He had warned them with the words of prophets and melted their hearts with the poetry in the Psalms of David. He had charmed and inspired them with stories heroes and heroines of old, of Joshua, Gideon, Ruth and Esther. He had read to them lovingly, over and over, the stories of the coming of the Christ to earth, the Lamb of God who would take away the sin of the world. He read these to them until the names of places like Bethlehem, Jerusalem, and Galilee of the Gentiles were more familiar to the Britons than the names of distant cities of their own island. More familiar, and more real. When this priest baptised a child, a man or a woman, or when he blessed the bread and wine, sealing this people to their Lord as one, he did so gravely, but sweetly.

The younger man was a Briton. A layman, he was not as well educated as the older, regularly ordained priest. Even so, he spoke in a voice that implied an even greater authority. He administered sacraments in a perfunctory way, rushing through the mysteries that blessed the people with the sense of God's grace so that he could hasten his way to his favoured time of discourse. What he taught was less of God and more of beliefs, understandings. He was full of opinions about Christian doctrines: which ones were correct, and which ones were not. He alternated between denouncing perceived errors held by others and floundering through explanations of his own perceived truths. His teaching was tortured, complicated, and full of thunderings about judgement upon anyone who believed a heresy. He was nothing if not certain, but those hearing him grew less and less certain of their own understandings. He pondered aloud, confusing them in the wanderings of his ponderings. He was intensely concerned that they should grasp his explanations about the nature of God and the Trinity, or the functions of Divine grace in dealing with their sins. He used Scriptures that seemed to say whatever he was sure of. Even some of his listeners, Ninian among them, were aware that he deliberately ignored any passages that indicated something slightly different, something fuller, something that might lend a warming understanding to his calculated, icy points. Somehow, although there were true things in what he said, his teachings as a whole were not truth, because they were not whole teachings.

People began to avoid the practice of their faith. Some despaired of understanding the man, and others declined to be part of the troubled mood that invaded the once-holy place. The old priest, ready to take his leave from the area, increasing in deafness and in frailty, was pushed more and more in the background. The new man grew louder, more domineering. The church was not, any longer, a place of refuge for the soul, a place of enlightenment to the mind. It was an assault to be endured. The heavy lectures began to drown out memories of the Biblical stories that had brought the people in the beginning to belief. They could not grasp what was important in the new doctrines, and their faith was failing.

Those who became disaffected by the philosophical ramblings and fiery discourses of the man who patently did not care for whether they lived or died, or how they did it as long as they listened to him with respect, wandered away elsewhere to seek solace in their troubles or guidance for their pathway. They went wherever they thought their needs might be met. The gentleness of Christ had drawn them slowly, but held them to Him for generations; tragically quickly, pontification from one who claimed to represent their Christ dispersed them. They returned, in ones and twos, sometimes in families, to abandoned shrines, mysterious deep wells, and finally to the giant stones that marked the movements of the glowing, life-giving, healing sun.

Ninian despaired when he saw the signs of the people's abandonment of Christ. It was not for the rulers of a people to teach them their faith, though sometimes rulers affected the life of the church as arbiters. The Emperor of Rome could make final decisions in great doctrinal disputes, but only after an open hearing, after an international gathering of all church leaders had discussed all points in question and sought God's way in earnest prayer. A prince in Britain, not a king, as a younger son not likely to become a king, even though he were a man of learning and promise, had no such right or power and never would have. In spiritual decisions, he should honour those who were appointed within God's providence to serve His flock just as his people were expected to do. But Ninian could not rest in peace with this reality, for he nursed a genuine fear that his nation was beginning to wander from God. What would be the benefit of exercising leadership among such people, guiding them into a safe and peaceful time, if he had no influence in matters of faith and if his safe, peaceful, even prosperous subjects were to lose their souls in the end?

The young prince was confused. He became preoccupied and increasingly agitated. None among his friends or family understood what had happened to him, what had so unnerved and distracted him at such a time of promise in his life. Some of the wise, older men advised his family that they had observed in soldiers, after particularly harrowing war experiences, a kind of delayed reaction that seemed to be a suffering of the spirit. They muttered together, and watched him. Others suggested that the balance of his mind was, perhaps, disturbed because of some hitherto hidden frailty embedded in his nature, something only now becoming apparent. There had been other young men of apparent brilliance who sometimes had come to nothing. Still others considered, and offered the opinion, that the freedoms of youth could not be easily set aside by a type of person who was determined to be forever young, and that perhaps the weight of impending responsibilities was proving to be too much for the young, rather slightly built Prince Ninian.

His family, uncomprehending of the reasons for changes in his attitude, realised that none of the offered diagnoses were correct, but they did not know what was brewing within his thoughts or how they could help him out of the darkness he was experiencing. He refused food, did not attend worship in the church, and became sullen whenever the subject of plans for his future were broached.

~~~~~~~~~~

The day arrived for the departure of the old priest. Ninian sought one last audience with his friend. Against all that was decorous, he clung to the ancient man, weeping as a child would weep.

"What can I do?" he asked through his sobbing.

"My son, you are greatly blessed by God. He is granting you an important position in life. You must not fear to follow His will. He will not fail you and if you trust Him, you will be given strength and wisdom enough for a king's work."

"My heart craves that my people follow Christ more than that they obey me."

"As a king, you will have authority to set such an example that they will surely follow you."

"Not so, my father. Each person must find Christ for himself, not because of a king's commands. They will not find Him if claims about Him confuse them. The story must be truth, and it must be clearly told. It was this way when you worked among us. Christ must be lifted up before them, in His dying, as Moses lifted the serpent in the desert, or there will be no healing for my people. This is not the work of the king, but of the priest, and we will have no true priest without you."

The old man blanched. Was this young prince, the one whose tongue could cut in an eagerness to speak truth, accusing him of abandoning God's flock, leaving it in danger? He whimpered, deep inside himself, and writhed. He must leave. He was too old. Death would come to him before he was reunited with his family, before he saw Rome again. God was merciful, surely, and would grant him this rest and peace for his last days. He had served so many years in this dark northern place, and he was done. He had no more to give.

"Ninian!" He spoke more sharply than he had ever spoken, more sharply than he had ever thought that he could. "You must not condemn the servant God has sent into this place. He has given up all he has, all that is familiar, to come to your people in this way."

The distraught prince persisted. "I cannot bear to hear him

harangue the people and watch while they scatter from him in confusion. These are my people, my family, my tribe. It is a tragedy that they move back to the old ways. This man does not know the Scriptures as you taught them, and they cannot learn what he does not know. He toys with truth, and enforces opinions. He is destroying the work you have established!"

The old man stared at him. "Would you walk his path, my proud young prince? You cannot seem to find the courage to walk your own."

The accusation of the priest shattered him into silence. Finally, Ninian stammered his farewell, and left. He fled alone to a secret, sheltered place. There, he spread himself before God in a deeper anguish of spirit than he had ever known. He was broken and ashamed, and he was full of pleading.

From the storehouse of his memory, the words of the betrayer of Jesus, the disciple Peter, came to him, "Lord, you know that I love You." Nothing else remained from his weeping, no other words or thoughts. It was all he could offer. In the moment of helpless abandonment before his Maker, the moment when he had nothing but the deep inner core of his love, he saw what he must do.

Rome. He must go to Rome. At the place of learning and empowerment he must himself learn to save the souls of his people and be ordained to serve them as their priest. If he remained in his own land, married, established his own dynasty, occupied and ruled a kingdom, he could do a good work. By becoming their priest, he could do a better work, one that would bear more important fruit. A kingdom on earth was a temporary place; the kingdom of heaven was eternal.

He walked, following tracks through dense forest where graceful deer fled at the sound of his footsteps. He watched birds feeding their young in nests, fish swimming in the clear waters of winding rivers. He soaked in the sun, tasted the rain, set his face into the wind, and communed with his God. He looked over the beautiful world of his father's kingdom from its upland heights. He travelled to the sweeping shoreline and looked across the waters to the distant kingdom that had been assigned to him and his sweet, promised bride.

He waited in patience as the tide retreated, and then on until it returned to its former place. He drank in the sights and sounds of the world of his birthright, a rich and pleasant land. Sometimes his heart would sing with the sense of glory he was finding. Sometimes he would curl into a ball and weep with sorrow, because of what he was losing. Then he would cry again to God, and he would sleep.

Finally, peace came to his heart fully and deeply, a peace that would remain. His mind was clear. His will was set. It was only then that Ninian returned and sought audience with his father and his mother.

~~~~~~~~~~

It was a terrible argument, more terrible than he could have imagined it would be. He expected the anger of his father, but not the desolation of his mother. Worse than his rage were her tears, sobbing as though her heart would break.

"I must go to Rome," he announced with calmness that he again possessed. "It will be necessary for me to study a long time, so that I can be ordained and return to serve as a priest for the people." Stunned silence preceded the verbal assault.

"You will do no such thing," roared the king. "You will do what you have been prepared to do. This is madness!"

"I am sorry, Father," said the prince, simply and humbly, but not retreating. "I must go."

His father's laughter was cruel and cut him. It sounded even dangerous. "For this you were baptised a Christian? So that you could disobey God by dishonouring your father, your mother? So that you could ignore the needs of your people and the calling of your birth to pursue your own weak preferences? What kind of selfish Christian did the old priest make of you? It's well for him that he is out of reach now, or I would examine him!"

Again, "I am sorry; but I must go. It was not the priest. It is my own choice."

He was not asked to explain what had driven him to this desperate decision, but he was threatened:

"You are not fit to be my son.".......

"You will no longer be owned as my son"......

"You will not bear my name, or any name identifying you with your family.".....

"You will have no royal privileges until your dying day."........

"You will be buried without royal ceremony or marking.".......

"Your land will be given to your brother, who will rule instead of you."......

"Your promised wife will be given to one more worthy. She will hate you for the shame of your rejection.".........

"You will not be protected by royal privilege. You must find your own way."......

"You are cast out.".........

"You may not return..... ever.".........

"You will not be forgiven and may not seek mercy".......

"You will inherit nothing, nor will your children."......

"You have shamed us, and you will make a mockery of us.".........

Even Macsen could not alter the determination of Prince Ninian, now only Ninian, forever Ninian. His distinguishing Latin names were not to be used henceforth to identify him. He was declared a lowly freedman, with only the personal name given at his birth, the name by which his familiars knew him, to identify him. Nobility and every dignity that was born with it were stripped away forever. His brothers and sisters were instructed to ignore his presence among them. His personal weapons, those given to him as the warrior son of a king, were removed. His famous horse, the one that carried him in war and answered his bidding to ride against the Solway's tide, was taken from him. He was given a lowly pack horse and allowed to take only his most personal belongings as he left his home and family. To the last, his family believed that such humiliation would cause him to regret his actions and seek restoration to favour, restoration that would happily have been granted. But he did not change his mind. His will was like something of iron. His purpose was fixed.

Most prized of the things he carried away into his new life

were the scraps of Scripture and other carefully copied writings. In them he found solemn words:

"The enemies of a man, the members of his household.
The one loving father or mother beyond me is not of me
worthy;
and the one loving son or daughter beyond me is not of me
worthy;
and he who takes not his cross and follows after me is not of
me worthy.
The one finding his life will lose it and the one losing his life
for the sake of me will find it.

~~~~~~~~~~~

Medana closed her eyes, and I was disturbed to see an escaped tear drop on her cheek. Her voice was low. I could barely hear what she said and scarcely believe the words that came. "I was the promised wife," she said. "But never could I hate Ninian. And never would I marry another."

FOUR: Journey's Beginning
"So animated by the inspiration of the Holy Spirit,
scorning wealth and spurning all human feelings,
the noble youth began his pilgrimage."
"Vita Niniani" by Ailred of Rievaulx,
trans. by Winifred MacQueen

The words of the Lord instructed Ninian,
" If you bring your gift to the altar
and remember that your brother has something against you,
leave the gift there, in front of the altar, and go.
First be reconciled to your brother
and then come to offer your gift."

He could not set out for Rome to offer the gift of his life to
God while there was one owed, by him, an apology.

Thus, no more prince, only Ninian, he began his journey as a
penitent. He travelled north to the settlement near to the wall of
Hadrian to make peace if he could with the king whose daughter he
was deserting. Moving toward that place was a slow, dutiful trudge
on feet that felt lead-weighted. He must do this, he knew, but he
dreaded the experience he faced. There would be pain for him in
rebukes he was sure to receive from an angry father, but that was a
pain he felt would be a rightful punishment. Worse for him would
be any exhibition of anger, or even sadness, exhibited by the young
girl herself. She had done nothing to deserve his rejection of her.

When he reached the town, he was not recognised. He was
denied entry through the gates. In his earlier visits, he had been a
hero soldier first and then a princely bridegroom, accompanied by
an impressive retinue, readily acknowledged by all. As a simply
dressed stranger, all alone, he was the object only of suspicion. It
took some time for his identity to be verified and the gateway to be

opened to him. The guards looked at him with curiosity. He felt the shame of it, and knew that this would not be the only time in his life, in this different kind of life, when he would be treated thus. He was now an ordinary man, no royal being. It would be good for him to learn this humble walk, he wryly told himself. His Master had walked more humbly than he would have to do, having come from a greater glory but descending to the deepest depths of shame to accomplish His purposes.

He braced himself for the next, more difficult part of his visit, and he prayed silently for grace to do it well. Ushered into the presence of the chieftain, he knelt before the man whose daughter he had rejected. He asked, simply, that he might be forgiven for having broken his contract of betrothal, for the offence of wounding the family's pride.

His request was met with silence, only silence. He looked up to find the man just looking at him in a puzzled way. There was no trace of anger on his face. Finally he spoke, "It is strange that you should be bowing in front of me, Prince Ninian."

"I am no longer Prince, only Ninian."

The chieftain's eyes glinted with something akin to amusement. Then he said, "The man who saved the life of my son in such a display of courage while kings merely watched, displaying none, will always be a prince to me!" He offered Ninian his hand.

"But your daughter. I have offended her."

"Ah! There you speak some truth. She will weep over you. She did not have to be pressed to accept the betrothal bond, in spite of her youth. Even so, she is only a child. She will recover, will marry someone else. She may even forget all about you!"

"May I speak with her?"

"Do you feel this to be necessary?" asked the kindly father. "I would not ask this of you. She might turn on her tears. You needn't bother!

"I would prefer to speak with her, if I may," persisted Ninian.

In a while, the young girl was ushered into the room. She seemed pale, and was quiet, but her eyes flew straight to Ninian's face, and there was light in them. Then they filled, as the father had warned. She struggled, and kept her dignity, greeting him politely and asking for his family.

She meant to make it easier for him, but her sweetness, and her unexpected strength, made it worse instead. What a dear wife she would have been to him! He knew this, and the look of such knowledge was on his face for both the girl and her father to see very plainly. "I regret......" he began.

"You are free, " she interrupted him. "I have been informed that you have chosen to follow God, and you go with my blessing. I will always pray for you..." and then her voice trembled. She lifted her eyes to his again, for a moment, until she saw that his eyes has flooded as her own. The betrothal was broken and the marriage would never take place, but the tenderness between them, as long as they lived, could not die. It was instinctive and natural. They were two birds that might seem to fly freely but would move, by instinct, in unison. She dropped her head and slipped from the room.

It was done. He spent that night as a guest of the household, perhaps for the last time in his life being treated with the courtesies due to a prince and a hero. His future was an unknown path. After he left the hospitality of this home, life would be very different for him. No one he met in the wider world, from now on, would understand if he were alone, poor or insulted that this was not his natural place accorded by birth, for he would be a stranger. Other people he encountered would not know, as these people knew, that he had given up his royal rights to follow his God.

In the morning, when he gathered his pack for the journey and slipped out into the soft light of dawn, he found someone waiting for him. It was Lugo, the son of the chieftain, the one whose life he had saved from the Solway tide, now his friend.

"Farewell," said Ninian, clasping him.

"No," was the reply, and Lugo grinned at him.

"No?"

"I am going with you to Rome."

"Oh, no. No, you are not!" Ninian stoutly countered the suggestion. "This is something that I must do, and I will do it alone! There's no need for anyone else to suffer for my decisions." Reading the heart of his friend, Ninian insisted, "You owe me nothing. I did what anyone could have done if he'd had as good a horse as mine! You will prove this to yourself some day when you find that you are saving someone's life. Then you will understand that these moments don't require repayment!"

"Whatever, " Lugo grinned on, adding his pack to that carried by Ninian's baggage horse, carefully adjusting the weights, carefully checking the straps and ropes. "You can explain more to me about all this as we walk, if you like."

At first, Ninian felt a surge of panic. Then he stumbled as he tried to catch up with Lugo, still protesting. Lugo said, "Father agrees with me. I'll never have an opportunity like this to see the world... Rome! If I fall into some river crossing, he knows that there's someone who will rescue me!" And he laughed.

They passed the women's hut, and the tiny form of Lugo's sister appeared in the doorway. She beamed at her brother, threw her arms about his neck, and murmured to him. Ninian knew his first twinge of loneliness, but the feeling vanished the moment Medana looked at him with eyes that were shining, no rebuke in them.

~~~~~~~~~~

With a heart a thousand times lighter than he had expected it to be, Ninian set out for Rome in the company of a friend. In an unexpected surge of happiness, he sensed the pleasure of God all around him. It was as though God Himself was carrying him in His arms, like a father would carry a child over rough ground. Ninian's feet would not feel the stones of the pathway, his bones would not grow weary, he would not be hungry, and he would not thirst. He was blessed. Not just absolved from guilt, not just allowed to go freely, but sent on his way with an abundance of kindness, blessed with loving friendship. Blessed. So blessed. He had feared the loneliness. No longer.

~~~~~~~~~~

Their path led them across the Pennine ridge that formed the spine of the island. From the heights they saw in the distance the beautiful, mysterious mountains they knew so well, those lying on the western side of northern Britain. This familiar world was left behind. First they glimpsed below them the more open plains bounded by the eastern sea, a less familiar kind of country, and soon they descended from the uplands into broad, undulating sweeps of eastern land occupied by peoples of other tribal groups. Their own western peoples, together with the occupants of this northeastern part of the island lying beneath Hadrian's Wall, were designated in unity for the administrative purposes of Rome as the northern province of Britain. The easterners were different from westerners, nonetheless. Ninian and Lugo hardly dared to think how many peoples' lands, how many provinces, how many valleys, how many mountains, how many rivers and seas they must cross yet before they would come to their destination.

They walked with ease, for Rome had made the great roads that were under their feet, and had made them well. Not so many soldiers walked on the highways in these times, so travellers making long journeys could take advantage of their emptiness and walk on the broad surfaces unchallenged for long miles. Whenever larger groups of people appeared, be they military or trading trains, private travellers moved to the unpaved verges on the sides of the causeway, or paid for the privilege of walking on the more solid central ways. Milestones kept count for them and, though a single day's journey was reckoned as being one of 20 miles' length, the two young men leading their lightly burdened horse discovered that they could cover twice that distance on some days.

It was the early part of the springtime. The days were long, and the weather was good. They avoided lingering in towns beside which they passed, not able to afford too often the expenses of accommodation at wayside inns there. They found that they could be comfortable in open countryside, settling at the approach of darkness into a quiet meadow, some hidden place on the edge of a copse near the road, near a stream. They ate food they had purchased from roadside bread vendors or had picked from fields and bushes as they walked. Sometimes they caught fish in the streams. Sometimes they snared plump and unwary birds. A small fire cooked such food, and its dying embers warmed them in the evening chill. They slept on softening layers of foliage or bracken, wrapping themselves in their outer cloaks, and their sleep was sound.

The further south they went, the more roadside villages, walled towns, large villas, and groups of travellers, there were; and then they began to take turns in keeping watch during night's hours. There was little worth stealing in what they carried, but they were wary. The breakdown in the conscious grip of Roman law meant that there were renegades who now dared to roam the countryside and prey on travellers. It would not be wise for them to be too casual about their safety.

In four days, they passed a joining of roads and they followed the markers pointing toward the famed city of Eboracum. Capital of the northern province, it was a place of note in Britain's history representing, more dramatically than any other British city, both the military might of Rome's rule, and the triumph of the Christian faith. Constantius and Constantine had ruled there, one dying and the other being proclaimed Roman Emperor by his soldiers there.

It was a great city on the banks of a broad and busy river, safely encircled by towering walls of stones. Within the maze of her streets, the two travellers worked their way through throngs of people who were busy governing, buying, selling and gossiping. They had to shout at each other to be heard above the din. They finally found space in an inn and, after stabling and feeding the horse, they carried their packs inside. The hostel's public room was as jammed with people as were the streets outside. There were soldiers there, amongst the assortment of travellers from many areas. People were eating and drinking, some shouting, others listening to those doing the shouting.

A thickset soldier who was obviously full of ale, was bellowing to be heard. "We did it before! It was here. Constantine was declared Emperor and it happened."

Another soldier, with a different accent, tall and leaner, of different colouring, less affected by the drink, surveyed him coldly.

"Declared, maybe. It took years to make him so. Your declarations aren't anything like enough. No real authority."

The first man slurred, "But he was Emperor, wasn't he? Just took others longer to realise it. And it will be the same now, for sure."

"Never. Nothing like the same."

"Aye, I'll tell you! Just the same. Same bloodline too! Macsen will be Emperor. The rest of the Empire will know it eventually, just like before!"

"You fool. What claim has he got?"

"Best leader. Best soldier. Best strategies. And the bloodline. Don't forget the blood. He's born for it."

"He's a Spaniard."

"No! He's the son of Constantine's own son. The one nobody ever hears about. And his line goes back to Julius Caesar's family. I'm telling you. It's true. He's a natural. Now he's British, but he's born to it!"

"So he says. Rome doesn't seem to know much about it! Ha!" He laughed, but few joined him. He looked distinctly outvoted and noticed this, becoming uneasy.

Redder in the face than before, Macsen's admirer slapped the handle of the dagger in his belt. He moved nearer to the tall man, his once-cool opponent in argument. "I'm telling you. It will be."

Lugo was entranced by the exchange. Ninian was stunned. He was ashen-faced. His blood seemed to chill in him. He felt sick. Was this right? Would Macsen be carried to power in Rome by the men of Britain, hailed as Roman Emperor, lead the nation, and even go beyond the island to rule the Roman world? Could he, should he, have waited, served Macsen as had been planned for him, proved himself, come to power in Macsen's train? Then he would have been able to accomplish all his dreams and more from a position of great authority?

Later, in the velvet darkness of night, lying with the poor on the floor of the cheap and crowded inn, Ninian tossed on a lumpy, itchy pallet while Lugo slept soundly nearby. A voice whispered on and on inside his head, "Macsen as Emperor! You were his favourite. Think, think what this would mean. You could be riding alongside the Emperor of Rome. What power! ——Power a good man could use to create a Christian kingdom. Riches! —— Riches a wise man would use to build churches, fund priests, provide for them. Instead, you are living like a vagrant. You should not have acted quite so rashly. You're a homeless wanderer. Walking to Rome. You have no influence. You have no wealth. You walk where you might have ridden alongside the one in the purple cloak. You could have one day been dressed in purple yourself, commanding a city like this one, like Treves, like Rome! Instead, you sleep on the floor of a flea pit alongside drunken men. Silly, silly man. You fool."

Loose, wild talk should not have disturbed him, nor the voices inside his head, if he were sure about God's will. The question that had for the first time come to his mind was whether he was truly doing something that God had led him to do, or had rushed forward foolishly believing this to be so because he wanted to do things his own way. There might have been an easier, more acceptable way to accomplish his ends if he had only bided his time. If, in fact, he had made a mistake, it was too late for him. He saw that night the face of his father, and heard his voice. "You will not come back here, ever." There was no right of return. His choice was made, and it was irrevocable, whether it was right or wrong.

He prayed, and he reasoned. Before the light of dawn crept into the dingy place, he had regained his sense of certainty that he must follow God in this way, this way and no other. Even if there had been a way back, it was not the way he could take.

Peace would not come by a sword. One sword proving stronger than another in battle ended no fight. War-crushed peoples rose again to strength eventually, and it would all begin again. Peace must come another way.

Faith could not be imposed on any heart. A prince, a king, or an emperor might be able to force men to bow their knees or their necks, but human authority could not command faith in a subject's heart. That must come another way.

Wealth could build a church, but could not hold Christians together in faithfulness. This must come by God's work in lives, and money could not purchase that work.

Ninian had not made the wrong choice, but the right one. Accusing voices fell silent, and he slept.

The next day the subject of discussion in the inn during the previous night was the main topic of discussion on the streets of Eboracum. There were Rome's soldiers everywhere, and British men of leadership were openly in discussion with them in the precincts of the forum. Ninian caught a glimpse of the young king Coel, Macsen's brilliant lieutenant of battles past. "He will succeed in Macsen's train, " thought Ninian. "He is a natural leader among men, and a gifted strategist in war. God help him."

Coel noticed Ninian, in the distance, among the crowds. He knew that face. He could not remember where he had seen the young man, but he knew that he should know him. Unaccountably, he remembered a scene on the Solway shore where a young prince had ridden fearlessly into the tide to save a life while he, Coel of the Brigantes, had watched from the safety of the shoreline. This young man in Eboracum looked remarkably like the hero of that incident, but he was dressed so plainly and appeared to be walking amongst the poor of the city. "No prince under the mighty Macsen would dress so plainly, or walk among the poor," he thought.

Ninian and Lugo left Eboracum, moving southwards and slightly to the east, following the Roman road that gradually rose above the flat river plain. They had started late and thus covered less distance that day, coming only in the evening to the broadest estuary they had yet encountered. The road had led them straight to the crossing place, but the tide was out and there was nothing there but a rather rundown settlement of huts occupying a formerly proud fortress encampment on the steep bank above the ferry's jetty. The ferry's docking point was in the side of a muddy embankment below which trickled a tiny snaking stream. There were thousands of wading birds busy in a pecking search for food along the mudbanks of the low-tide shore. It was the strangest place! How could a boat arrive, or leave, from this point? It was nothing. There was no river here, not even a living, lively broad stream. There was only a narrow ribbon of water, one that could be spanned by a hand, down deep in the soft, reedy banks.

Any remaining light was fading from the blue-gold sky. In gathering darkness, they were pestered by swarms of insects. They slapped at what flew and scratched at bitten places. Finally they found a rough shelter further back up the banking, and they settled inside the wrapping of their cloaks to sleep.

They awoke at the first light of an early dawn to a scene that was nothing like that of the night before. The tide was almost fully in, still lapping into what had become a broad enough channel to invite the entrance of the heavy planked ferry raft that they could see was sliding quickly toward them across the full water, churning upriver on the tidal rise.

They laughed. How could the tiny channel of the night before hold this amount of water? Swallows in their darting dance were magical in the pale light, breakfasting on the bugs that had supped on the travellers the night before. Ninian and Lugo prepared the horse, grabbed their bags, shook out their cloaks, and made ready to board the boat as soon as the passengers and cargo from the other side disembarked on landing. They moved forward ahead of others who had been arriving to form a line behind them. The dour ferryman, a rough and ragged creature, old, weather-beaten and toothless, held them back. He shook his head and muttered. They could not follow his speech. He gestured at the water behind him, at the water beneath him, scowled and forbade them access. They wondered what would happen, and if they should trust their crossing of such a water to such a strange creature. Soon, though, the man's purposes became apparent. He was carefully watching the water lying full and flat under his boat, and then the beginnings of a swirling within it, the soft sign of a turn in the tide. "Now!" He shouted and everyone on the bank pressed forward, laden with packs, leading animals, even cradling babes. Onto the boat they crowded, and the ferryman's pole had pushed them away from the banking within minutes.

Fascinated, the two northerners watched a display of

wonderful skill in the seemingly rude and ignorant ferryman's manipulation of the clumsy craft. Just catching the water on the turn, the channel now in full flood but beginning at this very hour its return to the more natural flowing of downstream instead of up, the boat simply followed the motion of the water, turning with the bends of the channel, this way and that, softly moving between the reeded banks, and then slipped out and into the broad estuary flow. There, the man skilfully employed a pole prodding into the shallows of now submerged sandbanks he obviously knew as well as he knew the river's surface. The raft drifted slightly eastwards, seawards, with the outflowing tide, but moved steadily south across the estuary until it reached precisely the point of the hidden entrance to the ferry's port on the other side, a channel buried deeply within acres of reeds that waved in the wind. Carefully the ferry was guided, prodded, against the still full channel, moving less willingly against the turned outflowing of the tide, until it docked and was fastened safely. Ninian and Lugo felt like cheering the breathtaking display of expertise by the strange ferryman, but all the other passengers seemed unmoved, obviously used to the crossing and the man who so skilfully executed it. They moved ashore in their turn and looked back to see that the man was busy again, readying his boat for another crossing of the waters of the Abus River.

FIVE: Another World
"The sails filled out by eager breezes flew on,
until the rough timbers completed the journey
and the bark quit the sea
and fastened its prow in the yellow sands."
"The Miracles of Bishop Nynia" trans. by Winifred
MacQueen

The road to Rome ran on along a ridge that stood like another bony spine above surrounding countryside. It led as straight as an arrow in unhindered flight, stretching on and on and on and on, forever. The countryside to the left and right of them grew flatter as they moved further south, and as they walked, mile after straight mile, the world warmed. Hour after hour, counting the passing milestones, feeling the increasing heat, they wondered what lay ahead. In their northern land, there had been only a spring's first beginnings, the air sweetened by the earliest blossoms of the season, the merest hints of pale green tingeing the bareness of trees' winter branches. In this southern world, summer flowers bloomed to drooping already, their scent heavy and thick, and what trees they saw were weighted by dark summer foliage.

They talked, as they walked, of everything they knew, of everything either of them could remember as far back as memories could take them. They talked to fill the long hot hours, making up for the emptiness of the landscape with pictures they drew for each other in words about their lives and homes. Sometimes when Ninian talked, Lugo yawned, for Ninian spoke a great deal about his love for learning and memories of worship or study. When Ninian sang, it was always psalms, hymns, all that was to him worth singing. There was a haunting beauty in his voice, as in the solemn words he sang. Birds seemed to pause in their own trilling and cheeping to listen.

Lugo, by contrast, was all brightness, both in merry songs and in galloping stories. His memories were full of humorous incidents and confessions of childhood pranks. Often he laughed so hard that he couldn't speak. He laughed until the breath left him. Then he would start again, where he had left off in the telling of his funny tales, tears still streaming down his face from the crying that came of laughing. When he sang, the birds sang more loudly, joining in his joyful peals.

The two young British princes were as unalike in their approach to life as day is unlike night, as tall is different from tiny, as a tree contrasts with a river. Ninian was intense, grave, always thinking, always seeking to understand the mysteries of God's purposes in the tiniest details of his life and in the world around him. Lugo was easy, charming, talkative, unquestioning, enjoying and accepting what any day would bring. And yet, to strangers they encountered, they would seem to be as matching as any pair of brothers. Of the same people, both being men of the north and west, not much different in physique or appearance, betraying an identical accent in their speech, dressed the same, eating the same foods in the same ways, knowing the same peoples and sharing similar history, these external likenesses that others would notice bound them ever more closely as they made their journey together into an increasingly foreign world.

The few towns they passed as they travelled did not entice or hold them. Apart from the need to replenish supplies, they kept to themselves, only stopping to sleep. The further they went, the more people they encountered. The traffic increased until they found that they must walk always on the pathways to the sides of the paved areas. Progress slowed. There were more towns, more villages, more villas, simply more people, everywhere. There were more soldiers, and there were more people whose appearance, clothing and speech identified them as true Romans, not Romanised Britons. There were many more foreigners than they had seen in the north. It was apparent that conscripted foreign soldiers had remained in their retirement to establish settlements with those of their own kind in Britain. Some entire communities seemed to be peopled by tall, fair-haired families, unlike the native Britons, while others they passed were people of much darker complexions, smaller, equally unlike the British.

The long-fingered ridge of land ended at Lindum, and the road further southward veered away from that straight line, the causeway dividing in different directions, curving in any direction that could avoid a vast tract of marshy flat fenland. Choices of alternative routes began to make their journey more complicated, but more variations in the kinds of people walking and riding on the roads made travel more interesting. Wherever land would hold people and grow their crops, there were clusterings of houses. The south was a populous place, and there was an increasing amount of activity on the greater number of roadways as they approached the greatest city in Britain.

From the moment they arrived there, Londinium astonished them. Enclosed within its great walls, it was like a giant cooking pot, noisily bubbling with energy, steaming with heat, full of mysterious ingredients creating intriguing odours. They tried not to stare as they pushed their way down lanes in search of an inn. But they stared; they couldn't help themselves.

They were accustomed to the sights of foreign faces in their own part of Britain, for the area around the Wall of Hadrian had often had among those stationed there troops who had come from very distant lands. Dark-skinned soldiers from the Levant were a common sight; so were tall, blond people gathered into the army from lands east of the Rhenus; occasionally black African servants were among the households of administrative ranks of Roman officials; and even golden-skinned Oriental traders had found their way to those parts. Those exotic peoples, either dressed as Roman soldiers or wrapped snugly against the northern chill in enveloping woollen capes, had been entertained amongst the British according to British ways and customs, and had spoken Latin in their conversations.

Londinium was so different. The young northern princes had never encountered large groups of such people dressed in their own native clothing, eating their own strange foods, speaking their own languages with others of their own kind. Foreign women, foreign children, they were everywhere, elegantly and colourfully dressed, calling out to each other, laughing, playing, haggling over produce. These were transplanted from other climes and somehow, surprisingly, thriving in an alien environment, like delicate summer flowers blooming in mountain snowdrifts.

After they had spent some days gathering advice, learning the news of the world, and making arrangements for further stages of their journey, Ninian and Lugo began to enjoy the sights of the city. Sometimes they separated to explore. Lugo would go to the docks to enjoy all the colour of life. He was fascinated by the bustling river trade, and watched for long hours while goods were unloaded from ships that had sailed up the broad river channel. Cloths, foods, wine vessels, even strange animals came ashore in Londinium. Lugo was full of questions, and made friends of locals and foreigners alike as he haunted the place.

Ninian would go to the church, at least once in every day. Those who were devoutly Christian in Londinium were a hugely mixed group of people. Some were British, and some were foreigners. Most of the British people were from the city, and their lives were nothing like the lives of those who came from the wilder regions of the island. And yet, though British and foreign, country people and city inhabitants shared little in common in the physical ways that had bound Ninian and Lugo into naturally easy companionship and understanding, Ninian experienced a deeper bond with these people than he would have thought could be formed between complete strangers. Pale or dark, noble or poor, man or woman, aged or young, within the walls of the room that became for them the house of God, there was an instant sense of familiar kinship. In their prayers, their singing, the readings, the mysteries of the communion there was unity. The name of Christ was their shared joy, deeply, sweetly. Ninian, who had always worshipped among his own people, had never realised how powerfully this transforming bond could make strangers into brothers.

When Lugo and Ninian met again in the inn after their explorations, they shared all that they had done, all that they had learned. Their preparations were finally completed, and they left Londinium reluctantly, sure that no city could be greater, more intensely alive, more fascinating.

The horse had been sold to a man travelling northward from the city. The faithful creature would go back to cooler climes while the travellers, having parted with some of their heavier clothing and given away a few unnecessary burdens, would proceed on their journey more lightly dressed and carrying their own packs as soldiers would do.

They carefully crossed the ancient damaged wooden bridge spanning the broad Tamesis. The wooden superstructure of the bridge, erected in the time of Rome's first coming to Britain centuries before, was so timeworn that it was no longer considered a safe crossing for vehicles or troops. Wary foot passengers, moving from plank to plank with care, could still use the construction to reach the other bank where the Roman road continued in its straight course to Dubris, the port for the shortest crossing to Gaul.

Along this stretch of Roman highway, beautifully designed towns and handsome roadside villas set amidst pleasantly rolling garden landscape gave the impression of a softer, lusher kind of world than that of their familiar homeland, or even of the flat marshy landscape through which they had passed north of Londinium. The people themselves seemed sleeker, more elegantly dressed, than the people of harsher northern lands. This was a richer world altogether.

Britain ended in a dramatic coast, its shining white cliffs rearing up against the waves of the channel sea. For once, laughing Lugo did not laugh, and Ninian had nothing to say. They stood, just looking for a long time at the edge of Britain, transfixed by the scene. Ancient Britons had raised marker stones at crossing places throughout their island to signify the tribal authority of each area. Ports and fords all bore such simple signs and visitors knew by them whose land they were entering. The Romans, for three centuries, had created their own markers. Ignoring the native definitions of ancient British territory, they had claimed every important entry point to Britain, not with individual raised stones, but with fortresses created from thousands of stones, or of bricks. These enormous structures rose above the headlands and were intended to be seen from a great distance away, making clear to any who would come, or who would leave this place, that, whatever Celtic tribe inhabited whatever piece of the landscape, it was Rome that was overmaster of the island that lay at the western limit of the world.

The two young Britons finally dared to approach the famed port, while gulls whirled and dived, squealing at them. Men shouted, horses neighed, and goods being loaded on and off boats rumbled and clanked into position. A ship was ready to set sail, and places on its deck were readily negotiated for a crossing that would occupy most of the hours of one day's light. Sails billowed like wings of a great bird, and the gulls cried farewells to them as they plunged into the waves of a sea beyond which they would enter a different world. Ninian and Lugo both shivered a little in the wind, in spite of the heat. They blinked against the glare of the light that came from the sun's reflection off the great white cliffs, cliffs that first filled their view, but then grew smaller and smaller, until they disappeared under the dark waves.

They turned to look beyond the prow of the boat, searching the rolling watery horizon for signs of land on the other side. Only a crust of a headland ever came into view, and that was just before they drifted into a landing place at an inlet on a beach of rich golden sand in the late afternoon. This was low-lying part of the world, one barely raised above the sea. The travellers heaved themselves from the deck of the boat and out onto the land, scrambled along the shore to the beginnings of the Gaulish road to Rome.

More consciously strangers than they had ever been, an increased degree of unfamiliarity assailed their every sense. The two unlike, but so alike, Britons became all that was known to each other. Lugo wondered what he had done. Ninian silently gave thanks to God for Lugo. They found a place that was sheltered from the road, tucked themselves into their cloaks, and slept.

~~~~~~~~~~

It was a new world. Native people they met looked of a different type, and they dressed differently. Though the language of Gaul had first been considered by the Romans to be the same as that of Britain, the words of the Gaulish people were not quite intelligible to the ears of Britons. The separate Celtic races could only really communicate easily with each other in their universal second tongue of Latin.

The landscape was very different. It was flat, as the sections of the journey north of Londinium had been flat, but this was a dry flatness. It was not marshy wetland. The trees were different. The colours of the crops were different, much more roasted into goldenness by the sun, even though it was still early in the summer time. It was hotter than even in the south of Britain, and it grew even hotter yet.

As they walked, they found distinctive features reminiscent of their own homeland. The countryside around them might seem unfamiliar to them, but the Roman roads were the same roads, and milestones were marked just as they had been in their own land. There were soldiers of Rome, some perhaps marching toward Britain, and they looked like the soldiers that they had always known in Britain. There were ancient and largely abandoned settlements within sight of the roads. Obviously established in Gaul from times before Rome, as ancient British settlements had been, they crowned hills in circled shapes, and were surrounded by grassy ranks of ditches just as the ancient British Celtic fortresses had been. Roman roads and towns were often noted to be directly beneath these Celtic hilltop forts, on level ground and laid out in orderly rectangular form with impressive fortifications and formidable gates, just as in Britain.

They saw men toiling in their fields, or on buildings, or busily engaged in trading. They saw women walking, working, talking with each other, holding or scolding their children, just like mothers in their own land. Children, like children everywhere, helped where they must and played whenever they could, with whatever toy they could fashion for amusement.

Moving through the lands of Gaul, day after day, the unfamiliar became more familiar. The Gaulish words began to be more intelligible. The bread, the wine, the fruits, the vegetables, wonderful foods, some strange new foods, all soon seemed usual to them. Beautiful landscapes unfolded as they walked, and a sense of adventure grew in them as the sense of strangeness wore off.

All roads of the Western Empire north of the Alpes mountains seemed intent on leading all travellers to the great city of Treves. Treves was of ancient establishment, as Augusta Treverorum, having been founded by the very Augustus Caesar whom all Christians knew to have been Emporer of Rome at the time when the world's Messiah was born. Constantine, declared Emperor in Eboracum, had ruled from Treves before he had finally conquered and reunified the Empire. After his lifetime, the Empire had divided again into east and west, ruled from different places by successive emperors. The western empire now had no fixed centre, its emperors ruling from Treves, or even from Mediolanum, more often than from Rome herself.

The road they followed led them through changing scenery; flatlands, hilly lands, towns, agricultural workings, rich pasturages, and dense forests of giant trees, sometimes beside huge dark rivers. Rock changed from dark grey to golden as they travelled, the soil shadings like the stones, and eventually, as they approached the city of Treves, the stones and the soil were both rosy red. As side roads joined into the main route, there was a swelling of the traffic that accompanied them in a broad river valley. River joined with river until the waters became great, like the Tamesis. Unlike the Tamesis, there was no sense of the salted air of the sea about the waters of the Mosella. This was far inland, far from any sea, and yet as great a river as some of the estuaries of Britain. The highway finally came to an end in a huge bridge spanning the combined river forces that curved their way around the side of the famed and powerful city.

York had been a great city; Londinium had been greater; Treves would have been beyond their imagining if they had tried to imagine such a place. Its vast population, hundreds of thousands of people, flowed on beyond the original bounding walls, spreading over the landscape like an organism that could not find a way to stop growing. The dark sentinel mass of the Porta Nigra, the principal gate to the heart of the city walled from the days of Caesar Augustus himself, gave them entrance. Larger public buildings than they had ever seen dominated great avenues, and off these ran an endless number of side streets and tiny crooked lanes, each crowded with dwellings that were crowded with people from all over the world. Looming above them was Constantine's basilica, its thin bricks stacked higher and higher, as if to reach into the sky itself, the soaring height and vast length of the building leaving the Britons breathless. There was more to cause wonder. Within the nearby church founded by Helena, mother of Constantine, was treasured a garment believed to be the very robe of the Saviour. They prayed, prostrate, in the enormous sacred place, giving thanks for a safe journey and praying for the one yet to come.

~~~~~~~~~~

Treves stopped them. They could easily have forgotten that Rome was their destination, for it seemed that they had arrived at the very heart of the world itself, already. They explored it, day after day, never feeling that they plumbed the depths of all there was to discover. They followed the walls, walked broad avenues, searched intriguing secret lanes, and indulged themselves by taking time to simply observe what they could see of the lives of the people who lived in such a place.

They became somewhat bewildered. They had not expected this, when they had set out from Lugo's home in the far north of Rome's world. They had thought that they would walk through Britain, cross the sea, walk overland, climb a range of mountains, and eventually come to the one great city that was the centre of the world — Rome. There would be nothing memorable to experience before they reached Rome; everything of significance would be in Rome. Already, they had discovered in Eboracum that there were ambitions amongst their fellow Britons to rule Rome. In Londinium, they had then begun to understand the complexities of urban life in an Empire that was created from so many kinds of people. Now they had come to another Rome. It was a lesser Rome, perhaps, but it seemed to contain all that they had thought they would need to go to Rome to find.

This was one of the seats of power, one of the settled homes, of the young Emperor of the West, Gratian. Clever and sensitive, earnest and yet not sure of himself, some despised him and others adored him. He was emperor, regardless of their opinions, and all owned him as such. Gratian had recently moved his court across the Alpes mountains to Mediolanum, leaving Treves with only the imprint of his imperial reign, but a deep imprint nonetheless. Even without his presence, the air seemed to whistle with excitement. There was power in the place, and it was noisily exercised. Roles were greedily scrapped over by those left behind to fill his space. Claims of importance were paraded and bellowed by those who believed they had any claim to importance. Intrigues were whispered by those who intended on becoming important. Even in the church there were men of power, who walked with authority.

In Treves Ninian and Lugo experienced a more truly Roman world than ever before. They bathed in the huge Roman baths and attended games in the hillside Roman arena alongside those who were entrusted, from this place, to make decisions on Rome's behalf concerning their own now-distant land of Britain. Here there were scholars to consult, and books to read, both classical and religious. What more could be got from Rome?

As they developed confidence in their new surroundings, the two Britons began again to go their own directions during the days, pursuing their individual inclinations. They returned to the inn in the evenings to share their discoveries and to discuss their plans. Sharing discoveries began to take more time than the making of plans did. There was so much to see and to do in Treves. The future was stalled, postponed, perhaps even abandoned.

Within the central area of the city where many people from many lands jammed together in a confusedly fascinating mingled society, there was one area occupied almost entirely by one singular people, a people apart from the rest. They were the Jews.

In any of the nations of the world there were physical distinctions that made people seem different from each other. This was the case in Britain, where some tribal groups tended to be tall and red-haired, others, tall and fair-haired, yet others small and dark-haired, and many of medium height with brown hair. Peoples of any larger tribal groups vaguely resembled each other in such stature and colouring, as well as in facial structure. Dress varied, too, depending on where people lived, the warmth of their climate affecting their clothing styles as much as individual tribal custom did. Apart from the vivid darkness of the Africans or the golden skins and slanting eyes of the far eastern peoples, most peoples did not appear distinctive enough to be recognisable, as to specific tribal origin, if they were far distant from their own lands, especially if they dressed in the clothes of the region in which they were living. They could blend in amongst the natives if they lived with them long enough.

Jewish men, though, could be recognised wherever they appeared, however long they lived there. No other people were like them, and all of them were like each other. Though, like other tribal groups, they did share vague similarities amongst themselves in a physical, familial sense, these were not what made them so easily identifiable wherever they went. It was the style of their dressing and manner of their living that made them utterly distinctive in human society. The men had curls of hair that dangled against their faces between their full beards and rather long hair. They wore strange garments that proudly featured tassels of threads on the hems. When they prayed, in a unique rocking way, their heads and shoulders enveloped in huge shawls, there were straps wound on their hands and wrists, and mysterious capsules tied to their foreheads.

In Treves, the Jewish people occupied a little area of lanes just behind a busy central thoroughfare. Entering their space, though it was right in the heart of the city, was like discovering a completely different country. The Jews did not move in concert with those around them. Their calendar was their own. Their festivals were different from those shared by the rest of the population. Their week was the same, seven days in length, but the days bore numbers, not names, each beginning and ending at the setting of the sun. When the sky darkened on Friday nights, that part of the city went silent. The stillness was only broken when they moved as a swarm, in the curious rushing manner of a flight of starlings at dusk, to the nearby synagogue for their prayers. All day on Saturdays, the strange silence prevailed throughout their quarter. No outsider dared enter their quarter then, for the Jews appeared to be resentful of intrusion into their designated space on the holy day. Then, on Saturday nights, after the sun had set, they burst into life and action again, filling the street with their business and the noise of their living. When the rest of the great city ceased work on Sundays for the hours of worship, responding to the calls of the bells summoning them to services, the Jews were quiet enough, respectful to a degree, but they could be seen moving about within their own area, occupied in normal business.

They would not share meals with other people. They particularly despised anything that came from a pig, and would not consume any meats purchased in the normal markets. They did not marry except within their own communities. On the rare occasion that a Jewish person chose to marry a Christian, it was said that his people held funeral services for him and considered him as dead, entirely cut off from his own people all his days.

Lugo enjoyed observing the people of the city, and spent much of his time amongst the crowds that gathered in the Forum and the markets. People grew accustomed to seeing him there. A trader would call on him to help shift an unwieldy load. An old man sitting on the street, begging, would answer his greeting and be glad of an hour of his company, idle chatter making a day pass more sweetly. Children would tease Lugo, because he loved the teasing, and they could sense that he did. Women would flirt with the charming Briton, and he loved the flirting.

On a busy day, a young woman who was completely shrouded within her veils tried to slip through a narrow gap between stalls in the marketplace. A rough trader, a coarse man who was known for his short temper and punchy fists, blocked her way and leered at her. He would not let her pass. She quietly spoke a pleading word through her veils. He laughed and his bulk seemed to swell. Lugo, sitting down on the street with the old beggar, glanced up to see her plight. Her veil slipped, and he saw the fear in her eyes, as well as the mockery on the face of the lout. Just as the bully reached forward to grab the girl, compounding his offence, Lugo sprang. He knocked the man sideways, and created space for the girl to escape. The man crashed into his pile of vegetables. Lugo started to wail, "Oh, dear, oh help!" He scrambled about, arms and legs flailing clumsily as if making an attempt to rescue the man, and the vegetables. He stood on the man's foot, while pulling at an arm to raise him. The man bellowed in pain. He dropped the man's arm, as if giving up a hopeless enterprise, leaving him struggling to stand in the middle of all his vegetables. Then Lugo blustered about, loudly exclaiming that he was searching for lost cabbages, scattering the produce in every direction with his stumbling. The fallen man thrashed around, skidding on a pile of rolling onions, trying to gain a foothold so that he could stand up, and he roared at Lugo, who looked horrified, wailing even more loudly, "Oh, dear, oh dear!" A crowd gathered, laughing at the awkwardness of the British fool, immensely delighted as the rage of the fallen stallholder increased and the vegetables went on rolling down the street.

Suddenly the fool was gone and the milling crowd were left with the angry stallholder to sort out the confusion. Further up the street, safely away from the scene and sheltered in a doorway, the young woman was watching. She saw Lugo escape; she saw the laughter in his eyes; she knew that he was no fool. She waited until he was near her and then stepped out from shadows. She smiled at him, and shyly offered, "My thanks". He smiled back at her, and then he watched as she retreated under the Jewish archway, into her different world.

Lugo began to haunt that area of the city, and he saw her, sometimes in her own country under the arch, sometimes leaving that place for the main part of the city, but always in company. It was many days before he found her alone, near the entrance to the Jewish street. He asked her if she were recovered from her ordeal.

She assured him that she was, only thanks to him. She laughed at him, remembering his antics. He laughed at her laughing. They slowly became friends. She trusted him, and her trust was a precious honour to him. Without any warning, Lugo found that he was loving this woman, and he knew by some deep instinct that his love was returned. He was awkward. She became shy. The days went on. The world was full of mysteries and, suddenly, a more complicated place.

Ninian had learned of the floundering trader on the day this had begun. Lugo had shared the story with him, full of detail, full of fun. He had omitted to tell Ninian of the gratitude of the young woman he had rescued. He had no idea why he had kept that lovely part of the story to himself. Ninian was unaware of the change in his friend. He, himself, was absorbed in his own pursuits.

One day Ninian had walked outside the walls of the city, curious to know what life existed outside the gates. Though there were many habitations crammed between the river and the sheltering hill, there were also tended gardens and wilder places not as fully occupied as the area inside the walls. He found a small house, alone, and fell into conversation with the quiet man who was working in the vegetable garden adjoining it. He was intrigued to learn that the man was one of a group who had chosen to separate themselves from the city, from society, and from the world as much as they could. They were devout Christians who had dedicated their lives to serve God Himself, giving up all that linked them with their pasts to do so. Ninian had never heard of this. He knew of priests who were ordained to teach and to lead worship, but they lived in the midst of the world, not separate from it. They lived amongst people in order to serve those people for God's sake. These men in the small house outside the walls of Treves served only God, for His sake alone. It was an entirely new understanding.

Day after day he found his feet returning him to this place, the casa. He was introduced to others of the community. They had no rules but that they share what they held in common in their simple existence, and that all time and means other than those concerned with the barest essentials of living be devoted to God.

They had books, precious books. There were Scriptures. There were commentaries upon Scriptures. There were histories. There were accounts of the lives of men who had served God, as they wished to do, with utter devotion. The lives of the men of the casa spoke to the heart of Ninian, making him hungry to learn all that they knew of a world beyond his experience.

He learned of Antony, a monk in the desert. He had hardly heard what a desert was, and had never heard of a monk. He did not know that miracles, the kinds of miracles that happened in the days of the Bible, still occurred as they had done in the lifetime of the famed Antony, a life that had ended almost immediately before the time of his own birth. He learned the story of the life of saintly Bishop Hilary of Pictavia, of his sense of honour, of enforced eastern exile, of his return to Gaul, of his writings, of his teachings, of his influence on all who now influenced the most important people in the world, regarding the faith of Christ. Hilary had died when Ninian himself was a child, but many still remembered the man. The devout men of Treves spoke often of Ambrose, born in Treves, famed Bishop of Mediolanum, a charismatic and learned persuader for Christ. He heard of the intense-natured young scholar Jerome who had visited this city almost two decades previously, who had copied assiduously, more rapidly and yet more accurately than any other ever observed. Jerome's own translations were now prized, and copies of them were eagerly sought by every student of Scripture. Word had come to Treves that Jerome was preparing a new translation of the Psalms, a work awaited with buzzing excitement.

Ninian learned, too, of one called Martin, protégé of Hilary, now bishop of Turones in Western Gaul. Once a reluctant soldier, Martin had courageously won honourable release from the army and then become an influential missionary for Christ among the pagans of Gaul, deeply respected. His visits to Treves were marked by a church that bore the name of his founding, and in caves among the red cliffs bounding the mighty river of the city. In such caves, they said, he found solitude for times of communion with his God.

Ninian shared with Lugo the story of the casa on the day he discovered its existence. This was the very same day of Lugo's experience in the marketplace. After that recounting, Ninian only barely mentioned his visits there, saying less and less about what he was learning from the community's men and books. He was drinking deeply of the sweetest waters, feeding on the richest food, and he had grown to understand talking about such things for too long, the things that made his heart sing, caused Lugo to yawn.

One day another travelling Briton came to their inn. He was to be in Treves only briefly, returning in one week to Britain. Full of excitement, the man regaled his fellow Britons with all the news of the island that had seemed increasingly far away to them. He told them of the establishment of peace after the crushing of the Scotti and an alliance with the Picts. He told them the wonderful news of cessation of hostilities between Conan and Macsen. Eudaf had died, and Conan finally bowed to the widely acknowledged national popularity of Macsen's leadership. Macsen had not only secured his own place as rightful ruler together with Elen but, as father of Elen's children, was the founder of a new dynasty that would succeed him. In a movement of astounding generosity, Macsen not only forgave Conan for his devastating former rebellion, but made him a partner in his ambitions, promising him great things in the future. The confidence of the nation was increasing daily under the inspiration of Macsen's leadership. So was national prosperity.

The news from Britain shot a lightning bolt through the preoccupations of both Ninian and Lugo. Lugo realised that their people were in the midst of a time of significant change, and that he was far away while it was happening. He was excluded by distance from participating. He wondered whether he would be allowed, when he did return, to find a place among his own again, or whether his place in the greatly altered world of his homeland would have been forfeited, his seat taken by another.

Ninian also was deeply affected by the news. He had no desire to be included in the machinations of politics, the struggles for military or governmental supremacy now firing his race with ambition. Yet, he felt a kind of embarrassment, realising that his people would be regarding him as a deserter from his rightful post at such an important time. They, as they would see it, had fought nobly and done well, bringing the nation into a new time of peace and unity, where those in leadership no longer served foreign leaders but worked under their own chosen king. He, in comparison, would be regarded as merely a follower of his own fancies, a man with no spirit for the fight, no interest in the glory. He should be there with Macsen, with his brothers, they would think, fulfilling the destiny of his birth, not evading it, not wasting the prime of his life in wandering.

He remembered, in consolation, that others had been like him in their pursuits. Martin of Turones, had been so desperate to leave the life of fighting behind that he offered to go into battle with no weapon just to prove to his commander that he was no coward. Thus, he won his dismissal, with honour. Such faith. Ninian felt that he was a beginner only in this life of faith and following God, nothing more. It was a troubled night for him, as he wrestled with these thoughts, tossing from dark confusion to bright believing and back again. He realised that if he would reach his original goal, he must leave this place now, before British armies reached into Gaul, if they came. If they found him here, they would swallow him into their fold, and his freedom to find God's way for him in Rome would become an impossibility.

The next morning he announced imminent departure to the friend he had come to know so very well, fully expecting Lugo's usual sunny acceptance of this decision. He was stunned by the reaction. Lugo looked surprised, and then darkly sullen before storming at him. Nothing in the raging of his words made any sense at all to Ninian, whose reaction was to believe that Lugo must have decided to abandon the journey, to return Britain, to join the army, to join in Macsen's train. He asked if this were the case. "No!" shouted Lugo. " I don't care about that! I just see no reason to go further. You have plenty of opportunity here, Ninian, to do your reading and studying. You couldn't get through the books of Treves in a lifetime. Copy away, go to your services, learn to become a priest, but do it here. This is enough. You have said yourself that Treves seems to hold all that Rome would hold. Why, now, must we go on?"

There was some truth in Lugo's challenge, for he could satisfy himself with all there was in Treves. But he began to explain: Rome was yet the real place of learning, learning that led to credentials, credentials leading to the authority that Ninian must possess if he were to return to teach and minister to his people in Britain. It was more necessary to do this than merely satisfy his own cravings for knowledge. What he did not explain was that there was a more pressing need to leave; he could not find the voice to utter the words of real reason for the suddenness of the decision. How could he tell his faithful, brave friend that he wanted to be gone from this place in case his own people might arrive to claim him by right for their purposes? Their purposes were not the purposes he held as holy things in his heart. He was afraid, so afraid, of losing that which was of God within him.

There was a tension between the two as they parted for the day. Ninian went straight to the casa, determined to finish the work of study and copy he had nearly completed, and to inform his new-found friends of his departure for Rome. Lugo went to the market near the street of the Jews and waited for the appearance of Devorah. He knew that he must go with Ninian at his command. This was what he had agreed when he had joined him on the road to Rome at the door of his father's house, and Lugo would not fail in his word, regardless of personal cost. He seethed at the thought of leaving this place, and this woman. He had no real thought of what a future would hold for them here, even if he could have stayed, but the very intrusion of the word 'departure' into the morning had shocked him out of a long and blissful daydream.

When she appeared, smiling sweetly, openly, and teasing him for his strangely dishevelled appearance, his heart broke. He must leave her, and he could never leave her. The contradiction was a reality, both parts equally true. One was born of honour and the other was born in finally acknowledging the truth of this love. He told her.

Her face whitened, and she seemed to go limp. She leaned against the wall, pulling her veil over her face, leaving only her eyes visible. It would be over then, this impossible, beautiful, sweet friendship, this blooming of love. It would die. It would be forgotten. She would be contracted to one of her own people in marriage, as she had always known that she must be, and soon. The man who kicked cabbages around the marketplace to save her from coarse hands would fade into her past. She would wonder if she had dreamt him. How could she forget the youthfulness of his unbearded face, the wonderful openness of his expression, the mischievous notions that always betrayed themselves in twitching at the corners of his mouth, the huge grin that lit the world around him, the nut brown colour of his hair? She started to turn, to flee into her own place, but he stopped her.

"Devorah, I will come back. I will take you to my own land as my wife, if you will come."

Her heart seemed to stop beating. She, like Lugo, had never thought of the future. They were both people of a present moment, those who delighted in living as they lived. Forced to consider the implications of what he was saying, she turned again to look at him. The shock dried the welling of tears in her eyes and brought colour flooding back into her face. She looked at him fully, deeply, her veil forgotten. She knew suddenly that she, who had never once in her lifetime considered the possibility of leaving her own world to live in the foreignness of any world beyond it, a world full of gentile idolaters, of Christian blasphemers, of unclean foods, of unkept Sabbaths, of uncircumcised children who did not belong to the family ordained by God, that she could live in such a world, but only if Lugo were her centre in that world. She smiled, she nodded, and then she disappeared.

Lugo returned to the inn puzzled by his own impulsive words, but determined to solve the problem of how to fulfil his obligations to both of them. He was not angry with Ninian any longer, he realised, for he was not leaving Devorah forever. Of that he was certain. Ninian, when he returned, was relieved that Lugo was calm, almost normal, but still rather unsure of what he would do next. It was agreed that they could leave Treves immediately in the morning. The two men spoke with their fellow Briton at the inn, arranging that he would carry letters for their families back to their home country. Ninian would write an account of his travel thus far for his younger brother, so that word could be passed formally to his parents, and suitably dutiful filial respect be paid to them. Lugo would scratch a briefer letter to his parents, just to let them know that he was hugely enjoying his adventures. Both Ninian and Lugo wrote separate short notes to Medana, for they had promised, and she would be believing their promises.

~~~~~~~~~~

Medana was noticeably weary when she concluded this part of her story. She sat still, silently, for a while, apparently dwelling in the time of which she had spoken. "The letters arrived safely," she said finally. " I learned about their amazing journey from what Lugo wrote to my father, and later I learned more from Ninian's brother. Lugo and Devorah told me many more things when they returned. I treasured my own letters from my brother and from Ninian. I have them still, though the ink has almost disappeared from the writing." Her face suddenly sweetly childlike, she added, "I know the words even where I cannot find the ink. I memorised the lines. I prayed for them every day.... all day. I missed them so much." Then she sighed, and stood up, stretching a little as she gathered her cloak around her and turned to go. "It is good to remember the story. As I tell it, I remember more and more. Tomorrow I will tell you about Rome, if God will spare me. I think He will." She chuckled, and she moved away.

SIX: Greater Heights
"Then on foot he crossed the Alps....."
"The Miracles of Bishop Nynia" trans. by Winifred
MacQueen

It was now high summer. They had walked for a long time, between equinox and midsummer, by the time they arrived at Treves. When they recommenced their journey after a month in that city, they realised that time was passing very quickly. Fearsome, fabled mountains lay ahead of them. These must be crossed before the autumn snows sealed shut the passes through the Alpes. From the days of their childhood in Britain they had heard stories of these massive Alpes, how high, how dangerous, and how desperately steep the crossing paths were. Bold and brave young men of north Britain were not in the least daunted by such tales, for they were men of the mountains themselves. The west and northlands of Britain were full of mountains.

The next stage of the journey, though, before they reached the Alpes, involved travelling along the great plain that was the valley of the River Rhenus. Moving quickly among the red, vine-clad banks of the Mosella, through dense forests and along the sides of deep gorges, they made good time. They found that it felt good to be walking again, and they were eager to compensate for lost time in Treves. The landscape flattened, and broadened before them. They were soon in a much more open landscape. The Rhenus valley, defining an eastern border of this western empire, was so great an expanse that they could not sight where the river lay within it. Bounding them on the west were beautiful rolling hills, and a range of mountains could also be seen far to the other side of the great plain, within the dangerous territories occupied by unromanised Germanic tribes.

During the time in Treves, Ninian had begun to observe the

practice of private prayer during his daily routine. He had learned the importance of this from the devout brothers of the casa. This was something more personal than the prayers of formal public worship, and something more disciplined than the spontaneous experiences of crying out in moments of crisis or joy. This was regular, habitual, solitary prayer. Each morning he would slip off a little distance somewhere, hidden if he could be from the sight of a puzzled Lugo, just for a while. He would open his heart to his God, and lay the matters of each day before Him. Lugo said nothing about this curious activity, only shrugging his shoulders at the signs of excessive religious devotion in his friend who would now pray before he could walk. At night, when they had prepared their camp, shared their food, and were ready to settle to sleep, Ninian would creep off again to give thanks. Lugo was usually snoring by the time Ninian returned.

It took them an unexpectedly long time to reach the great boundary river, and then a good number of days of trudging alongside it before they reached the place where they were to cross to the other bank and begin their approach towards the mountainous area yet barring them from Rome. Already fully two weeks since they had made their departure from Treves, it was yet another three days after they had crossed the river, following a road sometimes pressed between other curving rivers and hills, sometimes stretching straight in a Roman way across winding green valley floors that led from one into another, before, at last, they began to enter the Alpes terrain. Higher mountains rose alongside the way, enfolding valleys, making of them secret, hidden places. When they reached a comfortable settlement at the edge of a large and beautiful lake, they barely paused in the place, for they saw more mountains, yet bigger mountains, still far off in the distance. For the first time they realised that the mountains were not a formed of a single barrier ridge of peaks, but that there were fold upon fold of bands of these heights, and that there was a long way to go before they would reach the other side of them.

Looking down at waters below them from the side of a gorge, they noticed that the river in the bottom of the valley was not the colour of any river they had ever seen. It was not dark, brooding grey, or the blue brightness of any sky-reflecting stream; it was green, truly green water, rushing and clean. Clouds came down, shutting out the day's light before its time, and though they walked in a gloomy darkness, the air was mild. It seemed strange to walk in clouds among high mountains and still to be uncomfortably warm.

They finally sought a resting place, exhausted from their travels. In spite of lowered clouds hiding the mountain tops from view, they sensed that they were surrounded by peaks that soared beyond any in their experience. For all the distance they had covered within this mountain world, they had not actually seemed to have climbed to any height. The road seemed content to move deeper and deeper into the range on the level, from one absolutely flat valley floor to another flat valley floor. Sometimes there was a little rise in level between successive valleys, but beyond any such rising it was always yet another flat valley floor. The mountains surrounding them climbed skyward, but they did not.

The stories they had heard all their lives about the vastness of these mountains, the strange sharp points of them, the terrifying roads that crossed through them, their deadly steep precipices, thundering avalanches of snow sweeping travellers to their deaths, all seemed to have been mere fantasies. Such tales had been told by Gaulish traders, Roman soldiers, in fact, by any and all who had ever seen this strange land of the Alpes. While level, quiet green valleys, ribboned by rushing green waters, endlessly wound their way in between admittedly great heights, the tales seemed unreal. They began to joke with each other about it all, about the storytellers who had obviously been teasing them. Lugo was confident, "It's the style of the people from these countries. They exaggerate everything they say. They get very excited."

Ninian agreed, but then remarked, "It's strange that they all said the same things. It doesn't make sense. Their stories matched. If they made them up, they should have said different things. Very odd."

They plodded on, musing about this. The beautiful Alpine valleys, lush with the deep golden grasses of late summertime, were being harvested by the families who occupied small huts here and there. Delicate faced, small pale brown cows, and goats too, could be seen in the higher pasture areas, grazing contentedly among blossoms. These cattle were nothing like the cattle of northern British stock, sturdy, black, woolly in comparison, cattle that were herded to rough moorland pastures in the summer and grazed on ever-green pastureland nearer towns later, until they would be forced to eat conserved hay over the dead time of the midwinter. These high mountain cattle were gentle creatures, more like deer. They seemed to carry abundant milk, much of which was obviously used in making the light creamy cheeses to be found at every table in the homes and inns of the people of these mountain lands. There did not seem to be much meat on their bones.

The travellers came to another huge lake. They could not believe that such a vast body of water could lie, filling its basin to the full below grimly steep tree- lined slopes, so far into the body of the mountain range. The sides of the hills were so vertical that no road could be carved into them along the sides of the lake, not even a Roman road. A willing boatman sailed them to the far edge of the water, landing on a shingle beach formed at a little opening. There they found the trusty road that began again its march toward Rome.

One night in a small village, the kindly local people who fed them and gave them sleeping room urged Ninian and Lugo to accept a guide from among their number for the next stage of their journey. This did not seem at all necessary. The road was a plain enough way, and surely if they simply followed it as one flat valley led to another flat valley, it would eventually lead them out into the southern side of the Alpes. Though they sensed that it would be a kindness to these people to pay them for the services of a guide, something that would obviously augment the income of such a remote community, the two young men did not have resources enough to feel able to dispense with any money merely out of generosity toward them. Another traveller would come along soon to welcome their services and fill their pockets, undoubtedly. They were not afraid to go on alone.

When they set out into the dawning of the next day, a slip of a lad, with an obvious expression of determination on his face, was waiting for them. They attempted to refuse his insistence of help, but there was concern in the look that darkened his face. Lugo attempted to brush him aside, but Ninian softened, remembering how Lugo, too, had waited for him in this way. He intervened, motioning to the boy to precede them on the road. Turning to his puzzled friend, he said, "After all, it is written, 'A small youth shall be their guide.'"

The boy seemed relieved. He was cheerful as they began their walking, but as time went on the weather changed and he began to appear anxious. Just then, the great shoulders of mountains seemed to close in more tightly around them, and the way became steeper. Walking was more difficult. Their breath came in sharp gasps as they ascended higher and higher. In an ominously treeless terrain, they had to pause for rest too often for their liking.

Toward the west, there suddenly seemed to be a space between the enclosing mountains. They approached a river bed between steep flanks of rock and the clear roadway disappeared in the ford. Across that water, still in the bottom of a ravine, they could see a path moving in the direction of the broader, lighter way, off to the left of them, and they tried to argue with their guide, who was moving forward, more to the right, across a rough, gravel-covered slope. Surely the left, eastern path, was the obvious way they should go. Ninian and Lugo dearly hoped it was the way to go. It looked, to them, like it was the beginning of the ending of the enclosing massif, and by this stage they longed to be at such a point, to begin their long-awaited descent to Rome. The boy stubbornly refused, stood his ground, and pointed across the patch of scree into an area of dark mountain, sheer cliff face, an area where there was little light penetrating the mountain spaces. He insisted that the road lay in that direction. They were forced to follow him, wondering where he thought he was going.

Eventually, the road appeared beneath their feet again, carved right into a rocky hillside. The road remained flat no longer, but climbed, and crept alongside yet another little valley, this time seen from a greater height, strangely green and fruitful in the bottom of an otherwise utterly barren terrain. The continued stringing of sweet green flatlands, increasingly far below them, seemed more and more incongruous in a world walled to the sky with mountains of solid grey rock, steeper and sharper by the mile. They dared not to ask if they were nearing the top of the pass, beginning to understand the stories of the travellers that were turning out to be not such fantasies after all.

There was yet more. Beyond a small hilltop settlement where they found brief rest and simple refreshment, the young guide began to urge them forward, this time with a strange grimness in his expression. As they rounded the next stone flank of mountainside, they saw that beneath this one there was no space for any soft green valley. The worn road under their feet had been hacked long ago right into the face of the rock and rose, dangerously steeply, above a deepening chasm. Following the boy, Ninian and Lugo clung to the inner side of the pathway, scrambling along it with hands as well as feet, struggling to stay away from the edge, to keep moving upwards. Lugo muttered, just loudly enough for Ninian to catch his words, "I hope you prayed well this morning." Ninian did not reply. He had no spare breath for speaking.

Far, far below them, pale green water foamed and churned its way the opposite direction, searching for the sea that was so very far away. The clouds above them broke apart, a brilliant blast of sunlight streaming down into the narrow cleft in the mountain slabs and, for the first time the two Britons clearly saw the soaring, jagged, snow-capped peaks of the tops of the Alpine range, like needles seeking to pierce the very sky. They stood in awe, bracing themselves in fear at the height. Then they sat, right on the road, gasping for breath and gazing in wonder-filled silence. No one had exaggerated. No one had ever said it plainly enough. This was both an exquisite beauty and a truly terrible power, nature in a form beyond anything they could ever have imagined. Only eyes seeing it could believe it. They looked at each other in silence, just shaking their heads, and then they began to laugh. They laughed until they shouted, a silly shared delight in the realisation of their own stupidity echoing like music from rockface to rockface. The guide just grinned at them. He had seen it all before.

Not long after, they noticed that the river below them was running the other direction, with them, southward, no longer to the north. At last, at long, long last, they were on the other side. They were on the Roman side of the Alpes. Their feet began to go downhill. The beaming sun glared off the rocks, warming them increasingly, welcoming them. They were dazzled, and deliriously happy. They had done it!

They now pressed their young guide to return home. They didn't want him to have to climb uphill again, or to remain so long with them that his family would worry about his safety. He refused to go. Danger was not fully past for them.

The descent, carved into continuing stone mountainside, followed the torturous course of a foaming river. Rome had machined her way along a route where from antiquity goats had skittered, mules had crept, and even humans had crawled, albeit in dread of their lives. The Empire had designed straight highways wherever in the world it could make them; this was not a such a place. Nonetheless, a decidedly brave assault had been made by Rome's architects on the Alpes, nature's barricade against Rome's expanding military authority, freedom of movement, and ease of trade. Slices had been taken out of rock where necessary, viaducts had bridged impossible gorges and, where nothing else would work, men had tunnelled passageways through solid stone. Such works, no doubt, had been created at the cost of many lives, but nature had, in the end, conceded passable ways through for Rome's use.

The Britons and their guide finally came upon valleys again, beautiful, green, flat, safe valleys. Vines grew beside the pathway. The ground itself seemed kinder. Breathing came more easily. In an open, meadowy space framed by a distant waterfall, so high and steep in its plunge to the valley that it looked more like a misty veil hanging than a torrent of water, they camped, rested, and regained their strength. Around a cluster of nearby huts, pigs squealed. Dogs barked. Birds cheeped. Geese honked. A local man riding on a white donkey nodded as he passed them.

Later, the boy recognised familiar faces amongst a group of travellers approaching on foot toward the pass they had just descended. At last he signed to his wards that he would return with these people. Ninian and Lugo were on secure footing now, and company for the boy on his return over the pass would be a safer, a more pleasant experience than walking alone over the hard places he knew so well to fear. His job was done. They paid him, grateful in spite of themselves for his guidance, and truly respectful of his work. To their mild astonishment, the reserved Britons found themselves embraced and kissed by the lad, and then he was gone.

~~~~~~~~~~

It was over. The northern men had walked to the southern coast of Britain, crossed the sea, traversed the whole of the length of Gaul, and clambered over the mighty, terrifying Alpes. They knew that there lay before them only one last stage of their journey. They must descend from sub-Alpine hills to the city of Mediolanum, home of famed Bishop Ambrose, and then travel on from there by a very ancient Roman road, one that would end inside the gates of Rome itself. Any day they would arrive at the most famous city on earth. They imagined the remainder of the way to be much the same in distance and time as they had experienced during the very first stage of their venture, from Hadrian's Wall to Eboracum, a walk of a week, or perhaps even a little more. Mediolanum, the first goal of this final part of the journey, might be a day away. And so they began to stride on more level ground again, eager to be arriving. They walked. And still they walked. There was no sign of the next city. The great mountains gradually opened out. Lakes filled the spaces. Sometimes they walked beside the lakes, or boats took them the length of the waters. The mountains retreated into the distance, day after day, until peaks merely framed the horizon.

It was fully another week before they reached Mediolanum, nowhere yet near Rome. The anciently proud city was raised a little above the level of a river's plain, ringed by walls studded with many gates. The two Britons had little interest in the place and no desire to remain any time there. They had known such cities before, and met interesting, even influential, people who lived in them. They had crossed the Alps, and had done so with only a boy guide. Wonders were losing any power to amaze them. They would, however, appreciate a good soak in a civilised Roman bath and a hot meal of rich meats, tender from stewing, flavoured with tasty herbs, dishes prepared by skilful hands. The gates were open, and they entered Mediolanum, just for a night.

The footsore and dirty travellers refreshed themselves at the public baths. Their fellow bathers were speaking about Ambrose. They ate a wonderful meal. Their fellow diners in the inn were talking about Ambrose. They were puzzled. This city knew the presence of not one emperor, but two emperors and a mother empress as well. Here resided, in such personages, the embodiment of all the imperial power of a world encompassed within the mighty Western Empire of Rome. Strangely, royal palaces and royal occupants of them did not seem to be the greatest influence in Mediolanum. Ambrose did.

In the morning, it being the Lord's Day, the two young British Christians made their way toward the church in the central plaza of the city. They walked in an increasing throng, the city's inhabitants all appearing to be walking together towards the large basilica. No one paid any attention to the strangers as they walked, or as they entered with the crowd. They managed to find space where they could stand, though they were pressed, squeezed, against a wall by the increasing mass of people crowding into the place.

The people began to sing, to their amazement. Britons did not sing in churches. Neither Ninian nor Lugo had ever heard people singing in congregational worship. They had heard Roman soldiers singing as they marched; they had been entertained by singers at banquets; they knew the sound of a priest intoning prayers, or of a mother soothing a child in song, but they had never heard a mass of people in song, in church. Nowhere had they ever experienced a feeling like that which swept over them when this sound began. Thousands of voices, swelling together in words that confirmed their faith in Father, Son and Holy Spirit, words that praised God, words that adored, that joyed, that prayed for blessing, rang out with the sound of heavenly anthems, filling every corner of the building, and flooding with emotion every heart within it. Sometimes the congregation sang as one; then they sang in parts, one half singing to the others, and being sung back to across the dividing aisles. Voices of men, women and children blended into the richest, most glorious music that could be imagined. The Britons could not sing because they did not know the songs, but had they known them, their emotions would have robbed them of their voices. It was like angels. It must be.

Then, at the front of the basilica, a slightly built man stood. All went silent, every eye upon the man, eager, expecting. He had a long face, a neatly trimmed dark beard, and large ears. His drooping eyes had sadness in their expression, and tenderness. His head tilted slightly to one side as he looked out over the people, as if listening for something in the stillness.

When Ambrose spoke, all else was forgotten. He talked in a way no bishop had talked before. He did not read his words, but spoke quietly, earnestly from his heart, looking into their faces as he addressed them. He looked at them like he knew them, and loved them, and his words were like honey.

This was no pretender. This man knew these people like a father knows his children or a shepherd knows his sheep, and that was how he addressed them. He told them of ancients who had been people just like them, but who had walked with their Creator, and been blessed by Him. He spoke of the beginning of the world, of the love of God and the schemes of the Devil. He told them of battles between good and evil, and the mercies of God in rescuing men and women who strayed from His path. He made the ancient Book of the Hebrews, stories in texts the people had known so little of, alive to them, and one in message with the more familiar sacred texts from the Christian era. He lifted before them the story of Jesus of Nazareth, the Jewish Messiah, the Gentile Christ, as the Son of God who had come to earth to redeem all men, for all ages, to the glory of God.

According to the plan of the Eternal Father, by virtue of the sacrifice of His Only Begotten Son, and in the power of the Holy Spirit, men and women and children should now live for God. Bishop Ambrose begged his flock on that Sunday morning to surrender their lives to Him. He plead with them to be honest, to be loving, to be humble, to give what they had to the poor, to bear responsibility with dignity and integrity in serving their God with all their hearts, souls, minds and strength.

He ended his discourse with prayers, and prayed blessing upon his people.

His words ceased, but the transfixed congregation remained silent and did not move at all. For many minutes they stood in this way, absolutely still, seeming to be barely even breathing. Eventually, still hushed, they began to creep out of their holy place and back into the world outside.

Ninian and Lugo were stunned. They had never experienced a time like this time, this short time, so full of emotion and spiritual power. They had never heard of such a thing happening anywhere but in the times of the Bible. What they had witnessed, and felt in their hearts, caused them to understand the curious preoccupation they had observed among the people in the baths, in the inn, even on the streets of Mediolanum. They realised why emperors and empresses were not regarded here as of supreme importance. What had the rule of an empire to offer in comparison with God's dealing with mankind? They wanted more of Ambrose, and began to ask everyone about him.

The beloved Bishop of Mediolanum, they learned, lived an uncompromising life. He was known for extreme frugality. He only dined twice in a week, and on feast days. Every day he shared Eucharist with his people. From the time of that morning sacrament until the night he would then remain in his chamber with the door kept open so that anyone who wished, anyone at all, could come to speak with him. A beggar might come; an emperor was welcomed. Appointments were not necessary, and no one would be refused. If there were a gap in time between visitors who sought his counsel, he would read. He could be seen reading, but not heard, for he read silently, his lips moving without a sound being uttered. It was a curious habit, all agreed. At night, after the doors were closed, he would diligently read, study, write, and pray. He slept very little. There was not time, for there was much to do.

It was said that Barnabas, the Biblical saint who had helped the Apostle Paul in his work, had established the first leadership of the Christian church in Mediolanum. From that time others had followed to lead the believers there, sometimes in periods of persecution, sometimes in peace. For twenty years a tyrant, an Arian named Auxentius had held the chair of bishop in the city, and many had suffered during his rule. When he died, his ruthless followers were determined to install another like him in his place, but those who were of orthodox belief, so long oppressed and yearning to rejoin their city to the mainstream of Christian understanding, began to object. Feelings were intense on the subject, on both sides, and neither party was willing to compromise its position. The heat of the struggle had reached boiling point, and civil war was imminent when the church met to decide upon the successor. The building was filled with determined opponents, each seeking their own candidates.

Into this dangerous scene of chaos had come the Roman-appointed consular prefect Ambrosius Aurelius. Descended from a long line of Roman nobility, his father having been praetorian prefect of Gaul, his inherited leadership credentials were sound. Even more, he had become known in the city as a good man, one with wisdom, of peaceful purposes, and possessed of honest intelligence. He stood before the people courageously and urged the disturbed throng to behave as Christians should, to seek a just, mutual settlement between them.

A child called out his name, and somehow the crowd were electrified. "Ambrose, for Bishop!" they demanded, in a roar. Ambrose was a catechumen, a seeker, student of the faith, not even baptised. He was horrified at the implications of what was happening and fled the place, even the city. Eventually, though, he returned and was prevailed upon to recognise what the people had seen and even his emperor could understand, that this was a true calling.

He was baptised immediately and set about to divest himself of his considerable inheritance of wealth and power. He took care to provide for any who would be dependant upon him, especially his devout older sister Marcellina who lived in the family home in Rome. His brother, Satyrus, gave up his own pursuits to oversee all practical matters for the new bishop. Ambrose, freed of temporal concerns, gave himself up to a long period of earnest study. He had studied Greek, rhetoric and poetry with the best tutors in Rome in his youth, so was possessed of an excellent classical education. Now, though, if he would be a good bishop, he needed to know the Scriptures, the writings of the Church fathers, and all theological works available to him. He prayed, mightily, and all his industry and prayers seemed blessed as he poured himself into his work amongst the people who had called him to serve them.

His devoted brother had died and a church was begun at the grave. The site also incorporated the graves of two Christian gentlemen who had been martyred elsewhere but whose bodies had been carried by those who had honoured them to Mediolanum for burial. This basilica was away from the central square of the city, near the Roman walls. Ambrose planned that this would also be the last resting place for his own remains.

The people of the city began to delight in the wonderful Biblical teachings and practical guidance of their teacher. They flocked to hear him, and so many came to be baptised each year that the baptismal services in Holy Week could barely cope with the numbers. Ambrose began to be sought within church councils and travelled to other parts of the country to help settle disputes between theological factions. His judgements were prized. He increased in influence as young Emperor Gratian sought his guidance in matters of faith. Ambrose developed a reputation for strength of purpose when he held firm against the rising demands of the famed beauty Empress Justina who, on behalf of her young son Valentinian II insisted that Arians be granted their own major places of worship among the churches of the city. The gentle bishop of peace was a man who had no fear, courted no favour, and obeyed his conscience above the imperious demands of any earthly ruler, however beautiful, however powerful. He would not bend, no matter who blustered or wheedled, when he believed that he was in the right. He feared, truly, only his God.

Since he had divested of all his wealth and titles to secular power, he was as poor as the poorest of his people. Any money that came to his hand, he gave to them, and called them his stewards. He sold gorgeous church plate to pay ransom for Christians captured by barbarians, for he declared that human lives were more valuable than metal or jewels. He lived as he taught others to live. For his sincerity and humility, even more than for his naturally powerful influence, the people respected and loved him. Bishop Ambrose had become the great heart at the core of Mediolanum, the delight and the pride of her people.

Weeks passed. The British prince and his friend fell under the influence of the Bishop's ministry, and they were reluctant to move onward. They shared the Eucharist with the people of the city each morning. Each Sunday they rushed to the basilica to hear Ambrose speak, eager to learn more, and more, and more. It was never enough. There were such riches here, riches of learning and power in experience. The words of the anthems and the melodies quickly became familiar to them, and they began to sing with the congregation. The more Ambrose read and taught from the Scriptures, the more they realised how little they had known. The prayers and scraps of writing that had been Ninian's most priceless possessions since his childhood seemed only bare, tiny little fragments in comparison with all that he came to understand could be studied and, with precious time, could be copied to be read and studied over and over.

The Britons also developed a sense of curiosity about the stories of the early Christians in this city during the times of persecution. Compared with Britain, where there were fewer Christians, scattered towns and smaller cities, the Latin peninsula seemed to abound with stories of hundreds, if not thousands of martyrs for the faith, from the time of the Apostles in Rome to the time of Diocletian and even during the reign of Julian the Apostate, times that could still be remembered by many. They remembered and they recited names, dates, and places, with horrid details of the suffering the faithful Christians had been forced to endure. The people of Mediolanum were descendants of those heroes in those times.

Ninian was always absorbed by his faith. This was the very reason he was in this place at this time. Here, though, even Lugo, a merely nominal Christian, was affected by Mediolanum's preoccupations. He forgot to haunt the docks and marketplaces. He, too, was drinking in the very atmosphere of a place that became, for the two of them, a City of God.

Eventually, though, news of events occurring in the world beyond Mediolanum began to disturb their peace. During their time in the city, letters were written and sent to those at home, letters expressing wonder and delight at all they were experiencing. Answering letters had finally reached them there. Conversations with travellers passing through confirmed what they read. As the power of the dying Eudaf waned, Britain had risen, almost to a man, in support of Macsen as king. The final crushing of the Scotti soldiers and the ruthlessly accomplished cleansing of their presence from within the lands of Britain, as well as the profoundly affecting national reconciliation between Macsen's followers and those of Conan, had caused the people to acclaim Macsen as the only rightful wearer of the purple within the island. Voices of ambition in Britain were declaring that their king, their own Macsen, must now extend his rule beyond their own shores, into the wider Empire. It would be better for Britain to rule Gaul, Hispania, and even over Rome.

Gratian, young, playful, questing, unsoldierly Gratian, was despised in the northern lands, considered a weakling who was unfit to rule. He had not brought the peace to Britain. Macsen had. Gratian evidenced no purpose to bind Rome in obligement to protect Britain in the future. Macsen would. Theodosius, enthroned in Constantinople, was seen as greater, far greater, than Gratian, and Macsen was deemed to be the equal of the younger Theodosius, even his better.

As word spread, the city of Mediolanum was stunned by the news. Gratian was weak enough, it was true. He had too easily

96

been persuaded to share his western kingdom with his baby half brother. He did not have a soldier's heart. He played his sporting games and paraded his wild Scythian bodyguard in the lands of Gaul when he should be ruling more effectively. He was learning, though, guided by Ambrose, and had a good heart. The child Valentinian II was growing up. The people had been content enough with their young emperors who were, after all, the rightful sons of a rightful preceding emperor. The city began to buzz with alarm, and annoyance. Such things should not be. Usurpers had no right to rule in such circumstances, and British king usurpers even less than others! Magnus Clemens Maximus might claim royal blood and powerful personal credentials as a warrior leader, but he was not, and never had been, the inheriting son of a rightful Roman Emperor.

No one noticed the two young Britons stealing out of the gates of the city to begin the last stage of their journey to Rome.

Second Part: To Follow Christ

SEVEN: Britons in Rome
" 'I will seek the truth which my soul loves'........
Coming to Rome...."
"Vita Niniani" by Ailred of Rievaulx,
trans. by Winifred MacQueen

It was fully autumn when Ninian and Lugo finally walked into Rome. During the final hour of their journey along the Via Flaminia, they passed for three long and eerie miles between cemeteries that crowded against the great Servian walls binding the city within its ancient space. There were many huge sepulchres lining the roadway, ornately carved stone memorials to the powerful and rich personalities of Rome's past. There were entrances, too, to underground caverns, catacombs, where rested the remains of thousands of ordinary people, poor people, often now-forgotten people, but proud Romans nonetheless. These reminders of past ages, silent sentinels, witnessed now the arrival of the tired Britons, ushered them solemnly onwards, along the straight, straight road, toward the gateway granting passage into the heart of the living city that had once been their own.

The travellers entered the Porta Flaminia in the softening, glowing gold of twilight, their first view of the city magically beautiful, forever remembered. Her famous seven hills were graced and greened with palaces and gardens; her spoke-like streets leading straight onwards toward the golden milestone in the Forum past broad side avenues lined with handsome tenements. The Tiber, snaking softly toward the Mediterranean, spanned by wonderful ancient bridges, provided lushness in her trail as she wound her way through the greatest city on earth.

They passed the mausoleum of Caesar Augustus, the man who had ruled from this Rome in the days when the Christ child was born in far-off Bethlehem. Off to the right of the die-straight road lay the brooding mass of the majestically pillared, soaringly domed Pantheon. The ancient temple to all pagan gods, all gods presided over by the greatest of them all, Jupiter, had stood for more than two centuries in its present form as designed by the Roman Emperor Hadrian. The emperor whose commands had walled their own British island, planting his name on the remotest Roman boundary in the world, had defied the claims of the Christ throughout his empire in his day. His famed pagan Pantheon was now neglected, even abandoned, for the city and empire once ruled by Hadrian in defiance of Christ had become Christian. Jupiter was fallen, and the presence of Christian Britons walking from Hadrian's Wall to learn of Christ in Rome bore witness to this fact.

Suddenly the Capitoline was straight in front of them, the Arx peaking at its side. They saw them just as the last light left the sky. They were truly in the heart of Rome. They had reached their destination. They had done it!

The Britons stood in wonder as darkness fell, gazing around them at the city that was like no other city on earth, like none had ever been. Ninian was born a prince of the Britons and Lugo was consciously the companion of a prince, but here, in this moment, they were less than nothing, and both felt as insignificant as ants.

Night had begun, but this city's life carried on regardless. Torches blazed on the street; lamps and candles gleamed their lights from windows; it could have been day. Thousands and thousands of people pressed on every side, rushing to and fro around the watching Britons, calling to each other, laughing, shouting, confiding, arguing, cajoling, threatening, loving. These were the sounds of every kind of human experience in concert. There was every possible human appearance, too: tall, and short, thin and fat, old, young, beautiful, ugly, brown, black, white, golden, some clothed in rags and some decked in silk. There were powerfully important people on the street as well as people who were trying to appear to be powerfully important even if they were not; and there were busy, attending slaves doing the bidding of all such. There were prosperous-looking common folk, plain and hearty, confident and purposeful. There were others who seemed more like scraps, the debris of something hardly recognisable as truly human, crouched along edges and huddled in darker corners. Their bones were like sticks, their eyes silently pleading, their hands outstretched for anything, anything at all. It was overwhelming.

Exhaustion made the young men seek shelter at last. They enquired of someone, asking where they might find space. They walked a few streets back from the foot of the Capitoline hill, going toward the river, and in a side lane they rapped on a door. It was a simple lodging house, and it had room for them. Assigned to a cubicle, coins clinking in the palm of the hand showing the way with an oil lamp, they had no words to speak with each other. They simply fell to their pallets, exactly as they were, sandals and all, and slept soundly, deeply, sweetly.

When the sun rose, a new world and life began. This time, they did not know how long it would go on, or how it would end. There had been no real stated plan, when they set out for Rome, beyond this goal, this famed destination. They had arrived. They truly had arrived in Rome. What now?

At the beginning, curiosity drove them to see all there was to see, to learn Rome as they had learned Eboracum, Londinium, Treves, and Mediolanum. They walked and walked, looked and looked, listened and learned each day until they could absorb no more.

The first day they went together to the Forum. They needed to touch the place of the golden milestone, the beginning point of every road made within the empire. Wherever Rome had forged a way, north, south, east or west, to the extremities of Britain and Hispania, as well as the far-off lands in the east, Roman road builders had marked their miles from this point. The experience of entering the Via Sacra seemed unreal, like walking into a fable. Ninian descended through the magnificent Arch of Septimus Severus as if he were floating; Lugo kept shaking his head, rubbing his arms, fluttering his fingers, as if he were trying to waken himself from dreaming.

The amazing Curia rose to their left. The voices of Julius Caesar and Cicero had rung out within this very building. These walls held those sounds. Such famous men and others like them had influenced lives all over the world with their philosophies sung out in passionate oratory, and the powers exercised from this place had touched lives to the ends of the empire.

The famous black paving marking the establishment of the city back beyond the mists of known time was there, in front of them, not merely mythical any longer, but solid stone they could touch.

There were temples everywhere, above them, around them, behind them, in front of them. Beautiful buildings, ribboned by elegant marble pillars, decorated with exquisite carvings, beckoned worshippers, but worshippers were few. Like the Pantheon, these pagan-purposed buildings held no meaning any more for most people, and served little purpose in the corridors of power. Once, in supreme confidence that it would always be so, they had governed the spiritual lives of those who reigned in the city and its empire. Those who still practised the ancient faiths did so now in emptying buildings, worrying as they did so about the fate of such places, saddened in contemplation of their future. What would become of the temples and, indeed, what would become of the throngs of women, bred and trained for generations to serve within them, vestal virgins, the royal princesses of religion from ages past? These once honoured and envied women who had walked with dignity and celebrity to their places of service were now sad-faced, rather pathetic, and merely scuttled between their ancient home on the slopes of the Palatine Hill and the temples of the forum. Those who yet observed pagan rituals needed these women, but those who needed them were becoming fewer. As the riches and power of the Church increased in Christian Rome, year after year, their hopes for a future restoring past glories to them were diminishing. Christians who loved beauty for its own sake could not take pleasure in the destruction of such glorious buildings, whatever they had once symbolised, and they faced a growing dilemma, for they could not really support them without compromising the integrity of their own faith.

Halfway down the Via Sacra on the left side was the

enormous Basilica of Christian Constantine. It dwarfed all other such buildings that had seemed large in the memories of the two Britons until this day. Even the Basilica of Constantine in Treves that had looked so very, very immense when they first saw it, would be small in comparison to this. Vast domes. Power. Greater power than could be imagined by anyone anywhere until they saw this structure and entered its space.

Ninian and Lugo stood before it, marvelling. Eventually the monstrous doors swung open, and they got a glimpse of the incredible interior that seemed to go on forever. In one apse there was a colossus, a figure of Constantine the Great himself, Blessed Constantine as Britons had always thought of him. The head of the statue was so high up, so far away from those standing at its feet, and so huge, that it could not seem like it could have been modelled on any normal human being in any way.

Ninian gazed at the distant head, bearing the face of the man said to have been the grandfather of Macsen himself. He knew the face of Macsen. Even though the features were something the same, this statue was the face of a stranger to him. Before this moment, when hearing the name of Constantine, a sense of goodness and greatness, even of kinship and familiarity would be carved into any imagined countenance. This face, on this colossal statue, was a brutal one. It spoke of power, not of any grace, not at all. The blank eyes were stony cold. This was awesome, unsettling. The inspiration of fear was obviously intended by this portrayal of the Emperor Constantine. But, thought the Briton who gazed on it, should any man be presented as this mighty? Even Constantine? Were all men, whether they were ordinary men, princes, kings or emperors, not just men? They were not gods! They were not giants! Why were they pretending to be greater than men? A stray cat slept, nestled between two toes of a giant foot of the statue. It was smaller than the smallest toe.

Outside the chill darkness of the massive Basilica, the sun warmed the scene and they walked on in the ancient sacred way that curved, down below the height of the basilica, joining with another road. They walked on eastwards, rising again to a higher level through a smaller archway, one that commemorated the historic Triumph of Titus. Rich carvings on the stonework portrayed his conquering of Jerusalem, the chief victory of this emperor. His reign had only begun, not long after he had destroyed the Holy City, when it was blasted by the eruption of a mountain, Vesuvius, with the resulting destruction of the famous cities of Pompeii and Herculaneum, cities devoted to pleasure and emperor worship. They were no more.

On the Arch of Titus were depicted captive Jews, led away in triumphal train to this Rome, their holy temple menorah raised high in the hands of victorious Roman plunderers. Lugo stood for a long time, looking at the carvings, remembering Devorah in Treves. In the home of his beloved there had been just such a branched candlestick, much revered by her family. She had once shown him when no one was there. She had explained that it was a small copy of the Temple's menorah, ever remembered by her people in lands of exile, so far away from their homeland, still honoured in domestic ceremonies long generations after any of them had seen Jerusalem with their own eyes. The Titus of this archway had destroyed their city and temple, but it was Hadrian, the builder of the wall in Britain, who had later banned the Jewish people from their land forever.

On the higher ground beyond the Arch of Titus, the Britons were amazed again, the yet greater Triumphal Arch of Constantine, the massive and infamous Roman Colosseum, and the Colossus of Nero all towered above them. Crowds were pouring from all directions into the tiered circle where men and women roared in approval while other men died in sport, for their amusement. Even Britons knew that fellow Christians had been among those whose deaths in this place had entertained throngs of Romans during the dark past times of persecution. They knew that still, to this day, gladiators faced death in the blood-soaked arena. The Britons had not learned to enjoy such sport, and hoped that they never would as they pushed their way out against the press of the gathering crowd.

Wearied by the unaccustomed heat of even autumnal sunshine and drained of energy by many conflicting emotions, they made their way back to the lodgings not so very far away, just on the other side of the dominating Capitoline Hill. Already it was becoming clear that the whole of Rome would not be seen, grasped, understood during a great number of such exploratory days. Every other city they had encountered in their travelling had yielded up its secrets in a short time, becoming quickly a familiar place to them; Rome was not just another city. There were not enough days in a lifetime to discover all her secrets, all her wonders. Rome grew before the eyes; she changed as quickly as the world changed. Tomorrow's history was developing in every today and planting itself brazenly on the top of another generation's cherished memorials. Romans born here, living their entire lifespan in this greatest of all cities, would accept naturally that there was something new, each and every day, within the city that claimed to be the centre of the earth. Those who merely visited her for a time could never plumb her depths, no matter how hard they might try.

~~~~~~~~~~

I was fascinated by the tale as it came from the lips of Medana, but puzzled at the detail within it. She seemed to know so much of the journeying of the two men, so long ago. She had not travelled with them, by her own account, and a long time had passed since these things had happened, much of a lifetime. Was she imagining this story? As she rose from her stone seat to stretch her limbs back into life, signalling the end of a session with me, I finally ventured to ask her.

"Dear Medana, you tell me the tale so clearly. How did you know it was thus? While you speak, I feel that you were there with Ninian and Lugo! Did you cross the Alpes mountains at some time in your life? Did you ever travel to Rome yourself? Did you see these places?"

Her face lit up, and she laughed. It was a sound as clear and free as a clean, fresh river running over rocks.

"No! I have been nowhere but this island."

She shook her head, and wagged her finger at me. "Do not

doubt, though, that I tell you only the truth!" She laughed again, full of good humour, and then, gently, she reminded me. "They wrote letters, and I learned them, more deeply in my heart than in my conscious memory. It comes back, even after all this time, so clearly. The pictures were inside me always. Love takes in the words deeply," she said. "Anyway, in later years I heard the stories again and again, and they were always the same. I asked Lugo, and Devorah, and Ninian to repeat them many, many times. I loved to hear of all that happened. Are you not glad?" With that, she twinkled a smile again at me, and slipped away to her prayers and the overseeing of the work that was left to her when Ninian had died. She had much to do.

EIGHT: Apostles, Martyrs and the Bishop of Rome
"....After he had shed tears as pledges of his devotion
before the sacred relics of the Apostles.....
it happened that he rose in favour and friendship
with the pope himself."
"Vita Niniani" by Ailred of Rievaulx,
trans. by Winifred MacQueen

For a few days they rested, too tired to walk any more, too tired to think. Then, as freshened energy filled them, curiosity burned anew and made them restless. Ninian and Lugo began to explore Rome again in earnest, but each in his own way.

Lugo was drawn to the banks of the River Tiber, where Roman-born mixed with people who had come from more exotic lands than he had ever dreamt even existed. This was trade, and trade cared not for nationality. From all the corners of the earth, the enterprising came here, to the world's trade centre.

The newly arrived Briton watched what went on, began to find out who people were, where they came from, what they did, and how they did it. Gradually he became a part of the scene in the riverside area of Rome. Charming them, friendly, happy Lugo soon was their companion in the baths, was being fed by their wives in their homes, was pestered for play by their children, and was never barked at by their dogs.

In amongst these peoples, so many families from so many places, he found a colony of Jews. They were working, trading, living and dying just like them, right amongst all the other people from all over the known earth. However much they were involved with other nations daily, more so in Rome than in Treves, they still seemed strangely apart from everyone else, a little distanced by their ways, a little different in their understandings, and a little annoying to others in their need to maintain, for some deep secret inner purpose of their own, an exclusivity of identity. They could not blend completely. They would not blend entirely. So marked was this need in them, and this perception of them, that Constantine himself had declared it must always be so. They remembered that in his laws he had forbidden them to do what they did not desire, in any case, to do, to intermarry with those around them. From earlier ages they had been commanded not to intermarry with pagans and to them, all who were not Jewish were pagans.

When Christianity had appeared in the world, it had come to Rome, as to other parts of the world, from amongst their own people, as a sect of their own Jewish religion. The new way was embraced, as the earlier form of Judaism had been embraced, now and again, by the pagans around them, and for many years Christianity had been regarded as a new form of Judaism by both Jews and gentiles. Much tension had arisen, from time to time, from group to group, about how Jewish this new religion was, or should be.

Since the time of Constantine, though, Christianity had become officially declared as a Roman religion, and was no longer seen primarily as an offshoot of Judaism. Its ways were becoming more gentile than Jewish. Many Christians still followed their Messiah's habits of worship on the Jewish Sabbath, but many others did not, preferring a Gentile Christian holy day, the first day of the week. Now Jews would not marry with Christians; to them, pagans and Christians alike were simply not Jewish. Christians had become gentiles.

Once Lugo would have felt excluded from such people and respected the barriers they erected against outsiders, but not now, not since love of one of their own was such an overwhelming consciousness in his life. He saw Devorah in them, and was drawn toward them as a people, as her people, as his people. He behaved towards them as naturally as if they were his kinfolk, but he could not tell them why.

They grew curious about this affable young Briton, in time, this strange gentile who did not seem to understand that there was a difference between them and him, so great a difference, so wide a gulf in their perception. It seemed that he did not understand, and he walked into their hearts right across the space that lay between them, as if he were a Jew. Eventually they allowed him entrance into their lives.

Ninian was walking a different course. He set out to find his old mentor, the priest whose departure from northern Britain had set in motion his own abdication from that land, his own coming to Rome. As he enquired and searched for him, he prayed that the man had lived. He longed to see him again. And when he did finally discover him, on a busy road not far from the Colosseum, sitting in a sunny courtyard outside his room in his family's house, touching the faces of children he had spoken of with such longing, touching their faces with love, Ninian was overwhelmed with emotion. The delight of the old man when he recognised the young Briton, and his joy at their reunion, were apparent. They were men, but unashamed by their weeping as they embraced each other.

"Ah! My young prince! How you have grown into a fine man! You crossed the mountains! You came to Rome, like you said you would. Ah. Ah. I did not think you could do it. But what of your people?"

Ninian, contentedly settled in at the priest's feet, just as when a child, protested, "No! Please! I am not known here as a prince. I'm not a prince any longer. I am an ordinary Briton only, in search of God's blessing and His instruction. That is a greater life!"

"Greater than those following in the train of Magnus Clemens Maximus?" queried the old man. "I've heard that he has risen so high! Like another Constantine, perhaps, do you think?"

"Perhaps, for sure, " answered Ninian. "But my people do not own me now. They made me promise that I would never claim my title among them again. I am outcast. I only hear what you may hear, news from travellers."

"You give up your rights lightly?" asked the priest. "You have no ambitions?"

Ninian remembered the statue in the Basilica of Constantine. He shuddered. "No, really. That kind of power does not appeal to me. It is no sacrifice to give up what does not appeal to you!" And he laughed.

108

Fresh grapes were brought to them by the grand daughter of the priest's sister. She patted the old man's head, beamed at him, and left them alone. The men munched the sweet fruit and enjoyed just looking at each other for a while.

"My father," ventured the youth, "Where should I meet with others in the city for worship?"

"Oh! You always did love the churches. So many churches here!" exclaimed the man, spitting seeds through the gaps in his teeth, wiping juice from his chin with the arm of his sleeve. Ninian noticed that the priest was not dressed in typically Roman clothes. He still wore a simple, coarse robe, just as he had in Britain. This one, though, was of lighter cloth. Woollen robes and cloaks were not so much needed here in a place better warmed by the sun, except for the nights, perhaps, and later during the rains of winter. Then, again, he would need to wrap his aged bones in heavier garments.

"Here, my prince," for the old man could not remember new ideas so easily as he once could, and Ninian had been his prince too long, "You have a great task to accomplish, a long chore ahead of you! So many churches to choose between! So many places to see! Ha! When I left Rome so many years ago, there were only a few places, simple places for worshippers in the city. Believers had met in rooms in the houses of Christians for long ages. Constantine, though, at the time of the coming of peace to us, began building grand churches. Now, it is all different. Believe me, it is very different! These old family houses are being turned into huge churches. Great crowds gathering in them." He chuckled, "It is no longer a danger to meet, or maybe they wouldn't gather so openly still! It's becoming very popular to be a Christian, young prince. In fact, if you have great ambition for your life, it is better to be a Christian now than not to be a Christian. This is a great change. Really. It is a wonder to me! What changes since my youth......."

He chewed a while, muttered and mumbled, and then went on. "You need to see the places where the Apostles met the early believers in the city, though. That would bless you, for certain. I know it would. Peter, the Lord's own disciple, and Paul, the great

Apostle, both. They were here, in this city. Even John, the Lord's beloved disciple. He suffered here for a while. Imagine. It always amazed me to think on that. Here. My own family became Christian through their witness, and kept faithful, in spite of the persecutions. The houses.... They met together in the houses all the time, you see. Their fellowship made them strong for each other. Rome could not destroy them."

Ninian was riveted. The places of the Apostles. They are here. Of course they are! Rome is not just a place of imperial power, or a place where learning takes place because of books and teachers; it is the place where the faith took root, the fountain spring from which the gospel's river had flowed throughout the world. All the way to Britain. "I'm walking in their footsteps," he thought. "On the same stones." His skin prickled, and tears started to form in his eyes.

Very near this house, he was told, was one of the earliest places of Christian worship in the city, the house of Clement. A leader in the early church, Clement had spoken with Apostles themselves. Clement had written letters of his own to another church, and copies of this letter were yet treasured by many Christians. He may have been the Clement named in one of Paul's letters, his name preserved within the very Scriptures.

"And further down there, " the old man swung his arm in the general south-westerly direction of the Via Ostia, " is the place where Paul died, a martyr. But here, just along here," he indicated the street behind him to the east, "the palace of the Princess Fausta was given by Constantine as the headquarters for the head of the church in Rome. There is a place of worship there; a basilica; a baptistery." His face darkened. "Humph. Damasus. Well."

"But there," the arm swept out again, the hand marking out the western side of the city, across the Tiber. "Over there is the place where a church was raised over the grave of the Apostle Peter, the fisherman himself, the one given the keys of the kingdom by the Lord. He is laid to rest near where he made his own life's sacrifice. God rest him."

Another grape disappeared into his mouth, another few seeds

popped back out, and he went on excitedly, "But did you see the prison at the Forum?" Ninian shook his head. In went another grape. "The place," the old man said, "the place," and his voice went into its intoning mode, the way he had always spoken when leading the Britons in worship, a sound so familiar to Ninian, so evocative of another time, another place on earth, singsongingly, "the very place where the greatest Apostles of our Lord were held in imprisonment before the fateful days when they were called upon to lay down their lives on earth, having finished their course, and from thence to enter the courts of heaven."

He stopped, swallowed, blinked, and reverted to his normal conversational tone, "Oh, so much you have to see!"

Ninian required no further urgings. During the next weeks, his feet flew from place to place as he saw all that the old priest had described, plus much, much more.

Immediately after he left the man's house, he walked along the same road eastwards, just as he had been directed, and he found the first church building he would enter in Rome. The old family house of Flavius Clemens had been constructed above a secret underground chamber devoted to the cult of Mithras during pagan times. Such Mithraic places existed in Britain, one very near the wall of Hadrian in Ninian's own home country. The distinguished Roman Clement had become a believer during the time of the apostles. After the death of Peter, and then of his successor Linus, he had been entrusted with responsibility to lead the church in Rome. He, too, died as a martyr, but believers went on meeting in his house, generation after generation, gathering in the room hallowed by association with its past, and with those saintly souls who had graced it. Now there was a huge church on the very site of the home of Clement, its walls and spaces beautified, its doors welcoming throngs of worshippers who gathered, not furtively, but openly, and regularly, at appointed times.

When Ninian found the church, it was past the time of morning prayers, and long before those of the evening, but a few worshippers were gathering for a simpler daily office as he approached. He joined them. The priest recited a prayer, read from the Psalter, and then sang a hymn before dismissing those faithful who had gathered. The other worshippers quietly left the sanctuary, but Ninian remained, alone. He could not understand the depth of his feelings. He was taken completely by surprise. He had not thought that it would matter where Christ was worshipped by His own. The whole earth was His, and His Spirit was in every place where two or three people would gather in His name, just as He had promised. How could this be so different? And yet, it was. For over three hundred years, it seemed, right where he was standing, Christ had been honoured. The place, not the building, but the place, had an air of sanctity. He felt it, but he could not understand it. Did God specially bless a place, as He specially blessed people?

From there he walked to the Circus Maximus, went beyond the beautiful gardeny Aventine Hill, and continued along the road until he had passed through the Ostian Gate in city walls. A little further on, he found a church built by Constantine over the former small shrine that had marked the vineyard burial site for the body of the Apostle Paul. This man had opened to the gentile world an understanding that the God of Jews had, in sending the Messiah of the Jews, revealed Himself to all people, not just the Jews. From that time and the preaching of the good news that came from it, no Jews or gentiles, no slaves or free men, no men or women, no group of people and no single individual in the entire world, could make the excuse that they lay outside the scope of God's love and redemption.

That joyful truth, that gospel, had first been understood clearly, and then faithfully spread through the empire by the very man whose body had lain abandoned here after his execution. Paul's remains, outside the walls of the city, had been gathered up by a Roman lady who had bravely undertaken to give him the dignity of a burial, and, understanding the importance of the place, to mark it. Ninian could hardly bear to stand there. He curled up. He knelt. He prayed. As a gentile, born to a nation once considered far from God's grace, the Christian Ninian of Britain owed much to this man, the man whose body was lying here.

Across the Tiber, beyond the huge mausoleum of Hadrian,

past the city's busier spaces in the Campus Vaticanus, was the great church erected to commemorate the Apostle Peter. The acknowledged leader of the disciples during the years following the resurrection of Christ from the dead, the same man who became then the father figure for the church in Rome, Peter had been crucified within the Circus of Nero. His body had been discarded nearby, and his remains had been carefully entombed there by those of Rome who revered him. More than two centuries later, the Christian Emperor Constantine had raised a large church there also, over the earlier simple oratory. Far, far removed from the first form of church in the city, a church that would be a simple room in a family house, or a place of any kind where meetings could be held secretly in fear of betrayal and death, this structure proclaimed with pride the honour it did to a fisherman whose life and death were part of the core beginnings of the establishment of a body of believers of the true faith in this, the greatest city on earth. How astonished would the rustic Galilean, a Jews among the Jews of Rome, a common man among the commonest men of the city, have been at the thought of such a building raised in Rome, of all places, to honour his name?

This was only the beginning. There were churches marking the places where other godly ladies and brave men had gathered their fellows for worship in the times of the Apostles; there were churches formed within the dwellings of believers who became famed as martyrs during the various persecutions that marked tragic periods of history down through the succeeding centuries; there were churches on the actual sites of executions, the places where apostles and martyrs had died, and others where it was believed that they were buried, inside and outside the walls; and there were churches where once pagan temples had stood, the conversion of such buildings being triumphal shouts that the God and Father of the Lord Jesus Christ now reigned over all in earth and heaven. There were more than two score early church houses, now formally acknowledged as organised churches, and many more, new churches, were springing up around the city all the time. There seemed to be no end of churches!

One drew Ninian again and again. It was referred to as Jerusalem, the Church of the Holy Cross. As far out on the eastern side of the city as it could be, tucked almost into the furthest point of the city wall, the building had been erected to house a piece of wood from the cross on which the Lord had been crucified. This wondrous relic had been brought to Rome by Queen Helena, mother of the Emperor Constantine, all the way from the city of Jerusalem where she believed a miracle had blessed her with its possession.

A hundred years after that crucifixion, after the resurrection, after the founding of the faith of the Christians, the Emperor Hadrian had searched out the holy sites of the growing Christian movement, and on them he had erected temples to pagan gods. He intended to stamp out Christian stories, as earlier Jewish ones, obliterating the memory of them by destroying the evidence. In their place he had given to the defeated Jews and Christians new gods, greater gods as Hadrian saw them, conquerors of their own failed Protector.

When Rome bowed its knee to Christ, at the time of the ascent of the Christian Emperor Constantine to the Imperial throne, the indomitable mother of the man who ruled most of the known world made a journey that few men would dare to make. Three hundred years after the time of the life of the Saviour, she combed the Holy Land in search of the places Hadrian had tried to obliterate forever.

The dusky-skinned, dark-eyed native believers of the Holy Land, people who spoke to each other in the language of their Lord, had kept the stories of the hallowed places from the hallowed times. Queen Helena had excitedly directed the removal of Hadrian's temples under their guidance, and she found beneath them the evidences from the Christian stories, just as the people descended from the first Christians had told her she would. In Bethlehem she found the cave where they said He had been born; on the Mount of Olives she found the secret hiding place where He had prayed with His disciples and had taught those who had come to Him. She found the place, too, where the church was born on the day of Shavuot, Pentecost, on Mount Zion. Buried in the rubble beneath Hadrian's Temple to Adonis, in the most holy place of all, she discovered the remains of old crosses of wood used in Roman executions. This was the place the modern generation of the cousins of the Lord said that Jesus of Nazareth had offered up His life for a sinful world and been raised from death by a Holy God.

Pieces of the sacred wood were carefully transported back home with her, along with the robe, Christ's seamless robe. Ninian remembered well the church in Treves where the robe said to be the Lord's robe was enshrined with honour, observed with awe by worshippers. Now, in a corner of Rome, removed some distance from buildings occupied by newly powerful Christian authority, he often knelt within the church built to cherish the relic from a cross. For those who believed, this place was a reminder that there was, and always would be, a power greater than any other: that was in the message of the Cross on which had hung the Christ, the One who could not be destroyed by all the powers of hell, the One whose death could not obliterate the promise of forgiveness, even to His murderers, by a loving God. Nearby, around the walls of the city, rested the bodies of many who had believed that claim, had bravely given their lives in defence of it, and who had believed that in the power of the Risen Christ they too would one day live again.

Among all the stories of all those who had given their lives for Christ in this city, none moved more people, or affected them more deeply, than the story of Lawrence. A greatly respected deacon in the church in Rome, the man had met a horrible death, it was said, being roasted alive on a gridiron. His life was so shining and his death so terrible, one of such unspeakable suffering, that the fame and sweet faith of the man had inspired widespread conversion to the Christian faith within Rome, and gone on to sweep throughout much of the Christian world. Constantine had raised a church over the place where Christians declared his remains to have been interred. Pilgrims flocked to the place to weep over the story, and to pray for strength to bear any suffering they might ever endure, in the same noble way that Lawrence had done.

Damasus, the Bishop of Rome, passionately involved in honouring the memory of all of Rome's martyrs of past times, was particularly devoted to the establishment of commemorative works for this man. Lawrence was to be remembered in the building of many churches, including one at his own private family home. The father of Damasus, a deacon and priest before him, had been born not long after the time of the martyrdom, and had told his son the story many times, even before the day when Constantine's Edict was delivered, announcing that such times would be no more for Christian believers. Lawrence was never to be forgotten by the Christians of his city. The mother of Damasus was named Laurentia. This was a passionate, personal campaign. Ninian could believe that it was a worthy one.

Not quite so worthy were other tales that he learned, as he moved about the city. The office of Bishop of Rome had not come to the powerfully ambitious Damasus in the same glorious, even miraculous way that the office had come to Ambrose of Milan. Ambrose had fled from the spontaneous, unison calling of the people. Damasus, by contrast, had pursued his appointment with vigour, an uncompromising kind of vigour that ended with him being charged as a murderer. Lives had been lost as his supporters, battling it out in a contest with the rival Ursinius, had flung much of a roof down into a church, killing many of their opponents in their determination that Damasus would rule. And he had ruled. He had separated himself from his wife and children, determined to consecrate himself wholly to the task at hand. Since then, again unlike his frugal and ascetic brother bishop Ambrose, he had enjoyed a lavish lifestyle. His fawning public entertained him as royalty. He openly enjoyed the company of the socialite women of the city. There were rumours of adultery, but he had been excused by the emperor from requiring to answer to the charges of a civil court, charges many believed, anyway, to have been trumped up against him by malign spirits.

He had, in truth, been a forceful and industrious bishop, accomplishing a great deal during his years in the chair of Peter. He had built more churches, established more memorials, overseen the writing of more testimonials, and encouraged more scholarship in study than perhaps any who had preceded him. But he was not an Ambrose in his effect on Rome any more than he had been an Ambrose in the style of his calling. Converts came to the church of

Mediolanum with deep soul searching, tears of sincere penitence, believing themselves to be taking up a cross, agreeing to embark on new lives of self denial, lives filled with charity. In contrast, people flocked into the churches of Rome in great numbers, but in this city it was a popular, socially improving exercise to do so. Many were baptised into the faith, but this was easily, happily accomplished in the place where Damasus was the bishop. They became Christians to further ambitions, to enjoy privileges, to meet important people, even to fatten their purses. Pagans in the city commonly made caustic remarks about the Christians of Rome and, worse still, about their priests, about their bishops.

As Ninian made his way around this city, seeking out the places where people had lived holy lives or died noble deaths in the cause of Christ, he was saddened to hear such stories. He was reluctant to believe them. Though his heart would almost break with sorrow whenever he learned stories of the sufferings of martyrs, and though he would weep tears at the places where the leaders of the early church had borne their witness, there was a sweetness and deep joy buried deep within such sorrows, such tears. However, when he heard of the lives being lived around him in the name of Chris; shallow, self indulgent, power-hungry lives, the sadness he felt had nothing of sweetness, nothing like joy in it. It was a dark sorrow and ugly pain, and he longed that these things might not prove to be true. That such things would happen anywhere in the world would seem wrong. That they happened here, in this setting, was a cause for deeper shame. In this church where the light had shone so brightly that its beams had stretched right across seas, there should be no dark, dirty, silly, sordid corners.

The day finally came when the money the Britons had brought with them was gone. On little enough hoarded between them, stretched out as long as possible by the simplest of living styles and added to, from time to time, by the generosity of those they had encountered along the way, Ninian and Lugo had managed until now. It had finally run out.

Lugo earned a little, finding occasional work down along the riverside in jobs his new friends gave him. Even so, the Britons discussed the situation and agreed that something must be done. In the first place, new accommodation had to be found. They could not afford the room they had rented from the time of their arrival in the city. They had to look elsewhere for a home.

The much-loved Bishop of Milan had an older sister who lived in a large house belonging to distinguished members of the Gens Aurelia for many generations. It once had been a grand dwelling, even palatial, as was expected for such a family's needs, but the devout sister of Bishop Ambrose lived very simply there now. She had long since devoted her life to God and in consequence felt that any allowance beyond that which provided for her basic needs should be given to the poor. Some of the poor, in fact, shared her home.

Marcellina, it had been said about the city, required a scribe to do some writing for her. She wanted one who could make a copy of a translation of the gospel composed by Christ's own disciple Matthew, a work recently completed by the famous Jerome. When Ninian heard this news, he enquired where she lived, and sought her out immediately. He boldly asked to be granted an interview with the lady.

One who was a prince among the Britons did not commonly need to ask for employment. The very idea of this situation arising would have been unthinkable to his family, but he was no longer one of the family. He was deeply embarrassed as he waited and realised what he was doing.

Marcellina, though, was gracious and welcoming, and he felt at ease in her presence. She was a straightforward person. She asked him quite bluntly who he was and where he had come from. He answered, quietly, "I am the son of a leader of the Britons. I come from that island. I am seeking education in Rome as a priest so that I can return to my people and lead them in their faith."

"But who are you? Who is your father?"

"I am Ninian, " he replied firmly, with finality.

She looked carefully at him. "Well, Ninian. Do you write well? Do you care to understand the meaning of what you write, or do you merely copy?"

"I believe that I will satisfy your requirements, my lady Marcellina," he assured her. "It is something that I love to do, and I have been told that I do it well. I have learned all the Scripture that I know in this way, and have always kept my own copies of any Scripture fragments that came into the hands of my people. I have done this since I was quite young. These matter more to me than anything else I possess."

"Please show me an example of your work," she said, indicating a table, paper, a quill and ink placed neatly nearby. She stood across the room and watched him. It was so hot here, and his hands were sweating, but as he took up the quill and prepared to write, as the paper stretched out under his hand, the request seemed as nothing. He loved the feeling, again, of writing. He wrote a Scripture verse from memory, and signed his name beneath it. Then she indicated a passage from a letter, and asked him to copy it. He did so, quickly and neatly.

"Do you live nearby?" she asked

Ninian blushed. "My companion and I really require a room at this time, if you have one to spare us," he admitted. We have been staying at a travellers' inn not far from here, but we have no more money.

She smiled. "That will suit me very well. If you live here, I will always know that you will have no difficulty in getting to the house, regardless of weather or riots, and the work can go on. There will be space for your friend too. I have a vacant room at the side of the garden courtyard, and I am sure you will be comfortable there. You may work here, in my library. I expect the books to be kept with care. Tools for writing are always maintained in good order, and you will find plenty of material to do your work here." She went on, eagerly, "I have hopes of gaining a copy of the Psalms which Jerome is revising from the Septuagint version at this present time. If you do well, you may do that after the first book is copied."

He could hardly contain his excitement. An entire gospel work! The Psalms —all of them! Jerome's latest works, under his own hands. His learning would begin in earnest, he knew, and in such a way. God guided his paths, without doubt.

Lugo wasn't entirely sure about the news. He was pleased for Ninian, and realised how delighted he was. This appointment to work for Marcellina would, undoubtedly, aid him on his way in his aim to study formally in Rome. The room and income would be a great help to them. There were two problems with this, though, in his thinking. The first was that Ninian was his prince, and Lugo should be supporting him, not the other way around. This was hard for his pride. The other problem was that he knew all about the household of Marcellina. She was famous for her austerity of life, her severe rules, her astonishing piety, and her strength of character. Even the Bishop of Milan did as she asked! Lugo loved life and laughter, food and friends, chatter and fun. He was not terribly sure that the lady Marcellina would like him very much. Still, he agreed. Ninian was so excited, and Lugo could not bear to dash the delight of any friend.

It wasn't as bad as he had feared. Sometimes Lugo did not manage to get home before the gates were locked at night. Sometimes he received some severe looks, some lowered eyebrows. Eventually, though, he won his place there, as he did everywhere. He was too delightful to annoy people for long, however strict-natured they might be. His laughter brought a new brightness to the solemn home of Marcellina.

It was almost too perfect a world now for Ninian. He was in Rome, right in the centre of its Christian life, doing the work he most loved to do. Hour after hour, carefully and beautifully, he copied the Word of God. This time, the word was not in fragments, breaking off in the middle of a sentence or starting in the middle of some profoundly mysterious thought. The work he copied was complete, and perfect.

During the work of writing Matthew's Gospel to the Hebrews, as the stories flowed across the pages from his quill, the eager copyist discovered that the tragic woman who had crept forward in a crowd to touch the fringe, or hem, of the garment of the Lord for her healing, had been touching the fringe of the tassels that the devout among Jewish men yet wore on the corners of their garments, the tsitsith, reminding them constantly of their obligations

120

to observe and fulfil the holy commands of their God. The Jews of Treves and Rome wore fringed garments. Jesus of Nazareth had been one with these people.

Marcellina not only provided her paid scribe and his friend with a pleasant apartment, but she gave them comfortable furnishings, and ample, decent food. She went beyond even this, far beyond it, in her kindness. She quickly seemed to recognise the earnestness and intelligence in the young Briton. In an act of supreme generosity, she granted him the privilege of doubled time, and doubled materials for his work. He was to copy the precious words, not once, but twice. She would keep one copy, and the other would remain in his possession, the beginning of his own library. By supporting Ninian in this way, Marcellina knew that she would possibly be providing the means for the Word of God to reach to the edges of the Empire, to Ninian's people. How could he repay her? He never could. God would.

In his own free time, Ninian still visited the tombs of Christians from ages past, and regularly attended worship services in the nearest parish church to his new home. This was a recently established church, the Anastasis, lying between the Roman Forum and the Circus Maximus. The Bishop of Rome supported this work on a site donated by a lady whose name had born witness to the Resurrection of the Lord. The Bishop was determined to change pagan festivals so that they would become known as days of Christian celebration. The midwinter festival, observed in so many idolatrous cultures, coincided with the day the Greeks had claimed as the birthday of their god of wine, Dionysus. By sheer force of will, Damasus determined to change the memory of this day forever, for all people, into a day that would celebrate the birth of the true Son of God, the Christ child, in Bethlehem. He chose the church of Anastasia as the place where, as the special day was born at midnight, the Christ's Mass would be celebrated.

Ninian was intrigued when he learned of this. Was this truly the way in which pagan behavioural patterns should be transformed into Christian ones? Some railed strongly against the very idea. Particularly, those who regarded the faith of Christ as something so

121

pure and new, so unique on earth, that it should never adopt, nor adapt to, any other consciousness, most especially anything tainted by idolatry, were angered at the Bishop's intentions. Those who had come to be known as Christians from among the Jews were the loudest in their protests.

Others, more pragmatically, perhaps, could see a validity of sorts in the suggestion. After all, they would say, Jesus Himself had turned water into wine, accomplishing in Galilee of the Gentiles what the Dionysian priests had pretended to do in ceremonies within their shrines. He had walked on water and calmed a stormy lake in the presence of His followers, whereas Neptune and his sons only did these things in fables. He had healed the sick in a place where pagans waited for their false gods to stir the waters for their benefit. He had risen from the dead, returning to life with a real body, something that Thammuz could only symbolically do.

Even the Apostle Paul, when he was in Athens, had chosen an idolatrous tribute raised to 'an unknown god', to earnestly declare to the people who sought such a one that the Unknown could be known through faith in His true Son.

At midwinter, on the 25th December, Ninian went to the Anastasis Church to honour the birth of the Christ child. Whether this was, or was not, the right way, whether it was, or was not, the right day, did not seem to matter in that dark hour of a winter's night. Those who braved cold and the disapproval of their Christian fellows to gather together sang in joy, just as angels had done on one special night four hundred years earlier.

Great Damasus heard about Ninian. It was inevitable that tales of the young Briton who was making his way so faithfully from shrine to shrine, from church to church, would reach the man. Ninian was reportedly affected by what he read on the beautiful memorial inscriptions carved by the aged, faithful Philocallus under the direction of the Bishop, and deeply engrossed in his worship in all the churches being established by the Bishop. The Bishop was gratified by such accounts, and sent word that the Briton should be brought before him. This was exactly the kind of devotion that Damasus was seeking to inspire in Romans. He had not expected it to be so remarkably displayed in a visitor from an uncultured part of the world. The young man would be favoured with an invitation to meet him.

With curiosity, Ninian answered the summons to the Lateran headquarters of the Bishop of Rome. At the approach of the appointed hour, he walked past the Forum, the Colosseum with the Colossus of Nero towering above him, past the doorway leading to the home of his old priest and on past the wonderfully atmospheric church of Clement until he reached the place that had belonged to the poor, damned Empress Fausta, the Lateran itself.

The Bishop of Rome physically resembled the Bishop of Mediolanum in not one single way. He was no ascetic, someone who seemed from another, purer world, nor was he given to humility. He looked much more like a wealthy man. Fuller of face and figure, with carefully groomed hair and beard, Damasus was attired in gorgeous robes. He seemed restless, and his large eyes were everywhere, taking noticing of everything going on around him. He expected guests to be impressed. In fact, he usually found people to be quite timid when first in his presence, at least until they became more used to him.

Ninian was not in awe of such a man, any more than he was impressed by the colossus he had passed on the road. He met the glance of Damasus calmly and squarely, his composure unaffected by either the Bishop or his palace. Ninian was, after all, born a prince. It was Damasus who was impressed. He had heard of the deep emotion exhibited by this youth when he had visited holy places. But he quickly saw that the Briton was neither moved by emotion, nor exhibiting signs of undue piety as he was presented to a man of such power in the grandeur of the Lateran. This young foreigner, apparently merely a paid scribe who lived in a room off the garden of the house of Marcellina, was very obviously no servant.

Damasus was not angered by the demeanour of this young man, as he might have expected himself to have been. Rather, he was deeply intrigued. He abruptly signalled Ninian to follow him as he descended from his seat of authority and strode across the majestically appointed room. In the more relaxed setting of a smaller chamber, he began to behave less like the public potentate he had previously thought he should appear to be on such an occasion, and more like the charmer he could be in private. He asked Ninian about himself, how he had come so far to Rome and why, what he was doing in the city, where he thought he would go from here, how he would pursue his ultimate goals. As they spoke together, he realised, as Marcellina had done before him, that this was an exceptional person. Ninian seemed to possess that uncommon blend of intelligence with purity of heart, and of unpretentiousness with iron purposefulness.

Hardly knowing why, the Bishop heard himself insisting that he must take responsibility for the education of Ninian, that this must be of the best quality, under the guidance of the finest teachers, and that all would be done at his, the Bishop's, own personal expense. Ninian immediately accepted the Bishop's offer for help with his education, responding with dignity, but honest appreciation. Damasus was well pleased, gratified at the reaction to his quite spontaneous suggestion, one that had surprised even him by its generosity. As for financial support, the young man refused, quite bluntly. Damasus was bewildered by this, even stunned. No one refused money. It was obvious that the youth was not dressing beautifully, nor eating richly. Anyone under his guardianship should be seen to have only the best, as befitted their status. Ninian was adamant. He needed nothing more than what Marcellina provided in exchange for his work as her copyist.

"But you will not need to work at copying," Damasus explained, as if to someone blind to the obvious. "You can give yourself, from now on, fully to your studies."

"My copying is part of my studying," Ninian replied, just as patiently, to someone patently blind to the obvious. "I will finish all that I promised to do for the lady. The work is begun in my hand, and it must end so. My own copying progresses at the same pace, and these works will be necessary to me in the future. I learn as I write." No more could be said on the subject. The Bishop of Rome yielded.

NINE: Powers on Earth
"The altar of Victory was ....
once more banished from the senate
by the zeal of Gratian."
"The History of the Decline and Fall of the Roman Empire"
by Gibbon

Under the watchful eye of his acknowledged patron the Bishop of Rome, Ninian made great strides in his studies. He had access, now, to many books and documents, copies of Scriptures, commentaries, histories, and maps. No one would dare, with the authority of Damasus approving him, to deny anything he asked.

On the surface of their relationship, Damasus was being wonderfully kind to a foreign youth who was nobody of any importance, almost a barbarian, only a degree above a servant in status. In reality, though, there was more thought behind the kindness of Damasus than mere warm-heartedness. The bishop read people very well; he had quickly recognised that Ninian was more than he claimed to be, and he was guarding himself by caring for him. Yes, his spies had reported to him, Ninian was as poor as he seemed. The Briton was without outside financial support, even secretly. His only means of survival in the city were provided by the comradeship of a friend and employment honestly served with Marcellina. But, Damasus knew, Ninian was not ignobly bred. There was a sure air of aristocracy about his bearing, evident in his features, betrayed in his speech. Who, really, was he?

His spies also found out what they could about Lugo, and one of his minions was assigned the task of befriending the second Briton to learn more from him. Lugo, though utterly open by nature, had developed a sense of cunning, had begun to learn the art of wariness in conversation. The secret of his love and pledge to Devorah had been kept even from Ninian. Those things were buried deeply within him, and other secrets, too, could be hidden as safely when they needed to. He was guarded enough to be instantly suspicious of a stranger who suddenly began to appear in the area around the riverbanks, one who so obviously targeted him with his curiosity.

Lugo reported his suspicions to Ninian late one night in the privacy of their shared room at the side of the house of Marcellina. "What does the man look like?" asked Ninian.

The man had a particularly noticeable feature, the fact that his eyes were not the same colour. One was brown, but the other was green, flecked with brown spots. Ninian knew immediately who he was, someone who often attended upon the Bishop in the Lateran. They laughed together at this undisguiseable choice for a spy.

"Good for you, Lugo, my friend. I always felt that the Bishop was watching me a little more carefully than was really necessary. His questions are just a bit too searching."

While they had been in Mediolanum, Lugo had thought that the amazing bishop of that city was just a bit overly severe in his demands for self denial amongst Christians. Since coming to Rome, though, he had already concluded that he preferred that fault in a bishop to the one of apparently unlimited self indulgence of lifestyle that was commonly associated in public conversation with the present Bishop of Rome. Powder, paint, elaborate robes and gowns, magnificent coaches, shining gold, flashing jewellery and overly plump flesh seemed a little incongruous when displayed so freely by the occupant of the holy office, and by those whose friendship he courted.

"I know that he is good to you, but I'm not so sure that I trust the man," muttered Lugo. He expected a rebuke, but received none.

"The Scriptures say that we shouldn't put our trust in princes," was Ninian's reply.

"Oh, well, I trust you!" Lugo assured him.

"I'm not a prince, remember!" exclaimed Ninian, "But since Damasus is considered a prince of the church, I was thinking of him."

"Or an emperor," suggested Lugo. "An emperor of the church."

"I'm sure he would accept that designation," said Ninian, but quietly.

Damasus was determined to establish a principle that he, as Bishop of Rome, had primacy over all other holders of the office throughout the world. Not all bishops, nor all Christians, were inclined to agree with him. Most in the Eastern Empire had refused to answer his summons to a council in Rome on such important matters as primacy within the church.

Ninian had overheard the discussions. Was Jerusalem not the chief seat of the Church of the Lord, even though the city where the Lord had died and risen was now technically under the rule of the See of Caesarea? Was it, then Caesarea? Or Antioch, which seemed to be over Caesarea in authority, Antioch where for the first time believers in the Christ had been called Christians? Or was Constantinople, Constantine's new imperial capital, the seat which could claim true episcopal authority over the Christian churches of the Roman Empire?

Not so, not any of them, Damasus would answer. To Peter had been given the keys of the kingdom, and he had the authority given directly from the Lord over all the rest of the disciples. The disciples had spread their message throughout different countries, and Peter himself had come to Rome. He had been recognised as leader of the church in that city until the day of his death. By virtue of his martyrdom on Roman soil he had become one with the city, and had later been declared, with the Apostle Paul, a true Roman citizen. The symbolic keys of the authority of this position were always revered as having come from the hand of Peter, and to and from the hands of each of his successors in turn until the present day. Never mind that the followers of Damasus had resorted to violence to gain those keys, that blood had been shed and lives lost before they were secured. They were, now, without dispute, his, whatever Ursinius continued to bleat from Mediolanum. No one listened to Ursinius any longer.

Thus, Damasus reasoned, as the throne of Peter was his, and

his was the supreme bishopric of the world, he was the supreme bishop over all Christendom. Eastern bishops, not agreeing with his reasons, or even the choice of him for Rome, had sent their apologies and stayed at home when they were summoned by him to council. Only three delegates were coming from the half of the Empire ruled by the good Theodosius. The worthy and greatly respected Paulinus of Antioch, yet denied his own rightful succession to the Antiochal See for political reasons, and his supporter Epiphanius of Salamis were coming. These men were to be attended by the famed scholar Jerome.

Damasus was delighted to learn that Jerome was coming to his court. The monk had written him some deeply respectful letters when he was studying in the deserts of the east. The deference of Jerome might have an effect upon others.

While he was engaged in pursuit of his own position of primacy within the universal church, the conscience of the Bishop of Rome was not particularly exercised with regard to the continued pagan practices that were conducted in the realm of public office within the city of Rome. Many of the senators and holders of important positions had never converted to the Christian faith in the train of their Christian emperors. Damasus was, in fact, a close friend and socially involved with many of the distinguished leaders in the city who often represented the most ancient and noble Roman bloodlines. These men, even those whose wives were now Christians, continued to observe pagan rites, to honour the gods and goddesses of their fathers as had been done in Rome's past times. They were among the last frequenters of the tragically empty pagan temples of the city.

The Emperor Gratian himself arrived in the city, attending the council with his spiritual adviser, the Bishop of Mediolanum. The city glowed with a newer, brighter kind of light, as if stars had conjoined in the sky, producing brilliance in the merger of their powers. It soon became apparent that the Emperor Gratian and his own Bishop Ambrose had spiritual designs on the city in matters that did not relate to the agenda for the coming council.

The proud, aristocratic men of Roman government, men

whose pagan rituals did not unduly trouble the present Bishop of Rome, welcomed the young Emperor Gratian to assume pride of place among them. They offered him the sumptuous, mysterious robes traditionally worn by the man who bore the title Pontifex Maximus, the one who held authority, from time immemorial, over all the religions that found their home in the world's greatest city. To their great annoyance, Gratian spurned the honour.

The youthful emperor went on, as he had carefully been instructed by Ambrose to do, to order the removal of the Altar of Victory from the Senate house. This pagan altar, in honour of a pagan goddess, had already once been removed by Christian Constantius but then restored by Julian and had remained unchallenged since. It was the place where the senators customarily swore their oaths of allegiance to the Emperor, and to the Empire, as they had done throughout all the pagan ages of Rome. Always, too, wine and incense were offered at the altar before the commencement of official proceedings.

When ordered by Gratian to cease this practice and remove the sacred altar, the senators were shocked, furious, and even frightened. Some feared the wrath of the gods of Rome upon them and on the world for which they bore responsibility. Many disputed, loudly and fiercely, when it was announced that there would be an immediate cessation of state funding in support of pagan practices along with the destruction of the altar and removal of the statue of the winged goddess. This would cause significantly increased hardship for the dedicated ones such as the vestal virgins who had no other role in life but to conduct the secret and ancient ceremonies at time-honoured shrines in the increasingly deserted temples.

Senators rallied in conference and arranged for deputations to seek a change in these decrees, but they were spurned. The most eloquent and influential among them, the prefect of the city, a famed writer and speaker, Quintus Aurelius Symmachus, was a close friend of the Bishop of Rome and had been a distant kinsman and kindly supporter of the young Ambrose in the days before his conversion. A convinced pagan, he was asked to appeal for toleration on their behalf to the Emperor. He did so. He was banished from Rome immediately, for a period of two years. The altar would not be restored.

There were some features of compromise, though. The winged statue of Victory was allowed to remain in the Curia, as long as the figure was regarded in the future as an angel, no longer as a goddess. Though pagan services could receive no official funds, the temples could remain in use as long as people wished, and supported them. There were over four hundred of them in the city though, like the Pantheon, many had already fallen into complete disuse.

One desperate senator proclaimed to the young and determined Emperor loudly and clearly, so that all could hear, "There will soon be another who will wear the robes of the Pontifex Maximus." A chill was felt in the air, more than could be explained by the covering of the sun by a little dark cloud.

Ambrose was pleased with the work done for Christ by his young Emperor. His own preferred approach to all such situations in life was not one of drastic or violent measures, but of quiet reason and sure faith. The removal of the Altar of Victory from the Curia was a great triumph for the Christian faith. In a mood of thanksgiving he visited the small memorial on the grave of the brave martyred woman of his own family line, Soteris. She was a woman who had borne so much, so beautifully, in the name of Christ. He wept quietly at the memory of her, and knew that she would be glad of this day's work that had been accomplished, by the influence of her own kinsman, one thousand, one hundred and thirty five years after the founding of Rome, about three hundred and fifty years after the Roman crucifixion and resurrection triumph of the Lord Jesus Christ.

The Bishop of Rome asked his brother, the Bishop of Mediolanum, to preside in the eucharistic services and to preach in the hearing of the people of the Church of Anastasis where Jerome often led the celebration of Eucharist for the congregation. As the visitor was staying nearby, in the old family home now the residence of his sister Marcellina, Ambrose readily agreed. Word spread through the city that Ambrose would be there, and that he would preach. People came from everywhere to hear him, and the church was filled to the doors. Those who came late had to stand outside, in the courtyard, hoping to hear something through the opened doors.

A woman who supervised the business of a bath in the neighbourhood near the church suffered from palsy and had become bedridden. She begged her family to carry her to Ambrose. They put her in a chair and struggled along the street with their burden until they reached the door of the overflowing church. The crowd there parted in sympathy, making an entrance for the helpless one. Ambrose, when she reached him, looked sweetly upon her, prayed simply for her, and touched her gently. She wept with emotion and thanked him movingly. The crowd were in tears. She was healed, and a sense of awe filled the city.

Some who came to attend the Council of Rome came from far distant places and brought with them news that King Eudaf had died in far off Britain. His son-in-law Maximus now reigned supreme, without challenge. A pirate king from Hibernia who had menaced the waters around Britain had been defeated by the new ruler, and the terrifying Picts had been suppressed. Britain was at peace, and Maximus was hailed by all as a great protector of the nation of his adoption. The two Britons in Rome witnessed the healing of the palsied woman, and on the same day they heard the news from home.

TEN: Jerome
"A worthy recompense indeed
for one who had scorned native land, riches and pleasures
for the love of the truth,
having been led into the very innermost shrine of truth
and admitted to the very treasure-houses
of wisdom and knowledge......."
"Vita Niniani" by Ailred of Rievaulx,
trans. by Winifred MacQueen

Only when he reached the years of middle age did Eusebius Hieronymus feel himself to be finding his true, best stride in life. He had struggled for so long. There was always someone, or something, to fight against. Jerome's swimming was always upriver, struggling against the water's flowing movement, waters that always seemed as cold and bitter as they were contrary in their current. All the disputes and all the sorrow that came from them had strengthened him and sharpened him, some would say had hardened him.

In spite of his difficulties, he had never ceased to apply himself to his studies. He had a brilliant mind and a voracious appetite for learning. He was driven by a deep, seemingly insatiable, hunger to understand the truths of God. His work had finally turned him into a man of greater scholarship than perhaps any other in the world. He was ready, finally, for whatever it was that God would assign him to do during whatever years remained of his life. Sensing that he was approaching some monumental task, one that would give meaning to the confused twists of his life, Jerome had travelled from Constantinople to Rome in the company of two esteemed bishops in answer to the summons of the greatest of all the bishops, Damasus of Rome.

Damaging gossip about Damasus had filled the air all over the world with dark whispers, but Jerome had refused to listen at

132

all, to any of it. He himself had been the object of gossip, nearly ruined by it. He loathed gossip. He simply would not listen. Anyway, what were such things that people might be saying in comparison with the fact of the primacy of the position of the man in the church of the world, and the good that was known of his work?

Years before, Jerome had established himself as a sincere supporter of Damasus when he had written to the Bishop of Rome that only his final decision, as the direct successor of the Disciple Peter to the chair of the See of Rome, would be regarded by him, Jerome, as absolute with regard to an important matter of doctrine. He had meant it. Whatever his own understandings, and he would in honesty argue them fully, he deliberately made the choice to submit himself, finally, to the decision of the Bishop of Rome. For his part, the Bishop of Rome was pleased to promote such a man to prominence. Those who would thus subject their will to his understanding made Damasus feel secure, bolstering the increasing number of claims for his primacy.

Pressing on toward the Council of Rome in the summer of 382, there was every reason for Jerome to believe with confidence that his day was coming. He was ready for it. He would soar.

It was true, and he did soar. The welcome of Damasus was warm and faithful to a friend. Jerome was embraced into office, and into fame. The delight of being in Rome again where he had first entered the faith in baptism during student days was sincere. The fact that his return so many years later was respectfully hailed within the Court of Damasus was overwhelming to him. Almost immediately, he was requested by the Bishop to undertake the greatest and most thrilling challenges of his life. This was even more than he had hoped or dreamed.

Such acceptance, such regard, began a work of healing deep inside the man. His emotions had been lacerated and his pride bruised by the actions and words of many of his former friends, people he had loved and trusted, but people who had turned against him. He had begun to snarl and bite back, his temperament soured. Now, though, that past and those people could be left behind. A clean, fresh future was beginning.

The Bishop Damasus and the scholar Jerome were so alike, and yet so different. Both were determined to accomplish their goals, and both had been capable of showing ruthlessness in the accomplishment of their goals, when required. Both men were truly devoted to Christian scholarship. Both passionately collected and preserved the truth wherever they found it, any understanding as they unearthed it. The lives of saints and martyrs moved them equally.

Damasus built churches and directed the work of elegant stone inscriptions to be set up all over the city in tribute to the Christians of past times, memorials for the instruction and blessing of future generations. Jerome made copies of valued commentaries, and had begun showing his genius for translation and commentaries of his own, so that the words of truth, the doctrines of the faith, could be passed, as well, to future generations.

Neither lived with a wife, or a family. Damasus had been married, many years in the past, and was the father of children. Due to the preference in those times for a celibate bishop to serve the people, he had shed his family in favour of the bishopric. Jerome did not claim to have always been celibate, but he had no wife, no children. Now, he urged everyone who would listen to be like him, living without the encumbrance of family distraction and responsibility, wholly free to serve God.

Added to their shared preference for an unmarried existence, both men were known for the apparent anomaly that they chose to spend much of their time in the company of women. That was the likeness, but the marked difference between them was the contrast in the types of women whose company they sought. Damasus preferred the society of wealthy, influential Roman wives and in fashionable social settings. He said that such women, whom he could, undoubtedly, charm by his personality, would bring their powerful, often pagan, husbands with them to the church. Jerome preferred to be with women who had left their husbands behind, if they had ever had any, women who lived harsh lives of self denial, women who eagerly wished to pursue studies of the Scriptures under his gifted guidance.

Now an elderly man, Damasus treasured the dream of one last major project during his lifetime. He could not accomplish this final goal unless he could inspire Jerome to share his dream and do the work. Damasus desired a newer, more accurate translation of the whole of the New Testament and Psalms, works which until this time had varied in content and in details of translation all over the Christian world. He planned to authorise one unified Latin version, as perfect as it could be, for the use of all Christian churches, to the edification of all literate people. He knew that Jerome was the only man in the world fit to accomplish such a task, and Jerome rejoiced to embrace the plan knowing that Damasus was the one man in the world who could ensure its success.

It was agreed. This would be a great work, and the results were eagerly awaited. When it was accomplished, the Bishop of Rome would surely never find his name linked again with murder and adultery. His name would be, instead, linked with his great triumphs. Damasus would be remembered for all time as the Bishop of Rome who established Rome in primacy over the world's churches, the one who gave to pilgrims of the world beautiful memorial churches and moving memorial inscriptions, and the one who endowed the finest translation of the Scriptures the Latin world had ever known.

The mind of Jerome was as sharp as the sharpest blade, and his understandings were truly profound, but his eyesight was poor. If the task of translation were to be accomplished, he would require the assistance of several young men who could serve as secretaries and write to his dictation. Because of the importance of the work, he insisted that they be men of bright intellect whose lives were unblemished in reputation. They must be willing to be devoted to the task for however long it would take, and prove that they would be absolutely fastidious in the work of copying. Only such would do.

Among those who answered this description was Ninian, the Briton. His work for Marcellina having been completed to her satisfaction, she had encouraged him and Lugo to remain in the room that had become their Roman home. Ninian had been freed to engross himself in his studies under the guidance of the Bishop, and was thus available to work as a copyist for the translation of the Scriptures by Jerome.

In this work, as in all other work he had done, Ninian soon was seen to excel. His beautiful, careful script, his tireless devotion to the task, and his genuine interest in the content of his assignments brought him to the attention of the great scholar. For him, this was obviously not a labour at all, but a matter of devotion. It was apparent that he loved the words, every single individual word he was privileged to write from Jerome's dictation. No detail, to him, was trivial. Such rich, sweet things he learned in the details!

In the process of copying the Psalms, the careful design of them, some crafted beautifully in the pattern of the Hebrew alphabet, was discovered.

The places mentioned in the holy pages had been unfamiliar names, as had the people, when he had learned them as a child. Now, because of the knowledge the translator possessed, and because of his visits into that part of the world, the names of places and of characters in the Bible became, themselves, lessons in the understanding of writings.

Letter by letter, word by word, line by line, page by page, as the writing progressed so did light fall upon the Scriptures in the understanding of the British prince who had come here, for this purpose, but had never dreamed how glorious would be the provision that God would make for his learning. The Bible came alive.

Jerome was a hard taskmaster, a critical judge of every work and every thought expressed, sharply speaking out against anything he deemed to be less than perfection in any regard. He was glad, though, that there was one among those who wrote at his command whose hunger for knowledge was like his own, and he gladly answered all the questions that came. Ninian loved every assignment he was given. There was never a complaint from him, to anyone. He had so long yearned for these things. In the new surroundings of his most privileged existence, knowledge flooded into the deeper reaches of his hungry mind as naturally as if it were soaking in through the very pores of his skin. He was awash with it, swimming in a deep and glorious sea at last.

136

In the hours when he was not translating, or busy serving as personal adviser to Damasus, Jerome was often found in the company of a group of devout Roman women who had established themselves into a fellowship long before his coming to the city. These wealthy and aristocratic women, inspired by readings about the austerity and devotion of the desert fathers, had separated themselves from the luxuries and self-indulgent spirit of their world and entered into a different kind of life. Accustomed to power, they had humbled themselves; accustomed to luxury, they given away all that they could, and had simplified their surroundings to the point of sparseness; accustomed to being sought and feted for their physical beauty and fine apparel, they had begun to neglect their appearance and dress in only the plainest of clothing, like the poor of the city. Within the confines of their individual homes, they lived as they believed their God would wish them to live, in a spirit of self denial, of generosity toward all who had needs, and of utter devotion to God Himself.

Until the time of Jerome's arrival in the city, they had encouraged and instructed each other. When he came, they asked him to accept them as his students in their Biblical study. He had never encountered any group more eager to learn.

Jerome knew the Bible like few men. He knew that His Lord had accepted just such a woman as these women seemed to be, Mary of Bethany. Mary had sat at the Lord's feet, and He had taught her. In His time, among the Jews, a student would sit at the feet of an acknowledged rabbi, and was acknowledged as being accepted by being allowed to remain there. Mary had been acknowledged, and commended. In time, even men of Jerusalem would come to her with questions, this woman who had been instructed by the Lord, her rabbi.

Thus it was that Jerome accepted the women of Rome who sought him as their teacher. He was loved by them, and he loved them in return, until their deaths. Marcella and her mother Albina; beautiful, gentle Paula with her lively daughter Blesilla and her meeker daughter Eustochium; Asella, Felicitas, Lea, and even Marcellina who, from time to time, joined in the Bible reading circle on the Aventine in the home of Marcella. Jerome taught them, and they questioned him. The rich truths he shared drove them to search the Scriptures more avidly, which searching prompted their enquiries and drove him, in turn, to deeper and deeper studies to provide full enough answers for such keen minds. He loved the searches the women provoked, for these caused him to dig for answers buried like the most precious of treasures, yielding themselves only to those who truly care to find them.

When the women were not studying, they were often praying. Sometimes together, sometimes alone in a simple, austere chamber, the door shut behind them to close them in with God. They would slip away, when they could, to the places about the city where the stories of lives and deaths of Apostles and martyrs would move them to tears and inspire them to greater devotion.

As Jerome's friendship with the circle of earnest pious women deepened, so did his regard for the young British scribe who aided him in his translation. More and more, Jerome spared time and pains to explain the rationale behind his decisions regarding the details of his choice of words and phrases with Ninian. This was a mutual delight to them. Like harvesters who would glean every single grain with meticulous care, determined not to allow a single one to escape ungathered, such minds could not bear to let one single scrap of truth that might nourish the soul fall by the wayside, to be trodden underfoot, unnoticed.

Jerome invited Ninian to accompany him to the home of Marcella for one of the study sessions. He realised how much the young man would enjoy the probing questions, and the replies that he would give them. Ninian was aware that Marcellina, his own benefactress, was sometimes present in this gathering. She had spoken of it to him. He went gladly.

In a grand aristocratic house on the beautiful Aventine Hill, the two men were ushered into a plainly furnished room where plainly dressed women of all ages sat quietly and expectantly in a circle, waiting for the arrival of their teacher, this new pastor of their souls. They evidenced genuine affection for the great man, this famed scholar, when he came into the room, but this affection

138

was nothing in comparison with the greater love they began to reveal when they spoke of their Saviour. They listened to Jerome with concentration and real delight. Then, as they read Scriptures together, discussed the teachings of the day, asked questions of their patient teacher, the Christ-centredness of their thinking began to be apparent. Their pursuit of understanding of Him made them fearless in their demands upon Jerome. As they prayed in a heartfelt, simple, spontaneous way, it was Jesus who was their object, their joy. It was Jesus on whom their lives centred, completely, truly. They were absorbed in Him utterly. They were plainly dressed and unadorned, it was true, but Ninian had never seen more beauty in any women than in these. Love for Christ so possessed them that their gentleness was strength, their simplicity was beauty, and their deep hunger, a kind of glory.

Paula, with her daughters Blesilla and Eustochium, were undertaking a special study of Hebrew together. They were determined to become fluent in this language so that they could know and sing the Psalms as Jesus Himself would have known and sung them. Under the guidance of their teacher Jerome, they were mastering the tongue at an astonishing rate. This was spoken of by the others, and their hostess Marcella urged the three women to sing together, to show the others present what they were working on. They sang the verses of the Aleph portion of the 119th Psalm, and the sound was like angels.

Jerome, who could not have been anything but astonished and proud at the ability of his pupils, who must have been delighted and moved by the very sweetness of their voices, suddenly became agitated. He looked about him like a trapped animal and, while the notes of the singing still hung in the air, he quickly excused himself, dragging Ninian with him, and bolted from the house. He seemed to be fleeing from some danger as he charged down the road in the direction of the Circus Maximus, and only slowed when he reached the bottom of the slope. Pausing to let Ninian catch up with him, gasping for breath and mopping his face, he looked very strange.

"What?" asked Ninian.

"Oh, dear!" he exclaimed.

"What?" asked Ninian, again.

"The singing. Oh, dear! Learning, yes, and praying, but not singing, my young man, not singing! Did Paul not say that women should remain silent in the church? It is distressing to hear their voices raised aloud like that. It is for men to sing. They may sing, of course, when they are alone, but we were there!" His eyes rolled, in exasperation. He huffed, and he puffed, and the sweat rolled down his face and neck. "They may sing when they are alone, but it is not fitting when men are present! I must have a word with Paula. The dear soul. She would not be thinking! Marcella should have known better than to ask them."

He marched on, wiping his face, mopping his neck, his arms, and muttering to himself, as Ninian trotted behind him, bemused.

That night Ninian told Lugo the story of what had happened in the home of Marcella on the Aventine. He told his friend of the wonderful, devout women, of their brilliance in study, of their deep devotion to the Lord, to each other, and even to Jerome. When he reached the part about the singing, he could hardly describe what happened because he started to laugh. As he laughed, Lugo laughed. They laughed until they wept. They laughed until they ached. They couldn't stop. Someone in Marcellina's house was disturbed by the sound and called, "Be quiet!!!" into the night air. They covered their heads with cloaks to muffle the sound until they could stop laughing.

"Imagine my sister Medana being told that she could study, and question, and pray aloud, but MUST NOT SING! ——— except in a cell!" Cloaks over their faces, they roared.

In the stillness of that night, as Lugo snored away in the corner, Ninian lay awake and remembered Medana. "She would be just such a one," he thought. "She would pray; she would read; she would understand so much if someone would teach her, she would be full of questions, no doubt! She would sing Psalms as sweetly and naturally as the birds praise their Creator God." And he, too, slept.

"I know," said Medana. "He thought such things. He told me. I did learn to sing the Psalms, just as the Lord Himself had done. Isn't it wonderful? My sister Devorah taught me herself.

ELEVEN: Another Turning
"The reign of Maximus might have ended
in peace and prosperity, could he have contented himself
with the possession of three ample countries,
which now constitute the three most flourishing kingdoms
of modern Europe.
But the aspiring usurper, whose sordid ambition
was not dignified by the love of glory and of arms,
considered his actual forces
as the instruments only of his future greatness,
and his success was the immediate cause of his destruction."
"History of the Decline and Fall of the Roman Empire,"
by Gibbon

A year passed, and more. Ninian laboured diligently under the dictation of Jerome on the work of the new Latin translations. Day after day, week after week, and month after month he joyed in this assignment. When Rome was hot, he worked where a breeze could cool him, for the writing must not be damaged by sweating hands. When Rome was cold, he wrapped himself in a cloak and sat as near to the central brazier in the room as he could, so that the script would not be affected by the trembling of icy hands. Ninian did not really care if it were cold, or if it were hot. He didn't care how early he was asked to begin, or how late he was kept at the task. He only cared that he make the work as perfect as he could, every letter, every word, in every line. It was a work of beauty and the words were words of life-changing power.

Gossip from the outside world only reached the ears of Ninian through Lugo. The banished pagan senator Symmachus had returned from his place of exile to Rome. There he met a brilliant young man from Africa teaching rhetoric, one who bore his own family name a connection of the gens Aurelia. Symmachus had supported brilliant young men before, such as Ambrose, another Aurelian, whose rise to power had resulted in his own banishment. Symmachus suggested to the struggling rhetorician that he would do well in Mediolanum, and helped to send him there. The young man was not a Christian when he left Rome, but he was seeking an answer to deep questions. His name was Augustine, and in Mediolanum the wondrous teaching of Ambrose began to create a powerful effect within his understanding. Soon he was baptised, his life transformed by the work of Ambrose, as that of many before him. In Augustine, though, Ambrose realised that he had discovered a newly rising star, one whose natural talents, hallowed by his commitment to the Christ, would illuminate the world.

News that made a greater personal impact upon the minds of the Britons, though, followed soon after. Theodosius, the Hispanic Emperor of the East, had named his small son as his successor. Something in this declaration had caused Magnus Clemens Maximus, Britain's king after Eudaf, to rise in protest. No one knew why. Macsen brought all the armies of Britain with him in a move of usurpation against Gratian, who had appointed Theodosius in the first place, and Macsen was claiming the right to rule the Western Empire from Treves.

Gratian, as was usual for him, was engaged in pursuit of his favoured sports in a lovely area of Gaul when Macsen swept into power in his own kingdom. It was there that he was cornered by a cunning follower of Maximus. He was tricked into believing that his young new bride was on her way to him and, responding to the cruel deception with delight, he galloped out from a place of safety to meet her. He was murdered and Macsen, now Emperor Maximus, ruled without challenge.

Ambrose had loved young Gratian, for all the softness of his ways, and had experienced the greatest spiritual triumph of his life while standing with the Emperor in defiance of pagan claims to a continued place of honour in the Roman Senate. Gratian had been brave then, just barely a year before, even in the face of the haunting pronouncement that he would soon die for his actions. Gratian was only twenty-four years of age when the supporter of an usurper to his throne now seemed to have fulfilled that prophetic claim. He had not yet been baptised. The tragedy of his death was compounded by that fact, and Bishop Ambrose of Milan was grief-stricken.

Gratian's half brother, Valentian II, still a child emperor ruling under the direction of his mother and advisers, was now in great danger. Maximus could move on from Treves to seize and re-unify the entire Western Empire. Rome waited anxiously for more news.

Ambrose was sent by the terrified Mother Empress Justina to plead with Maximus for the security of her son's throne. Though he often did battle with her and her Arian cause spiritually, the kindly bishop responded to her cry for help. The snows closed in behind him, and he could not return to Mediolanum. He was forced to remain in Treves for a winter, sharing the city of his birth with the man who claimed to be emperor, the man who had been responsible for the death of his beloved protégé. The snows that had closed the roads and mountain passes were not nearly as icy as the relationship between the emperor Macsen and the visiting holy man. However, in the end, Emperor Maximus agreed that he would seek no more territory than that he already controlled. Britain, Gaul and Hispania would suffice him. He would leave Rome's peninsula and Africa to young Valentian II.

Ambrose returned, when he could, to his own city, and Macsen, who intended to establish the succession of his newly-acquired throne within the next generation of his own house, named the son of his first marriage, Victor, father of an infant son himself, to be his heir.

While the lives and deaths of emperors, bishops and scholars continued to fascinate the ordinary people day by day, Jerome and his diligent band of copyists were focused on the major work of translation for Damasus. In what seemed an astonishingly short period of time, all four gospels were gathered, sorted out, translated, prefaced, and indexed for study purposes. This first section of the work to be completed was presented to the Bishop of Rome. There was joy on the day, and a sense of deep satisfaction, even something of pride. It was a considerable accomplishment already, but much, much more remained to be done.

Not long afterwards, as winter's chill settled in on Rome, the same winter weather that closed the Alpes against Ambrose, Damasus was stricken by a fever. He was an old man. In a matter of days, he was dead. He had prepared carefully for his own death. He had favoured a place of hallowed association for his burial, one where greatly famed martyrs' tombs were visited by pilgrims. When he realised that permission would not be granted for his interment in this place, he had a plaque made saying that he had wanted to be buried there, but would not be, lest he lessen the holiness of the site. His second choice of burial place, then, where he would be interred alongside his mother and sister, was an oratory already built and beautified by him during his lifetime. It would be further adorned by the epitaph he, himself, had written. This was an expression of his sure confidence that the Christ of the Galilee who had walked upon waters, who had raised Lazarus from the grave, and who, Himself, had triumphed over death, would one day, surely, raise Damasus to be with Him.

The body of Damasus had scarcely been lowered into the specially prepared tomb when factions formed in matter of the choice of his successor. During the last two years of his life, many had believed that Jerome, scholar without equal and essentially the voice of the aged Bishop to the world, would become bishop in his place. In that time though, even some who had benefited and been blessed by the work of Jerome, had grown to understand that this man, however brilliant his mind and uncompromising his dedication, was not as reliable in temperament, not as balanced in his opinions, not as generous in his approach to the understandings of others as a bishop ideally should be. He would never be called a peace-maker.

Thus, the quieter and more steady-natured deacon Siricius was chosen. He had served honourably under Damasus, and before that with Damasus under Liberius. He had never drawn attention to himself. He had always been trustworthy. He was deemed wise, and virtuous. Some were, perhaps, wiser but less virtuous; some others may have been exceedingly virtuous but not exactly wise. He, of all those who were known, exhibited the best combination of combined qualities, and his election seemed entirely appropriate.

The candidacy of Jerome was ignored. That of Ursinius, too, whose supporters had gathered about him from the almost forgotten past, the distant time of his loss of the bishopric to Damasus was by-passed. Neither the sharp-tongued reaction of Jerome, betraying the disappointment of his own expectations, nor the howl from the camp of Ursinius disturbed the confidence of the Emperor, the officials, the church or the people in general that the hand of Siricius was the right one to receive the keys of the kingdom that had been passed down through the church in the See of Peter.

The new bishop, who had seemed so quiet, so mild, while he had served in the shadow of others thus far, changed as soon as he stepped into the light. He reinforced the claims Damasus had made as to the primacy of the See of Rome. He declared that he, and he alone, had the ultimate authority to pronounce on matters of orthodoxy versus heresy. He, and he alone must be party to the appointment of all other bishops. His voice was the voice of decree, not proposition. The expression on his face remained as it had been, one of calm sweetness; the voice alone changed, and in it was the sound of the rumble of a thunder.

Jerome was incensed. His words began to cut. He would not be ordered. He would not. Damasus had sought his counsel, sought it earnestly and even humbly; but this formerly mild-mannered, always lesser, successor to Damasus would now instruct him?

Old insecurities began to haunt him. His work was less confident. Even more, he began to lose interest in the translation. The Acts of the Apostles, the epistles by Paul, by Peter, by John, and by Jude, as well as the powerful Revelation, all remained to be done before even the New Testament could be complete. The old Hebrew testament, beyond that, desperately needed an erudite translation from the Hebrew directly into the language of Romans to light up the understanding of Latin speaking Christians the world over. The task was a mammoth one, but Jerome, the only one who could accomplish it, was distracted.

When he did work with his scribes, he no longer dictated every word to them. He sometimes allowed them, instead, under his looser direction, to copy from other, earlier translations. He would merely add comments when he was dull, or criticise and correct impatiently when he was in a sharper mood. The change in him, and in the consistency of his work, embarrassed them, and confused them. It was quickly evident that the death of Damasus had removed all his confidence, that the election of Siricius had darkened his world, and that the great Jerome was floundering.

Jerome began to spend more and more time with his devout students among the women. Some of them were wary of him, but others became more and more dependent upon his teaching and his guidance. He became increasingly vocal in his complaints of the world as it was found in Rome. The city was no longer the dear, sweet centre of all that was best and strongest in the world of Christendom. The fact that he had held up the city, the See, in the time of Damasus the Bishop, as the seat of the apostles, the place of the authority of the faith, ceased to matter. Rome became, for Jerome and his more impressionable Christian sisters, Babylon on earth. The city was the great harlot. She sold herself for gain; she wallowed in her riches; she vaunted herself in her pride. She was a lost place, and those who lived in her were tainted by her. The Christians in Rome did not live pure enough lives. None were admired any longer. All were compromised by the city and everything she stood for. Everything was to be complained against. Everything, simply everything, was badly wrong.

As everything seemed wrong, everything began to go wrong. Someone reported that the relationship between the great scholar and one of his female followers, between Jerome and the widowed Paula, was less than pure. There was an investigation. During the time it was being held, an accuser was tortured to extract more information from him, but he revoked his claims instead. The accusation was withdrawn. Even so, people still talked, and complained against the man and his influence upon vulnerable women.

Blesilla. The lovely, lively daughter of Paula, had in earlier years ignored Jerome's encouragement that she, like other especially good Christian women, should spurn any possibility for marriage

146

and children to give herself, instead, to Christ. She was determined to enjoy her life and had begun by marrying well, entering fully into the whirl of the lifestyle that was typical in Roman high society. Her husband had died suddenly. She was determined still to enjoy pleasure and wealth. She was greatly admired for her beauty and spirit. Then a fever had struck her down, and she became terrified. She was only twenty years of age, but suddenly faced the reality that she was very vulnerable, very mortal. She was converted. She became serious, studied the Scriptures, and prayed earnestly. She denied herself any and all of her former pleasures; she fasted until her appearance was dramatically altered. The Romans of her former society watched all this with alarm. In four months she was dead. Jerome was publicly blamed for having forced an extreme lifestyle on such a young woman, and was reviled by many for the stern rebuke he delivered to Paula when she collapsed with grief at the funeral of her beautiful, brilliant daughter.

And there was more. The accusations continued, with events in the lives of Jerome's associates from the past suddenly remembered and brought to mind in common talk about him. People from other places remembered having heard from others, elsewhere, that a young woman, acting upon the strict principles urged by this same man, had virtually starved herself to death in another, distant, part of the Empire.

Within the city of Rome, public opinion turned against Jerome in a surge of unanimity not unlike that surge that had swept him so approvingly to fame and influence only two years before, when he had first entered the court of Damasus. Jerome had bloomed and softened then, when he was loved and feted. But that sweet day was gone, and it seemed that it would never return. He hated confrontation, and could not cope with rejection. An altered Jerome raged against his detractors in the presence of his friends. He raged when he spoke, when he wrote, and even as he walked; he raged as he had never raged before.

He hinted about his intentions to flee the city, to seek refuge in some distant desert place where he could find the inner peace to continue his work unmolested by rumour and unaffected by distress brought on by opposition. His secretaries, who worked with him whenever he found time or was visited by the mood to work, knew nothing of these plans. They only knew that he raged.

One day it seemed to Ninian that his whole world was blown apart. He was in the room beside the courtyard at the home of Marcellina, mulling over his situation, without Damasus as sponsor, without confidence that the work on the Scripture would ever be finished to the standard envisaged under his inspiration, when Lugo burst in.

Agitated, his friend announced, "I'm leaving Rome. I must return to Treves."

"What?"

"I have to go. Macsen is in Treves, and the place is full of our own people. Maybe even my brothers are there. Yours are sure to be!"

"So, he has been there for almost two years. Why do you need to go now?"

"There is trouble, Ninian. They say he has no intention of stopping there any longer. He might come right on to take Rome."

Ninian was stunned, but it made sense. Ambitions were never satisfied. They grew. He had learned that. Still, he could not understand how this affected Lugo, and what it had to do with Treves. "Why do you suddenly have to go to Treves, Lugo?"

Lugo looked at him strangely, and then stopped what he was doing, packing his possessions. "Sit down, Ninian. I need to tell you some things."

Ninian sat there listening, amazed. Open, sharing, easy-natured Lugo had kept so much from him. Devorah? He had never heard Lugo mention her name! He couldn't believe what he was hearing. He didn't know whether to laugh outloud, or to be angry that he had not been trusted. In the end, he just kept silence and listened and, as he listened, he began to understand it all.

It was true. Lugo had reason to be concerned. Britons were in control in the provincial capital, and no one knew how minority people such as Jews were faring under their rule. It was urgent, too, that Lugo go to claim her, in view of the pressures being put on her by her own people to marry one of her own, for her own security. Word had come to him of Devorah's plight through one of the travelling Jewish traders Lugo had befriended down at the river's banks.

As the tide of British military strength moved further into the continent, Lugo would move against that stream, right through that powerful concentration of British rule, going back into the quieter world of his homeland with Devorah, to begin a new life and establish a new family. There was no other answer.

Lugo packed what he needed to take and left Ninian alone for a while to scratch a greeting to Medana that Lugo would deliver. Lugo expressed his gratitude to the dignified and generous Marcellina, made his fond farewells to those of the household who considered him their pet, and set out to retrace his steps along the Via Flaminia.

Ninian accompanied him as far as the gate in the city walls. He was numb. They spoke little. He felt bereft already, unable to imagine life in this distant place without the company of his friend, his brother Briton. When they reached the parting place, they looked long and hard at each other, and embraced. They slapped each other's arms. "God guard you, and speed your way to your Devorah, my friend," said Ninian. Lugo just blinked, and tried to grin, but his grin was strangely lopsided. Neither could see very clearly, their eyes misting.

"When you come home," muttered Lugo. It was as much as he could say.

They turned away from each other, Lugo walking northward toward the mountains, toward Treves, toward home. Ninian entered the city that roared with the sounds of the world's most vibrant living, threading his way through the crowds that filled the busy streets, strangely exhausted when he entered his emptied room.

Later that day he was informed that Jerome was leaving Rome. The scholar was going to Bethlehem. He would complete his work there. He needed secretaries to accompany him, for his eyes were troubling him greatly. Without help, he would not be able to finish the Latin Scriptures.

Ninian walked between the Aventine Hill and the Circus Maximus until he reached the Porta Ardeatina. He followed the road until he came to the beautiful chapel over the tomb of Damasus. Oh, Damasus, what now? He sat in silence, in prayer, in anguish of spirit. What was Rome with no guiding, protecting bishop? What was Rome with no teacher, no completed Scriptures? In the depths of his being he knew that, if he were ever to return to his land and his people to lead them into truth, he must have with him the Scriptures, as perfect and true as they could be made.

He looked up at the lovely walls, so tastefully and richly adorned. His eyes fell on the epitaph of the Bishop, and he read the words. Christ had walked upon the waters of a lake in the land called the Galilee. Christ had called Lazarus back into life at a village called Bethany. Christ had risen from the dead in the city of Jerusalem, the city where God had said He would place His name. Ninian remembered from his readings of Scripture that God had called those who followed Him to rejoice in His presence in that place. To delight in His presence in that place. To eat and drink in His presence in that place. A light dawned in the dim tomb. Rome was not the holy city. Jerusalem was. He would go with Jerome to finish the work, and he would see the places described in it. He would see the Lake of the Galilee, the village of Bethany, the Holy City. The work of the translating would, indeed, be done, but not here. It would be completed where it had begun, in the Holy Land of God's choosing. Rome, for all her greatness, was a city built by men, for the glory of men. The new translation of the Scriptures would be done in the place where the Christ was born, the Messiah who had proclaimed that His kingdom was not, after all, of this world.

Jerome was raging and writing letters to express his great displeasure with Rome even as he was waiting on board, waiting for the departure of the ship that would take him to the Holy Land. Ninian, his faithful scribe, was on the other side of the ship, looking out across the waters that lay beyond the port of Ostia, toward the sea that would carry him to the land where the Lord had walked with men and women.

TWELVE: The Holy Land
"Of all the ornaments of the Church
our company of monks and virgins is one of the finest;
it is like a fair flower or a priceless gem.
Every man of note in Gaul hastens thither.
The Briton, 'sundered from our world,'
no sooner makes progress in religion
than he leaves the setting sun
in quest of a spot
of which he knows only through Scripture
and common report."
"Letter to Marcella" from Jerome,
on behalf of Paula and Eustochium,
written from Bethlehem, 386 A.D.

Paula and Eustochium could not bear to remain in Rome without Jerome. Their dependence upon him as a teacher and personal spiritual mentor was complete. Just before his ship finally departed from Ostia, message reached Jerome that they, too, were forsaking Babylon for the Holy Land. They would meet with his party at Antioch.

The travellers in both ships stoically disregarded sorrowing howls of protest from those who loved them, who needed them. They ignored more easily the whoops of delight from scandalmongers who revelled in new tales and speculations to broadcast at Roman baths and banquets. Those who sailed were determined to follow Christ and serve Him, regardless of weeping voices echoing from the shore, or what was likely to be said about them in the city.

Ninian understood better than most what drove men and women to forsake all in their pursuit of God's will. He remembered leaving his family, and the cost that he would pay all his life for that decision. Still, even he was disconcerted at the tragically strange news that a Christian mother was forsaking her care of an unmarried daughter and her young son. It was true that the forsaken children would not be alone as long as they had each other, that there were family and friends who would always care for them, and that they were richly endowed, not left without means. Nonetheless, a mother was leaving her children, going against the most powerful of all natural instincts, never mind moving in apparent contradiction of all Christian teachings about godly living and responsibility to others.

Jerome saw nothing tragic or strange in the news. He was ecstatic. At the last minute he knew that he left, not in defeat, but in triumph! The atmosphere of the city was souring his nature and destroying his ability to accomplish his most important work for God. The city was polluted, a pollutant, and he must breathe purity again to be restored for God's work. He had escaped to begin afresh, but he no longer faced his former fear of an unloved, lonely existence as a consequence of doing so. Paula and Eustochium! His own brothers! His most faithful scribes! They would be with him. He had saved more than himself; other precious brands were plucked from the burning blaze.

It was not long before they all met together in Antioch, refugees from another world. At the eastern end of the Mediterranean, in a place associated with the earliest foundations of the Christian church, they were reunited in fellowship with each other and with the old revered Paulinus, their friend. Jerome would very gladly have remained there for a good while. Contentment and peace were restored to him.

Paula, though, now evidenced a driving passion to discover the land of her Lord, and she would not remain any longer visiting in Antioch. In the time of winter rains and chills, they set out on a pilgrimage through the Holy Lands of the Bible. Jerome was deeply impressed by the spirit of Paula from the start of the journey. Having been used to seeing her being carried about the streets of Rome in privileged style, always cocooned in a litter borne by strong eunuchs, he was amazed to observe that the Lady Paula was perfectly delighted to be riding on the back of a simple little donkey along the roads of Syria.

On the coastal route to the south, they passed through Roman towns and native villages. They met soldiers, travelled alongside peasants, and encountered traders from the familiar west as well as from the more exotic deeper eastern lands. They descended from hilly terrain into the broad, rain-greened sweep of the plain of Megiddo. Their donkeys galloped across the flatness toward the tree-covered mountain and ridge of Carmel, the natural barrier from northern approaches to the heartlands of ancient Israel.

Narrowed into single file, trudging again up along the rock-strewn pass that curved through flanks of the mountain, they spoke little with each other. Elijah had wandered in these places, sometimes all alone, cowering in fear. It was near here that he had challenged and defeated the followers of the cults of the Baal gods. Such faith had been rewarded by the sign of a miraculously fired altar, and by rains sent from heaven to bless back into life a land dying from drought.

They emerged out from the hills and descended into a coastal region. They were now within the lands of ancient Israel. At the tiny harbouring place of Dor they discovered a mostly ruined settlement of people. Once Syrian, it had been claimed by the Romans and ruled by them as part of Palestine. There was a little promontory to the side of a lovely tiny bay. At a factory there, slave workers were making purple dye, the precious colouring that could only come by a process of crushing the life from one specimen of the myriad kinds of sea creatures to be found in this area of the world. It was a stinking, horrid business. The travellers were hypnotised as they watched. This was the colour made for kings. Much purple had been in evidence in Rome.

The voice of Eustochium, who was standing beside Ninian, was very soft. "So much purple was worn at home. I wonder if it came from here? Perhaps it was not so common in your country?"

Ninian smiled, but succeeded in not laughing outright. He looked down at her and answered in a kindly way, "No, not so much in Britain."

"It is very rare, so valuable," she added, her eyes widening as she looked on the scene.

"And I might have been wearing it now," thought Ninian, "I alone of all these people." He had given up his right to be adorned in such a glorious hue, a colour that would have identified him to all at first glance, to Eustochium, even to Jerome. Instead, he was wearing the clothing of a commoner, and travelling the world as a servant. His Lord, too, he reflected, had given up the wearing of purple.

A little distance away, Jerome saw the exchange between the two young people. Something inside him sounded a danger signal. Eustochium, the dear reflection of dear Paula, must never be tempted away from her devotion to a life of virginity for the sake of Christ. No. After that, he always carefully positioned himself between her and Ninian, no matter where they were, or what was happening around them. He would answer her questions himself.

Caesarea was laid out as a Roman city, all her component parts copying, as all other Roman cities did, those important elements of the mother city of the Latin world. Anciently named Strato's town, it lay wedged between grassy dunes and the eastern edge of the rolling blue Mediterranean. A massive harbour, magnificent aqueducts, a perfect hippodrome along the waterfront, straight streets, grand palaces, the theatre, the amphitheatre, baths, a forum, temples, statues and pillars, elegant colonnades, all made the city an impressive one, an elegant one, one that shouted about the power and influence of far-distant Rome. But this was a tiny version of that Rome, Rome among sand dunes, Rome with the sound of the sea crashing in her ears, Rome without hills, Rome without the Tiber, Rome never green enough to be Rome. Not really Rome, at all. Those who walked on her streets would never mistakenly feel that they were in Rome, not even for an instant.

The city had been constructed in its Roman form by Herod the Great in honour of Caesar Augustus. It was the city over which Herod Antipas had reigned, the provincial capital from which Pilate had exercised the authority of Rome over the Jewish world. This was the city where the distinguished Roman Cornelius had received Peter in his home. That famed, gentiles who believed in the Jewish Messiah's coming to earth were filled with the same Spirit of God as believing Jews had been at Pentecost. Paula wept at the house identified still as the home of that man whose faith and experience had signalled the opening of the door of God's grace to such as herself, a gentile. Paul had witnessed to Christ as he been imprisoned here later, and Philip had evangelised among these streets. Paula, remembering all these things, gazed in wonder as she walked the streets and gave thanks to God aloud while devout Jews, passing her by, drew their cloaks more tightly against their bodies. They feared that they might inadvertently touch her clothing, causing their own prayers to be ceremonially defiled.

Jerome was in his own special kind of blissful reflection. He had long admired the mind and work of Origen, and this was the city of Origen in his mind. Eusebius, too, the great historian of the church, had filled the world with his fame from Caesarea. The manuscripts these and other great intellectual Christians had amassed created a library here that was almost unequalled in the world.

Caesarea could have held them for months, but Paula surged on. There was so much to explore. They passed on southwards, through and beside others towns and villages, some lively, some mere ruins, all bearing witness to the past in some way. The strangers from so far away were told endless stories from local history by natives of the land as they rode through it. They recognised the names of some who had lived in these places, the names of those who had fought over them, recalling from past teaching of history and readings of the Scriptures the deeds that had been done in them.

They finally reached Joppa, the ancient port that served Jerusalem. Houses cloaked a single rocky ridge that rose behind the harbour there. The steep streets and lanes of Joppa had been the route of the fleeing prophet Jonah on his way to an appointment with the insides of a whale. They had been familiar to the greatly loved lady Dorcas who had died, but whose miraculous restoration to life had proved the power of the name of Jesus. They had been just as familiar to Peter who, having received a vision when he napped somewhere on a rooftop, in a tanner's house, had hurried along these streets, away towards the house of Cornelius in Caesarea to open faith's door to the world's gentiles. In spite of the delight of hearing all these stories, and the fables of other peoples connected with Joppa, the town held them only briefly. Looking eastwards, nearby hills could be seen framing the lush plain of Sharon, hills that called the travellers to walk on, to come, to enter them, to climb, and in them to find Jerusalem at last.

The journey to Jerusalem took them a day. A long day. The travellers from Rome crossed the flatlands and climbed up into the higher ground beyond, moving slowly, winding through valleys. They passed beside the tombs of Hasmonean heroes. They entered a world above the coastal plains where it seemed that every mile held a scene straight from the pages of the Bible. Every turn in the road, every rock beside the way, every view and every tree seemed to shout, "Come! Look! It happened here! I bear you witness!" The lives of prophets and kings, of shepherds and warriors, of tribes of Israel and invaders without mercy, all were lived on the ground they crossed. Even the Lord Himself had walked here before them. The Bible's stories that they had learned while they lived in other, far-distant worlds, had been sketched and brushed into their consciousnesses by the powers of limited understandings and faulty imaginings. The Bible's words had been trusted to be true; they had been believed because faith had chosen to trust, to believe them. As they walked through the settings of Biblical tales, meeting and observing the native peoples of the land, there was a huge change in their understanding of their Scriptures. No longer pictured by the powers of imagination alone, no trusting in blind leaps of faith alone, now they could see, and hear, and touch, and taste, and feel the reality of it all. Everything they had learned was true, vividly alive for them forever. They walked through their Bible, which now spoke more clearly, more powerfully to them, than it had ever spoken before.

They passed the high place which marked the grave of the

great prophet Samuel. They passed Gibeah, just a name, little to be seen there, where tall, handsome Saul, the first to wear Israel's crown, had lived while he changed from a majestic natural royal into a pathetic obsessive, one who would plot the death of a talented youth God had chosen, and Samuel had anointed, to be his successor. Beyond that sad place, the road dipped as it approached the city of the Great King. Beside the road lay the tomb of a foreign queen who had blessed the Jews with her generosity in their time of need. Then, they entered Jerusalem.

They did not pass through the city's northern gate unnoticed, for the proconsul, a connection of the famed Roman family of Paula herself, had learned of their approach and sent an escort to offer the use of sumptuous apartments in his residence. This would be a place befitting her rank, and enhancing his own as the bestower of such a privilege. Paula refused. She had not come to Jerusalem to be feted and pampered, but to abase herself in the presence of the cross. Jerome was full of pride, for Paula acted exactly as he would have hoped, and never dared to request.

Simple cells, such as the kind the poorest of pilgrims would afford, were their accommodation. These were damp, chill places, and the food that they shared, men together in one room and women gathered in another, was very little, very plain. This, to Paula, to Jerome, and to all who knew them, was as it should be. They were entering into their Lord's sufferings with Him, in the place that had witnessed those sufferings.

In the morning, they approached the entrance of the great church that Constantine had caused to be erected over the site of Golgotha discovered by his mother, a church also encompassing in its vast space the site of the nearby garden tomb. There was a sense of awe as they entered the sanctuary of the greatest memorial on earth. Paula was overcome with emotion when she saw the rocky height looming above her within the church, a cross on its summit. The emotions of Paula were freely expressed, her sobbing and groaning, her exclamations of love and gasps of wonder witnessed and remembered by all who saw her there. Those with her, though they were more reserved in their manners, were equally moved in their hearts. Ninian, born of a race that prided itself in not displaying emotion, in never giving way to embarrassing expressions of rapture, and certainly not to indulge in superlative descriptions, felt his legs give way before Calvary. He found himself bowed low, kneeling on the floor behind Paula, in the midst of others, with tears streaming down his face.

One at a time they entered the tomb where the Lord had lain, the place from which God had burst the bonds of His death and returned His Christ to never-dying life. And, one by one, the pilgrims from Rome, the pilgrim from Britain included, experienced a glory. Truth imparted far away from here in gospel witness, faith sincerely born from the hearing and accepting of such truth, were all that had been necessary for their souls' salvation, and they had never expected anything more than the joy they had already known in believing. Yet, in this place, all that past experience seemed to belong to a time when they had walked where the light was dimmer. Now there blazed a fire, brilliant in its illumination and life-imparting in its heat. They touched the stones with wonder. They had wept, at the place where He had died; now they kissed the ground, for here He had been carefully wrapped for burial; now they shouted with delight, for here He had risen. Finally, exhausted, they stood together, silenced, cherishing the realisation of newer, deeper understanding. All they had heard and all they had believed, far away across the seas in other lands, was now so very, very real.

From this place the travellers eventually climbed on, up the steep lanes that led to the western gate of the city on the high point of the ancient citadel. The massive towers built by Herod the Great for his palace on Zion, all that remained upright after the city's destruction by Titus, loomed against the skyline.

Quietly, for in such a place there were no words in them, they walked along the ridge from there to the extreme southern point of the hill to the place where the Christian church had been born. Here, on the Day of Pentecost, there had been the first harvest of souls into the Kingdom of Christ who was acknowledged as the promised greater Son of David. Jews had been mourning at David's tomb, as they always did on the anniversary of their most beloved king's death. While they mourned, fire had fallen from heaven upon wondering believers in their nearby upper room. This miracle had been witnessed by fearful unbelievers who had become believers when Peter had risen from among the disciples to proclaim the Christ. The king had died. Long live King Jesus!

Here had stood the building known as the first church in all the world, the Church of the very apostles who had continued meeting in the upper room where they had gathered with their Lord Himself and then experienced the Holy Spirit's baptism at Pentecost. The building that stood there now had been erected by the next generation of believers in Jerusalem, on the very same remembered site, when they had crept back into the city after its destruction by Titus. These were mostly Jews, but their church building had not been placed to face in the direction of the destroyed Jewish Temple, as might have been expected of them. The alignment of the stones was toward the place where their Lord had died, and had risen from the dead.

Since that time, they had worshipped there together, allowed to continue during the purge of Jews from the city by Hadrian. That Emperor had exempted them from the enforced exile from the land, understanding them to be Christians, not the same as Jews. Yet, more than two hundred years after that time, this congregation were still regarded as the Jews, the natural descendants of the first believers in the city, those Jews who first proclaimed Yeshua of Nazareth as their Messiah. As more and more gentiles had become followers of this Jewish Messiah, and had been designated Christians by a Greek-speaking world, the Jewish Messianics meeting on Mount Zion had become known as the Jewish church in Jerusalem. The believing gentiles, who over the years gathered strength in greater numbers, met for their worship at Constantine's Church of the Holy Sepulchre.

Recently, under the rule of Bishop Cyril, the Jewish believers had come to be regarded as annoying schismatics. They had been forced by his heavy hand to submit to the orthodoxy of the wider Christian Church. The Church of the Apostles, the Jewish church, surrounded by a separating wall in a vain attempt to keep its ancient identity, ways and independence, to keep faith with its Jewish origins, had lost its battle. A new church, a large church, was to be built there by Theodosius, brushing against the side of the ancient little first church of the world. The new church would dominate the old, overshadow it, but not quite absorb or overwhelm it. The Church of Jerusalem was now, newly, one church for Jews and gentiles. It was forced into being so by the decree of authority. It was not a marriage of love.

The Roman party left Jerusalem. They descended from glorious Mount Zion into the sad, dark Hinnom Valley below, a place where idolaters of old had sacrificed their children in fires. This hellish practice had been banned by a loving God, the One whose own Son had gathered the children of this land into His arms and uttered threats against any who would abuse them.

The road to Hebron began on the other side of the valley. In only two hours they came to the childhood home of King David. A thousand years after David's lifetime it had become the birthplace of His promised heir, the Lord of Glory. There were fields where widowed Ruth had gleaned under the kindly gaze of Boaz. Shepherds guarded flocks of sheep nearby. David had been a shepherd here, exactly in this place, and that it was here, too, that other shepherds, perhaps some of them even descended from the brothers of David of Bethlehem, had heard the angels singing about the birth of a child in a stable.

The travellers passed the tomb of Rachel, beloved wife of the Patriarch Jacob, mother of Joseph and Benjamin among the tribes of Israel. This tomb memorialised Rachel's sorrow at the approach of a death that would tear her away from her newborn son, Benjamin. The walls of this tomb stood within hearing distance of the cries of sorrow from other mothers, those whose children were torn from their arms, slain by Herod in his desperate attempt to destroy a promised Messiah.

The pilgrims walked on a path made by many footprints, and in that consciousness they approached Bethlehem Ephratah. The village itself was small and its houses unremarkable but just at the end point of a ridge, rising above all the surrounding structures, was the huge church that had been built by Constantine over the place where the local Christians had told Queen Helena that Mary had given birth to the baby Jesus. They entered the little doorway one at a time, and stood for a while together in silence inside the great interior space. They walked on mosaic floors between great pillars to the far end of the sanctuary. Steps curved down into an underground cave, the stabling place for the beasts that had carried visitors to the inn of Bethlehem long ago.

Down in that grotto, they adored. It was not the magnificence of the building above them that moved them to worship, but the knowledge that here, in this small dark place, down underneath the confusion of a troubled world, a child had been born. This was not just any child, however precious any and every child might be. This was the only child whose birth was a gift for all people of all time, for those who had lived in the ages before His coming, and for those who would live in the ages right to the end of the world. That night, angels had carolled with joy to shepherds. The very stars of heaven had been drawn together in a blaze of light that could be seen and understood by astrologers away in another land. And now they, themselves, stood, knelt, wept, kissed the stone, prayed in a kind of ecstasy, all together but each alone, and they worshipped Jesus. The fame of Him had reached the ends of the earth and drawn them to the place of His earthly beginnings.

Paula cried out that she could see Him there. Faith gave her eyes to see the past as clearly as she could see her own daughter, Jerome, and the others. He who had been born here was yet here. From that moment, this must be her home. "This is my Lord's native place," she murmured, "And I will live here until I die."

Before that work and that new life could begin, the rest of the land must be visited. They next travelled to Hebron, passing through lush, tree-clad, vine-embroidered valleys. They visited every place that was associated in local memory with the lives of the patriarchs: where Abraham had walked and talked with angels, where Sarah had kept her home, where Isaac had lived in contentment with his Rebekah, and where Jacob had tended his flocks. Familiar stories of men and women who had walked with

God and fought with men came alive as they passed mile after mile along the roads of the land. As it had been during their approach to Jerusalem, it seemed here there was hardly a placename that was not, in some way, associated with someone or some event recorded in a Bible story.

On a desert summit south and east of Hebron, they came to a high point where they looked out over a scene of strange desolation, into and across the massive rift in the landscape in which lay, below the level of the seas of the world, the Sea of Salt. Once, more lush than the land through which they had come, so lush that it was chosen by a greedy Lot as his home in preference to the higher, hilly world he left to his uncle Abraham, this was the part of the world where cities had been blasted out of existence by the judgement of God, blasted to salt and sand. The party were awestruck. This was a harsh, frightening world, full of rocks, gullies and haunting emptiness. David, fleeing the crazed jealousy of King Saul, like a goat had scampered among the ravines and caves and refreshed himself at the sweet oasis place of EnGedi alongside the strange, lifeless, heavy blue waters of a deadened sea.

They moved back toward Bethlehem, passing Tekoa, just on the desert side of Bethlehem, where a sheep owner had once become a prophet. Amos had lamented over the self indulgences and idolatrous practices of the people who claimed to follow the God of Israel. He had warned them of coming judgement on them, the ruination of their land. The travellers shivered in the winter wind, feeling a chill that reached further than their bones, into their hearts, as they remembered the words he had written. For those who had come from Rome, the world that they had recently fled, with all its wealth and stubborn affection for idols, as well as the claim to be 'the place favoured by God', the life of their own contemporary civilisation was not unlike the world of Judah and Israel in the day of Amos. Would Rome now, as Israel had then, know judgement on its ways?

They moved quickly on, passing Bethlehem to reach their next destination, the Mount of Olives on the east side of Jerusalem. The travellers ascended that steep hill on a path that rose between ancient, gnarled olive trees, trees under which the Lord Himself had wept and prayed. Tombs of generations of Jews lay beyond the olive groves, on the southwestern knuckle of the mountain. The devout believed that those in the tombs awaited the shofar sound from God which would come at the final judgement, when God would, here, right in this place, judge the whole world. The Day of the Lord. Jerome talked, as they walked, lecturing them all about all the things they should know when they looked on what they passed. Panting as he climbed and spoke, he filled their ears with understandings and their hearts with wonder. They toiled their way to the summit of the most solemn of all the hills on earth.

From the top of the Mount of Olives, facing across the Kidron Valley, they could see the mound on the eastern side of Jerusalem where the ancient Temple of Solomon, replaced by the Temple of Herod the Great, had once stood. This Jewish temple had been a golden place of glory until Titus had destroyed it. Now, its massive blocks of honeyed limestone lay in heaps, in tumbled piles in the bottom of the valley underneath the Temple Mount, just as they had lain since the day of destruction. They would lie there forever. It had been intended that all who saw the ruin would wonder at the sight, and they did.

Nearly at the top of the mountain there were some caves where it was said that the Lord had taught His disciples to pray to the Father. There he had also met with the fearful ones who crept out of the city under cover of inky night darkness for fear of the Romans, and of the Jews who were plotting with the Romans against Him.

At the very top of the mountain was the place from which the Lord had ascended into heaven. His followers had watched as He disappeared into clouds with glory. Christians in Rome now, three centuries later, made constant reference to this ascension of their Christ in any doctrinal creed. "He died, He rose the third day, He ascended into heaven," were words that came naturally to the tongue, were recited from memory as poetry would be recited. Standing together on the Mount of Olives in a little encircled space, a bell-like room built of stone planted over a rock, Christians from

Rome found that the truth of the often repeated doctrine struck them with a physical power. It had happened here. Right here. Those who loved Him had witnessed the event. On that day there had been an angelic promise to the witnesses. He would one day come again, to this place, this very place, out of the heavens. Those who loved Him then in this place would witness that scene too.

On this holy mountain there were two monastic establishments. Melania, whose reputation Jerome had known, and whose example he had encouraged Paula to follow when they had been in Rome, looked after women who came to Jerusalem seeking God. Nearby, Rufinus, a friend of Jerome from their earliest student days, worked to guide the men who came to make a devotion of their lives in this place. Paula and her women companions were guests of the famed Melania, while Jerome with his brothers and group of scribes went to eat and sleep in the place over which Rufinus presided with gracious hospitality.

Several days were spent there, those who had come from the Latin world sharing news with those who were hungry for it, and the two established monastic leaders communing with those who had come to them, giving them a taste of the spiritual delights of being in such a place. This was exactly the kind of environment for which they had yearned when submerged in all that was Rome.

The two monasteries were near enough to beat as one heart in purpose, but distant enough to avoid any appearance of compromise in matters of chastity. This had proved to be a worthy and workable approach. Men and women did not meet at all for meals, any social experience, even for worship services or prayer, but only occasionally for teaching and study, or to discuss practical realities in their work. Men and women were believed to experience equally validly a call to follow and serve Christ. They needed to live completely apart from each other in order to be able to follow Him without distraction, as well as to maintain the reputation of absolute holiness in their lives. Yet, men needed the women to help in many practical matters, and to share with them in spiritual insight. The women needed the men for other practical matters to be accomplished, for the sense of safety that their presence provided, for the administration of the sacraments in public worship, and for an equal sharing in developing the spiritual insights that came when they spent so much time in seeking to know their Lord. This was the pattern that both Jerome and Paula had instinctively sought for their chosen working place of Bethlehem.

Already in Bethlehem there was a place for men who wished to live a monastic kind of life. It was small, ill designed, with no leadership of note and no room to grow. John Cassius and his friend Germanus had spent time there and been enriched during the time, becoming part of the routine of prayers that was accepted and followed by those who sought God together in this way. From early morning until the hours before sunrise these men had formed the constant habit of prayer, at set times, in set ways. They read psalms. They remembered the events in the life of the Lord. They had confided to Jerome during the earlier visit there that the two of them wished to leave to pursue an even more solitary desert existence. Bethlehem required new leadership and Jerome's coming meant that there would be a fame and an influence there had not been before.

Ninian was absorbed in his own thoughts as Jerome conferred with the pleasant Rufinus and Paula consulted with the impressive lady Melania. The Briton had been eager to begin work in Bethlehem, work he knew would prove to be profoundly important in his own future ministry among his own people, as much as for the Roman Christians in every part of the world. He had expected to live in Bethlehem, in the new monastery where Jerome would be leader, as he did so. During this time on the Mount of Olives, though, he had come to realise that he did not want to leave this place. He wanted to sleep here, to rise each morning with a view of Jerusalem before him, to see the sun sink behind the city, its stones turning from milky, creamy white to warm gold in evening's light. He wanted to sit at night, when he could not sleep, under the olive trees that had witnessed His Lord's praying and teaching. He wanted this so much that he ached. Still, he was reluctant to provoke Jerome from his current mood of serene pleasure. "Let it be; please, let it be," he prayed.

And it was so. Jerome himself decided that there would not be enough space in the cramped accommodation for monks at Bethlehem, at least until Paula could accomplish the building of a new home for him. His brothers could accompany him there; his young scribes were fit enough to walk to and from Bethlehem each day and, indeed, the walk might do them good. They could stay in the larger monastery of Rufinus for meals and sleeping. Ninian and the others were not disappointed. They would rise in the place where the Lord had ascended, the place to which He would return; they would spend their days writing the translations of His words and truths in the very place where He was born, walking between Bethlehem and Jerusalem daily in paths made by the feet of Ruth the gleaner, by David the shepherd, by Mary and Joseph, and by all who loved the Christ ever since His time. Not only that, but they would escape the moods and imperious demands of their employer for the sweet hours of darkness. "He restores my soul."

Such matters decided and planning for the future commenced, the pilgrims took to the roads again to complete their journeying through the Bible's lands. They plunged down the back of the Mount of Olives, skirting a steep wadi. They passed the place where the Lord's donkey for the triumphal procession into Jerusalem had been found tethered, the colt of a donkey that had never been ridden until the Lord Himself climbed on its back. Beyond that place was Bethany, with the home of the sisters the Lord had loved, and the tomb of Lazarus that had been robbed of its prize by His command that Lazarus come alive again.

Down, further down and beyond to the east, they entered desert lands. Their way wound through wild desolate valleys, normally barren hillsides temporarily feathered with green grass because of the rains. They were grateful for the comparative coolness and freshness of the season because, once they reached the level of the deep sunken sea at the bottom, they realised that even now there was a heat unknown further up in the hills. As they plunged down the rough road that led through the wild landscape, they realised that they were in the area where another traveller, in another time, had been beaten and robbed. Left for dead here, along this roadside, his own most religious kinfolk had ignored his plight, rushing on past him. He was saved by the kindness of a despised kind of foreigner. Ah! Then was this the reason why the Lord had been so determined to walk in Samaria, to work among these people, to fold them back into one within the family of Israel?

Jericho was beautiful. Lying at the head of the strange salt sea, near the River Jordan and between two mountain ranges, she was a ravishing oasis. An abundant stream of water, cured of bitterness by Elisha, bubbled and danced its way through the unexpected bowl of lushness, of fragrant balsam, fruit-bearing palms, and proud sycamores growing within a desert world. The heap of an ancient tel bore witness to the ancient story of a city that fell to rubble when new-born Israel, for once in unison, shouted in obedience to God. This was the city, too, of a brave and believing prostitute who threw in her lot with the invaders and defied her own people, becoming an ancestress of the world's Christ. This was the hometown of the tiny, crooked and despised Zaccheus who had clambered up a tree to see Jesus walking by, and of an uninhibited blind man who somehow knew that the passing man of Galilee was the Messiah and dared to cry out for help.

The River Jordan, where the Lord was baptised, spoke also to them of Elisha, of Elijah, of David rejected by his people, of Joshua, of God. They climbed away from the hot, desolate desert landscape, back into the hilly country to the west, back to towns and roads. There, in the land of the Samaritans, they passed ancient Bethel and came to the well of Jacob. It was a deep well. It took a long, winding, pulling time for a pail of fresh water to be drawn so that they could be refreshed by its waters. A little dog ran around barking at them. They remembered, as they drank, a woman who had come here when the day was at its hottest, in order to avoid staring eyes. Here she had met the stranger who knew everything about her. Her witness about Him had brought her town, even those who had despised her, to believe in Him.

They passed between green Gerazim and the rocky bare heights of Ebal, two mountains that faced each other across a valley. Once, all Israel had gathered here under direction of Joshua. Half of the people on the slopes of Gerazim had chanted across the valley the list of blessings that would crown these people if they obeyed the laws that God had given them through Moses. The other half, on the slopes of Ebal, had chanted the curses that would visit their lives, their nation, if they forsook their God. In a dramatic moment they had, as a nation, freely chosen, loudly proclaimed, that they would serve their God. It was a covenant that they made with Him. The covenant had been soon broken, and was too seldom renewed.

Northwards they trudged, amazed by all that they saw. Mount Gilboa was made of richly coloured earth. Its soil, washed to lower lands over the centuries, reddened and made fertile the huge plain of Jezreel that lay spread out in a sweep beneath its slopes. Beautiful Tavor was an isolated dome rising from the plain, and nearby were the cluster of hills that encompassed Nazareth. As they wound up the steep, pine-clad road that led from the plain of Jezreel into little Nazareth, they fell silent again. It was here that their Lord had played as a child, had grown into manhood, had known family and friends, had heard the readings and teachings of His Scriptures in his own home synagogue. They left the sweet dusty hamlet by a road continuing northwards, and soon came to Cana, where Jesus had worked His first miracle, had 'displayed His glory'. Water from abundant springs nearby had been channelled away a short distance to the west, where the capital city of the Galilee in Herod's time had proudly and beautifully perched like a bird on a hilltop, singing out over another plain that lay beyond it. Carmel rose blue in the distance. Sepphoris had been burnt after a rebellion by the people of the city following the death of Herod the Great. The Baby Christ had been hidden away for safety, just then, far off to the south in Egypt. When Joseph and Mary had returned to Nazareth to live, the city of Sepphoris, less than an hour's walk away, was being rebuilt by the son of Herod, foxy Antipas. Had Jesus learned the building trade at his earthly father's side here, constructing new palaces fit for a king and his court? There was a Roman house there, built in more recent times on the site of a more ancient house. Its floor was a beautiful mosaic, depicting scenes from the legends of the life of the Greek god

Dionysus. The son of a god and of a human mother, lover of life with all its delights, kind to children, one who was feted in a triumphal procession by his followers, Dionysus, it was reputed, could turn water into wine with the aid of sunshine only. The water that flowed from the springs near Cana to this city in great channels carved out of rosy solid rock flooded Sepphoris with life.

Full of wonderings, the travellers moved on, down again to the lower level where the Jordan River fed into and out of a great lake, the beautiful, living Sea of the Galil. Along its shores lay the community Mary of Magdala had known as home, and further on was the city where Peter had lived as a fisherman. It was his home the Lord had shared, for a time. The streets and homes of Kapher Nahum, now abandoned ruins of basaltic rocks, had been blessed with miracles of healing, and its still-pillared synagogue had been illuminated by the words of Christ. There were mountainsides nearby where He had taught of blessings on the lives of those who followed the ways of His kingdom, and of woes that would pursue those who defied their God. There were rocks from which He had preached, and table meadows upon which He had fed the people who listened, miracling a handful of bread loaves and little fishes into food enough for multitudes.

The travellers hired a boat, and crossed the hill-cupped water of the lake, straining their eyes to see if He would appear striding towards them on the waves, the Son of the God who could hush a storm with a word. On the far side, cliff slopes reminded them of a man who had been delivered from the demons of his insanity, a deliverance so astounding that it had terrified his village. They had begged Jesus to leave them.

Near the southern end of the lake, they docked and wandered through the remains of Tiberias, the city built by another Jewish king in honour of another Roman Emperor. It had been built amongst Jewish graves so that the devout among the Jews would not come near enough to witness their king disporting himself in a manner that the Romans might approve but Jews would not.

They climbed back up to the higher ground behind the western shores of the lake and came again to the plain of Jezreel. They passed the place where the Jesus had taken pity upon a widow woman whose own beloved son had been stolen from life by death. The Son of God had taken note of her tears, and had given him back to her. They pushed themselves up the steepness of the path that led to the summit of Tavor and were rewarded with a view all around them as well as the sense that they were, here, above and beyond the noise and confusion of a world full of worldliness. They were nearer heaven. Was it away up here that God had spoken of the need of men to listen to His Beloved Son?

They had seen so much, and heard so much, and thought so much, and they thought they would always remember it all. In the future years, whenever they read their Scriptures, they would see in the pages what they had never seen before. There was new life in familiar words, meanings now so clear. They would understand what others, who had not come here, could not see. Few of the world's Christians might ever be able to walk where they had walked, to breathe this air, to touch these stones, to taste this milk and honey. With the privilege of having seen, having felt, having tasted, would come great responsibility. All the weary band of travellers who walked together through the land of the Bible felt the same. Words would be their only tools to share what they learned in these days with any enquirers of truth they might meet in other lands in the future. If only they could find words enough! But words would never be enough.

Immeasurably enriched, Ninian planned to return eventually to his homeland and to share such treasures, faithfully, among his people. As he walked, and learned, and yearned to remember all the lessons he learned, he was suddenly struck by the sense of his own powerlessness. In spite of the promise of precious Bibles in his homeward pack, in spite of the vastly increased knowledge in his head, and in spite of the good will of godly men and women who would always support his mission to his people in their prayers, his life could still turn out to have been of no avail. There must be something more. Preaching the Gospel, teaching the truths of the Scriptures, however knowledgeable the preacher was, however earnestly the shepherd worked, would only have a true effect among his fellow Britons or those in the lands beyond them if the Holy Spirit of God breathed life into the work. Without that, the words from the wonderful pages of truth would fall as dead as stone on the hearts of the Britons, accomplishing nothing of any eternal consequence. For the sake of the eternal destiny of the souls of his people, he would need to know the anointing of God upon him; only then could these truths strike a living root in the hearts of others. This was not something he could work to attain, or something that could be imparted to him by any human agency. Only by the grace of God could anything of eternal value be accomplished.

Third Part: Preaching the Gospel

THIRTEEN: A Great Commission
"....The pope of Rome,
hearing that some people in the western parts of Britain
had not yet received the faith of our Saviour......
consecrated the....man of God.....
and sent him as apostle to the ....people."
"Vita Niniani" by Ailred of Rievaulx,
trans. by Winifred MacQueen

One last journey of pilgrimage was scheduled before the group would settle down in Bethlehem to begin the work for which they had come.

In his earlier years, Jerome had sought monastic solitude in the Syrian desert. During those times he had researched and written a biography of Paul, the first hermit monk of the Egyptian desert, a man whose devotion to God had been spoken of throughout the Roman world and whose life had served as a model for many aspirants to a holier way. For years Paul had sustained his solitary existence in a cave. A palm tree and a pool of water were his only luxuries. There were occasional visits from a bread-carrying bird, but nothing more, for years and years. His clothes were of woven palm fronds. His food was the fruit of the palm and the occasional gift of bread from the bird. His drink was the water. His company was his God.

Antony, another hermit who was dedicated to the pursuit of holiness, had thought himself to be completely devoted to God and living the most severe lifestyle possible until he heard the story of the aged Paul, yet more devoted, living even more austerely, and more holy in his manner than he could hope to be. He set out on a journey to meet his ideal.

The hermits discovered that they were of a single mind and heart. It was a joy for them to be in this fellowship of two, two the

172

same. The aged Paul sent Antony away to fetch a certain cloak which would soon be needed for his burial. Antony rushed to complete his mission, longing to see his friend once again in life, but Paul died just before his return. As Antony mourned, two miraculously understanding lions dug a body-sized hole in the sand and the simple burial was accomplished by Antony as Paul had intended. It was a sweet story, and Jerome had delighted in writing it for the encouragement of others.

Jerome had left such desert existence and returned to the softer life of a more populated world, but his understandings and preferences were marked forever by that time, by such lives. He had been determined to continue to live according to standards of heart purity he had embraced while living like a hermit, and never to forsake the underlying principles of austerity. While he had gone about his ordinary work as a scholar in Constantinople, and then even in the midst of the opulence of noisy, riotous, teeming Rome itself, there had always been something of the desert hermit about him. Now, in retreat from Rome to Bethlehem, he sought a life where he could live as purely and truly as a desert monk, but still be enriched by the fellowship others, albeit those only from a select band of his choosing, and finally be able to pursue unhindered his work of scholarship to the benefit of the world-wide church. Before that work would begin, Paula must meet the hermits. She would understand that all he had said of them was true.

As plans for this final journey were discussed, Ninian remembered how he had learned of these holy desert men when he had been in Treves with Lugo. Long ago. It seemed an age in the past. Ninian had been challenged to think of men who would so devote themselves to God that they would creep away into lost and lonely wilderness haunts to spend the rest of their lives with God, and God alone. Now, so far away from Gaul, further from Britain, he was making preparations to visit the very desert where the monk Antony, the man of miracles in his own, Ninian's, lifetime had lived, and to do so in the company of the famed scholar Jerome, he who had written the life of Antony's mentor, Paul, the first hermit. Ninian could hardly believe that such riches had been given to him.

All the hermit monks of Egypt seemed to have learned of the approach of the wondrously devout, wondrously wealthy, widowed Roman matron, Paula. They knew that she had left her all to follow Christ, had left even her children in a supreme sacrifice. They had heard that she bestowed gifts freely, with abandon, never regarding her own needs but only those of others. Paula was overwhelmed by the multitude of holy men who rushed from their desert places to meet her. She declared that she saw Christ's likeness in them, all in their own individual ways. She loved to speak with them. She did not often speak with men, not even very often directly with Jerome, her guide and teacher, but she conversed freely with these monks from the wilderness. She gave them all she could. She loved to be there. She could have stayed forever.

Jerome, who usually was singing the praises of self-denial, virgin lifestyles, and monastic existence, became very uneasy very quickly. He grew noticeably impatient. He did not seem to see Christ in the faces of the monks who so eagerly sought her out, as easily as Paula did. He seemed to see greed there, instead.

It became very, very hot in Egypt and suddenly Paula felt the need to return to Bethlehem. The task facing her and Jerome in Bethlehem was a pressing one. They flew back more quickly than they had come, taking a boat instead of retracing their steps. Soon, they were safely engrossed in building plans for the great work about to commence in Bethlehem.

It took three years for the monasteries to be constructed. Paula ensured that the place needed to house Jerome, his students, his assistants, and visitors to Bethlehem, was completed before her own accommodation was provided for. She shared unsuitable and uncomfortable quarters with her daughter and the other women in her company during those three years. She did not care what hardship she endured.

During those years, Ninian and his fellow scribes rushed out to Bethlehem from Jerusalem at the break of the working day, normally returning in the last dying light of the same days to their cells on the Mount of Olives. Sometimes, though, they remained in Bethlehem, working late into the night by the light of candles and lamps. They would sleep for a few hours under the tables where they wrote and begin to work again at day's break.

In the monastery of Rufinus, they found a peaceful, orderly world. It was a plainly furnished place, but solid, with a kindly atmosphere that gave refuge to body and soul. The first prayers of the day were said together before the copyists would leave.

They would recite familiar Psalms of David.

"Their delight is in the Torah of Adonai and in his Torah they meditate, day and night......" so true, so real.

"......Like trees, they are planted beside a stream of water; they give their fruit in season; their leaves do not dry out; what they do prospers......." God, make it so.

"For the Lord, Adonai, watches over the path of the righteous, but the way of the evil workers is doomed." Thank you for daily protection.......

"I will sing of the mercies of my Lord forever; with my mouth I will make known Your faithfulness to all generations........" Oh, Lord, let this be.

As he walked between Jerusalem and Bethlehem while the morning sky opened into light, or from Bethlehem to Jerusalem when the night deepened and the stars began to shine from the blackness, Ninian would wonder with the Psalmist David, who had walked this scene before him, *"Who is in heaven that can be compared with the Lord?"*

In Bethlehem, each morning, in the monastery occupied by Jerome and made the scene of his work, the beginning of the day was marked by the first full morning prayers in which the work of the day was consecrated to God.

The Roman Psalter was no longer to Jerome's satisfaction. It was not, he realised, Jewish enough. From his new home in the city of David, the birthplace of the Messiah of promise, with the understanding imparted to him by friendly Jewish guides and teachers of Hebrew, and with the advantage of having works from Origen's Caesarea library available for study, he realised that improvements must be made in his earlier work. The light of this holy land cast new light on the pages.

Jerome's Psalter was translated afresh very carefully. Any weaknesses of word choice, any lack of absolute clarity, any clumsy shaping of phrases, any vagueness obscuring underlying meanings, were dealt with, with infinite patience. As gemstones gleam when polished and reset, the truths of passages of Scripture glowed.

As the translations were refined and settled upon, copies were made with great care. Copies were made of the copies, each one eagerly awaited by someone, somewhere. The Christian world was hungry for its Scriptures. Teachers and students alike were writing, asking, pleading, for more of the Word of God.

As some of the scribes worked on these, Jerome began to translate more of the Septuagint to others. He worked at a furious pace. He went over the translation of the New Testament from Greek into Latin, revising what he had previously neglected to oversee when he had delegated some of the work to his 'Latinus interpares', as he had fondly called them in their days in Rome. Now, he was in complete control again. This was more his true style of work. He dictated the work, word for word, not encouraging advice, suffering no alteration in his work.

Copyists wrote on, and on, producing translations and revisions, but Jerome did not wait for them to finish. He began to dictate commentaries. He covered the mysterious meanings hidden within Ecclesiastes and the practical teachings of Paul found in epistles to churches that had formed in scattered cities throughout the pagan world of the diaspora. Jerome even translated the commentaries of others, whom he admired, from their original Greek into Latin for students in an increasingly Latin-literate world.

Gradually there grew within Jerome the determination that the whole of the Hebrew Scriptures, the entire canon of the Old Testament, should be translated afresh. Even Jews, for nearly seven centuries, had read their Scriptures more often in a Greek version than in their own original language. The Lord Himself had known and quoted from this Septuagint version. Only Hebrew scholars maintained the purity of the understanding of those writings that existed before the period of Hellenisation, Scriptures still considered by the most devout among the Jews as the only pure words from

God. Jerome had already discovered that the translations of the Old Testament from the Septuagint on into Latin, having passed from Hebrew through the medium of Greek and then on into the tongue of Rome, had lost a certain degree of clarity. Therefore, Jerome would go back, right back, and learn from the Jews what their Scriptures said, translating them from that base into modern Latin, by-passing the intrusion of Greek thought. This was a massive undertaking, one that he, and only he, could accomplish.

Among the Christians of this land, as among the Jews of ancient times, prayer was habitual, regulated by and defining the hours of every single day. The dawn prayers, said collectively in the minutes before darkness had abandoned its hold on the world, sought blessings on the day. The morning prayers at the third hour after dawn sought strength for the day, remembering then the coming of the Spirit upon the Church at Pentecost at that very hour. There was a pause, in the heat of the day at noon, time to lift up the heart to God. At the ninth hour past sunrise, in the middle of the afternoon, the hour of the death of the Lord on the cross was acknowledged in solemn devotion. At sunset, the time for the lighting of the lamps, people gathered together, wherever they were, for the public evening prayers. Finally, there were prayers to quieten the heart before God, to begin the long vigil through silent darkness until the dawn, the light as of another resurrection to another day.

Not only the hours of the days, but the days of the weeks were lived according to a pattern in the Christian life. Fasts were observed, commonly on Wednesdays, marking the day that Judas arranged to betray the Lord, and on Friday, marking the day of His death upon the cross. Different groups of people observed fasts on slightly different days, but they all followed a pattern of some kind making a week of seven days.

Many Christians observed the seventh day, as the Lord had done, as their Sabbath. They continued past their Sabbath into the celebration of the resurrection on the first day of the week, as the earliest believers had done. Others, those who had come from a gentile world into the faith, those who had not come by the way of understanding taught by believing Jews, disregarded the Jewish

Sabbath and kept only the Lord's Day on the first day of the week. Each group understood the origin of the observance of the other.

Each group had, also, its own style of worship. In Jerusalem and among the monasteries of Bethlehem there were devout Christians from differing traditions who worked and worshipped as brothers, as sisters, in different tongues as well as differing routines. Those who came from Rome prayed, read, and spoke together in the Latin language. Those who had come down to Palestine from the cities of Asia prayed and spoke together in the Greek language, the language of the New Testament writers. Those descended from the first believers of the region, and those converted by their successors, spoke together, prayed and sang in Aramaic, the family tongue of the Lord Himself. When the priest uttered the words, "We are so bold to say......", the recitation of the Lord's own prayer by His own people would be recited in unison, but in many tongues, on any day of worship in any assembly.

In the churches, liturgical responses from the congregations would come from all of them at the same time, each in his own language. The litanies of "Hallelujah" and "Hosanna", "Kyrie Eleison" "Gloria in excelsis", and "Te Deum Laudamus" filled the sanctuaries in turn, or together. Such prayers made in unison were reminiscent of the style of early Jewish worship as found recorded in the Psalms of David the Jewish king. One such psalm, in twenty six verses that remembered the goodness of God to Israel His people, invited a communal voice to cry out, "His loving kindness endures forever!"

Whether at the same hours or different, the same days or alternative days, in the same form or individual style, Christians gathered, worshipped, made supplication, and celebrated being in the presence of their Lord as they followed Him through the year.

On a winter's night, all Christians would process to Bethlehem to view the place of the Lord's incarnation. The Bishop of Jerusalem, together with all the monks and priests, joined with the throngs of the common people who loved the Christ to celebrate His coming on this precious night, a holy night. At that same time of the year, the Jews would light candles to celebrate the gift of light in the temple at Jerusalem, a miracle born in the time of persecution for their people.

In the springtime, as the anniversary time of the Passion approached, there was a quiet, devoted solemnity in the Christians. On the day when the triumphal procession from Bethany into Jerusalem was re-enacted, there was unbounded joy, and all, whatever their native tongue, sang glad 'Hosannas' to the Son of David, "Blessed is the One who comes in the name of the Lord," as they waved their palms in descent of the Mount of Olives to make their entrance through the city gates. On the night He had prayed in the garden, the night He was betrayed, they went to the place of His sorrow, and shared His burden. On the day that was the preparation for the Sabbath, the day of His execution, they flocked to the Church at Golgotha, and they wept before His cross. From that time until the glorious first day of the week, they kept vigil. The hours of inky darkness were lit by their certain hope. The first day exploded into light and ecstasy as the story of the Resurrection was read to them in the place where it had happened. Here He had triumphed over death's claims, and won a victory for the dying world, proving the reality of eternal life. Bells rang; greetings were shouted. "The Lord is risen!" "He is risen, indeed! Hallelujah"

At that same time of the year, the Jews observed Pesach, the anniversary of their deliverance from the slavery of Egypt, the miracle of their redemption from hopelessness to life in this land as a people, a people whom God had declared would bring Gentiles to Jerusalem to worship Him.

Fifty days after the time of the Passion and Pesach, the Jews and the Christians, on the same day, celebrated the Pentecost. Thus, on one and the same day, Jews mourned the death of their king and celebrated a new harvest, while Christians celebrated the new kingdom's birth, with the beginning of a harvest of souls world wide. The Jews celebrated the giving of the laws of God, written on stone; the Christians celebrated the giving of the Spirit, with the laws of God written by Him on the human heart.

When the heat of the summertime began to subside, at the time when the later harvest was gathered in, the Jews of Palestine and the Christians of Jerusalem again became absorbed in festivals. For the Jews, there was the triple observance of the beginning of a new year, the solemnity of seeking the forgiveness of sins on the Day of Atonement, and the joyous gathering of all their people home to eat, sleep and celebrate for a week of days in their branch-bedecked Shavuot booths. For the Christians, there were three days of festivals to rededicate the three holiest churches in all Christendom, the Church of the Resurrection, the Church of the Cross, and the Church of Mount Zion.

There was one singular day that belonged to the Jews alone, the day of their greatest sorrow, the day when they cried with their grief. Barred now from entering the ancient city walls since the time of Hadrian, they were allowed by the authorities on one day in the middle of the summer time, the 9th day of the month of Av on their calendar, to enter the place in order to commemorate the destruction of their city, their temple, their time of past glory. It was for them a day of unmitigated tragedy and unbearable longing. Wailing the verses of Jeremiah's Lamentation, they would mourn without restrain, weep long and hard and publicly. Those who saw them pitied them.

Nowhere else on earth, not even in Rome, did the liturgical year so powerfully frame the days, the weeks, the months and years as it did in Jerusalem, and in Bethlehem nearby. Months of work and worship rolled through the circle of a complete year, and then another, followed by another. Ninian's existence blended into this passage of time in the rhythm created by worship that became familiar, as familiar and natural as that of the sun's rising and setting.

He learned steadily, as he worked on the Scriptures and commentaries for Jerome. He learned by the faithful repetition of psalms and prayers while walking, by the regular recitation of prayers and responses with people of all tongues in public worship. He learned earnestly as men of God preached in the long hours of Sunday worship. All that had seemed new and foreign to the Briton who crossed the sea from his own land became here beloved, familiar, second nature.

What now? Ninian might stay here forever, in this place.

Pilgrims from all over the world increasingly flocked here, like birds in migration. They came, they perched, they rested, they fed, and they flew off again. Ninian was of use here. He copied Scriptures, and there would never be too many copies of the Scriptures in the world. He shared what he learned with visitors, made them welcome, guided them in worship, helped them when they needed help. He loved this place. He loved being in the land where God had planted His name and spoken, on occasion, in an audible voice. He loved walking where Christ had walked, touching the stones he had touched, hearing the songs of the birds descended from the birds that had sung to Him, marvelling at flowers sprung from the seeds of the lilies of the fields that He had described. There was no place on earth like this place, and his roots as easily sank into the pale soil as the roots of the ancient olives he passed by whenever he climbed the Mount of Olives.

Visitors from Rome brought news from the outside world. People were shocked and amazed, and there was the buzz of concerned talk in Bethlehem, as in Jerusalem. Maximus, Macsen of Britain, had besieged Rome. He had not been content with less than the Eternal City after all. Ninian was benumbed by the news. The strangest to his ears, though, was the recital of a tale that Macsen had been offered the title of Pontifex Maximus at the city gates. Gratian, it was remembered, had refused this honour. Gratian had gone on to challenge the altar, statue and whole pagan influence on Rome. Gratian had been cursed. Soon after that he was murdered by one supporting the claim of the usurper of his place as the Western Emperor. This very usurper, at the gates of the city, already possessed within his name part of the title that Gratian had so stoutly refused. Maximus. Pontifex Maximus. Had Macsen remembered? And yet, Magnus Clemens Maximus had also refused the title. He had not spurned it, as Gratian had done, calling it a title unworthy of a Christian. Rather, he had offered it, as if it were his gift, to the Bishop of Rome. The Bishop of Rome, it was said, would sanctify this title by his bearing of it in the name of Christ, the rightful Head. The Bishop of Rome was now the Pontifex Maximus of Rome.

Macsen, then, was slain. Theodosius had ordered his death in order to reclaim and restore to young Valentinian II that which was more rightfully his. Macsen had been destroyed more as the result of his own treacherous nature, his own voracious ambition, than by the will of Theodosius, his one-time friend, a man who would rather be building a great church on Mount Zion in Jerusalem than killing fellow emperors.

Macsen had disappeared from the world, and the hoped-for security of Britain within a Roman frame had vanished with him. Ninian wept before God when he received this news. His abdication from family and from royal privilege did not in any way lessen his sense of love for his family and his country. Macsen was king, much loved. The members of his family were part of this drama, would be filled with sorrow and with their sense of loss. Ninian's nation would be reeling, and he shared in their emotions. There were huge practical considerations for his people. Macsen's troops were stranded in Gaul, could not find their way home without his leadership and authority. Britain herself was denuded of thousands of her men, and lay abandoned, vulnerable, and uncertain of the future.

A letter from Lugo reached the hands of Ninian. Bless Lugo! He had managed to rescue his Devorah from a forced marriage within her community, had persuaded a dubious wandering cleric to perform a dubious garbled blessing over the pair of them, and was fleeing with her to his home.

Ninian could scarcely believe some of the letter, and had to read it over and over to be sure that his eyes were truly telling him what Lugo had written: "While here in Treves, I learned that the famous monk Bishop Martin came from the west to plead with Macsen. He did not wish some heretics to be executed, and Macsen gave his word. After he left the city, though, Macsen ordered them killed anyway. Macsen was not very pleased with the bishop. He had made a powerful impression on the Empress Elen and on Peibio. They were converted, it is said, and became very pious in the Christian practice you speak of, many prayers, much reading. They now lead a simple life, wearing simple clothing, and give alms to the poor. Since the death of the Emperor, they have left Treves, as we are doing. Gossip was that they were intending to establish houses in Britain of the order of the casa you visited outside the walls..."

It seemed to Ninian that a work of God had begun, in the strangest of ways, within his own people. He was deeply affected by the news, and began to think again of his return to his homeland. He had not left his people behind for the purpose of pleasing himself, but so that he could prepare to serve them in the future. He had been led by God, he had no doubt, in these years. He had been protected by the bishop, educated by the finest scholars, privileged with understandings in the Holy Land, and enriched by fellowship with God's people from all over the world. He had now reached an age where ordination for him was possible. Was this the time?

Jerome was ordained as a priest, but had refused to carry out any longer the priestly functions so that he could devote himself, as a monastic, to his work of scholarship alone. If he agreed to serve as a priest, involved with people in pastoral care and eucharistic service, he would not be as free to give himself wholly to his work. Ninian, who had lived in the monastic life during these years of his training, realised again that his calling was the opposite to that of Jerome. He was not to escape the claims of people, but be devoted to them, to be their shepherd for Christ's sake.

As if to prise him loose from the present situation, turbulence broke out again in the life of Jerome, disagreements erupting between himself, his long-time friend Rufinus, and John, the Bishop of Jerusalem. All three had been admirers of Origen the scholar. Jerome had written in praise of him at many times. In recent times, though, the pursuers of orthodoxy had targeted some of the thoughts and works of this man. It was no longer considered desirable to praise Origen. Jerome made statements against works of Origen that he had decided he could not support. This pleased the orthodox-minded critics of Origen. John of Jerusalem was adamant in his determination to approve those riches from Origen that had blessed him. That did not please the orthodox. Rufinus, friend of Jerome but serving under the direct authority of John in a way that Jerome was not required to do, was not pleased with the uncomfortable situation he had been placed in when Jerome insisted that he, also, turn against Origen. Rufinus, instead, defended the position of his bishop, John, and reminded Jerome that he, too, had loved Origen, not so long in the past. Jerome was furious. He was scathing.

The bitterness that developed made the very air prickle. Each day Ninian faced an ordeal when he arrived, as he had always done, from the house of Rufinus to begin work with Jerome. Some caustic remark would float to his ears, usually directly after the morning prayers had ended. It was implied that he should consider moving into the beautifully appointed, larger place that Paula had funded for the monastery of Jerome in Bethlehem. He could then not only work on the copying, but he could also help Jerome with the teaching of classics and Scriptures to the young children who were sent to him. Ninian would be with Jerome virtually every hour of every day: morning, noon and night, working, helping, eating, praying, worshipping...... everywhere all the time. He would be so busy and so far removed from what was taking place in Jerusalem that he would no longer be able to be part of that city's worship and fellowship.

There was a deep inner sense urging Ninian, whispering within him, prompting him. It was time to go. He gathered his few belongings and his great bundle of precious writings. He had the Gospels now, the Psalms, and many other treasured works of the Scriptures. He took leave of Jerome, who was not pleased. He bade a fond farewell to the monastery on the Mount of Olives. He visited the holy places in Jerusalem for one last time, places he loved so deeply, would have loved forever as deeply. He was called elsewhere, not to this place. He must return home.

~~~~~~~~~~

Ninian returned to Rome and soon it was forgotten that he had left at all. His room was still his own, just as he had left it, the garden room beside the house of Marcellina. She was older, a bit frail, glad to see him and eager to hear all that he had experienced. The news of the division between Jerome and Rufinus with John did not seem to surprise her. She was very concerned to hear how Paula was faring. Ninian, for his part, was eager to learn all that had happened during his absence.

He was impressed by the beauty of the churches being erected in the city under the direction of Siricius. It seemed that the Bishop of Rome was intent on outshining his predecessor, however great that challenge. One of the most ancient Christian places in the city, near the Basilica Liberiana, had been the ancient tituli church known as the home of Pudentiana. In Rome, this was remembered as the original site of the home of the Roman Senator Pudens. Converted to the faith, he, his British wife Claudia, his son Linus, and his daughters Pudentiana and Praxedes, had given gracious hospitality to both Peter and Paul during the time of their stay in Rome. Referred to locally as 'the British palace', it had been regarded with a certain reverence by Ninian as the place where the faith had first made its claim on those of his own race, even though they were here, in Rome. The house of Pudenziana had been replaced by the Bishop's establishment of a church beautified with Roman columns. In a strange but glorious apse mosaic, the Lord appeared in the form of a Roman god, the apostles as Roman senators with buildings in the background clearly meant to be Jerusalem. There was an intriguing symbolical depiction of the coming of the gospel of Christ to the women of the world through the ministries of Peter and Paul, the two great Apostles receiving crowns of gratitude from the hands of two women. One of the women was clearly Jewish and the other, a pagan gentile. There were many other such works going on in the city that never stood still, that always grew, that always changed.

Rome, though, stank. Rome bawled with noise. Rome was gaudy, and bawdy. The huge churches might rise high on the skyline, many churches in many streets, but the people of Rome seemed to live through their days and nights as if they were not there. Before the official hours of worship and after them, Rome was unaffected.

Rome was not Jerusalem, a small pale gold and dusty place whose every stone spoke of the reality of a living God, whose hours were filled by so many people with the worship of Christ, some of whose people were His distant kin and spoke to each other, even when they bought bread or scolded each other, in words of the language He would have used.

Still, it was here that Ninian must be. He must serve his apprenticeship to be recognised as worthy of ordination. Hands of authority must be laid upon him so that, when the time was right in the purposes of God, he might return to his people to begin the work among them that God wanted him to accomplish.

Very soon he was made a deacon, and assigned to assist in the Church of Clement. He served the needs of the people, and led them in responses. Then, after an appropriate time, he was ordained. As priest he read Scriptures, he shared the eucharist. As a teacher he explained the meanings of the mysteries of the words he had read, unfolding the word of God so clearly that all could understand. When he led in worship, his voice rang out clearly, and the people could hear him. When he cried out, "May we be so bold........." with one voice they responded, "Pater noster........" There were no Aramaic voices, no Greek phrases, no other foreign tongues, for in Rome all worship was conducted in Latin. Ninian spoke the Latin with no betrayal of a foreign accent. He read, he recited, he taught, and he prayed in Latin that was always perfect, as perfect as that of any Roman.

Siricius was aware of Ninian, as he had not been before his departure with Jerome. When he had served under Damasus, though that bishop had regarded Ninian so highly, Siricius had not seemed to notice him. The difference in him was due to Macsen. Since the appearance of the then usurping Emperor Maximus at the gates of this city, Siricius had come to realise that Britons should not be underestimated. They could be powerful. Furthermore, since Macsen's gift to him, the title of Pontifex Maximus which he felt was rightfully bestowed upon the Bishop of Rome, he had taken the title seriously. He was the head now, not only over the see he considered to have primacy over other sees, but of all religions within Rome and her empires. His interest was more piqued by the state of religion everywhere throughout the empire. Thus, Siricius had begun to watch the Briton whom, his instinct could have told him, had more of the air of a prince about him than that of a commoner.

He marked the progress of the young priest where he had been placed at the church near the Lateran. Ninian was reported to be orthodox in his faith, consistently virtuous and disciplined in his life, clear in his teachings, winsome in his manner, and a naturally gifted leader as he presided over the worship of the congregation. He was not neglectful of his work. Those who sought guidance or help from him were fully guided and helped. Those who required catechising were well taught and emerged from their baptism into a life of faithful observance. The Bishop of Rome finally summoned the young British priest to speak with him.

Ninian had not been in the audience hall of the Lateran Palace since the days when the very kind, very direct Spanish-blooded Bishop Damasus had counselled and guided him. Bishop Siricius was altogether more reserved, more Roman, more refined than Damasus had been. As he stood before his pontiff, quietly and with respect, but as little awed as he had been when a youth in the presence of the predecessor, Siricius was struck by the thought that his young priest could go far in the Church at Rome. Perhaps too far.

He sat Ninian beside him and began to draw him out. Slowly, carefully, very deliberately, he questioned the Briton about his life, his people, his experiences since he had come to Rome and gone to Palestine. As Ninian answered, though he answered truthfully, he betrayed nothing about his royal origins, only about his heart as a priest, his call to evangelise and teach amongst his own people.

To his surprise, Siricius learned that there were yet parts of the islands of the Britons, the extreme edges of that remote land, that had never yet heard the claims of Christ upon them. They knew well the reputation of Rome, he understood, but perhaps had never even heard the name of Jesus. The long ringed fingers of the bishop began to stroke at his silky silver beard as he thought and thought again about what he was hearing.

"Is it right, do you think, that such people are left in ignorance of the Gospel? Are they such barbarians there, do you think, that they have no souls to redeem?"

Ninian blushed at the words, "No!" he replied instantly. "Of course they are fully human, and have souls. They speak a form of the language my own people speak. They are brave people and skilled in many ways. They have wonderful ornaments, artistically designed. They use intelligent strategies, and they are capable of forming alliances to their advantage —— as well as breaking them."

"Then, Ninian, go to them. Be the man to take responsibility before the Lord to fulfil His command to His own disciples. Ninian, go and tell those people of Christ. I believe that the people you describe must be the ones who inhabit the places meant by the Lord Himself. Remember His words to His disciples upon the Mount of Ascension, 'You will receive power, the Holy Spirit coming upon you, and you will be my witnesses both in Jerusalem and in all Judaea and Samaria, and unto the extremity of the earth.'"

Ninian froze. He had stood in the place where those words had been spoken. It was as if he stood there again, was part of the scene. He had never realised until this moment that this command of the Lord had not yet been fulfilled! The islands marked on the maps showed where the ends of the earth lay, but Ninian knew that the wild people who lived there had not yet been taught of the coming of the Christ.

The challenge of the Bishop was to him, but for an instant he recoiled against it. He was not a great apostle! He was simply Ninian. The work that he expected to do, the work he had prepared to do, would be as great a one as he could undertake using all his skill and strength, requiring everything of his dedication. It was enough that he would shepherd his own scattered, frightened, almost abandoned people. Would God ask more of him than he was able to do?

Waves of memory swept over him. He was suddenly a soldier again, desperately wielding a sword that sliced into the flesh of strangers the leaders had called his enemies, crying out in horror as he did so that there must be a better way. There was. It was peace with them through Christ. They could be brothers in faith. The same sense of helplessness that had filled him when he stood on the holy mountain in the Holy Land came to him again. This was not something that he would be able to accomplish, whatever talents he possessed, whatever learning he had done. Only a miracle of God could cause this to happen.

Yet, Christ had said, "All authority was given to me, in heaven and on the earth. Therefore, you are to be going out, discipling all the nations, baptising them in the name of the Father, and of the Son, and of the Holy Spirit, teaching them to observe all the commands that I gave you. And see that I am with you all the days, until the completion of the age."

Ninian's eyes finally met the questing gaze of the Bishop. Ninian knelt before him. It would be, for he believed with all his heart that it could be. This was God's perfect purpose for him. This was the task for which he had prepared as he yearned and prayed, toiled and studied for years. Christ had promised to be with him, all the way to the extremity of the earth, all the way to the end of the age. For love of Jesus, and of his own people, he would do his utmost to fulfil the great commission of Christ the Lord.

FOURTEEN: The Mentor
"The pillars in the tabernacle of the Lord
are joined one with the other,
and sometimes borne aloft on the wings of their virtue
they soar up to God,
sometimes standing and folding their wings
they confer seriously together."
"Vita Niniani" by Ailred of Rievaulx,
trans. by Winifred MacQueen

Though Rome's eastern and western empires were separately ruled by very individual emperors, it was the eastern Emperor Theodosius whose power had prevailed as supreme within the bounds of the formerly united whole. Other emperors, as they rose to power in the west, looked to Theodosius for confirmation of their rule, and went to him for help in their time of difficulty. Theodosius had proved to be not only a man of integrity in his leadership but also a sincere Christian in his faith, both publicly and privately. When he was given the honour of a triumph in Rome the year after he deposed Macsen, the extravagant display of pomp in the city seemed more a spontaneous celebration by the people from their own fears than a self-congratulatory display by an emperor intending to become, as others before him had purposed to become, a colossus in history. His entrance was made in a chariot drawn by elephants, the gift of an eastern king who paid him tribute. Even in such a setting, there was nothing vainglorious in the manner of Theodosius, a man of essential goodness and, astonishingly, of sincere modesty.

There may not be pride in the man, but there was no weakness, either. His authority and resolve had been well proven. He had maintained peace with some whose nature was war, had executed fellow emperors who had pushed too far, and had resolutely closed the pagan temples throughout the whole of the Empire in spite of loud protests from people of influence.

He was so powerful, and so unchallenged, that he could afford to be kind. This emperor had exhibited incredibly tender mercy and care toward the families of some regarded as his most threatening enemies, had established Christian works of great merit throughout the world, and had performed penance, when required, with the meekness and sorrow of a child rebuked by a loved parent.

However completely Christian their emperor was, and however much the people approved of that fact, they, themselves, as a whole, were not so thorough in their devotion. They were nominally Christian, but attended the spectacles in the arenas, the games in the stadii, and the races in the hippodromes in greater numbers than they attended upon their fasts and their religious observances, or came together in the churches for worship.

Arbogast the Frank, one of those whose power had served Macsen's purposes, had pushed the young Valentinian II to commit suicide. Arbogast himself had promoted one Eugenius, gifted and educated, to be the successor to Valentinian. Arbogast advised and backed Eugenius cleverly and even won a certain acknowledgement of him from Theodosius. These two, Eugenius on the throne and Arbogast as the power behind it, were in sympathy with the remaining pagan faction in Rome, those whose hopes for a resurgence of their powers had never completely died out. Heartened by the support of the new usurper and his powerful ally, an attempt was made by the pagan faction yet another time to return the Altar of Victory to pride of place in the Senate House in the Forum.

Ambrose had grieved greatly the loss of a second young Emperor. Once again, the Bishop of Mediolanum resisted with ferocity. The arguments of the two now-aged Aurelians, Ambrose the Christian and Symmachus the pagan, did duel in a written debate. Ambrose won, for Theodosius was true to his faith, strong in his purpose. This time, Theodosius took hold of the matter with a final air of certainty. Not only were the Altar of Victory not restored, and the pagan ceremonies within the Senate not reinstated,

Theodosius established the Christian claims against the pagan hopes even further. The Olympic games, because of their pagan associations, were abandoned. The sacred pagan fire in the heart of the city, tended by the Vestal Virgins, was allowed to die. It was all over. Finished. No longer merely neglected, threatened, deprived of financial support, the whole system of pagan observance was erased, not to be resurrected in yet another, later, change of circumstances, of heart, of rule. No more. Eugenius and Arbogast were killed in a final clash, and there was no one again to support the pleas of the likes of Symmachus, the last powerful and respected pagan voice of Rome.

A year later, Theodosius himself was dead. The Empire was bequeathed to his two sons, Arcadia in the East and Honorius in the West, a division that would prove to remain until the day the Empire finally collapsed. Alaric, the Visigoth, who had observed a treaty of peace with the powerful Theodosius for sixteen years, declared that peace was at an end. He was free to engage in war.

Ninian was very aware that in a very dramatic way everything was changing around him while he made his final preparations for a return to Britain. Not only was the political ground altering beneath his feet, but the Christian world was also experiencing great upheavals.

Another Briton had come to Rome, a brilliantly gifted nobleman who was teaching in the city. Pelagius expounded strong views about the nature of the relationship between God and men, and his opinions were spoken of by everyone. He challenged the commonly understood belief that men were helpless in the matter of their salvation, that even their faith was a gift of God's grace. He declared that God had given men free wills, that they must exercise these wills to choose Him, that if they were lost by not doing so they could not blame God. Some of his hearers were liberated by this opinion, for it stirred them to reach out and take hold on the offer of salvation; others were terrified by it. Could their faith, if it was produced by their own sinful natures, ever be strong enough, hold on truly enough?

At the same time, Augustine, the gifted rhetorician whose

very public search for God and eventual conversion in Mediolanum under the influence of Ambrose, had returned as a priest to Africa. His doctrinal writings were the exact opposite of those made by the Briton. Augustine declared that man was so helplessly dead, lost and in darkness because of his sinful nature that only intervention by God could awaken him to his state of need, never mind save him. Every awareness of the need for salvation, every instinct to cry out to God, every uttering of the cry, came from God's grace operating upon the soul. It was all the mercy of God. Some were liberated by this opinion, feeling safe in their dependence upon the mercy of a merciful God; others were terrified, terrified that they would not be the ones chosen to receive this mercy. Were they altogether helpless in the matter?

From Jerusalem came news. Jerome had completed the work of the Latin revision of the New Testament and now had declared, as it had seemed that he would, that the entire Old Testament canon must be translated afresh into Latin directly from the Hebrew. There must be no reference to the Septuagint in the work. His version, when completed, must stand clearly and strongly as it did in the original Hebrew.

Ninian was consecrated by Siricius, Bishop of Rome, now an aged man. The Briton was set aside and commissioned for the work it was agreed that he had been called upon to do among the people of his own British islands. That there would be Christians there one day, beyond the boundaries of the world Rome had conquered, was not a question in the minds of Ninian or the Bishop of Rome. The Scriptures convinced them that there would be, for Christ Himself had said, "I have other sheep, not of this flock, which I must bring. They will hear my voice, and there will be one flock." Such 'other' people must be sought, right to the ends of the earth. The believing Jews who had been first to acknowledge their Messiah, knew the salvation of God, the coming of the Holy Spirit upon them, in far-distant Jerusalem, in far-distant days, had eventually realised that gentiles, too, could believe, and were joined to them as one family in faith. To these first gentiles had been added more far-away gentiles, even those in pagan Rome, the ones to whom Peter, Paul, and many others had ministered. That spread of the gospel throughout the Roman world had seemed complete, until now. Yet there remained the fringe of space beyond the edge of the world, the northern and western edges of the islands of Britain, as yet untouched by the sound of the name of Christ. This last part of the world must be reached by the message that Ninian would bring. In those places would be the final flock to be shepherded to Christ, and their bishop would be a prince from among their own people.

Before his departure from Rome on this mission, Ninian was blessed and heartened by news that came from Jerusalem. A sweet kind of miracle had happened in the Holy City. There was peace in the church. Jerome was reconciled with Rufinus and Bishop John. Even more wonderful, there was reconciliation between the Jewish believers of Mount Zion's church and the gentile believers of the Church of the Holy Sepulchre. Bishop John had gathered them all together into one family at last, not by force but by love. He had blessed the altar honoured by the Judaeo Christians, their kapporet. Once despised for their 'strange altar', once treated like outcasts, once forced to submit to decrees of the 'foreign church' by a determined will to dominate, these brothers of ancient tradition were now embraced and honoured. Possessing unique gifts, their historical memories and cultural understandings would enrich the whole of the church. There was one flock in Jerusalem.

Fifteen years after he had passed through the city of Mediolanum on his journey towards Rome, as a young man driven by hunger for truth, Ninian the Bishop passed again through the same city on his journey homewards, returning with truth to his own people. The influence of the godly Bishop Ambrose had remained with him. Ambrose still lived, and his influence had become greater than ever in the intervening years. His own country and the entire world now honoured this man. Ambrose had counselled with love; he had guided with wisdom; he had wept over the lost with tears; he had drawn those who strayed back into the safety of penitence and restoration; he had gathered wanderers into the arms of God. Three emperors had called him their spiritual father, and he had deeply loved each of them, like sons. He was yet grieving over the death of Theodosius, who had died in his arms.

Other emperors had not loved him. Twice, usurping emperors had killed those he loved. Against these, he had been courageous in argument and by them he had been considered a daunting foe. Maximus of Britain, had defied and taunted him. Arbogast and Eugenius had banded together against him but they could not prevail. Ambrose had stood his ground with dignity and determination against the world's greatest rulers in his time, the kind of men who expected all other men to give way to them. In the name of His God, and for truth's sake, he had not compromised. Ambrose had affected the lives of many emperors, and he had outlived them all.

Within the walls of the city of Mediolanum, by virtue of his status as a visiting bishop, Ninian was given hospitality by the church. His kindly hosts and those who served him eagerly spoke of their own bishop, of his life and work amongst them. Ninian learned that on several occasions, in disputes between Ambrose and the Empress Justina, their bishop had been incarcerated within the buildings of his own churches. She had demanded that one of the churches of the city be handed over by him to the Arians, like herself, who wished to have their own place of worship in the city. Ambrose had always refused. On one occasion, surrounded by troops doing her bidding, he had prayed, preached, and led the people in singing praises to God until finally the shamefaced armies had melted away. This was a victory over force won miraculously by the sound of the singing of believing "Hallelujahs".

There was talk of all the new and splendid church buildings that had arisen in the city. Some of these were now hallowed by the presence of the remains of martyrs for the faith who had died in the ages past. The discoveries of some of the graves of people whose names had previously only been known as 'obscure legends' had been deemed a sign from God. Miracles of healing had occurred as relics were transported to their new places of honour.

Ninian learned about one great new church building that had been designed especially to replicate the shape of the cross of Christ.

This was to serve as a great architectural memorial to the sacrifice of the Lord Christ on behalf of sinful humanity.

In the short period of time he remained in this city, Ninian learned several new hymns, hymns composed by Ambrose intentionally to anchor central truths of the faith securely into the memories of his people. Tuneful in melody and natural in harmony, they were sung in worship together and sprang to their lips as they walked or worked during the weekdays.

Everything that Ambrose did was good in their eyes. They loved him.

"Ambrose........"

"Ambrose......."

"And Ambrose........."

His name began their sentences, his thoughts coloured their attitudes, and affection for him shone from their faces. Yet, there was a strange, sharp poignancy in it all. Ambrose was a candle burning down to its last flickering light, in front of their eyes. They knew that he would soon be gone from them.

The elderly Ambrose gave his blessing to the young bishop. "The leaders of the Britons have forsaken their post. The people will need you. God make you a light amongst them, and beyond them, reaching out to those beyond, at the edge of the world. The Lord bless you and keep you, giving you grace to fulfil all He calls you to do."

As Ninian walked out from Mediolanum towards the Alpes mountains gleaming white against a blue, blue sky, there was a singing in his heart:

Splendor paternae gloriae,
de luce lucem proferens,
lux lucis et fons luminis,
diem dies illuminans.

Verusque sol, illabere
micans nitore perpeti,
iubarque Sancti Spiritus
infunde nostris sensibus.

Votis vocemus et Patrem,
Patrem perennis gloriae,
Patrem potentis gratiae,
culpam releget lubricam.

Confirmet actus strenuos,
dentem retundat invidi,
casus secundet asperos,
donet gerendi gratiam.

Mentem gubernet et regat
casto, fideli corpore;
fides calore ferveat,
fraudis venena nesciat.

Christusque nobis sit cibus,
potusque noster sit fides;
laeti bibamus sobriam
ebrietatem Spiritus.

Laetus dies hic transeat;
pudor sit ut diluculum,
fides velut meridies,
crepusculum mens nesciat.

Aurora cursus provehit:
Aurora totus prodeat,
in Patre totus Filius
et totus in Verbo Pater. Amen.

O splendour of God's glory bright,
O Thou that bringest light from light,
O Light of Light, light's Living Spring,
O Day, all days illumining.

O Thou true Sun, on us Thy glance
let fall in royal radiance,
the Spirit's sanctifying beam
upon our earthly senses stream.

The Father too our prayers implore,
Father of glory evermore,
the Father of all grace and might,
to banish sin from our delight:

To guide whate'er we nobly do,
with love all envy to subdue,
to make ill-fortune turn to fair,
and give us grace our wrongs to bear.

Our mind be in His keeping placed,
our body true to Him and chaste,
where only faith her fire shall feed
to burn the tares of Satan's seed.

And Christ to us for food shall be,
from Him our drink that welleth free,
the Spirit's wine, that maketh whole,
and mocking not, exalts the soul.

Rejoicing may this day go hence,
like virgin dawn our innocence,
like fiery noon our faith appear,
nor know the gloom of twilight drear.

Morn in her rosy car is borne:
let Him come forth our Perfect Morn,
the Word in God the Father One,
the Father perfect in the Son.   Amen.

It was easy to walk and sing. The hymns of Ambrose, eight pulses to a line, four lines to a verse, could be sung, in fact, to the tunes of Roman marching songs. Each line, thus, was eight steps, four Roman paces. Singing a hymn of eight verses' length would lift Ninian's thoughts to God and at the same time carry him exactly one hundred and twenty-eight paces along his long road home. By the time he had sung the glorious praises of God ten times, he had passed another Roman milestone, was well on his way into a second mile.

At night, when he rested, he committed his soul to God. In the morning, when he wakened with light, he bowed before the Lord and asked Him for strength for the day. When he paused for refreshment in the middle of the days, he read from Scripture and gathered strength, again, in prayer. He was on the road to his home and he walked the road with God.

~~~~~~~~~~

Ninian returned by a different route over the mountains. He had first heard the fame of Martin, the Bishop of Turones in Gaul when he had discovered the casa in Treves. Jerome had never spoken of him, for Martin had written no books. Bishop Ambrose had not been close to Martin. Ambrose concerned himself greatly, all during his ministry, with the souls and behaviour of emperors; Martin had avoided emperors, whenever he could, like a plague. Ambrose was greatly influential in councils of bishops and councils of doctrine; Martin had avoided them like another form of plague. Bishop Siricius had spoken disparagingly of Martin, even had said that none who had been soldiers should ever reach such heights in the church.

Yet, many others had spoken of him; the fame of Bishop Martin drew Ninian toward him like that of Paul had drawn Antony in the Egyptian desert. Ninian remembered how the holy man had been reluctant to serve as a soldier, had hated the life so much that he had pled for release from it, had faced battle with no weapon to prove that his motive was not born of cowardice. Ninian could remember the screams and blood of a battleground, and he understood why someone like Martin would hate it all. Yet, it had been the news that Martin had so greatly influenced Macsen's Empress Elena, and also Peibio, that had affected him most deeply. He had been determined from that time that he must speak with Martin. Without doing so, his travels and training would not seem complete. Thus, he walked the road homeward from Mediolanum toward Lugodunum.

As Ninian left Mediolanum, he saw the waters of the Ticino River, fresh waters running from a mountain lake that was sourced in snowy heights, waters so clean that colours and lines on the stones that lay on the bed of the river could be seen from the road. For many years he had lived in Rome where the waters of the Tiber had moved heavily and darkly, thickened by the debris of the great city, toward the nearby sea. He had lived for a time in the Holy Land where water came as a gift from heaven or was drawn from the springs hidden in the earth, where the few rivers there were ran through deep wadis only during infrequent rainstorms, or ploughed their way through desert sands until they dried again and left no sign that they had been there at all. He had not seen such lovely, abundant water for many years.

The great northern valley of the Padus River lay before him, sweeping on and on in a flat plain until it came to its end against the mountains that divided this Mediterranean land from its northern neighbours. On the distant horizon at sunset, peaks were outlined against the red-blazed sky. He remembered these mountains. Soon, as days passed in quick succession, the mountains rose to the south, the west, and the north of him in peaks that looked like broken, jagged teeth. A tree grew, all alone, in the middle of the river beside the road, a river now turquoise in colour, foaming as it bubbled its way downstream in the direction from which he had come.

Sometimes alone, sometimes in the company of others who travelled the road with him for a while, the Briton entered into the mountain passes, one after another. Following the course of the river, the road remained level for a long while, the valley of the river narrowing as bare, rounded slopes of creamy coloured stone folded in more and more closely together. Between gaps in the mountains could be seen other mountain ridges, some formed from strange gnarled shapes of rock, rock that growled as it blocked any hope of passage through to Gaul beyond.

Suddenly, though the road seemed not to have ascended to any height, it dipped downwards, further into the heart of the mountains. A beautiful valley opened out to view, lush with foliage, ribboned by the windings of a green river, framed by a beautifully shaped ridge of creamy, marbled rock. This was a lovely place. It invited the traveller to stay, here, not to move on. Ahead lay steep roads, darker rocks, colder days, wind-howled nights. This valley was safe. It was still on the edge of the part of the world that was Mediterranean, a world of blue seas, of olive groves, of luscious fruits, of heavy scented blooms. "This," the valley cried out with seductive sweetness, "is your last chance to remain where life is rich and the land is soft."

Ninian marched on resolutely, singing psalms now, crying out,

> *O Lord, who shall abide in Thy tabernacle?*
> *and who shall dwell in Thy holy mountain?*
>
> *He that walketh blameless and worketh righteousness,*
> *speaking truth in his heart,*
> *Who hath not spoken deceitfully with his tongue,*
> *neither hath done evil to his neighbour,*
> *nor taken up a reproach against those near him.*
> *In his sight he that worketh evil is set at nought,*
> *but he glorifieth them that fear the Lord.*

No sweet valley would hold him back, even for a day. He was disciplined, and he made good time. Beyond that place, the air, the ground underfoot, the surrounding mountains, and the water of the river seemed to grow wilder. This was a barren world lying out and above the warmth of lower regions now left behind. Here were flinty dark rocks, gravelled streams, raging waters, steeply climbing pathways, and dark, dank tunnels. Ninian walked on, climbed on, scrambled upwards, and sang.

One day he emerged from a place where the road passed between solid rock walls so high that they blotted out almost all view of the sky, and he discovered that on the other side of the cleft the river's waters were running in the opposite direction. He followed the new stream as it drove its way through folds of butter stone until a valley opened out. There were soon signs of cultivation in the terraced hillsides.

Still high in the mountains, foothills of Alpes peaks but uplands to the world that lay below and beyond, the landscape seemed strangely reminiscent of home, the wilder areas of northern Britain. Ninian had been barely a man when he had last walked in such a place as this, and memories began to flood in upon him. From the dark recesses buried deeply within him for long years, he began to think of his people. His mother? His brothers? Lugo? Medana? Who lived and who had died? He would soon know. He began to pray for them as he walked, and as he remembered.

Finally the mountains were left behind him, and, following a mighty river whose banks were of black cliffs shot through with rose coloured markings, the road soon brought Ninian to an ancient Celtic tribal centre, an ancient foundation now for long centuries growing into an ever greater Roman capital. Lugdunum was an enormous city tucked in beside a very broad river. Both the original tribal fort and the later Roman buildings, perched high on a cliff above the Rhone, were impressive.

There were memories in this place of an early church, one of the earliest organised church communities. The faith of the Lugdunensis was strong and sure. Some had died horrible deaths because of their belief, but they had died giving clear witness to their unshaken faith. More than two hundred years after those terrible times of persecution in Lugdunum, Christians regarded with respect the names of Potitus, of Blandina, and of their great scholar bishop Iraenus, student of Polycarp, who before him had learned his faith from John, the beloved disciple of the Lord Himself.

Ninian set out again, on the straight-as-arrows-flying roads made by Rome, heading westwards for the capital of the country of the Gaulish Picts, Lemonum, the city where the renowned Hilary, the mentor of Martin of Turones, had been bishop. Gaul was beautiful. There were valleys, heavily wooded slopes rising from magnificent rivers, and such breadth to the open plains that it took many days to cross them. This was not a country narrowed into a strip bounded by seas, like the Latin peninsula, nor had it the confines of an island like Britain. There were so many miles in Gaul between the mountains and the nearest shore that there was no smell, look or feel of sea at all, the land seeming to stretch forevermore. There were curving valleys enriched by dense forests, bejewelled with serene meadowy spaces. There were deep gorges, hidden and dark places. Sometimes the earth became red and the lushness of greenery growing there made the world all of brilliant hue.

Guided by gentle-mannered local people who spoke amongst themselves in a Gallic dialect he found that he could understand, Ninian finally diverted off the straight road that led from Lugdunum to Santones, onto a lane that wound down to a tiny hamlet nestling into a curve in the course of a secretive river. He had come to find Locociacum, the monastery first built by Martin. This monastery, founded at the site of an abandoned Gallo-Roman villa, its church built on the floor of the villa's cellar, was the first ever established in Gaul, and had become famed throughout Christendom. There was an air of sanctity about the space. Miracles had happened during the time of Martin's leadership over the community. One of the early catechumens was brought back to life by the fervent prayers of his master, just as in the days of Elijah, and a slave was revived after an attempt at suicide by hanging.

In the area that had developed around the simple church, in buildings made of soft rosy local stone, huts of wood, and in caves along the riverbank, Ninian encountered a colony of monks busy with work and prayer, and full of nostalgic memories of their founding father. There was peace, and order in this place. It was a beautiful retreat from the world, a refuge for men on whom the world had ceased to exercise its claims. They gave themselves to prayer, to reading, and to the making of simple mats, gathering together for worship on Sundays.

Although the style of their lives seemed as holy and separated unto God as those of the monks in the desert of Egypt, these men were somehow still connected to the world around them. Martin had longed for such a place, but was not long allowed by the Spirit of God to remain in this seclusion and peace. He was kidnapped by the people of the city of the Turones and consecrated there as their bishop. Those from whom he had been stolen were, and always would be, vaguely resentful. They missed him. He was their father. This was the home he loved. In his absence, they continued in his ways, and God blessed them.

Ninian, refreshed in spirit by the fellowship at the little casa, followed the road that led straight from the little monastery, the place affectionately called Locociacum, to nearby Pictavia, the Roman regional city of Limonum in the land of the Pictones tribe. These Gallic Picts, as he had suspected from their language, were not unlike the northern people of his own land. There, in another city perched on a bluff over the confluence of two rivers, a Roman presence had been stamped over a Celtic centre. In this place the godly Hilary had famously ministered as bishop of the church. A son of the city, the pagan Hilary had been converted simply by reading the Gospel of John. Later, while contending for the purity of his faith on the matter of the doctrines of the Arians, he had been exiled into Phrygia where he had learned more of the influence of that Apostle on the church that honoured John in the east. Returning to his own people finally, Hilary had died here, after many years of fruitful ministry among his own people. Jerome had spoken glowingly of him, reluctantly sometimes, but admiring nonetheless. He had referred to his stature as a learned man, dryly commenting that some of it came from the height of the soles of his rustic boots. Sometimes he had professed to have gained nothing from Hilary, but other times he deferred to him, quoted his example as precedent, and called him a 'master of eloquence.' Clearly, Hilary must have been a very great man, and Ninian visited the places where he had been born, had lived, had worked, and had ministered, finally also praying at his tomb.

There was the familiar Roman rectangular brick structure, one that had been adapted from a former public use to serve the bishop as his baptistery. Inside, the central feature was an octagonal pool of water. Carefully instructed and counselled catachumens descended three times into this stone pool to receive the sacrament, water poured over their heads and shoulders three times, the bishop declaring them cleansed in the name of the Father, Son and Holy Spirit. In this three-time descent and arising from the deeps, they proved that the faith was one that delivered a believer from the claims of the netherworld, the feared underworld, and brought them back to life. In the power of the name of Jesus of Nazareth, they were new creatures, and members of Christ's body, the church. Ninian was moved to realise that, over many decades here, in this very place, many had come from pagan belief to enter into a new life, all through the influence of one faithful man, a truly godly man. The fact that the fame of the scholarship and talents of such a man had impressed Rome and all the empire, was, here, acknowledged to be of lesser import than the fact that this was a man whose ministry had reached out from his city into the surrounding countryside to claim many, many souls for Christ, the Son of the living God.

Ninian set out on his journey again, facing northward always, walking more and more eagerly, more quickly, until he reached the broad Liger River in the beautiful Liger valley. In the golden autumn season, when Gaul was still warmed by the late autumn sun, Ninian found the one he had longed to meet, Martin the Bishop of the city of Turones.

A man may look into the face of his parents and trace there the likenesses to his own. The texture of hair, the colour and shape of the eyes, the definition of the chin, a gap in the teeth, the flap of the ears, even a peculiarly distinct tone of voice can eerily make it seem that a son is reflected in the face of his father, or of his mother. When Ninian, Prince of the Britons, protégé of Bishop Damasus, Latinus Interpres of Jerome, the newly commissioned bishop en route to become the Apostle to the Picts under the authority of Bishop Siricius, first saw the face of Martin of the Turonensis, he saw himself in the countenance of another man.

The Bishop was alone, high above the river and the surrounding cluster of monastic buildings of his great monastery, outside his own simple wooden hut, sitting on a three-legged stool. He was an old man, as old as Damasus had been when Ninian had walked into Rome full of youthful purpose. Bishop Damasus had been sumptuously robed, groomed, oiled, scented and sparkling with gems. Bishop Martin was garbed in a robe of black cloth, simply woven of coarse fibres, tied carelessly with a rope. His hair looked as if it had been cut with an unsharpened garden tool. The area above his forehead had been shaved, giving him an exaggerated baldness. His eyes were creamily dulled with age.

Yet, when those dulled aged eyes lifted to meet the gaze of the approaching visitor, there was such awareness, such understanding, such serenity, such wisdom in the expression of them. In an instant, Ninian knew that he would have to explain nothing to this man, for all that he understood, Martin would also feel.

Martin, seeing Ninian, had an identical sensation. He remembered all the other Britons he had known. There was Brioc, here, with him now, an awkward person, a goad to the spirit and flesh. There had been Macsen, charismatic, naturally a leader of men, but deeply treacherous. There was the Empress Elena, strangely moved to behave with the humility of a serving girl when he had accepted her invitation to dine and her youngest son the prince Peibio, a seeker of truth, having no heart to rule but, like his mother, determined to give his life to God. Martin remembered the visit of Pelagius, brilliant, devoted, passionate, questing, always questing, probing.

Here, before him now, was one who combined all the best of those Britons, but one whom he felt had none of the major flaws the others had exhibited. Naturally, this one would be a leader of men, but he would not betray any nor ever be capable of cruelty; easily he would serve, even the poorest, and with grace; God would command his heart, always; eager to learn, but not keen to challenge all, always, at every turn, just for the sake of it. Not this one. If he had ever had a son of his own flesh, it might have been this man.

Words flowed easily between them. One could have begun

the sentence and the other finished it, for their minds were attuned to the same note of music. They could have spoken in unison, for what one thought, the other said, and it did not seem in the least a surprise to them that this was so. Silences between them were natural and deeply filled with peace. Each communing with God, their thoughts continued to flow as one.

This immediacy of relationship was noted by others. Brioc, the Briton who had been raised by Martin from his childhood and was always with him, noticed it first. Brioc was steadfast and loyal to the bishop, serving him faithfully in every way, like an ever-present rock. Yet, nothing of Martin's temperament, or manner had ever seemed to influence that of Brioc. It was as if he had been formed in a kind of contrary motion. Brioc was always thinking, speaking, and running about in a way that was completely unlike any thinking, speaking or behaving that would have been typical of his master.

Brioc, the opposite, immediately recognised in Ninian something he had seen in no other, the reflection of Martin in every way. He could not understand how this could be in a stranger. Was this man a relation of the Bishop? Had Ninian visited Martin before, perhaps sometime when Brioc had not been in his company? That had not been mentioned when Ninian was introduced upon his arrival. But how could the British bishop and his own master seem to know each other, so easily, so entirely, otherwise? It seemed very odd, and he did not feel at all happy about it.

This was the month when the monks remained at the monastery. Their summer had been occupied with journeys further afield from their own area and with projects that could only be accomplished during good weather. In September there was time to recoup spiritually, to retreat from the world, to gain guidance and strength from God for the coming winter season of ministry within their area of immediate pastoral influence, in the city and in the villages nearby.

Ninian took care that he did not tax the elderly Bishop Martin with many questions. He did not overburden him, either, with demands for time in his company. Rather, he established a simple regime of sharing the frugal daily meal with him, watching closely, so that he could learn all that there was to learn, and sleeping in one of the huts nearby. Even in the nights there was much to learn. Martin's habit of praying often during the day and in the night was not inhibited by the fact that others could overhear his conversations with his God. Those near to him could eavesdrop, as well, on his arguments with the devil.

Martin made no difference between people. Whether he was in the company of the powerful, the highest in the land as he appeared at the courts of emperors or synods of bishops, or in the company of the lowest, the poorest, the most despised examples of humanity, he was the servant of all men.

Services on Sundays in the church of Turones, the church first formed by a Bishop Gatien in times of persecution, were rich experiences. Beggars and foreigners, the sick and those disturbed in their minds gathered to meet Martin and his monks on their approach to the city. Others met them in the porch of the church, where instructions had been issued to allow such to find sanctuary. The bishop did not shun these people. He treated them with wonderful natural dignity. He would close himself inside the church with them, unafraid where others would have feared. He would lie down on the floor in the midst of them, engrossed in prayers for them who, like all the others in his care, needed the grace and help of a loving God to make sense of their disordered lives.

Bishop Martin did not look like a man of power or influence. He always wore a coarse black robe with a tunic of goat hairs to keep him warm. Only during the celebration of the eucharist did he appear in more dignified garments, but even then he had merely added a simple white robe over the top of his usual layers of rougher garments. Neither in his dress, nor in his speech, was he elegant, but his ministry was profoundly effective. His sermons were straight, simple truths delivered without the skills of entertaining oratory. They were not contrived and polished in order to delight. They were meant to instruct people, to result in increased faith and practical changes of behaviour among the congregation. The simplest soul who listened to him understood his every word and meaning just as easily as the most highly educated scholar.

As the nights lengthened and winter's cold increased, visits were made to the surrounding parishes. Walking alone in prayer, or together in conversation about God and His work in the world, Ninian learned much of the effect of Martin's ministry in the area. Pagan shrines had been demolished everywhere. They had not been handed over for public use, the common practice in places where Christianity had become established in other parts of the Roman Empire. Instead, they had been completely removed, all remnants of pagan practice erased as stones of superstition were smashed and trees of veneration were cut down. Churches were erected on the sites where they had been. The Bishop of Turones was ruthless about this. He declared repeatedly that nothing of idolatry must remain in evidence anywhere, for as long as it did, some poor soul would live in terror of the consequences of not bowing down to it.

The sick were visited, each one treated with loving care. Disputes were settled in judgements that might have come from Solomon's own store of wisdom. Sins were rebuked. Wrongs were recompensed under direction. Holiness was blessed wherever it was seen, and encouraged where it was not. The world was not perfect in this area of Gaul, but anything that was less than perfect was challenged in the name of Christ to become so. The church was at the core of the lives of the people, and it was a good, uncorrupted church.

When the winter reached its darkest and coldest point, and when the rivers were in spate, the monks of the great monastery of Bishop Martin retreated to their cells to prepare for the searching season of Lent, to pray, and to read. Solemnity was the tone as the passing of those dedicated weeks moved the people toward the holiest celebration in the year's calendar, the remembrance of joyful resurrection accented by the springtime warming of the world.

A nobleman had come to Turones for the purpose of writing the story of the life of Martin for the blessing of future generations. Sulpicius Severus, whose name and writings were well known to many people of influence throughout the Roman Empire's Christian communities, accompanied the old bishop day after day, shadowing him, speaking with all who knew him, and faithfully recording everything he learned. Under his patient, gentle proddings, details of Martin's life from earliest childhood were drawn out from the recesses of his memory. Ninian, hovering near, always as near as he could be without intruding his presence into the consciousness of those around Martin, would listen carefully, and hold each word as a man will gather tiny pieces of gold found in a mountain stream, storing them safely into a pouch.

Ninian was often overwhelmed by the sense of the privilege of being in this place, of walking with Martin of Turones. Each day dawned with such a sweet light, because he knew that in that day he would encounter the one he knew he would forever acknowledge as his truest spiritual father. He would be blessed by something Martin did, by something he said, by the effect he had on someone around him, or just by walking near to him. The delight of being in his company when they communed together in the Lord, even if this took place while they shared a meal of rough vegetables in a cold hut, was more glorious than a rich banquet in a gilded, silken-draped palace warmed by a blazing fire. He knew that this was true, for had been there, at rich banquets, in gilded, silken-draped palaces. If there were a time when earth seemed like it could be the porch of heaven, this was that time.

Leaving Martin was the most difficult parting. Like Elisha, realising that his mentor Elijah was to disappear from his life, Ninian wanted to cry out in grief at the thought of abandoning such a place as this. And yet, he must go. The time came when the world grew lush and warmed again, when the days began to stretch in length. He knew that the season to travel across the sea back to his northern homeland was upon him. The sun called him on.

As preparations were made for his journey, it was decided that three monks among the community of the monastery who were skilled in stonemasonry would travel to Britain. A church would be needed for the northern Britons, for where there was a bishop there must be at least one individual building consecrated as his seat of authority. Ninian would send for them when he was ready to build his church.

Ninian assured his mentor that he would live simply, as was done in this place, spending much time in prayer, studying the Scriptures faithfully. He would be eating not much more than vegetables, and a little fish now and then. He would give himself to the people, preaching to them of Christ, planting churches in places where superstitions still terrified them. He would not become entrapped by ceremony or enmeshed in synodical confrontations. Martin advised him to find a cave for the sake of his soul, a place where he could creep away and pray alone. Perhaps by a river. Ninian nodded. Surely.

"Without the power of the Spirit," began Martin......

"Anything I do will be done in vain," finished Ninian. "The only really important thing for the people...."

"Is to know the love of Christ, and His power in their lives," agreed Martin. "How I wish that I could go with you," he croaked.

"But you will. I have truly found my way here, in this place. I will be guided by your wisdom. I will have you with me in my heart," and Ninian knelt, kissing the gnarled, cold, roughened hands of the man, hands which then lifted to rest on his bowed head, one that was anointed again, this time with tears.

" Go, my son. May the Lord bless you, and keep you. May the Lord make His face shine upon you, showing His favour. May the Lord lift up His face toward you, and give you peace."

FIFTEEN: Returning Home
"When he reached his native land
a great crowd of people gathered to meet him.
There was great joy among them all and amazing devotion,
and everywhere praise of Christ resounded......"
"Vita Niniani" by Ailred of Rievaulx
trans. by Winifred MacQueen

The River Liger first carried Ninian downstream toward a part of Gaul now occupied by his own kinspeople, the Britons. In the time when Macsen had been emperor, under the kingship of Elen's cousin Conan, those Ninian knew as his cousins had settled in the northwestern point of the continent. After Macsen had died, Conan had ruled on as king here while Elen, his cousin, had returned as Macsen's widow to her own homeland island. Her sons and daughters were with her. The sons of Macsen's first wife had perished with their father in his attempt to take more of the western empire than had been meant to be theirs. Macsen's rule in Gaul had ended completely for himself and his heirs, but his one-time rival Conan, succeeded by Conan's son and his grandson, continued to hold this remote outpost, the land known as Armorica, the land of the people of the sea, a country now known as little Britain.

The waters of the Liger emptied into a gulf of the western ocean. Not far from the mouth of the river was an almost entirely landlocked bay. It was as though the curving, extending stretches of narrow land, together with numerous tiny jewel-like islands had formed themselves by agreement into arms, enfolding in their fond embrace a thus gentled turquoise sea.

The city of Conan was perched on a hill just inland from the lovely, naturally harboured ocean, and in that city Ninian encountered his own people for the first time in nearly twenty years. None of them would recognise him, even if they had remembered that he had existed. A prince of the Britons had left his home as a young man and disappeared into the world of Rome. An older man returned, changed in speech and ways as much as in appearance. His Latin was effortless and elegant; his British tongue was halting and its accent affected. He was not a royal now. He was a simply dressed, gravely mannered, cautious and quiet servant of God returning home. Whoever he was, they were glad of the diversion of a visitor so lately come from Rome, one who had travelled so widely, one who had been a close witness to the work of the famed Bishop Martin.

The king was now Selyf, grandson of old Conan. His wife was the daughter of a Roman, and the court of the royal family in the capital of Vannetais, a city perched on a hill, was very civilised. There were two princes in the family. Aldrien was quiet, content, well pleased to be the heir to the throne of such a beautiful realm. Constantine, the second son, was searching for a better place, a more significant role, a greater entitlement than that of a second son. He was young, but he was beginning to move forward in the world. Discussions were taking place for his marriage, one that would unite the household of his great grandfather's cousin in the island of Britain with his own, that of Conan in Armorica. He was to marry Severa, youngest daughter of the widow Elen. Macsen, who had ruled Britain to acclaim, who had ruled as emperor of a part of an empire for a few years, who had even caused Rome to fear, had been her father. Marriage to such a princess was exactly what young Constantine, son of Selyf, needed to give him standing. A future could be built upon just such a beginning. It was all he asked. He would do the rest.

Watching these people, hearing what negotiations were taking place in the world of power struggles, experiencing the edges of the rich life of a king's place made Ninian feel uneasy. He was weaned from such ways and such thoughts, well and truly. They did not, to the slightest degree, draw him back. He was anxious to be on his way and about his work. He did feel a vague sense of concern for the young British princess Severa, about to be offered to the wan-faced discontented prince who would happily make use of who she was for his own ambitious purposes. Any sister of his, he had hoped, would be married to one who would cherish her for more than the status she would give her husband. He was in no position to interfere in this matter, he noted ruefully. He could only pray for them.

Ninian explored the beautiful area around the city for a little time. He discovered an astonishing site near the sea where ancient peoples had erected great lanes of giant stones, mile upon mile of them, eleven rows of them in their largest manifestation. He was very aware, when he saw the stones, that wherever Bishop Martin had worked, he had insisted on pulling down any stones and destroying any trees regarded as sacred places by the local people. In this area, this little Britain, there was nothing that anyone could understand any more, the stones remaining regarded merely as a mysterious memorial of some forgotten purpose for a long-vanished people. Disjointed, confused tales were muttered, locally, some even claiming that the Romans themselves had been responsible for the stones. No one bowed to them, sacrificed upon them, or observed any rituals within them. They were just there. A mystery from a forgotten age.

The stone avenues and circles of Britain marked the passage of the sun and of the moon through complicated cycles of years. Those served a practical purpose for local farmers, and even to passing travellers. Unlike such sites in the homeland of Ninian, the alignments of the stones in Gaul were not established in the same shapes and patterns, and seemed to serve no practical purpose for those who systematically marked the passage of years, days and hours by Roman history, by Roman calendars, and by Roman sundials.

Also dotted around the landscape of this beautiful land were the places of the dead, from times of equally long-lost antiquity. Some were covered by mounds of earth, small hills. Ground-level passages through them were entered by intriguing stone-lintelled doorways. Others had been fashioned of careful stonework, beautifully crafted windowless homes of the dead. The most dramatic were those that looked like stone tables made for giants, massive slabs of rock resting on huge standing stones. Such places had been plundered for many generations, emptied often not only of any gifts that had been left with the bodies of the deceased by those who grieved for them, but sometimes even emptied of the bones themselves.

Through beautiful wooded valleys, across rivers teeming with fish, through meadows brilliant with flower, from settlement to settlement of Britons who now resided in perfect contentment in Gaul, Ninian walked on. He came, at last, to a small port at the north-facing shore of the land, where the channel of sea running between Gaul and Britain was much broader than that of his first crossing. He found a boat that was loading and made arrangements for his passage. This was, finally, his homecoming.

There were dark cliffs heavily covered in lush grasses, and pebbly shores of dark sand when the ship eventually came to land. A rising tide carried the vessel into a broad bay within the lands of the southern Dumnonia tribe. The boat was skilfully guided into a narrowing river channel until it reached docking at a settlement marking the beginning of the Roman highway.

The light seemed strange, as if the sun were obscured. There was no cloud in the sky, and the sun rose high in the sky overhead at a spring noontime, but the light was dim. Ninian had forgotten the darker light in a northern world.

The scenery was beautiful, and the familiarity in the sense of the place tugged at his heart and his memories. The road led straight in a northeasterly direction, past villas and towns, toward cities established by Macsen at the height of his powers. There were stones as in the lands of Gaul, some in circles, some in cairn graves, much like those he had seen in Armorica. He knew that this road would pass near a giant stone circle, the greatest on the island, but before he reached that place he turned at a junction onto the road that led straight northwards. He carried greetings from Bishop Martin to both the Empress Elen and her son Peibio. These two royals, who had learned to prefer simplicity and service for Christ to pomp and the power of Rome rule, were living in casas of their own establishment, among their own people, having retreated from the great cities of the world.

If none others would remember him, these two would. Elen, with a mother's heart, embraced the long-estranged British prince. They spoke together of the years that had passed since Ninian had set out for Rome. So much had happened! Macsen was reigning with her in Britain, in the last days of Eudaf when Ninian had left. After that, there had been such stirrings, and such risings. They had entered Treves in triumph, but left with nothing. And yet, there she had found Christ to be, after all, the whole meaning of life and its sufficiency, so she had left enriched with her nothing. From heights, having endured such losses, it had been proved true that Christ was all to her. During her remaining years, Christ Himself, and working for others in His name, would be everything. She could not hear enough of Ninian's experiences and of Martin, her own father in the faith.

Elen, daughter of Eudaf the high king, widow of Macsen, one who had been Empress of Rome's western rule, was busy in this place. In spite of her desire to live in peace according to her religious devotion, she had been forced, for a time, to lead armies into battle. Too late to save her eldest son from the mortal blow inflicted by one jealous of his northern kingdom, her command had held off the rebels until Stilicho could arrive from Gaul to restore and maintain order. Returning again to her place in the western mountain land, she had busied herself, between times of prayer and study, in designing and funding Roman-style roads to connect the communities of this lesser Romanised part of the island of Britain. Her prayers and concerns for the future were concentrated on her daughters, women who, as the wives of kings, would be a part of the governing of the nation as her father and husband had been, but as her sons would not.

Peibio, too, warmly embraced his brother Christian, the Bishop Ninian. Together they conferred, eager to learn all that had happened in both their lives and to share understanding of the work they felt called to do. Peibio, like Ninian no longer identified with the privileges or responsibilities to which he had been born. He was living near the once-great Roman fortress where his parents had met. The military had been withdrawn to follow Macsen, and the unguarded countryside was exposed to danger from invaders who sailed on the seas. The pirate king Niall returned to threaten, and his Scotti were bound to come. The people were truly afraid, all the time. Peibio would not defend them with weapons of war. He could not. He had no heart for that, but he would stand with them in his prayers for them. He would serve them as he served God, with all his heart. The faith of his people was his only concern. He left the governing of them to others with an easy grace, a deeply honest humility.

If Ninian could have remained there, in their company, it would have been a sweet life. Amongst his own kind of people, with the fellowship that can only be shared between minds and hearts so alike, and with the challenges of much work remaining to be done in establishing the faith among the Britons living in such beautiful mountains and valleys, there could have been a rich fulfilment just there. But Ninian's inner sense of calling as well as his commission from the Bishop of Rome drew him out and away to the lands yet further north, to the boundary world of Rome and into the unknown world beyond it, out of the comfortable, away from the familiar, to the furthest edges.

He took his leave of them, though not entirely easily, and walked on. The population became sparser and the light yet dimmer. Strangely, where the light grew fainter, it lasted longer. In the north lands, the long spring days stretched and stretched until, at their peak of midsummer's day, darkness barely managed to claim the world at all before the rising sun appeared again.

The grass was not as lush and flowers were less in evidence. The trees were not as fully in leaf as further south. The summer season came later to these regions, and the shivering man who was accustomed to a sunnier Latin climate found the air to be very chilly. He had forgotten how cold it was. Perhaps, in his youth, this had seemed normal.

Then, one springtime evening, Ninian arrived at the place he had loved in his childhood days. Word had been spread along the road before him by travellers who encountered him, people moving more quickly than he did during the days the journey took. When he approached the last miles he was met by one, then two, then a group, and finally a crowd who would walk the final paces with him. At first they smiled at him shyly, for he had become a stranger. They spoke his name, smiling, gently. When more gathered, they began to laugh, to call out to each other, to chatter excitedly, and he could not always understand their words. They spoke so quickly! Old men stood by the roadside, raising their hands high in greeting. Old women, beside them, wiped their eyes. Children were running around him, dancing with excitement. They did not know this black-robed man, but knew that they should, for all the adults were greeting him with cheering cries.

Then in the crowd he saw Lugo. His friend had heard of his coming and raced to be there. They embraced, pounded each other on the back, and shouted at each other at the same time, neither hearing what the other one was saying. Lugo then beckoned toward the little lovely, dark-haired, dark-eyed woman at his side, and proudly introduced his wife Devorah. Several dark-haired, dark-eyed children clung to Lugo, and to Devorah. One little girl with tumbled mop of black curls looked at Ninian with huge eyes. She was half hiding behind her mother's skirts, her thumb firmly anchored in her mouth. Behind the tiny Devorah he saw a taller woman, one whose face was achingly familiar, though he had last known it as the face of a young girl. He recognised the expression in the eyes of Medana. Ninian was home, and Medana's heart was, at long last, at peace.

~~~~~~~~~~

I could not restrain myself from expressing a growing curiosity. I asked Medana what had happened to her during all those years when Ninian had been away. She had been a child, just approaching womanhood, when he had abandoned the marriage contract and left for Rome. I realised, as she was telling me the stories of his experiences in other lands, living amongst other people for years and years, that she would have been growing up, living through the time of life when other girls married, other women bore children. His return promised no belated wedding, no family for Medana. What had she been doing and thinking during that time?

She did not betray even the slightest embarrassment at my blunt questioning. The radiant expression on her face while she had told of Ninian's return did not change a bit. "Oh! My father had pressured me for years," she said, laughingly. "He wanted me to marry this man, then another, and still another one. He was always bringing eligible men home for me to meet. So desperate he was for a grandchild from me, he said! I always refused. Loudly! I even learned to stamp my feet and sulk publicly enough to make his life miserable when he did this. He eventually stopped scheming and accepted that I would not marry. He became quite grateful, really because when my mother died he had someone to organise his household for him."

"When Lugo and Devorah returned from Gaul, that helped even more. Devorah gave him enough grandchildren for the two of us, and mine would not have been as beautiful as hers were!"

She stopped for a while, remembering those days, I imagined. She mused, "It was hard for Devorah. Especially in the earliest days. We loved her, though, and the children coming helped her to settle amongst us. The children were part of her, and part of us, and they were such adorable children!"

"Were you close to her?" I asked.

"Oh, yes! I had no sister. She was as easy to love as Lugo. They were very alike, you know. It was strange, because they came from different civilisations, different countries, different religions, and yet they were so alike!"

"The worst of it for Devorah was the cold weather — and the matter of her religion. We could do nothing about the cold. She eventually grew accustomed to it, and always wore more cloaks than anyone else. There was no-one with whom she could share her religious observances, so she just did what she could all alone. She explained much to me about such things. It was amazing, though. One day, she understood something we could not have explained to her. She always lit a candle at the setting of sun on

219

Friday night. She would say a special blessing none of us understood, in the Hebrew language. One night she was doing this, alone in a corner by herself, when she suddenly looked up and exclaimed, 'But He is the Messiah!'

She had thought that Christians worshipped the son of a pagan god, the one they called the Christ, the one after whom they were named. She did not know Greek, and that was the Greek name for him. It didn't mean anything to her. That night she realised that this One we call Jesus was one she called Yeshua, and that He was truly the person the Jews looked for and prayed for as their Messiah. After that, she named Him HaMashiach all her days. She was ecstatic that she had found Him. She wrote a letter to send to her family at Treves to tell them of her discovery, but she said that they might not read the letter if they knew it came from her. They considered her dead since she had left her people and married a gentile. She was sad, so sad about them. She had to, at least, try to tell them.

"I was very busy with all the family during those years and when Ninian returned the time folded in on itself in a strange way. It was as if he had not been away at all. It seemed so normal to have him with us again. What joy! I still recall that joy! " She beamed.

"Did you not want him to marry you then, when he returned?" I asked, scarcely believing that I could ask such a question.

She smiled at me. "Oh, yes! Of course! But he wouldn't have. He couldn't have. He had too much work to do, and God claimed all his life. There was another joy, though, because I knew that I could serve God with him. He might go far away, and I might never see him again for years, just as before, but we had the same purpose in our two lives and, though it might seem strange to you, my traveller friend, it was enough."

"Ninian..learned in a foreign land
what he would afterwards teach in his own."
"Vita Niniani" by Ailred of Rievaulx
trans. by Winifred MacQueen

Macsen had drawn thousands of the men of Britain in his train across to Gaul. Hardly any of them had returned. Ambitious to rule Rome from Britain, they had apparently vanished in Gaul; they did not rule Rome, and they had not returned to rule in their own land.

Those too old to go with the adventurers had remained behind and tried to carry on as normal in life. Those too young to go had grown into men very quickly, in ten years, but they had not had their fathers to raise them, only their ageing grandfathers. Their grandfathers could impart wisdom to them, skills from generations past, but they could not train them to fight very well. The people of the land were, thus, weakened and dispirited. Old and young alike realised the vulnerability of their situation.

As the old Roman priest had done, those who accompanied the Christian army of the Christianised empire, had begun to retreat to their homeland and the churches were as denuded of leadership as were the armies of the people. Though they considered themselves as Christian, the people did not meet together in congregations for worship as they once had. The most faithful in believing spoke together as friends and family would, encouraging each other in the way of the faith, sharing what truths they knew. Some still prayed. There were a few, probably one or two in every community, people like Medana, who drew others to them whenever there was a need, or a questioning, or a fear. Those who forgot how to pray found those who remembered when they needed them.

Falling away from the faith, many had begun to revert to the observance of only half-remembered rituals at shrine places, at wells, within dark groves of oak. They needed to venerate something, anything, and to seek help somehow, anywhere they thought they might find it. Some said that the recent neglect of ancient spirit understandings, had offended gods whose names they had forgotten. These thoughts began to haunt those who were nervous or who looked for a reason behind the plunging of the fortunes of the nation who had ridden out proudly for Macsen.

Ninian now had no spiritual leader from whom advice could be sought. He was on his own. His instincts took over. For a while he felt the need to say nothing, to do nothing, just to be there among them. He sat where they sat, and he listened to them; he walked with them along the roadways, and he watched; he ate with them; he toiled with them in their work; and he considered what he saw, what he heard, and what he felt in his heart.

In a short time he seemed one of them again, his accent like theirs in speech, his manner reflecting their manners, his understanding in tune with their hearts. He knew why they were staggering and falling, what made them weep, and what made them laugh. He knew their hopes, the dashing of them, and the fears that haunted them. What they hadn't told him, he could feel without words. He began to carry them upon his heart, and in his prayers, as if lifting a great weight with his arms, he raised them to his loving God in simple faith that believed they would be saved.

People began to seek him out, as they had sought out Medana and others like her. They realised that this was a holy man, and they came to regard his words as truly as people of the Bible times had regarded those of their prophets. They knew that Ninian cared for them. They respected his truthfulness. They responded to his gentleness. They trusted him. His ministry could begin, for they opened the door to him.

In this place, in the heart of the north of the land, Roman roads crossed the pathways of the Celts. Roman stations and towns lay alongside the hilltop forts of the Britons. Roman commanders and technicians had long mingled with foreign conscript soldiers from exotic places. Local British tribes quite commonly encountered travelling tribespeople from further north, or further east, or further south. Ninian began to call any people who would come, from all these groups, for regular times of worship. Morning and evening they gathered at the ringing of his handbell. Prayers were said, Psalms were read, hymns were sung. On the Lord's Day, he would tell them of the coming, the life, the death, the resurrection and the ascension of the Lord. He would preach to them about the deeper understandings of truth from the Bible. He would tell them of the history of their faith, the great shining lights of the Apostles, the moving stories of the sufferings of martyrs, and the establishment of churches among all the people in the world. He would explain the statements of the creeds that were formed to protect them from false teachings. He would challenge their behaviour, their day and daily walk in life, calling them to live perfectly and purely in an imperfect and impure world. There was so much for them to learn, but he was a faithful, patient, and a very determined teacher.

He taught them to pray when they were together, giving them the words of their Lord's own prayer, "Pater noster........." He explained the words, carefully, in their own dialect. He answered questions the words prompted. They prayed the words with him over and over until they could pray them without his leading, and pray them with understanding, from their hearts.

He taught them to sing.

"Te Deum laudamus,
Te Dominum confitemur,
Te aeternum patrem,
Omnis Terra veneratur......"
"We praise you O God
We acknowledge you to be the Lord,
All the earth now worships you,
the Father everlasting."

No more, the wooded darkness; no more the shrines of stone.

He taught them the marching hymns of Ambrose, so that when they walked on the roads they acknowledged their God and remembered that He who had made them would protect and guide them on the pathway. Sometimes he sang to them; sometimes they sang to him; they sang while they worked; mothers sang to lullaby their children and to confirm the faith within their own hearts.

Ninian read to the people from his precious Scriptures, books that had travelled with him over hundreds, thousands of miles of walking or riding and sailing on waters. He read the carefully scripted Latin, hearing the voice of Jerome in his dictation as he read. Then he translated the words into the dialect of the people. In time, they began to understand the words so clearly in the Latin that when he translated they heard and understood a second time.

When he addressed the people on Sundays, he spoke to their hearts in their own language. Whenever Roman soldiers or foreign traders gathered with the congregation, he would speak in Latin. His Latin was beautiful to hear. Because he was speaking always about God, whom He worshipped, to people, whom he loved, the words were clear, and earnest, and sweetly uttered. When Latin soldiers spoke, they barked roughness in authority; when Latin merchants spoke, their voices wheedled and whined. Ninian's Latin was a singing sound, a delight to the ears, rich and lovely and good. The hunger for words that added a sense of glory to the world made quick learners of those who listened.

Some wanted to learn to read, and wanted copies of some of the Scriptures of their own. Classes were formed, and scholars gathered. Ninian allowed anyone to come, if they would work hard. Men, women, boys, girls, leaders and slaves, Romans and Britons, anyone at all might come.

He did not find it natural to thunder at the people when he learned of any straying from the path of righteousness, any insisting on strange interpretations of the truth, or of anyone discovered tying strips of cloth to branches at roadside wells. His ways of dealing with his people were altogether gentler, the continual faithful correction of a steady, careful hand.

Horses could be broken to ride by merely jumping on their back, whip in hand, and clinging there, if possible, while the frightened animal would run, writhe, twist and leap about. Finally coming to a standstill through exhaustion or the eventual understanding that it could not unseat the rider, it was a tamed mount. It knew that it was dominated by the more determined will of another.

There was another way, though, to ride an unbroken horse. Touching it, stroking it, accustoming it to the presence and voice and touch and smell of its owner took time. Leading it with a rope, teaching it to respond to signals and directions, took more time. Placing a blanket on its back, walking it around in circles while it carried the blanket, talking to it in a comforting voice took patience, but the animal soon accepted this as natural. Eventually it would accept the weight and feel of a saddle without any concern. After leaning the body's weight on the saddle, again encouraging the animal with voice, with touch, over and over, finally the rider could slip on the horse's back. Such a person acquired a steady, willing mount, a better horse than if he had used a quick method of brutal domination. There was no resentment in an animal broken to ride in this way. There was acceptance. Completely, and naturally.

Ninian did not seek to dominate and break the wills of the people by the use of his authority. He worked, slowly, patiently, and lovingly to win their confidence, then their understandings, and finally their willing hearts to God. His was a soft, kind breaking in. Under the wise gentling influence of his work, what was muddled became clear; misconceptions were abandoned; crookedness was straightened. To the people, truth shone like light into their minds, then glowed warmth into their hearts, and finally produced fruit in the ways they lived their lives.

The shrines became neglected again, for those who had prayed to a stone or a piece of strangely shaped wood found more reality in praying to a living God. Springs and wells, before feared as powerful, dreaded entrances to the nightmare netherworlds, no longer frightened the people who passed them on the roads. These places had been blessed in prayers by Ninian, and their waters served for the quenching of thirst, for refreshment.

Soon, the church was filled. Mornings and evenings it was filled. On Sundays the people met outside when they could, if the weather were kind, because there was no room inside for them all. A larger public hut was built. It, too, was soon filled.

Those who came to their bishop to confess their failings and unbelief were formed into the ranks of catachumens. During the winter months, when there was less work and less travelling, these seekers were schooled regularly. They were urged to spend time in prayer, to fast and, as the Paschal season approached, to prepare their hearts for commitment to their Lord in the sacrament of baptism.

When the great day arrived, people thronged to the fountain that had been dug out more widely for the purpose. Stone steps led them down into the water where, while voices of friends and families sang their Hallelujahs, new believers in Christ each descended three times over, being baptised in the name of the Father, of the Son, and of the Holy Spirit. Lugo was one, and Devorah was another.

There was joy among the people.

There was joy in the heart of the Bishop Ninian.

The Scriptures said that there was even greater joy in heaven.

SEVENTEEN: *Reaching Out*
"With wise words the famous bishop taught his native land,
never relaxing his efforts
so that, when the dangers of the present strife were
overcome,
they would wear purple crowns at the coming of
Christ."
"The Miracles of Bishop Nynia"
trans. by Winifred MacQueen

The Carvetti — Cumberland, Westmoreland

Ninian found a quiet place in the curve of the river Eamontum, a hollowed cave hidden high up in the wooded embankment. He crept away into its space whenever he needed to be alone. And there, God would restore his soul. He gave out to the people constantly, and was learning to understand the story in the gospel which described how Jesus felt physically that virtue had gone out from him into another when one needy, bleeding woman tried to touch Him secretly in the middle of the press of a throng of people. Ninian would be drained by his efforts but then, alone in this riverside retreat, God would renew him.

He was in prayer there one day, and had just uttered the words, "What next, my Lord?" when he was distracted by a voice calling his name. He peered out to see a man gesturing wildly in his direction, the man he could hear shouting. He left his hiding place, annoyed at the distraction. He needed to pray. He was muttering to himself, "Bishop Ambrose would not be annoyed by this, Ninian. Who do you think you are to be annoyed by a seeking soul?" as he clambered down the banking. He retrieved his little coracle and crossed the water to meet the man in the meadow on the other side.

The man dropped to his knees, seized his hand, tried to kiss it. Ninian smartly withdrew his hand, forced him to stand, and made the man meet his eyes. "What do you want?" he asked more kindly than he truly felt. The man was dirty, tousled hair and ragged clothes, rotten sandals flapping from his reddened feet. He smelt.

"Please, sir. Come to my people. We are not far......" He gestured along the river's course toward the east. "Into the next river, and then, a bit downriver, up into another. Not far."

"Why?" asked Ninian.

"The people fear so much. Distracted by fear, they are." The man was wringing his hands together. "Peace they need some peace. Not from the Romans. In here." He patted his rough hands over his chest. His eyes flooded with tears and he looked away, ashamed, ducking his head.

Ninian put his hand on the man's shoulder. "Come," he beckoned him to follow. They returned to the town. Everyone greeted Ninian when he passed, hailed him with joy. He reached his hut and signalled the man to enter. He gave him some food and, as the man ate and drank, he gathered some books and a cloak. He made a secure bundle and then left. He walked through the lanes until he found a group of men near the church. He spoke to them for a time, instructing them to lead the people in prayers that night, then morning and evening the next day, perhaps more days, until he returned. He would be back by the Sunday meeting for the sharing of the Eucharist and the preaching.

Returning with the stranger to the river, Ninian beckoned for the man to join him in the coracle. There was just room for the two of them and the bundle. They struck out into the middle of the stream and Ninian guided the vessel there until that river joined with the faster-flowing, deeper River Ituna. There again, floating in the middle of the channel, using the paddle to avoid any eddies that would draw them against rocks that rose here and there, they passed for some miles under trees, in open places, following the valley made by the river in its approach to the Solway. Another river joined the Ituna and the man directed that they should turn into its waters. The current was too strong there for them to make any progress against it, so they drew into the bank. They lifted the coracle out of the water. The stranger hoisted it over his head and led the way along the path. Ninian followed with his books. The path led to a somewhat neglected Roman road and the road led very soon to a place where the river curved its way around a great, high bluff of land. The coracle was here hidden in bracken, and the two men began to climb.

At the top, in a scooped out space large enough to hold a town, a place that had once been a Roman encampment at a lookout point over the valley road and river far below, a community of people perched in their poorly-constructed huts like birds forgotten in their nest. They seemed dull, spiritless folk, and evidenced very little interest in the return of the man or the presence of the stranger he had brought with them.

When evening came, they gathered around a common fire in the centre of their cluster of huts, these poor, lifeless souls. Ninian sat amongst them and began to talk. He wasn't sure that they were listening, for they gazed at the fire with no expressions on their faces. He spoke in their own tongue and told them of a land far away from here, of the struggles of the people against foreign invasion and occupation, of struggles against sins of their own hearts. He told them of the coming of God's son to these people, born as a baby among them, of the miracles He did, of the wonderful truths He taught, of His tragic death and of His glorious resurrection. When He described how Jesus had held the children in His arms, how He had healed the lepers whom no one would touch, how He had rebuked proud people and honoured humble ones, and how He had fed those who were hungry, something like a light began to shine in the eyes of those around the fire, and from their faces. As the fire died away, they sat on, reluctant to move, pressing him for more. There was a kind of wondering hope about them that late night.

For the next few days, Ninian remained there, among the people on the hilltop. He touched those who were sick, who were simply wasting away, praying for them. He gave some money to one of the men and sent him for some fresh grain to augment the community's dangerously dwindling supply of food. He gathered the wild little children, clothed in scraps of rags, some covered in the kind of sores that formed on the skin of people who had no proper nourishment. The children listened to his stories, answered his questions, and responded to his teasing play with laughter that rang like music in the silent place.

His own people could help these people, he knew. They could share some of their plenty. This group of Britons had been abandoned, like so many, when their soldiers had left with Macsen but here, so starved of leadership and strength, so few in number, they had never returned to anything like normality and no one seemed to know that they were there anymore. These people had lost hope when their men had not returned after a few years. The older ones had died of grief. The younger ones, with no memory of how to make a better life, had carried on the best they could, but there was so much illness, weakness; they were tired. Then one man had heard news of a holy man teaching at the place where the Roman roads crossed, and he had gone to find him.

Ninian went back to his own place, but he returned, not many days after he left, and this time he brought others to help him. One young couple from his own community made the decision, after prayerful fasting, that they should leave their home and come to live with these people. The man would instruct the men and boys in skills they had lost. The woman would work amongst the mothers and their children, helping them when they were too weary to care. Others came, from time to time, to bring gifts in love, to lend support in whatever way they could. Medana was one who gave her time to this place, and she witnessed the gradual return to normal health and strength of a village that cherished its return to dignity. Peace came to the hearts of the people, the peace the tragic man had wept for when he went to find the Bishop.

Believers were baptised in a spring at the bottom of their hill, near the river. They built for themselves a little hut at the entrance to their lofty enclosure. That place was hallowed by their prayers, their hymns of joy and thanks to God, and by the sounds of the readings from the Scriptures. Some of the children learned to read, and some of the people from Ninian's town copied portions of Scriptures so that these could be read to the congregation. When

Ninian visited he would share the Eucharist with the new church. He would teach more stories from the Bible, more of the creeds of the church, and speak of other Christians whose lives could be an example to them. These people particularly loved the stories he told about Bishop Martin, the man who had cut his cloak in two to provide warmth for a stranger who begged.

Word of the miracle of the town in the old Roman fort site spread throughout the region, and others came seeking Ninian. Even from the other side of the Hadrian's Wall they came, people from communities and tribal groups beyond the gathering stone of Mabon.

Ninian worked amongst them, wherever they asked, restoring the faith that had existed in this region long before, in the days of frequent Roman marching and ever-present traders from abroad. The faith had spread from place to place in those times by gossip, had been established fully by decree under Constantine. It had almost been extinguished in the recent years, though, when the men had disappeared from the land, riding with Macsen to an elusive glory or massacred in stormy seasons of Picto-Scotti invasions.

One by one, family by family, hamlet by hamlet, village by village, town by town, Christians found their footing again. Slowly, slowly, their faith was renewed to them. The sun of light and warmth returned to bring some strength to their hearts and purpose to their darkened existences. The sounds of preaching, of praying, of singing came again to the valleys and meadows and poured down from the heights of ancient Celtic forts. The southern side of the Solway was again a Christian place.

In some cases, the faith took deeper root than it had before when it had been confessed as a matter of form, when it was the imperial fashion or politically wise to be a Christian. Now, after all they had been through, the people found the faith again, but like a drowning man would find a rock he could cling to, a rock that would save him from being washed into a powerful sea. There was more security and everlasting promise in this Rock that was Christ than there had been in the rock that was Rome. They had found a sure place, and they would not let go again.

One community led him to another, and that one on to the

next. The work spread into the lands on the northern side of the Solway. One day Ninian and his companions in the mission venture reached the summit of a bleakly rocky, heathered hill, and looked down on a scene that caused Ninian to stand still, like a statue. Memories flooded over him. This was the place where he had ridden as a prince with the Britons into battle under Macsen. He saw again, as he had seen then, the last broad rolling sweep of grassland and moorland that reached as far to the west as the land would go. Below this hill, he knew, there was a beautiful, sheltered valley that embraced the curves of a river called the Icena. In that valley, so much blood had been spilt. So many cries had torn into his heart. Hell had been sampled by a youth who had never entirely forgotten the taste of it. That terrible turning place in his life had put his feet on the road that led him to come to this place a second time.

The valley was quiet now. Birds sang. Somewhere, there was a splashing sound. Oxen lowed. A lamb scampered away to its mother. Swallows darted past, chasing whatever they only could see. Gulls flapped their way down from the sky to settle into a rocky patch of land a man was struggling to plough. Bushes bloomed a blinding gold blossom. It was a beautiful place and, in spite of the rocky mounds that marked mass burials near the road, the nightmare here had ended.

There was a path leading upriver. The river was forked here, two streams joining, and in between them there rose a typically fortressed settlement on a high point of land. Friendly faces peered at them from above as they climbed into the place. These were hospitable people, easy with life. As long as they could have peace, they would have plenty. There were fish in the streams and in the sea; there were many berries, and vegetables grew readily in the soft climate. There was game. Life was comfortable. Rough hills rose behind them, and the sea stretched out beyond them. To the south and west was the machar land. It was a good place. As long as they did not come as soldiers or pirates, the visitors were welcome.

In contrast to the people in other places, these were not eager to hear Ninian's gospel, or to listen to his readings. They were eager for him to eat his fill, and to drink their ale. They were rather curious about him, about the fact that he wished to pray as much as he did, but they yawned when he tried to explain his mission. No need. They were fine as they were. They had enough gods and spirits already.

This was the beginning of the boundary world between the Christian island and that which was not Christian, not even in name. Ninian was aware that between this place and the Antonine Wall further north, there were others of his British race called Christian, as they were called Roman. Here, though, were some like most of those living beyond that wall, people who had never been touched by the faith. For the first time in his life, Ninian met people who had never heard of Christianity; and with a shock he realised that these lovely people didn't care whether they heard or not. They were content as they were.

EIGHTEEN: The Chosen Place

He chose a place where he might live,
close to the sea in Galloway....."
"The Life and Miracles of St. Ninian",
an anonymous Scots poem of the 15th century
(trans. by C.E. Palmer)

"....in the place which is now called Whithorn......
built a church....."
"Vita Niniani" by Ailred of Rievaulx
trans. by Winifred MacQueen

""Bishop Ninian,
a most reverend and holy man of British race,
who had been regularly instructed in the mysteries of the
Christian Faith in Rome..........
built the church of stone,
which was unusual among the Britons......
his own episcopal see named after Saint Martin....."
"A History of the English Church and People" by Bede
(trans. by Leo Sherley-Price, revised by R.E. Latham)

Novantae — (Western) Galloway

Ninian had taken time to work among his own people within the protection of the Empire's walled boundary, but the Bishop of Rome had laid hands upon him in consecration for a task that was yet unfulfilled. At this point he must truly begin his work as an Apostle for Christ, evangelising and establishing a church beyond the Roman empire of Christian consciousness, right at the edge of the inhabited world. This was to be his greater calling.

Since his return to Britain, Ninian had been an Ambrose,

working among those who owned and claimed him. Now he must be a Martin, never content to rest where he was loved by his own if there were lost people to find and bring to Christ. In this land on the northern Solway shores, there were lost souls. These were not the kind of lost souls who knew where they belonged but had temporarily strayed from their fold. These were the lost ones who did not know there was a sheepfold made for their safety, and did not realise their souls' danger while they wandered outside it..

Before he returned home to prepare for this mission, Ninian took his companions with him to explore the land on the other side of the river, a long, rolling, grassy peninsula they had seen from the hill above the bay. There was a road leading southwards, strangely straight and true in places, causeways bridging some of the dipped marshy areas they passed. It was eerie. When had Rome been here? Not ever, to his knowledge. As the peninsula broadened, the road was more inland from the shore and rose to give views over a low-lying stretch of tide-washed meadowlands that were carved by a river's snaking channel. They passed a little to the west of a high hill that was crowned by a thriving settlement overlooking the bay. They came to a river. The tide was fully into its channel, so they were forced to wait until the flood of waters returned seaward making the ford passable again. There was a cluster of huts there, by the side of the river, and while they waited for the tide to retreat they talked with the amicable local inhabitants. Ninian and his companions then forded the river and carried on southwards.

They walked on, following more straight roads, wondering where they were going. They passed hilltop forts and duns of stone, ditched enclosures with inhabited huts, and came to rocky bays at the tip of the land where fisherman and seafarers lived and worked. At the end of the land they looked across the Solway to the hills that rose south of Hadrian's wall, and out at sea they could see the hills of the island kingdom called Mona. Further around the coastline, far in the distance, they could see the faintly outlined hills of the large neighbouring island of the Scotti people. To the north of them, looking back on the direction from which they had come, the land was encircled by a range of rocky hills. They were fully enclosed into this place, by sea on three sides and by mountains on the fourth. This was, surely, one of the ends of the earth.

The largest natural harbour they discovered featured a rocky point that stretched into the sea. It was a curious place, shaped like a head, connected to the land by a doubled strand, a narrow neck.

They walked further around the coast, turning south and westwards. After passing through a landscape of scrubby growth and stony meadows, they reached a beautifully lush place sheltered by wonderful trees. There was promise of richer, deeper soil there. Nearby they discovered an abandoned rectangular fort site hacked into the northern end of a humped hill that rose from the lower land around it like a larger wave within a gently rolling sea. Protected by very deep ditching, the place was reminiscent of many old Roman-built encampments. The top was heavily grassed over, unmarked by signs of building that must have once covered the central area. A little burn ran alongside.

From the height of this artificial plateau, Ninian looked across the lovely countryside in all directions. His eyes followed the line of the little stream northward. In the distance, only about a mile away in his estimation, there was a small mound that was sheltered from view behind ground that rose on every side of it. If he had kept to the roadways, he would not have seen it at all. Though this was the tip of an almost sea-bound peninsula, people from eastern or western seas would have no view of this place in their approach. It was quite hidden away. Apart from this vantage point, the little hill would seem to be hidden from every approach but that of those who walked toward it directly from the north on a more inland route.

Ninian remembered another hill that lay protected in this way, rising behind another small stream. It, too, was sheltered by surrounding hills of a slightly greater height, guarded and protected within their encircling presence. It, too, could only be easily approached from the north. Jerusalem was just such a sheltered place.

He softly began to recite a song of ascent from the Psalms:

"Those who trust in the Lord
are like Mount Zion,
which cannot be moved
but remains forever.
Jerusalem!
Mountains all around it!
Thus, the Lord is around his people
henceforth and forever.

For the sceptre of wickedness
will not rule the inheritance of the righteous......"

God had, Himself, chosen Jerusalem, a city of milky white stone.

Far from Jerusalem, this sheltered spot that had been called Leucophibia by Greek geographers, was by name a white place. A gleaming white city. In Ninian's language, it was the name of the place of Peibio. The prince Peibio, like Ninian himself, had given up his titles, any claims on rulership within the lands of Britain in the service of Christ. Leucophibia was left to any who would claim it.

The indigenous British people still had numerous settlements in this area, but they were not alone. They had been neighboured by groups of people who had come from other lands and established a foothold where they found any emptiness. The northern Solway was a cooking pot with many ingredients. Around this coastline there were Scotti Picts from across the sea, called Creenies, and even some of the Scotti families themselves whose fortresses, though often left empty for long periods, proclaimed their foothold on the land that lay opposite their own. Each community ruled itself in practical terms, only occasionally forced to reckon with the rightful British overlords who ruled such remote places from a distance.

So mixed, and so loosely governed, this land that lay beyond the limits of other, more centralised kingdoms, and yet on the edge of all of them, drew people from all the places who looked for an area to settle away from their own kind, for whatever reason. Rebels looking for freedom, criminals escaping justice, the hunted fleeing their persecutors, the poor seeking a new beginning, and even those just curious about what lay beyond their own shore, such people, speakers of different tongues, found their way to this land that had no resident ruler. They formed little clusters of shared language, and built new lives wherever the land would supply their needs. Occasionally neighbouring groups of strangers would have spats over boundaries or intrusions, missing cattle or stolen crops, but normally they remained tolerant of each other, wishing others to remain tolerant of themselves in return. Sometimes they merged in marriage, or joined for some practical purpose, and then they became one tribe, a mixture of two, in another generation.

In this place were representatives of all the kinds of people that Ninian must reach with the gospel, all the kinds of people that occupied the lands in the extremities of the Roman world. Romans, Picts, Scotti, Mona islanders, Britons who had never been Christian, or who had been Christian and fallen away, were all living near each other in this land that was surrounded by mountains and seas. In Peibio's intended kingdom, abandoned by his abdication, there would be a new church, its diocese encompassing all those lands that lay beyond this place. As John presided in Jerusalem, Siricius in Rome, Ambrose in Milan and Martin in Turones, Ninian would preside in a newly founded city, one that would be centred on his house of God, his casa, his shining white Candida Casa.

Ninian must be known here to the people as a Roman bishop, not as a British prince. For centuries Latin privileges had been granted to colonies that acknowledged Roman overlordship. Such rights pertained to this remote peninsula that lay between the Hadrianic and Antonine walls, but the privileges of Rome's protection implied within these rights had not often been claimed by the disparate, independent-minded tribes occupying the landscape. For the security of the work of Ninian in this place, it must be established as fact: Rome ruled. Spiritual authority, too, must be seen to emanate from Rome, for its bishop had consecrated and commissioned him to carry out this work. Ninian did not come in his own name, of his own will, to establish a new work for Christ.

He had been sent by those who had authority to send him. In the name of Christ Himself who had commanded that His disciples should go to the ends of the earth, his personal calling was confirmed by laying on of the hands of others, as the Scriptures had ordained that it should be.

The vision fully formed in his imagination while he stood alone on the high empty plateau. He knew now what he must do, and how he must do it. He gathered his companions and followed the Ket stream to the place he had seen, the little hidden mound on which his church would be built. This church must be rectangular, built of stone, in the Roman style. There would be a baptistery nearby. Martin's skilled monks were waiting for his summons. He would write now to request that they come to him here.

He took note of the many kinds of people living nearby, scattered about the land, not gathered into any walled cities. Fishermen were at the natural harbours and river inlets. Clusters of huts occupied by agricultural workers were established near the tilled, richer pockets of land. Rulers of the differing groups occupied small fortresses, often perched on shoreline clifftops. The homes of those who did their bidding snuggled for safety near these strongholds. Others occupied hut dwellings in the middle of lochs, secure there in case of invasion. All these people would be his first congregation. The site Ninian had chosen would be near enough to all of them and, when God's grace reached their hearts, they would hear the sound of his bell pealing out in the stillness, calling them to come and worship.

Quickly, the sense of purpose increasing his speed, Ninian returned home. The people greeted him with delight. His return was always a day to celebrate, a festive time. They rejoiced in all the news of the triumphs of the gospel's power among the people who lived on the other side of the Solway waters. He told them, then, that he was leaving them in order to establish a new work, a church and a city for God. There was stunned silence, and then a great clamour erupted.

No! He could not leave them, not to stay. It would all be for nothing.

Ninian was shocked by their reaction, and could not speak while voices shouted out in argument against him. They had not understood, from the beginning. He hadn't made things plain. It was his fault. No, it was not his fault. They should have sensed, in recent times if not in the beginning, that his place was not really here with him. He had done for them all that he could do. Men and women he had taught were now capable of carrying on the pastoral work. They had such riches of leadership among them and rich teaching as their heritage. What were they thinking? There were others, and they had seen this, who had nothing at all! Did they want everything while others had nothing? At first he was angry, as angry as they seemed to be with him, but then he saw that the flushed faces were wet with tears. He softened. This was sadness agitating them, not selfishness.

He quietened them down and opened the Scriptures to the gospel written by Luke. He silently pleaded with God for the words, and for strength, and began to read aloud. "What man of you having a hundred sheep and losing one of them does not leave behind the ninety nine, there in the desert, and go after the one that has been lost until he finds it? And, finding it, does he not place it on his shoulders with rejoicing and carry it back to the family's home where he calls together his friends and neighbours, 'Rejoice with me because I found my sheep that has been lost!'? I tell you that there will be greater joy in heaven over one sinner repenting than over ninety nine just people who need no repenting. ' "Ninian looked up to see that the people were hanging their heads before him with shame.

They wept still, but knew themselves it was with sorrow, not in anger. He was right. Many souls were lost, more lost than they had been with their fragments of knowledge and memories of worship. If they had strayed so far, even when they had once known of Christ, if they now knew the joy of returning, how could they resent Ninian's departure to others in a worse state of darkness than their own had been? Such ones had never heard of Christ, had never known of the forgiveness and cleansing of heart and life He offered, never known the relief of the peace He brought when

He came into peoples' lives. Of course he must go to them, and with their support.

Letters were written and sent with willing messengers. They must have flown along the roads, for word came back quickly from Peibio. He was overjoyed to learn of Ninian's vision for a church in the land that bore his name. Peibio promised to come when all was ready, to share in the prayers of dedication of Ninian's church and to support his brother in his missions from that place. He sent his blessing, and noted a verse from the prophecy of Isaiah to encourage his brother in the new work beginning.

"I will bring the foreigners who obey me to my holy mountain,
and make them joyful in my house of prayer;
their burnt offerings and sacrifices will be accepted on my altar;
for my house will be called a house of prayer
for all peoples."

Ninian had once copied these very words in dictation from Jerome. He knew them well. He realised that the prophet had foreseen a day when non-Jews, gentiles, people like himself who had come to believe in the God of Israel, would make their way to Jerusalem and pray there. At the ends of the earth he believed that there were others who had and would find God's salvation, but it would be unlikely that any of these would ever have the joy of seeing Jerusalem with their own eyes as he had done. On his knees he prayed, "God, please make this simple casa of my dreams another house of prayer for all peoples."

Before the season had passed, the promised trio of mason monks from the Turones community in Gaul arrived in the north of Britain. They brought with them news that made men weep. Martin had died. Journeying, counselling, ordering the works of God in the Turonensis region right to the moment when he drew his last breath on earth, the body of the abbot had been carried at night upstream from Candes to Turones, to its last resting place. The funeral was attended by thousands who grieved and mourned aloud the loss of their spiritual father.

Ninian grieved and mourned the loss of his mentor. Yet, there was a powerful sense of light shining within his sadness. He might so easily never have met this man, and the sudden realisation of that flooded his being with gratitude to God. Martin of Turones had become to Ninian the inspiration for the work he was about to begin, the model to follow. Because of this aged man, he knew what he should be, how he could work, how deeply he must care. On his knees, alone in his cave by the river, he wept his tears, acknowledged his debt, and vowed that as wherever his own ministry might be established, the name of Martin would be remembered.

A large party set out for the locus of Peibio on the north side of the Solway's waters. With Ninian and the Gaulish masons, there were some who had consecrated their lives to God during the ministry of the man who returned from Rome, and who now walked on with him into the next stage of his life's work. They were ready to be used by God as missionaries among those who had never heard. There were also some who wanted to continue learning, for their souls were hungry. Where their teacher went, they would follow. Yet others accompanied them because they knew that Ninian would need them for practical purposes. The Gaulish masons might build a church, but Britons would be wanted to construct huts for the others who gathered. The land would need to be tilled. Food would need to be prepared, however simply monks ate. Livestock would need to be tended. Clothes would be required, however roughly the Christian monks were garbed, and there must be shoes for their feet it they were to walk through the land in the name of Christ.

It was a small invasion army, a Romano-British army, a Latin-speaking tribe, but these carried no swords. Scriptures, a hand bell, spinning and weaving devices, agricultural implements, wood-working and masons' tools were their weapons. The songs of God were their battle cries, songs that echoed back from the hills that bounded the sea as they passed.

~~~~~~~~~~~

"Medana? Did you come with them?"

She smiled, shook her head, and brushed her small hand across her face as if to clear her vision of past memory, to return to the present where I sat waiting. "My father had found another suitor for me. He had promised that he wouldn't try any more, but perhaps he was afraid that I would be going with Ninian, leaving him alone. He knew that I would want to be going with Ninian! How could I have, though? This time it was an older man whose wife had died. He was hunting for a replacement and discovered me. He developed an obsession of sorts." She chuckled, then frowned. "Oh, dear! It was terrible!"

"What happened?"

"I pled with him to understand that my heart was not his. But he would not give me peace. Eventually I ran away."

"You ran away? Where? To this place?"

"Probably in this general direction," she nodded. "He caught me. He said that he would never be able to let me go. He was very determined! My eyes, he said! ..... 'Your eyes, Medana, they haunt and draw me!'

"I scratched my eyelids with my nails until they bled, right there in front of him. I poked my fingers in my eyes, too, and pulled out some of my eyelashes." She winced and shuddered. "It was terrible, but my eyes were very red and there was blood about. I looked horrible!" She laughed again, softly, shaking her head. "It seems a foolish thing now, but I was so desperate for him to go away, to leave me alone!"

"What did he do?"

"Actually, my crazy frenzy seemed to upset him as much as my ugly eyes did. His passion cooled to nothing!" Again, she laughed. "See, some of the lashes never grew back." She showed me. I saw. I shook my head. She smiled, "It worked. When my father died, soon after that, I was free to leave. I did, then, come here. No one would have ever wanted me as a wife after that anyway, would they? A crazy woman? No. Peace."

Fourth Part: To the Ends of the Earth

NINETEEN: Shining Light
"So the light set upon a candlestick began to shine
.... to enlighten dark minds
... and to inflame minds that were ice cold."
"Vita Niniani" by Ailred of Rievaulx
trans. by Winifred MacQueen

The work began then, in this place, in a green place which had called them to come. The varied clusters of peoples who lived in the surrounding enclaves welcomed those who came to them from the Roman world. They expressed wonder at the sight of the clay-bonded stone walls that rose into the form of a rectangular church building, the first such building any of them had ever seen. The walls were high, and the corners were squared. The roof was timbered, and was covered with heather branches like their hut homes. The outside of the stone was coated by a creamy lime paste, something, again, they had never seen. When the painted surface dried, the church on the top of the little sheltered mound bounded by the Ket gleamed white.

The community of workers that had come with Ninian built homes for themselves and their families near the church, a cluster of the usual rounded huts of wattlework. The men of prayer who had come to live as monks established another place. Further east along the seaward flow of the Ket stream, they built simple shelters for themselves and the bishop out of the sight of the church and away from the noise of the growing new town.

There was another place, Ninian's own solitary refuge. Three miles in distance from both the busy church town and the monastic community, he discovered a beautiful little wooded glen that led down to a rocky shoreline. Along at the far end of the rocky beach there was a cave formed in the cliffside. Bishop Martin had urged Bishop Ninian to remember the place of private sanctuary, to seek it, to frequent it faithfully. In hours of complete solitude, God only as his companion, he would find wisdom for his work and the strength to complete it.

The cave was a cold, hard place, looking out onto a cold, grey sea. This was not a lush, soft valley in a golden southern world; there was seldom any shining bright sunlight bringing comforting warmth here. The cave looked into dark days and out over the dark waters of a northern world. In winter, the sun would barely rise from the sea before it would slip beneath it again. The wind was strong. The rocks on the shore were difficult to tread. The stone floor of the cave was an unyielding bed.

Ninian embraced it all. If God called him to a dark, cold northern world, God would Himself be the light and the warmth within it. Against a gloomy, chilly backdrop, the glorious blaze of the Gospel would be even more easily seen, more eagerly accepted.

The lands to the east of this place, those belonging largely to the Novantes tribe, lay just within the Romanised, Roman-protected world. To the north, over the mountains, lay the lands of Damnonia tribe, the most northwestern families of the British, never completely absorbed into the world of Rome, but never uninvolved in its affairs or unaffected by its workings, either.

Westwards, in an easy day's walking, lay the extremity of this part of the world, a double-headed promontory facing out toward the lands of the Scotti invaders across the turbulent Hibernian sea. Anwn, the eldest son of Macsen by Elen, had been forced to concede his lands near the wall of Hadrian to the powerful Coelings. He had retreated to his other territories near to the area where his mother lived and that to where his religious brother Peibio served God. Anwn's eldest son Tudwal, still a young man, had married the heiress who held title to more southern lands of the kingdom of Madryn, as well as this strangely shaped promontory in his distant northern kingdom. In the name of his wife the Princess Morvad, Tudwal ruled there as king. The kingdom might be small, just a foothold here with his greater lands another in the more southern kingdom, but Tudwal played at being king in both places with grimly powerful determination.

King Tudwal of the fortified place of Madryn, was always very conscious that he was the grandson of a Roman emperor, the son of a king, and bore the name of a greater king of the southern tribes, his uncle Tudwal, husband of his father's sister Gratiana. It seemed to him that royal power had not come to him as fully as it might have, quite as largely as he deserved by the strength of his bloodline. His kingdom was comprised of only narrow points of land in reality, but he ruled his narrowed points of land as if he were ruling the world. He was fierce. He was not so very rich as he would have liked to have been, for these were difficult times, but he squeezed what he could from his small lands and the impoverished people so that he could appear to be richer than he was. He did not rule over a great number of people, at least not yet, but he used what people he dominated to their maximum potential. He was a natural tyrant. He did not care about his soul. That was soft business. Women could do that. Princes might choose to become monks, but such would not command his respect. Power was all he respected. His grandfather, his father, his uncle Tudwal, all who ruled as they did, who had warred, who had ambition, these he honoured. His grandmother, other uncles, those who gave up their titles and who lived humbly to serve the cause of Christ, were openly mocked by him.

The news of the establishment of a Christian church to provide a centre for worship and learning, and to serve as the headquarters of missionary evangelism near his stronghold in the north annoyed him. He did not openly oppose the place for fear that other rulers, more powerful than he, might come to the aid of Ninian and cause him problems. He despised the work done by the holy man who had despised his birthright.

Inevitably, for the distance between the two peninsulas was not great, the effect of Ninian's work began to be felt in the kingdom of Tudwal. Souls in need of God's salvation, keen-minded youths who longed for education, the sick longing for a cure, all such people began to go to the shining white church. What they found there, and what they heard from others who lived in the vicinity, seemed to affect them deeply and they returned to spread the news at home, back among Tudwal's other subjects.

246

In no time, word of the work of the Latinus man, the Roman-educated, Latin-speaking, Roman-ordained preacher and teacher was on the lips of any whom he met. The songs beloved of new Christians were being sung out loud within his kingdom.

The king who abhorred Ninian and what he represented did not speak out against him, but set his face like flint to oppose this work. People who became more devout in their faith were punished for it. Those who did not speak of it were allowed to live in peace, but those who enthused, or who practised their devotions openly, were made to suffer. Tudwal was cruel and he showed no pity to anyone. His heart was icy cold. He did not care that he ignored natural justice. He had the power to behave how he wished, was answerable to no one for his unfair rulings, and he used his powers vigorously. However wildly he pursued his intention to stamp out the fire of living faith, though, it spread on, and the more it spread the more aggressive he became. He would not be beaten.

It was the birthright of his wife Morvad the heiress that gave Tudwal the powers he wielded so viciously in this place. When the day came that she, herself, began to speak with something that sounded like reverence about the man who had come from Rome, he exploded. He sent armed men to the place of Candida Casa with instructions that they drive the religious men from the land and destroy their settlement. The monks were banished. The people of the new town gathered near the church might remain, for they could serve the King, providing revenue and soldiers.

While the people of the town and district argued and plead with the soldiers along the route of the forced march, Ninian and his men were escorted from the district. They were warned severely that if they ever returned the population would be slaughtered, the men with their families. Their homes, too, would be destroyed, and the church would be pulled down. Nothing would remain. There was no doubt that the armed men meant what they said.

Ninian calmed those who clung to him and sent them back to their lives in the shadow of the church. God would come to their aid. "Don't be afraid," he assured them. He was so calm that he seemed almost uncaring. They were terrified that they would never see him again.

For a time, Ninian and his fellow monks visited the communities in the lands of the Novantes where they had ministered in previous years. They preached in hut gatherings. They prayed with people who had need of fresh faith, or of healing. They comforted the distressed. They taught those whose souls were hungry for truth. When his fellow workers asked him why he was so unconcerned for the work they had left behind, wondered why he could not protest or rally help from another king to enable them to return, or worried aloud about those they had left behind, he quietened them sternly. "Trust in God," he commanded them. "Wait on Him."

Tudwal was well pleased with his coup. The banishment would work to his advantage. He had increased his grip on the land. He became more proud than before, and strutted more grandly. He did not relent in his harsh policies against his people. He did not soften to the entreaties of his distressed wife. He did not flinch when one he respected warned him that he walked on thin ice. "Ha!" he roared, when full of drink and intoxicated with his power. "Let anyone dare to defy me. God is on the side of kings and emperors, not on the side of the mewling poor!"

Something cracked, loudly, inside his skull. There was no explanation. Tudwal was afraid.. The pain was terrible. It increased, becoming unbearable. He knew that he would die. He writhed and he bellowed, calling for someone to help him, quickly. No one could. No one could do anything. The pain, already greater than he thought he could bear, increased yet again.

Then, in a single instant, his world went black. He screamed in terror. He was blinded. People rushed about him. People tried to help him. His wife tried to soothe him. He could rage no longer; he merely whimpered.

Finally, in a moment when all had gone quiet, when everyone had finally left him alone, when he was swallowed up in the silence as in the darkness, he began to wonder. Was this from God? Was it because of what he had done to Ninian?

The humbled man called for his wife and meekly asked her if this might be so. He could not see the soft smile on her face, but he felt the comfort of her soft touch on his face. "Send our son to him, with an escort," she suggested. "He will not refuse the child. They say that God answers the prayers of Ninian."

Eagerly, Tudwal agreed. The young prince Tudrig was sent with an armed escort to carry a message of contrition and appeal to the holy bishop of the shining white church. The child was advised by his mother as to how he should behave on such an important mission for his father.

Even though they left early in the morning, it took the whole day until the darkness was falling, riding on horses that galloped as far and as fast as they could, before the soldier and the young prince found the banished monks. When they finally did reach Ninian, and were granted an audience with him, the child prince knelt at his feet and bowed to kiss his shoe. Ninian protested and raised him to stand facing him.

"For God's sake," the solemn-eyed child cried to him, "Please forgive my father. He is dying. Can you help him, sir?"

Ninian opened the seal of the written message he was handed and read it carefully. Tudrig watched his face intently, anxiously, for he expected some outburst of anger. In his experience, all men had tantrums of rage when they were tense or confronted with anything they disliked. It happened all the time. He steeled himself. Ninian looked up at him again, and Tudrig realised that there was no anger in this face. The frightened boy's eyes filled with tears of relief, something of a reverence filling his heart.

"Of course," Ninian assured him. "Of course I will come to your father!" He saw the welling of water in the eyes of the child, and closed him into a kindly embrace. "It will be fine. Don't be afraid, Tudrig. God is kind."

Ninian made sure that the weary travellers were fed and given a place to sleep. At first light, upon his instructions, they set off again homeward at the gallop, commissioned to bring assurance of pardon and the coming of one to pray for the suffering monarch.

When they reached the Icena River, Ninian sent the other monks on homeward. They sped southwards eagerly, leaving him to go alone to the king. The people in the church would gather, by the time Ninian reached the western fortress, to add their prayers to those of the bishop for God's mercy and help. Ninian reached the high place of the king late that night and was ushered directly into the room where the chastened Tudwal waited in helplessness and pain for him to come. Ninian reached forward and touched the head of the man, right in the place where he had heard the cracking in his skull. Immediately the pain ceased. Ninian marked the sign of the cross of Christ on his brow, and light returned to the king's eyes.

Tudwal could see the shape of the man he had hated outlined against the blazing of torches behind him. As his sight cleared further, he saw the face of one who did not hate him in return, and did not triumph over him in this moment of undoubted victory. He saw the face of a man who was worried about him, and his heart was melted.

The pain had ceased, and he could see. "I can see! I live! God is greatly to be praised!" With healing of body came healing of heart. Proud King Tudwal of the high fortress of Madryn, having bowed himself before God, having faced the reality of his sin and repented, and having begged in absolute poverty of spirit for help of a man he had deliberately and coldly wronged, was forgiven. He was at peace. He was truly a changed man.

There was a miracle. The tyrant king was a good man from that day. His wife was blessed. His son had a new kind of father. His people lived under a just and kind ruler. The tiny northern part of the kingdom of Madryn, a sweet garden place on one of the world's edges, was one of order and peace. The light that had shone new life into this place increased in fame, more and more people began to travel to the new church, the Candida Casa.

TWENTY: Sanctuaries
"........Inside that little circle under divine protection."
"Vita Niniani" by Ailred of Rievaulx
trans. by Winifred MacQueen

The Damnonii — Carrick, Ayrshire, Clyde Valley

Word began to reach across the mountains that there was a holy Christian man in Tudwal's kingdom. Pleas came, first one, then another, until there was a flood of requests into the quiet world by the Solway where Ninian was blessed in the establishing of his church. "Please, we have need of the preacher."

"Please, we want to copy the Scriptures."

"Please, we have problems in our world. We seek God's help."

"Please, my wife is sick. There is not much time......."

He went, a small company of his students with him, leaving the people of Leukophibia to the ministry of others who had learned to serve. They struck out northwards, into the wooded cleft between hills formed by the waters of the Icena. At the edge of the forested valley they emerged into the open high moorland where rugged mountains seemed to barricade their way. They were guided by a shepherd who knew the path across the mountains. This took them to the head of a long valley, wound up the shoulder of a hill and then, through a land notch passed them into the other side of the range. Descending in another river valley, and then climbing the opposite side of it, they could see, stretching away in the distance, a land that faced westwards around a great curving bay, land that was home for the many people of the most northwestern tribe of the Britons within the influence of the Roman world, the feisty, determined Damnonii. Client kings of the Empire they might be, but they held their strongholds with ferocity for their own sakes, not for the honour of Rome.

Ninian preached. The people here were already Christians, Christians because they were the subjects of kings who were Christians, kings who were Christian because they were told they were Christians as clients of the Empire that was Christian. For many years no one had bothered to tell them, either the people or their kings, what it meant to be Christian. Ninian preached to those who came to listen. He told them of the coming of God's Son to earth four hundred years before, at the time when Rome had come to Britain. They knew stories of their land before the time of Rome's coming. They knew of the world before the time of which Ninian spoke. Their ancestors, whose names and exploits they well knew from their cherished traditions, were part of this story, because they were part of the time.

The Messiah of God had come to bring all people, all tribes on earth, to God, their Creator. The wayward heart of mankind had long before lost the way of truth, had worshipped stones, springs, rivers, mountains, the wind, even the sun. These were not gods, but were what they seemed to be: stones, springs, rivers, mountains, wind and sun. They were all made by God, made for the blessing of the world and now this wondrous God sought reconciliation with them by making a further gift to the sinning world that had forgotten Him. He sent His own Son. At this great cost He had wooed the world. He had allowed His Son to be killed, as if He were a great wrongdoer. God had not, then, visited the murderous world with revenge, but raised His beloved Son to life again, after sin had done its worst work against Jesus. He now called to mankind through the proof of His resurrecting power and still-forgiving love. This was the news that Ninian brought.

When challenged by the sceptical, he assured them that he knew this story to be true. Witnesses had written it down, and it was their very words he read to them. He had seen the places where the story had taken place. He had visited the town where the godchild was born, visited the home of his childhood, and walked the path the condemned Son of God had walked as He was led to His crucifixion. Yes, the people there knew that the Son of God had died. Ninian himself had knelt within the tomb carved out of rock, the scene of the resurrection from the dead. He had climbed to the top of the mountain overlooking Jerusalem from which the risen Son of God had been caught into heaven, the place where angels had told those who had watched that He would come again, one day, to earth. Yes, there were still people living in these places who were descendants of the witnesses to all the stories. Yes, there were those who were descended from the kin of the Messiah Himself. Yes, they believed in Him. Yes, it was true.

Some were wary. "It sounds a strange story."

Some were unconcerned about the teaching. "Rome is Christian. I oblige the empire's preference. I am Christian. I don't need to understand."

Some were puzzled. "If we are already Christian, what more do you want of us?"

Others were moved. "Is this all really true? I must learn more."

Those who had sent for the bishop crowded around him, followed him from settlement to fortress to homestead, hearing him as often as he spoke. He prayed for their sick, he ensured that those who could read to others were given copies of passages of the gospels, selections of psalms, written prayers, so that others could hear what they read. He held discussions with leaders who sought him out, both about the spiritual needs of their people, and about the troubles in their land. He counselled. He set aside a place, central to all the people but apart, separated by the curve of a river's course. He marked the space with a cross carved on a stone. This was the place for preaching and hearing, the place for coming to lay sins before God and a place to receive together the eucharist. This was the place where they would learn the teachings of Scripture, and the songs of God's people. Near this place, within a separate enclosure, the dead would be laid to rest, the faithful who awaited the resurrection that was promised. He found quiet nooks, too, in each district he visited, where he could go to be alone, to lift the people before God. He asked for wisdom to know the paths he should take, and strength for the task of the declaration of the gospel to the whole of the land.

Further north of the great sweeping bay, Ninian and his companions followed a route that led between hills and moors until they reached the plained valley of the Cluith. Here, in the lush terrain that stretched along both sides of the large river, was the farthest northwestern reach of land ever claimed to have been part of the Roman world. The terminal stronghold of this northern part of the populous kingdom of the Damnoni perched on a massive rock jutting out at the northern shore of the river. Truly Roman Briton had never existed north of this point. Just to the east of the fortress was the western limit of the wall of Antonine construction, a wall that reached to the Bodotria estuary on the eastern side of the country. The wall was not powerfully built of stone, as that of Hadrian. It was not as straight, either, but meandered its way eastwards enclosing to the south of it the world Rome had claimed centuries before and secured again recently by Stilicho's legion. Beyond this wall to the north, in Rome's understanding, was the whole of what remained of the barbarian world, unconquered, uncultivated, unknown and undesirable.

Near the grass-covered barrier line, Ninian marked out another plot of green ground, setting it apart for the use of the Christian community who wished to be identified with each other in living worship and with Christ in their deaths. None would dare transgress the space for any other purpose, for it was sealed by the symbol that had empowered Constantine' and that sanctified the work of Ninian, the cross of Christ.

A young prince sought audience with Ninian. The Bishop could sense his distress before a word was spoken. "What is it?" he asked, quietly.

"I am a coward," whispered the young man, almost too quietly to be heard.

"How so?" asked Ninian, answering in almost the same whisper.

"My father wishes me to fight for my people against those who attack us from the land of the Scotti. I will not fight them." His bowed head dropped yet further, as he curled in upon himself in his admission of such shame.

"Why will you not fight them?" asked Ninian, nothing altered in the tone of his voice, no shock, no accusation, no challenge.

The young man dared to lift his head, just a little, to look at him. "Some of them are our kinfolk," he said, his voice imploringly raised. "If they attack us, it is because they don't understand that this is wrong. I would rather go to them and share what you have preached, that in Christ we are brothers even more than in the flesh, and I would ask them to make peace with us. I have faith that this is a better way!"

Ninian's heart and mind flew back to the time of his own youth, and he smiled. He knew the heart of this lad. "Come," he invited, extending his hand. "Come, and follow me. Then be prepared to honour your heart's calling. One day your father will understand, perhaps and, if he does not, your people will."

Other people, of other kinds, came in droves in some areas, and in ones or twos in others, all with problems or needs of their own. Ninian and his companions walked on, preaching, reading, praying, healing the sick, caring for the poor, negotiating with rulers, caring for the poor, dealing with injustices that were laid before them, teaching the curious and heart-hungry, comforting those who sorrowed, and rebuking those who lived far from the ways of the God they professed to serve.

The Votadini — the Lothians, Lammermuir Hills, the lower Tweed Valley

As they approached the eastern end of the wall, they crossed the beginning point of the highway that led beyond northwards into the territory of the Pictish peoples. There were clusters of Picts living in more southern territories, but they were strangers, immigrants, in the native British areas. North of the wall lay the true Pictlands. These had long ago been claimed for Rome; they had been claimed but not conquered, occupied, and possessed for Rome. They had never been claimed for Christ at all.

Facing that unknown world across the broad waters of the firth, there was a rocky, projecting knob of land behind which dipped a sheltering hollow. Here Ninian preached to the curious shore-village people that gathered around any passing stranger. Inland from their village was a hilltop. They told him that there was an important settlement there. The missionaries toiled their way to the place the next day. From the summit, where a field of great ceremonial stones had been raised by a people of as great and forgotten antiquity, just as he had seen in northern Gaul, Ninian could see miles to the east, to the west, and to the north across this great sweep of land at the boundary place of the empire. His heart went out to the people who inhabited all these mysterious northern places, a land that shone with almost unending light through its summers, but endured long darknesses during the winters, a land of mysterious shades and frosted mists that created breathtaking vistas. This was a land where cold settled into the very bones, but where there were unexpected pockets of green beauty and richness, meadows heavy with beautiful blossoms, fields producing abundant food, and deep, sheltering groves of trees.

Further east they came to a space where impressive hills drew back from the shoreline, curving into a protective backdrop for a large opening, many miles across. In the very centre of this area, tucked between several smaller hills that looked like the hills of Rome might have looked before Rome's people had covered them in buildings, the people of the tribe had established themselves on the ridge of a black outcrop of rock rising dramatically above a small loch. Just a few miles in the distance, down a long slope from there was a little port where a fresh water river met the salty waters of the firth. Fisher people were living there. Nearby these British habitations there was a large Roman encampment which connected this place to the main Roman road to the eastern end of the Antonine Wall.

The king of the whole of the firth's southern coastland, even into some of the lands beyond the eastern edge of the Roman wall, was Cunedda, born of Roman stock. His wife was an heiress, daughter of the famed Coel with his wife Ystradwal. These tribal lands had anciently belonged to Ystradwal, and had been passed to her daughter, establishing Cunedda's rule in the region with both Roman and British authority.

Ninian ministered beside the lake to the people who came

down from the town on the rock to hear him. He visited another small tribal settlement on the slopes of one of the inner hills. He spent time with the fisher people at the river's mouth. Those who heard him talked about what they heard and as the days passed, more gathered from other nearby places to hear him.

Eventually Cunedda himself, with his sons in his train, came down from his great house within the town on the rock to hear the preacher. Ninian saw in the man the signs of leadership in his manner and in his effect on those around him, the same rare natural abilities that men such as Macsen had exhibited. He was one whom men would follow.

Cunedda had many sons, and among these princes there were a number whose eyes began to shine as the one-time prince of the Britons, one who had once been so much like themselves, told them the story that had captured his own heart. This story had torn him away from his own royal pride and privileges when he had been just their age. It did not seem so long ago to him when he looked on young men so much like himself. A generation of years had passed, but he had scarcely noticed its passing.

There were princes of Cunedda's family among those who flocked around Ninian after his address, asking for more, begging humbly to be allowed to hold his precious copies of the Scriptures, reading for themselves the words that Ninian had so carefully copied when he had been in the company of Jerome, long ago, far away.

Further along to the east, the lands were very fertile, garden lands, and many people fed well off them, as well as off the richness of the nearby seas. There was a huge outcrop of rock jutting forth in the middle of the low-lying landscape. An ancient fortress of the Celts situated on top of the rock had become a Roman-British settlement serving the purpose of a trading oppidum. The people of Traprain had been told of Ninian's approach in advance. Having clambered to the top of the curious formation, he was grateful to find that the people there were friendly. Anyone standing near precarious precipices edging the fort on all sides could have been despatched to a certain death by a simple push. There were those in this eerie birds' nest of a place who were eager to hear him, but others who were relieved when the time came to escort him back in a scrambled gallop to the bottom of the cliffside. His teachings demanded lives lived in accordance with a creed of discipline not all were eager to follow.

Progress was made, but slowly, around the northern curve of land where the firth merged with the Germanic Sea with its icy bitter winds and dense sea mists obscuring the way in spite of a summer's long day. The missionaries preached and taught, prayed and discussed, here and there, in open spaces and in chieftain's huts, as they travelled southward on a major Roman route through the Votadini lands. They came eventually to the great widened-out vale formed by the Tueda and other rivers that blended into its waters. There were villages and homesteads there where the ministry of prayer, preaching, and reading of the Scriptures were welcomed. The people here, as on the other coast of the northern lands of the British, had been baptised as Christians already, and lived under the rule of nominal Christian kings. As in other comparable kingdoms, many lived in great ignorance about the truths of their faith or the practical claims it should make on their lives. Here and there Ninian and his men met people who were eager to learn more, and whose hearts were open to a belief that would engross their lives, not just label them.

Alongside the river, there were miles of impassable marshlands, so they kept to higher ground above it until they finally reached the settlements where east coast Votadini and upland Selgovae tribes abutted against each other.

There was a town on the wooded banks of the river a little distance from three dramatically conical peaks that provided a major Roman station with its name of Trimontium. Near the town and its Roman outpost, within a little sheltered loop of the river there was a green patch of meadowy land which provided Ninian with a gathering place to address those who would come to hear of God. They came, and they did hear. Some who had not been baptised asked to be baptised. There, in the river, the converts were named as Christ's. Spending some time in the area so that those newly-born into the faith could be spiritually nourished and strengthened,

Ninian found a tiny quiet glen behind the back slopes of the coned hills, and there he would seek God alone for further strength, further wisdom, in what seemed to be a never-ending journey. He wondered if there were years enough left to him to accomplish all that he felt he should do in his life. There were so many people, and every nation, every group within each nation, every individual within each group, had needs that should be addressed with care. He came to realise that his vision was too big for one man's accomplishing, no matter how many years would be given to him to work, no matter how strong he was. There was too much to do.

Already, as they moved along, he had gathered up followers, one from this place, another from that place; and he knew that there would be more. Young men, mostly, but others not so young, determined to join the company of ministering missionaries, these had begged to be allowed to travel with them on the journey, and on to the Candida Casa for further instruction. The small company had swelled into a larger company, like a snowball growing as it rolls down a slope. When they reached their destination at the new church's monastery, these would need to be settled in, observed and, if suited to the task, educated for a long period of time before the bishop would feel they were ready to be missionaries working on their own account.

Down in the grassy cleft formed by a little stream, hidden away for just a little stolen time from the demands of a hungering public, a kneeling Ninian bowed his head deeply into his chest, and there he pled with God, yet again, for wisdom, for strength, and for time.

The Selgovae — upper Tweed valley, Southern Uplands

The Selgovae lived only in upland areas. Many Roman roads from the south, leading toward the lands of the Damnoni in the west and the Votadini in the east, crossed through their territory to shorelands the Selgovae did not occupy. Many Roman forts on the many Roman roads were carved into their landscape. They were not the most entirely willing of the tribes termed as client kingdoms of the Empire, but neither did they risk mighty rebellions against a power they knew they could not defeat. They hunted their high grounds and kept to themselves as best they could.

Wherever Rome had withdrawn troops from an encampment, as in other and neighbouring tribes had done, the Selgovae occupied the spaces. Alongside rivers, in old marching camps, high above them in former lookout situations, they made use of flattened ground and ditches or embankments that made their own cuckooing settlements more secure than they might have been if they had built them from scratch. A number of settlements had formed in a ring around the Beltane mountain of Tinto. This conical hilltop could be seen for many miles in the upper reaches of the lands where the young Cluith and Tueda rivers almost kissed at the places of their springing.

Ninian preached. With all his heart he preached to these lonely-living, neither Romano nor barbarian, neither Christian nor pagan, neither eastern nor western, middle people who called themselves Christians while they watched with diligence over the pagan fires on their fearful mountain. Some heard, and changed their ways, delivered of their superstitious bondage. Others nodded, in respectful acknowledgement, but went their way to carry on as they had before.

Following the Tueda River inland, up a long valley made beautiful by the winding waters, forested banks, green meadowland, and framed by the rising hills in every direction, the travellers came to a broadened space that was the gathering land for the chieftains of further hidden glens.

Peibio was one of the faithful company travelling with Ninian, supporting his brother's message with his encouragement, and strengthening Ninian through constant prayers on his behalf. In most places, he had remained a silent co-worker. In this one place, he seemed to enter a ministry of his own among the people. Somehow, it was Peibio who spoke with the curious men who came into the valley to learn from the simply robed men of God who had come upriver to this remoter world. It was Peibio who shared with them the truths of Scripture, who read to them, who dealt with their questions. Ninian was exhausted, and his brother was the only one who had noticed the fact.

There was much work to do. These people, like those among

the other Romano-British tribal groups, were joined to Christ by tribal declaration but knew little about their faith. Some were won in reality to truths they had not really known before, and these newly genuine believers formed themselves into fellowship. They asked for one to be trained and sent to teach them in the future. This was agreed. It was good.

Further along the way, Ninian sat by the roadside with his Psalter opened, seeking to refresh his heart by reading what he felt he should be singing, the praises of his God. His eyes would not focus on the words. He thought of Cunedda, of Tudwal, men who could have been his sons. He thought of their children, who could have been his own grandchildren. He began to muse over the fact that he was older than he had realised, and that he was alone. He had no children who could stand in his place when his work was done. He had followers, willing and eager disciples, but they were strangers, not of his own blood, not his own family. He began to feel the want of family to come after him, and it was becoming a painful sense of want. His thoughts went to Medana. He could picture the sons they would have had, the grandchildren. Like himself. Like Medana. Little children who had her eyes. Little children with solemn faces, seeking God as he had done. Most of the allotted years of a lifetime had already passed for him. He stared at the pages of his Psalter, not seeing the words at all. A rain cloud had gathered over his head, and before he realised what was happening, the precious page, so perfectly copied, so carefully guarded all the years since, was splattered with drops of rain. The words began to blur. With horror he gathered his cloak over the pages, and jumped to his feet. In the dry shelter of an overhanging rock, he examined his precious damaged book.

Peibio appeared, and saw what had happened. "What were you doing there?" he asked his brother.

"I wasn't doing anything," Ninian replied, shortly. "I was just looking at my Psalter when the rain started to fall on it."

"But you usually guard that work with your life," pushed Peibio. "What were you thinking about that you didn't see the rain coming?"

Ninian looked at him, blankly. His face reddened, and he dropped his eyes. He had always been so strong, so focused. God was everything. God's work was everything. His own needs were never mentioned. Never had been. How did he admit that he was thinking of himself?

Peibio saw the blush and the expression. "Ninian, you are tired, more tired than ever I've seen you. You are human."

"Peibio, I was sitting there thinking what life could have been like. I was wondering if I have truly needed to give up everything. Do you realise? I could have been a king of sweet, rich lands, and had grandchildren by now. So could you. We could have ruled people well, for God's glory. I should have had children. And Medana. She should have had children. I abandoned her and all that could have been. I felt that I had to. She was so good about it. Now, suddenly, I find that I am wishing I could have had a normal life, at least in some measure, and that I'm sorry for her as much as for myself."

Peibio looked hard at this strange brother who had never seemed likely to have doubts about the work he did, or the need for everything else to be submerged into it. Ninian ate little, drank only water, dressed in the roughest and oldest of garments, walked where he could walk, mile after mile, slept but few hours, prayed until he was white with weariness and hunger, studied, preached, wrote, and planned. He had never seemed to have any frailties of the flesh, longings, urgings, ambitions. Never. Not even when a child. Here, now, in this wild region of the world Ninian was wanting children to dandle on his knees!

"Face it," said his usually mild brother. "Ninian, you are past the age for that kind of life. So is Medana. You gave yourselves to God. You cannot take back what you have given."

Such words from any other would have seemed cruel. Peibio was the softest of the family, the kindest, the most sparing of any feelings. Where he got the strength to speak such words, such hard but entirely true words, was a wonder. Ninian received them as from the Lord Himself and knew that they were dealt out to him, not in rebuke, but in love and assurance. He would have nothing of soft humanity in his life, not ever. But God was all, and He was enough. There would be no more rain on his Psalter.

Novantae — (Eastern) Annandale, Nithsdale

Further south, having crossed over the rugged mountains that to the Romans had first seemed to indicate a world in which no man could live, the missionaries descended into a land of two parallel valleys, each one leading to the waters of the Solway, the waters that bounded the sweet peninsula that was their destination, their home. The rich and fertile valley of the river Novius was the eastern boundary of the kingdom of their own Novantes people. They were so near now, only a few days' journey from Candida Casa. All felt the lure to reach home, and would have hurried on if the Novius people had not opened their hearts to hold them.

There was a powerful ancient fort on a hilltop overlooking the valley. Below the fortress, alongside the water, there were tribes living who had heard of Ninian and eagerly flocked to meet him. These people lived beside a main Roman road, and they had heard news coming from every direction along that road for days. He must not pass them by. There, strangely, his work struck a deeper root than in any of the other places that he had visited. He felt it immediately. It was something working within the people, something that had already prepared their hearts before he had arrived. Their hunger was not a simple curiosity, as if they would be just as curious again the next day if something very different, very new, very exciting were to pass by their doors. This was a true yearning, as one would find from time to time in the heart of a single listener among a crowd of hearers. This yearning was in them all. Men, women, children, old crones. All were desperate, deeply desperate, to hear his words. This was the work of the Spirit of God, something Ninian had heard could happen, something he knew could happen, but something he had never witnessed. It was not Ninian that drew them in this way. It was not that they were different from other people, either. It was, it had to be, of God. There was mystery in it. There was a sense of awe in the place.

In a sheltered spot down by the river, within the reach of a number of tribal encampments and agricultural homesteads, not far from the Roman highway, Ninian and his company met together with these prepared hearts. For long hours, for long days, for weeks, the work went on. These enquirers were determined to hear all there was to hear. Their eagerness meant that they barely bothered to eat, and their excitement meant that they could not sleep during the hours of the nights. They were filled to satisfaction with the words of the living God. They were transformed, and they felt it within themselves, the individuals, and families, the extended family groups of the main tribe, and beyond these into the whole of the neighbouring tribes. Beyond the quiet place that lay on the banks of the river Novius, a border valley between the Selgovae and the Novantae, the sense that something exceptional was happening was spoken of by travellers when they passed through other valleys.

Visitors began to arrive, begging that they might be allowed to come to the table of feasting. Among them were not just British peoples, but isolated groups of Picts who had come south and settled here, in hidden parts of the uplands of the Selgovae tribe. These were a different kind of people from any others in Britain. They were tall, large and loose limbed, with heavy golden red hair, pale complexions, and pale blue eyes, some of them strangely tattooed. Handsome, beautiful, and altogether daunting people, the Britons usually avoided contact with these strangers as much as they could. Picts, like the Britons, experienced the drawing power of the Holy Spirit in this place, and many became Christians, baptised publicly in front of those whose lands they had occupied. Strangers, interlopers, Picts became like brothers and sisters to their fellow Christians among the Britons. There was no difference between people in the church that the Christ called to Him out of a mixed humanity. All barriers were melted. All hearts were one within the sanctuary of fellowship formed by the sign of the cross.

Not days, but months passed as the gospel truths took hold in the lives of men, women and children and formed the people into a living congregation, a church. They built a building for their gathering. There Ninian ordained as serving priest and pastor of a flock one of the number of those who travelled in the company of his fellow evangelists. While they remained in the place, any who could write took part in the work of copying out Scriptures so that the people might hear the Word of God. A local smith lovingly forged a ringing bell so that the priest could call his people to prayer morning to evening, and to services of worship on the Lord's Day.

Finally, though there were tears at their departing, Ninian and the rest of those with him set out on the final stage of their journey. They had travelled within the tribal kingdoms of the northern Romano-Britons right to the very edge of the Christian empire. As they passed through the countryside of the western Novantes people, they were hailed along their way by those who had heard of God's work in the land, and by those who eagerly awaited their return to the gleaming white church at the tip of the land. The men were tired, and they needed to rest, but they knew that the work to which Bishop Ninian had been called had only barely begun. Beyond the Antonine wall lay other lands, with other peoples occupying them, lands and peoples where Christ had never been preached.

~~~~~~~~~~

I was afraid to say anything. Medana had revealed very personal thoughts. I was curious to understand how she had learned them. She knew this would be and told me simply, dispassionately. Peibio had sought her out on their return to Candida Casa. While others had been learning of all that God had done in the lands of the Roman-Britons, of souls won to Christ, of kings established in the faith, and of sanctuaries that now dotted the tribal lands, she was listening to the grave words of the monk about the state of mind and body of the bishop on whom this work depended.

Medana understood, she said, that her presence was more necessary than ever before to guard and care for the state of Ninian's health in his work but that, at the same time, she must be more distanced than ever so as not to provoke him, in his weariness, into any weakness of purpose.

She resolved, she said, to be everything he needed, but to be entirely invisible in her ministrations to the one she cared for with all her heart.

I commended her for her selflessness.

She responded that this was not selflessness at all. She was devoted to the man, and to no other, only more so to God Himself. If Ninian needed her serving, but needed not to know that it was she that served, that would be her joy, entirely. And it was.

Some of the women helping Medana in the work at the community formed around the new church were the wives of some of the men who had accompanied Ninian as evangelists. Others were married to men who worked in the community as smiths, as builders with wood, as growers of food. Those who had families to care for lived with their families. Medana and other women who were unmarried or widowed had formed their own household but, already, she had decided that they must move away, a little distance from the main settlement. Single women together should not be living so near those men who were determined not to marry for Christ's sake. For men were men, even those who longed to be holy.

Less than an hour's walk to the south and the west of Candida Casa, tucked into a sheltered piece of land under a rocky outcrop overlooking a small lake, there was a place where the women could live together. Further to the west of this place there was a lovely bay where they could worship together. Beneath the headland that lay between the women's house on the rock and their seaside house of worship, there were caves, beautiful caves, facing out across the water. There they could seek God in peace, alone, away from the distraction of any human voices. Only birds would sing in accompaniment to their prayers.

Medana easily gathered a group who would accompany her in this effort. Some of the husbands would build them huts, places for living and a gathering place for worship. Anything they were required to do for God and for Ninian in service of the work of the church could be communicated to them by the married women living in the town. This was how it came to pass, and this was why Medana lived a little distance from the main community that Ninian had established. I understood better how things had come to be as they were, and I thanked her for sharing this story. She dipped her head, acknowledging my thanks, and slipped away back to attend to her work.

I sat alone for a while. I thought how much we normal mortals make the mistake of assuming that because some people serve God all alone, all their lives, they must have wanted things to be like that. We, well, I suppose I should only speak for myself,... I might have envied them the freedom to accomplish important things during their lives, things that were sure to be remembered and respected after their death, even by those of the generations to come. I would think, in a sloppy sort of reasoning, "Well, I also could have done great things, but my livelihood and my family came first; my wife has held me back." I felt unaccountably saddened by Medana's story, and yet awed by it too. No touch of a hand on the skin. No physical relief or secret delight, no pride in the children who came from loving. These people had nothing but their work for their entire lifetime; after their lifetimes, those who carried on their work would not bear their names.

Then I remembered all the people that had streamed across the countryside to grieve, as if they were Ninian's own family. They were, in a sense, his children. And Medana's too. In the end of the day, they were not children with his face, or her eyes, as she had said to me. No one could point to one of them, or another and say to me, "That boy is like his grandfather Ninian; that woman is like her mother Medana." The human likenesses of Ninian, and of Medana, of all those who lived life as they had done and were doing, would never be able to be traced in the physical features of descendants. The souls of those they inspired, though, would never die.

TWENTY ONE: Beyond All Walls
"Meanwhile the blessed man,
vexed that the devil..... had found a home for himself
in a corner of this island in the hearts of the Picts,
armed himself ...to put an end to his tyrannous rule.....
He invaded the empire of his strong-armed opponent
to rescue from his dominion countless vessels of his
captivity...."
"Vita Niniani" by Ailred of Rievaulx
trans. by Winifred MacQueen

When they returned to Candida Casa, those who had been away so long on their mission to the nation learned news of what had been going on in the wider world. Gaul was in terror of the barbarians sweeping through their lands. Stilicho had withdrawn his troops from Britain to engage in more pressing business on the continent, and Britain, though her peace had been restored by his actions, was left again to face her fate without the security of Rome's protection.

Coel was pressing against the lands of Anwn in the Solway region. The king of Damnonia, so recently engrossed in spiritual matters under the influence of Ninian, was calling his men to arms in desperation. He must halt Coel in an ambitious move toward the next obvious target, his own kingdom on the Cluith. Were there not enough dangers from pagan foreigners threatening the country to engross a king of the Britons? Must he be so greedy for an increase to his power that he would risk the lives of his men, and cause others to sacrifice theirs as well, draining away their few remaining resources in a crazed ambition to steal another's lands? Ninian was bewildered by the cupidity and stupidity revealed in the behaviour of his contemporary, the so-called Christian king.

News within Tudwal's northern territory was heartening.

That formerly selfish and cruel king was transformed into a godly man, the conversion born of fright having proven to be lasting, not a temporary one. The kingdom that had cringed when he came to rule now celebrated his arrivals, and worked contentedly under his authority. A mason monk from Turones who had helped to build the church of Ninian, earlier deputed to serve the royal house of Tudwal as priest, reported that a congregation in that place was faithful and growing. The church of the kingdom of Garth Madryn rang with hymns of praise.

Peibio, once they had all settled in and rested for a while, announced that he would return to the southern lands. His own monastery required his attention. Ninian nodded, though he wished his brother could stay longer with him. It could not be. He would have felt the same.

Medana and the other single women quickly established their own new monastery, not far away, but no longer within the community beside the shining white church. When he was told of this plan, Ninian bowed his head. He was strangely silent.

The men who had followed the missionaries home added greatly to the number of those already residing at the Candida Casa. They had not come to settle forever, but to learn so that they could return to their own tribal communities. Buildings were constructed to house them, some near the bishop's monastic home, and others nearer the church. Lessons were organised for them. Those who would teach others had much to learn themselves, first. Prayers, creeds, and hymns must be learned. The Scriptures were taught fully, and more copies of them were made. Each church must have its own copies, and there were many more churches in the northern part of Romano Britain than there had been the year before.

All the while these spiritual tasks were being pursued with diligence, there was practical work to do as well. Some men were busy building new huts, while others toiled in the gardens to provide the food that would feed the growing population. Food grew easily, and grew so quickly in this blessed landscape that it seemed to be a miracled garden. A great granite millstone turned ceaselessly, always sunwise, the miller thus providing flour from grains grown by the farmer so that a gifted baker had plenty to bake into cakes of bread for the tables of the hungry members of the growing community. There were men skilled in herding the cattle that provided so much that was needed: milk for butter and cheeses, meat, and leather for the shoes and harness straps. Cattle were particularly prized for furnishing the vellum and coverings for books being created by the scribes of the monastery. Shepherds tended the sheep that would produce wool for garments and blankets, as well as meat; others were responsible for the feeding and fattening of noisy, rooting pigs. Always, it seemed, the animals thrived, just like the vegetables and fruits. Occasional rustlers found it impossible to steal the beasts that grazed under the protection of God upon the work of the Latin teacher.

The streams, the rivers, and the surrounding seas competed with each other to provide most nourishment for those who came to this place to seek God and to serve each other. There were new boats to build and old boats to mend. There were pots to make of clay, and there was wood to gather for fires to bake the clay. There was a smith, always busy clanging at his anvil, shaping blades for ploughing and cutting, nails and pins for building. Skilled metalworkers made locks for safekeeping, bells for ringing, ornaments for beauty, and even trinkets for pleasure. There were a great many employments occupying a great number of people in order that the day-to-day existence within the little part of the kingdom of God on the Solway might run smoothly.

Such was the plenty in the place, so sweet was its fame, that the enemy of souls must have seethed. Something must be done to spoil the work for good in some way, in any way. A young unmarried girl became pregnant and she whispered to her friends that a protégé of the man of God, one of the young men in study for ministry, had fathered her child. In truth, the son of one of the local chieftains had seduced her, beguiling her with promises but this crass young man had totally shunned the girl since he learned that she carried his child. He had a temper, and she was too afraid of both her lover and his powerful father to dare to name him. The young trainee priest seemed a safer, kinder option for her future. He protested his innocence when he was charged with the crime, but she insisted that she spoke the truth. The babe was born. Ninian, grieved at the accusation, and really fearful that it might be based on reality, went to see the mother and her bairn. One look assured his heart. He called a public meeting and there, in front of the packed crowd, he lifted the tiny child from the arms of the frightened girl mother into the view of all. "Whose child are you?" he asked.

The baby had a thick crop of dark hair, dipping to a v-shape over its brows, and a little cleft visible in its little chin. The crowd gasped. The accused student was very fair-haired, his brow broad and high. The son of the chieftain, on the other hand, was a youth with a thick crop of dark hair, dipping to a v-shape over his brows. He had a marked cleft in his chin. As the people looked, and gained instant understanding, the little baby let out a growling cry, and his eyes seemed to fasten on the man he so much resembled, the young man whose face was reddening as his father turned to scowl at him. Everyone began to laugh, delighted, and the crowd was filled with wonder at the wisdom of Ninian.

A visitor arrived at the tiny harbour port near the town and walked inland to the place of Ninian's church. Ninian was astounded when he recognised Brioc, the successor of Martin at Turones. They embraced, and went where they could be alone in peace to speak with each other about all that had happened in their lives since they had parted company in Turones.. That city was caught up in the wave of barbarian invasion across Gaul and Brioc had abandoned his charge, fleeing home to Britain. He knew that he could not hide in his homeland for very long. He knew that he must return even though he might lose his life at the hands of the foreign marauders. Turones was his responsibility before God. While he waited to see what news would come from his beleaguered see, he had visited fellow Christians in the more southern parts of Britain. Glowing reports of Ninian's work had drawn him north to see for himself.

Ninian described to Brioc all that had been accomplished, by the grace of God, since his return home. Brioc commended him, heartily. "You have done well, Ninian. It was as Bishop Martin would have expected from you."

"I have not fulfilled my commission," Ninian said with insistence. "This has only been the beginning work, you understand. The people within these lands I have visited already bore the name Christian. I was told that I must reach those who have never acknowledged Christ, and I haven't begun to do that yet. I built thus far on the work of others."

"Ah! We all do that, to some extent."

"No, but there are more people to reach yet."

"You have gone to the very edge of the civilised world, my brother," said Brioc, gripping Ninian's arm in encouragement, feeling bones covered by little softening flesh beneath the rough cloth of the robe. "You don't look particularly strong. You've given your all. That will suffice."

"No!" insisted Ninian. "That is not enough. I must go to the very edge of the world, not merely the edge of the comfortable world."

"God does not ask us to go to such extremes," offered Brioc.

"Oh, yes, He does," countered Ninian. "To the extremity of extremes! I must go back, and I must go on until I finish what I was sent to do."

Brioc sat in silence for a while, poking a stick in at a small warming fire in the hut, remembering a monk who had been shamed by his own master Martin for warming himself too well on a chilly day. He, himself, had been determined to pursue a softer life than Martin's and to enjoy any warmth he could while in the service of Christ. It was not proving to be as easy as he had hoped. He sighed, and then said, so quietly that Ninian was not sure that he had heard rightly, "I will go with you then."

"What did you say, Brioc?"

"I said that I will go with you," the unhappy man grumbled the words more loudly. "You are more like Martin than I ever could be. I served him. I will serve you. But only for a while! I know that I must go back. It would be good to serve God here, though, for a while, in a way that my Bishop Martin would have approved, amongst my own native people."

Brioc was as good as his word. He started immediately,

preaching to some of the neighbouring communities who responded with delight to him. They loved his gruff, straight talking. He loved them loving his gruffness. He was home amongst his own, just for a while.

Others gathered themselves into readiness too. Word had spread that the gospel was going to march the roads again, and this time it would extend beyond the wall of Antonine. Trainees joined Brioc, Ninian, and others who came from other churches to be part of the campaign. Much to Ninian's astonishment, to everyone's astonishment, word came from Medana's monastery tucked into the rocky height above its own secret shore that a group of women, too, would accompany them. Eyebrows shot up. There was silence wherever the news was received. But Medana was insistent. They would be needed. It was necessary that they go, and they would go. They would not travel with the men, but separately. They would remain close, and would be ready to help in any way that they were called upon to serve. Some of the married women with their husbands would form part of the group, so the single women would not be unnecessarily exposed to danger. Ninian finally agreed, though it was obvious that she intended to defy him even if he didn't. His monks would split into two groups, since the company of them was increasing each day. Some would go in the front. After a space, the women would come, and then there would be others monks behind them. In that way the three groups could move independently of each other, but provide protection and help if any one of the three experienced difficulties. There would be safety in such numbers.

And so the day came that the threefold group of God's servants set out from Candida Casa, provisioned with warm capes and some basic foods, with several horses to carry the bundles of necessary items, with sticks to aid in the walking, and with hearts prepared by prayer. Within each travelling company, they spoke together as they walked the roads, or sometimes they sang as they passed through the beauty of the countryside. Sometimes one group could hear another singing, and they would join the song. Sometimes each group felt entirely alone. At night they camped, near each other, but out of sight of each other. Men and women would not eat together. Ninian remembered Jerome and Paula, so close, but never familiar. He was grateful to Medana. Her presence comforted, but her distance meant that she did not distract him.

Epidii — Kintyre, Argyll, Bute

As they moved northward through now familiar countryside, the people who had been affected by the first journey of Ninian through their lands, learning of their approach, came out to meet them. Progress was slowed. Each area wanted, even begged, that Ninian would stay, that he would preach, that he would abide with them, at least for a while. He spoke kindly to all who came, never spurning them, but doggedly refused to be hindered in his forward progress. The travellers moved on, and on, through the lands framing the great wide bay on the other side of the mountains. As they approached the high moor that separated the bay from the Cluith inlet, messengers came to him from one of the small islands that dotted the estuary.

"Please, come to us. Just this one time. We have need."

Something in the appeal arrested his attention. He looked across the glowing waters toward the place they were indicating, and saw that it was a lovely green island with beautifully shaped hills not far away. This was one of the homes of the Epidii tribe whose people were Picts. Hiberni Picts were different, he knew, from those of the northern lands of Britain, but they were truly Pictish nonetheless. These people were among those who had never received the gospel. Leaving most of his own group behind, and instructing those who would remain to lead the other groups on to wait together at the fort of Dumbritton, he allowed himself to be ferried across the water. He was gone for a few days, less than a week, but he returned to the valley of the Cluith with a glowing face. The people of the lovely little island had turned to God. The first of the lands of the Picts had been claimed and won for Christ, whose cross was now firmly planted in their world.

Damnoni and Miati — Stirling, the Ochils

They left the valley of the Cluith again, three separate groups, three groups with one heart and purpose. They crossed the Antonine

Wall and headed directly north, following a road that led in a direct line to the tribal lands that lay beyond Roman Britain. Eventually they came over a rise and looked down across a huge valley that was as beautiful as any place they had ever seen, any of them. There was a river winding its way through the heart of the green space and near one of the bends in the river, right in the centre of the plain, there was a huge rock outcrop rising from the flat land, so large that it could accommodate both a great fortress and a city too. The view was magnificent. Beyond the massive fortress site and the surrounding flat greenness of the plain, wooded hills enclosed the area, behind them a framing of sharp snowy peaks in the distance. To Ninian, it was more like a miniature version of the Alpes world than he had ever seen in Britain. To the others, it was the Alpes, for they had never seen higher mountains, and could not imagine any rising higher than these.

In this land, neither fully Roman British nor fully Pictish, and yet both, Cunedda was king and Gwawl, daughter of Coel was queen. The visitors thus approached a fortress they knew would receive them, with no fear and with great expectations. They were hailed; they were welcomed; they were eagerly entertained; but there was news in the place from further abroad that unsettled them. Cunedda was being urged to withdraw his people from this place, to move to lands further south, to encourage the Britons to abandon all the lands north of the wall of Hadrian. Rome's management had deemed this world so far north no longer necessary to their purposes, no longer worthy of their efforts.

Here it was that deep discussions must be held and grave conclusions drawn. As Brioc had experienced even in distant Gaul, no northern parts of the Roman world were safe from barbarian ambitions for territory. Rome herself, right within her seemingly impregnable centre, did not always reign unchallenged; how could she hope to secure her far-flung corners against such determined aggressors? Britain must consider her future alone. British Christians must consider their responsibilities within the context of this new understanding. To survive as Christians, would it be better to retreat into an enclave where they could more successfully hold out against raiders from north and west? Or should they at all costs hold the ground that they knew to be Christ's here, where they stood, in the region near the northern wall?

Indeed, what was the point of this journey? Should they, must they, need they, expose themselves further, beyond the wall of a now threatened empire, in regions unknown. Perhaps there they would all be killed, exposing the peoples and churches they had left behind them to a future without prized and necessary leadership? "They might even eat us," offered one trembling voice from those gathered in the circle of discussion. The rolling laughter that followed a shocked-to-silence-moment was sweet relief.

Ninian, at last, spoke. "Our fear is rooted in these people. We fear that they will invade us, conquer us, occupy us, and destroy our faith by force. Rome retreats before them, and we cannot see how we could stand against them. But if they, themselves, become our brothers and sisters in this faith, then we will not fear them. Remember God's work on the banks of the Novius river? Picts there joined our Britons in one family of faith. What did you then fear from those with whom you sang praises to God?"

Those who had been there knew he spoke truth. They nodded. Those who had not been there looked at the faces of those who had, and they were convinced. Miracles were not beyond their God. They would go on.

In this place, first, as they were welded into unity of purpose for the newly-understood, very precarious work ahead of them, the local people gathered to hear what they would say. The evangelists went out into the surrounding land, visiting the homesteads and the guard forts along the roads that radiated in every direction like spokes of a wheel. There were many groups of many kinds of people here, and all were told the news. God's Son had come. God's love. God's willingness to forgive. The call to repentance and faith rang out in the broad river valley.

One by one, two by two, family by family, clan by clan, they came to signify their belief, to acknowledge their allegiance, to ask for baptism. Before the band from Candida Casa realised what had happened, the work having gone on so quietly and in such a dignified manner, there were a great number of believers gathered into the fold, meeting together for the eucharistic service, learning to sing, memorising the prayers, and learning to live their daily lives in a sincerely Christian way from those who had come to instruct them.

Medana and the women spoke with women, gathered their children, nursed those who were ill, and helped to provide food for the men who were out walking and speaking and counselling during so many hours of the days, right into the nights.

A Christian church was constructed on a graceful mound of land not far from the rock-top fortress. It was near the main highway, looking out over the glorious valley and across to hills in the distance. An area of land around the church building was marked with the cross. The bodies of those of their number who died would rest in the enclosure gathered around their beloved place of fellowship, waiting together for the promised resurrection day.

Naturally gifted leaders within the new congregation were appointed to serve the people. One of those who had come with the company from Candida Casa offered to remain in the place, to serve as priest, and his offer was readily accepted. He was capable. He was sincere. And he was the one who had feared being eaten by the Picts of the north.

Fib — The Fife Coast, south to north

The missionaries went forth from there, carefully guided in single file as they threaded their way across the river's ford and marshy plain. Reaching higher ground beyond the northern shore, they turned eastwards. Homesteads dotted the sloping fringe of land that was tucked below the knuckled fist of a mountain barrier into the northern world of the Picts. The river beside them broadened into an estuary that increasingly distanced them from the safer lands of Rome's Britain on the southern shore.

They preached and prayed their way from homestead to fort, sometimes to clusters of huts of fisher folk. Across the estuary they recognised features, the hills, the fortress-crowned rock, the strange shape of Traprain, the sharply conical hill, and the islands between the worlds.

So near to lands and people they knew, they walked here in a foreign country. They were among people of pagan ways. The speech of the district was strangely accented but understandable if they listened carefully to what the people said. A tribal family who lived around one rocky cove greeted them warmly and gave them a glad hearing. These Picts listened with obvious curiosity to the gospel message and easily, strangely easily, agreed to accept it as truth. Happily they submitted to whatever the missionaries told them to do. The leaders were baptised, in the name of the Father, the Son, and the Holy Spirit, in the waters of a nearby running stream. As the days went on, the new converts came, as they were instructed, to morning and evening prayers. They listened to readings from the Scriptures. They heard, and they obeyed. They promised to forsake their old religion, to honour God alone, to guard the sanctity of His name, to keep a special day for worship, to respect their parents, not to murder or lie or steal or be promiscuous, or even to envy. The children were instructed to obey their parents. They did. They were a very obliging people. In a cave nearby, where he found solitude to pray, as he always did, for wisdom and strength, Ninian said, "Keep them, Lord." One of the sons of the clan was sent to accompany the evangelists. He would be taught by them and, as was agreed, return to teach his own people what he had learned.

This was easy. It was nothing at all. Walking, talking, and praying. Where people accepted the truth, here and there along the way, a small church was formed, and where the truth was simply ignored, they moved on to the next place.

They worked their way around the coastline until they found themselves on the southern shore of another estuary, a narrower body of water. Moving westwards, they came to a large Pictish capital where they encountered a king who ruled over all the Picts of the north. Talorg was reaching the end of his days, an aged man. The next in line to rule, according to the opinions of the people, would be his nephew Drust, a fierce warrior. The unsettled state of the world with a declining Roman power, the occasional opportunities extended to the Picts to band together with the Scotti, and the threat of the men of the east encroaching into their territory meant that these people had cause to fear the movements of the world around them. A fighter was what they needed. Strength. Muscle. The clan family of Drust held nearby lands, with those north across the broad river, those of a rich valley further inland, and those of another great, rich valley that lay beyond the hills.

In a quiet den of a place sheltered from the view of the estuary by surrounding hills, on the borders between the two tribal entities of the quiet Fib and the powerful Fortrenn, those tribes together being the Venicones of the Pictish people, Ninian felt moved to mark out a sanctuary for any who might come to believe. The people here showed greater wariness, as if they feared to catch the notice of the young man about to become their king. This Drust had a younger brother, yet a child, who heard that strangers were gathering near the capital town and came with some of his friends and protectors out of curiosity to see what was happening.

Ninian placed markers with crosses carved on them around the edges of a mound encircled by a stream and marshy ground. This formed a sanctuary. "Let none who seek refuge within this space be harmed by those who oppose the power of Christ," he prayed. "May they, their loved ones, and all they possess be under the protection of the God and Father of our Lord Jesus."

He spoke quietly, but the young princeling Nechtan, sitting on his pony nearby, grinned. "What strange people!" He turned his pony away for home, and those who had come with him galloped off in his company.

There was a shelter made nearby, and the monks with their followers settled down to sleep, trusting in the power of God to protect them and all that pertained to them. As they slept, some young men from the prince's court crept back to the spot, looking for some sport and, perhaps, for something they could steal to enrich themselves. They had no fear of the words pronounced in the ritual they had witnessed as they entered the cross-marked space and began to look through what they could find of the baggage carried by the Christians. A staff. A horse. Some food. They would not be made wealthy by such finds, but they were prizes of a sort.

The young man who untied the horse received a blow to his

head when the animal unexpectedly bolted. He dropped unconscious to the ground and the alarmed horse trampled him as it escaped. The others shouted with alarm, gathering in sudden terror around their fallen comrade who lay lifeless on the ground. There was no breath in him.

At the sound of the commotion, Ninian rushed out of the hut where he was sleeping. The robbers fully expected an outburst of fury from the man, but Ninian spoke gently and stooped to touch the lifeless body of the boy on the ground. He turned him over, and checked to see if he was breathing. He prodded him, knelt close to him, then firmly took hold of the shoulders of the unconscious boy and prayed loudly to his God. The youth suddenly spluttered and then groaned. His hand reached up to touch his sore head.

Watching monks quickly rushed to provide the injured one with water and a covering, since he shivered in the cold. They took him inside the house that was sheltering them to care for him until he might regain his strength. There was shame, and there were apologies from the would-be robbers who had received the booty of forgiveness instead of blame and punishment for their folly, and were offered healing sanctuary in the place they had despised. They waited until the day's light reclaimed the world, and then they slowly set out for home with their injured fellow. As they did so, they passed the horse, standing calmly just outside the cross-marked place. When they moved down the road, the horse walked back into the enclosure, nickered gently, and placed its muzzle in the hand of Ninian.

The inhabitants of the Pictish capital were amused, and a bit awed, by the story that quickly spread throughout the lanes. Many came to see the place of sanctuary, and to listen to the monks as they read to them from their holy books. Among those who came was the young prince Nechtan. From that time, he was careful to defend the rights of the place of sanctuary, and to respect any who went to worship in the secluded, sheltered hollow where forgiveness was granted to trespassers.

Fortren — Forteviot, Dunning, Ardoch, Comrie, the Gask Ridge

More willing students gathered into the company of those

who travelled together. Knowing the lands they walked, these were useful as guides to the visitors who otherwise would have been travelling in ignorance on roads that no one had been sure of. Inland from the Tava's narrowing, they followed the line of a Roman road that ran south of the Eren River. This was the area boasting the tribal seat of a powerful Pictish family. There were forts and homesteads all along the sides of the rich valley. Tucked beneath a hill, there was a strangely shaped high earthen mound, long and oval, like the hull of an upturned ship. Local people claimed that the Romans had built the mound. Clambering onto the top of the height, Ninian found that it was a superb place for preaching and, as word of his coming spread throughout the region, more and more people joined him on the top. Eventually, there were too many people for the top of the mound to hold, and meetings had to be held in more open meadowlands.

There were several Roman roads in the area. Many years before, in the ages when the Romans had believed that they could hold the entire island of Britain, they had forged highways right through this countryside and built great camps for the soldiers who guarded those highways. The roads remained. The camps remained. The Romans had long since given up any pretensions of holding the area they had thus marked by their presence.

Near to a great many-ditched Roman site, Ninian had his first hostile encounter with a Pictish chieftain. As he proclaimed the truth of Christ, the man exploded with rage and attacked the preacher. Ninian took to his heels to avoid the violence that was threatening him, and leapt over a rushing stream at a narrow point. The old man gave up the chase. He was beyond leaping, though he roared on in temper from his side of the water. Further inland from this place, the Eren's valley was narrowed in by mountains. Here, Ninian made another sanctuary place, earnestly praying for protection for any who found refuge within its marked space, protection from angry old chieftains as well as all other forms of opposition that would rise against those whose hearts opened to the love of Christ.

Caledonii — Glen Lyon

A Roman road led the length of a slight ridge at the north side of that valley and at its end, where the Eren joined the Tava, other roads took them northwards into another range of hills and valleys. Past yet another Pictish capital, they wound further in along the sides of rivers where little settlements clustered in remote places far from the greater centres of tribal population. Household by household, Ninian worked his way up the length of one such beautiful secret valley. Many people came to Christ with eagerness, simply, gladly. They escorted Ninian, whose voice had become as beloved to them as the message it had brought, to the place of honour among them, a rock shaped like a throne atop a curious mound, by the side of a musical fall of water on glistening pebbles of white. Nearby, in the shadow of a dramatically conical mountain whose very shape inspired fearful superstitions, Ninian marked out another cross-bounded place of sanctuary and there commended the people of the hills and valleys, the meadows and mountains, to freedom from fears within the safe-keeping of Christ's love.

Venicones — Strathmore, Arbirlot

Retracing their steps toward the area where the Tava opened into its estuary, Ninian and his companions entered the broadest, richest, most beautifully sheltered valley they had yet seen. This was a lovely, lush world. Higher peaks to the west glistened with snow caps but there no icy chill from the mountains was felt in the broad sward. The wildness and chill of the eastern seacoast winds didn't reach it either, as softly hilled lands to the north and the south of the valley protected it completely.

The fame of Ninian had reached there before them. Their women were here already, and had already begun to minister to the needs of the mothers and children of various clusters of settlements nearby. The gathering bell was rung and a crowd began to assemble, some running at the sound of the dinging. Standing before an eager throng on a south-facing slope to the side of the great, sweet valley, Ninian felt entirely inadequate. What could people who lived here want? They had soil so rich that it grew more food than they would ever be able to eat. There were forests so deep that abundant game was there for every hunter. There were rivers teeming with fish. There were fat birds pecking at the ground, so fat and so placid that one could walk right up to them. There was beauty, peace and plenty here. The people had everything and yet, without having Christ they had not yet had anything of eternal worth. Could he help them see this? Only the work of the Spirit of God could create a soul hunger within the hearts of such people.

"You pray to springs and mountains and trees? You sacrifice to your gods on the mountains?" he asked in ringing tones.

"Yes!" they called in answer.

"The mountains cannot see what you bring them. The springs cannot answer your prayers. The trees cannot save you," he said, boldly, sadly. "These are beautiful things, but they are without knowing. They do not live. They do not breathe. They have no ears. They have no eyes. They have no thoughts. They cannot help you."

The people looked bewildered. How could this be true?

"There is a God in heaven," he cried out, "And He does live! He sees! He hears! He thinks! He loves! It is this God who made all this beautiful world. He made mankind to be part of it, to be blessed by all that He had made and also to share in His company." He told them of the first man and woman, and of the garden world given to them by their Maker. The Picts of the broad, lush valley shook their heads in disbelief when they learned that these first people had been so foolish that they would disobey the God who had given them the gift of life and placed them in a garden, like their own. This God had walked as a friend with those people in that garden, and still they had disobeyed Him!

"Did He kill them with fire from the sky?" shouted one eager listener.

"No," said Ninian. "He promised to help them find their way back into the life of walking and talking with Him and promised that the evil power that had fooled them would be destroyed."

They cheered. "Did it happen?" shouted out another.

"Yes!" answered Ninian, in a joyful shout, matching their own, his hands thrust to the sky in a gesture of triumph. "Yes! It has happened!" He went on, then, to tell them about God sending His own Son to earth, born of a human mother, to make them one with Him again as the Son of God was one with them.

"He lived in the world as a man?" a woman asked.

"Yes, He did."

"When? Where?" Cries came from all around.

"Just about the same time that Rome first came to Britain, and just before the roads were built by Rome here. And the forts. That was when He came to earth. Far away in another land ruled by Rome."

"How do you know this is true?" asked one canny soul. "Have you met anyone who saw Him? That was a long time ago."

"Yes, I have spoken with some of the people whose ancient fathers remembered seeing Him, and I have seen some people who were His kinfolk. I have visited the places of His life, and know these things to be true. The people there still remember all the stories and the places."

Again, they cheered. It was a true story. It was an amazing story!

"Was he the king of that country?"

"No, He was not their king, though some wished Him to be. They killed Him. They rejected Him, and the Romans nailed Him on a cross. Many watched Him die."

A hush fell upon the crowd. They looked afraid. Many looked at each other, horrified. A woman pulled her shawl over her head and crouched down low. Tears welled in the eyes of a child.

"Surely God sent fire from the sky to burn them up this time!" There were eager nods, shouts, fists punched into the air in agreement.

"No," said Ninian. He looked at them in silence, solemnly. They hushed again. "There is a book that tells this story to us. Some people who were there wrote some of the book. Other parts of the book were written by their friends. The book says, 'God loved the world so much that He gave His Son so that anyone who believes in Him will not perish but will have an everlasting life.

For God did not send His Son into the world to condemn the world, but to save it.'"

"He died," someone said, so forlornly.

"Yes, but He could not be contained in the lands of the dead," smiled Ninian. "He came back to life from the otherworld, and many people saw Him."

"Did He get old and then die another time?" asked a young lad.

"No, He went up into the heavens in a bright cloud and heavenly beings told the people who saw this happen that He will come back to earth again, one day."

"When?"

"We don't know. First of all, the whole world has to hear this story."

And a little girl, her skin the colour of cream, her eyes the colour of the sky, and her hair the colour of a beech tree in autumn glory, asked him, "What was His name?"

"He was named Jesus," said Ninian.

Many people who heard the story believed it, embraced it, and these new Christians soon built a church for their gatherings of worship. Their voices rang with the same melodious, rhythmical hymns that Ninian had sung as he had marched towards his homeland on the Roman road out of Mediolanum. The tunes were the same, but the words were refashioned into the tongue of the one-time enemy of his people, now his brothers in faith, the barbarian Picts.

One of the number of missionaries offered to stay here, in this broad valley, to teach the Picts. A school of learning for those who would read, learn to understand, and make copies of the Scriptures was established on a curving hillside facing out to the sea. While all this was being organised, word was spreading further into the places of the Picts, and people came along the old, infrequently trodden Roman roads of the northern country to find Ninian. "Come, sir. Tell us too."

After many months and countless miles of mission, the season changed. The world grew colder. Brioc began to speak of leaving, of returning for Gaul. It was time for him to take up the cross that had been appointed for him in the city of his spiritual father Martin. The women of the company, too, had travelled far enough. It was time for them to return to Candida Casa. Their supporting work had been of paramount importance to the establishment of Christian communities among the Pictish tribes, but the lands further north, places of greater cold and darker legend, could better be explored by the men unhampered by any concern for the needs of women travelling with them.

The whole company of Christian missionaries gathered together on the morning of their parting from each other. Scriptures were read, hymns were sung, the bread and wine that bound them to Christ and one another were shared, and fervent prayers were uttered, by each group on behalf of the other. Tearful embraces were exchanged, the kiss of peace, the sign of love.

With Brioc and other returning men to guide and guard them, the women of Medana's company set off in golden autumn towards Candida Casa, back to their own sheltering homes for the approaching winter. Ninian and the hardiest of the men with him settled into a tribal town in a river's plain to wait out the season, knowing by the reputation of the north that they would soon experience the coldest nights and shortest days they had ever known.

One young man had attached himself to the band of travellers when he had embraced the faith in one of the earliest approaches to the Pictish people. Already he had become a keen winner of souls to the faith. He had left behind a young family, left behind everything, to follow Christ in the steps of Ninian. Adopting the Christian name of Paul at his baptism, he sought to emulate the Apostle of that name who, though he had not known Christ in the flesh, but only in a vision, had served him as greatly as those who had walked with the Master. Like this Paul of the Scriptures, Paul of the Picts longed to be part of this work, the opening of the door of salvation to all who lay outside the Christian world. In the wintering place, he found a young nobleman of another tribe who eagerly heard what he said, and truly believed. Pauloc taught him everything he knew, and was given the privilege of baptising his convert. Ternan grew in faith under his guidance, a son in the Spirit given to Paul in the place of the sons he had temporarily abandoned for Christ.

The winter passed. Before the grass greened and thickened, as the gorse sprang yellow gold in the light of longer days, the travellers set out again, speeding northwards in their determination to reach the edge of the world with the gospel's claims upon all mankind. The road led them along a high edge of land facing out to a bitter sea. Even in a tiny crevice of land where they refreshed themselves with cold water from a well, the blessing of the name of Christ was faithfully proclaimed. The well would always be known, from that time, as Ninian's.

Taezali — Aberdeenshire

They reached an opening out of the land and where a city had formed near the mouth of a deep river, a docking place for ships entering the river from the sea. The people here were much the same in their habits of life as those in the tribes through which they had passed in the late autumn. They were people who greatly prized metal ornaments, especially armbands, and who made offerings of their greatest treasures to the gods of pagan understandings. Here, amongst them, as amongst their cousins to the south, the word was proclaimed. Some believed. Others turned away.

A great stretch of open land, in some places settled and in others empty of any occupation, was coursed by the faint track of a Roman marching road. At every original Roman station site along the route, some part of some tribe had settled into the encampment spaces levelled and entrenched by soldier shovels in a time before their memory. Roman troops had not set foot on this land since they had battled against the now-fabled King Galdus, centuries before. Rome had then hoped to hold and rule these people. Rome could not.

Ninian prayed that God would now hold them. His purpose was vastly different from that of Rome before him. His was a message of freedom, not of enslavement; of divine love and tenderness, not of human pride and arrogance. In a grassy meadow beside a quiet stream, he established a place for converts to this message to gather in the name of the Christ who had loved them, and given Himself for them. The descendants of the people who had never bowed their hearts to Rome, even when crushed for a time under her mighty boot, bowed themselves willingly to this Christ in this place.

Vacomagi — Fochabers, Nairn, Inverness
&Caledonii — Loch Ness

In the days of a still early springtime, the men from Candida Casa reached the shore of another estuary, broader, more open to the winds of a yet colder sea. The southern side of the water was one of fertile land where there were many communities eager to hear the news they carried. The spiritual soil was as sweet and as good and the earth was here, and the fruit that came from their work was as quick to form. Churches were built. Bells began to ring out summoning believers to worship; and they came.

The greatest stronghold of the people though, where the southern shore met a river, refused them entry. No one would hear them. They were told to leave the place. Just as they prepared to cross the river and move on, a messenger came from a settlement along the shore of a long lake entreating Ninian to come to them. There were arguments among those in the evangelist band about this request from the edges of the lands of the Caledonii, for the place was not regarded as safe. It could be a trap. Another problem was that Ninian seemed to be unwell. The long hard winter had taken a toll on the leader. Physically he seemed to be more frail than any ever thought he could be. It was Ninian himself, though, that insisted that the group travel down the length of the loch to the place where there were enquirers. "Christ's message is for all," he rasped. "Even the Caledonians!" Coracles were found that would carry them, and the entire company paddled, with their guides, to a village that clung to the edge of a body of water that seemed to go on forever into the inner heart of a wilderness landscape.

At a lakeshore settlement and in homesteads up in a tiny slit of a valley leading inland from it, the gospel was again proclaimed to those who had sent for the messengers. These people were in earnest. They grew quickly in understanding of their faith. Ninian baptised those who believed and promised to follow Christ. The brightest sons of the tribe were sent on with the missionaries, the leaders begging that these be taught and then sent home again to serve their own people as priests and teachers. During the journey back up the lake, Ninian began to lose his voice, and then his strength began to fail. The great man whose faith and sense of purpose had powered the mission into these foreign parts, the father figure for all those with him, became as weak as a child and then fainted.

There was an urgent conference, and arguments broke out. Some said that they must return Ninian to Candida Casa at once. Others said they must remain where they were until he was improved, so that they could continue the work. He had been so very determined to reach the ends of the earth and would never forgive them if he woke from his semi-conscious state to find himself back where he had started, the great journey of his career uncompleted. Still others said that they should go forward, leaving him behind with some to care for him. They could not come to any amicable agreement. Finally, when the arguments were being repeated yet again in whispered ragings in the very room where the leader lay apparently unaware of what was happening around him, Ninian was heard to call out from his pallet, "To Thule! We must go to Thule! Put me on a horse and take me with you." Then he was asleep again, and they wondered if they had imagined his words.

Decantae - Fearn, Portmahomack

It was a decidedly subdued group of men that set out again, their beloved Ninian propped by cushioning blankets and tied into security on a horse's back between them as they walked. The first promontory of land they encountered beyond the great estuary was one where the people were fearfully superstitious and decidedly antagonistic to them and their message. Pagans they were, and pagans they would stay. It was a bonny place, but there was a blackness about it. Christ's light, they believed, they prayed, would one day shine here. Perhaps, if Ninian had been able to speak to them, the people would have listened.

As they walked on, ashamed of their failure and of Ninian's

inevitable discovery of it, they prayed. Sometimes some of them wept. They were a sorrowful train, and deeply fearful. They came to another promontory and stopped. To enter this land, another chief's domain, to try to speak, to be rejected again, were the miserable prospects that faced them. They were on God's business, but seemed ineffectual in carrying it out. This, to them, was a horror, and their shame. Without the courage of Ninian, the power of the Spirit of God that was so apparent upon his ministry, it seemed that their work was useless. They gathered around the groggy man on horseback, looked at each other, and shook their heads. Should they go back?

Ninian had no guidance to offer them. He was too ill. They knelt together, and they pleaded with Ninian's God to help them. They truly prayed. They prayed until they had no more words. They prayed until they could not kneel any longer and then they prayed on, finding themselves stretched out, on their faces, lying on the sandy shore near the place where they had crossed a river. Something, then, happened. A stillness. Sunlight broke through a cloudy sky. Birds began to sing. The men looked up and saw a group of women and children, small clusters of them, approaching. There was a strange sense of peace, and a deep well of joy, not in one or two, but in them all, and they did not need words to exchange this knowledge with each other. Ninian slept on, still propped on his horse, while his men began to speak with the people who gathered. Ninian still slept while the women went to gather the men, while the communities settled into crowds to listen to the readings from the holy books brought to them by the strangers, while wonder-filled souls recognised truths their hearts told them that they must acknowledge, while Christ was confessed, sweetly, truly, and with great joy, and while the sons of Ninian the Baptiser baptised family after family who professed their new faith and began to walk new lives in the steps of Christ's teachings.

Lugi — Clinging along the coast, Navidale

The monks had moved further north, surging along with songs of the purest happiness accompanying their every step. There was a sense of glory in them. The Spirit of Christ had flooded them, had proved the validity of their ministry, too, theirs as well as Ninian's. They began to understood what Ninian had always known, that any spiritual work being done was not accomplished because of his personality or his own charisma. It was a work of God, or it was nothing at all. This was what Ninian had known in practice and had always told them. He had realised it fully, but they had only accepted it as part of his teaching, a theory. Now they, too, knew that any work that was truly done was done by God alone. Even the greatest of men were only God's channel into the hearts and lives of others. Only channels, nothing more, and God could use all kinds of men, and women, even children, as His channels.

It was an awakening to increased joy, when he came back to them. He would have offered his apologies for having forsaken them for a time in his weakness, but he realised, and he laughed aloud when he realised it, that he had slept so that God could reveal Himself so newly, so fully, to the disciples of the Bishop for the good of them all. In a tiny foothold of a place along a dramatically high sweep of coastline, thanksgivings were made to God by a group of men who had proved His power and love afresh as they moved toward the place marked on the maps of the world as the very ends of the earth.

Cornavii — Wick, Thurso

The band of evangelists reached, at last, the furthest point of the island of Britain. The days were stretching out, so that there was very little night-time darkness for sleeping. There were people here too, the Cornavii who lived near the edge of the world. Many were seafarers, fisherfolk, adventurers. There was some agricultural work and produce, but this northern world was more sky and sea than it was land. For a little time, as Ninian's strength flowed back, they sat with the Cornavi in their main town, spoke with them, read to them, and prayed for them. Some believed.

Ninian found an inlet nearby, a little hidden finger of beach somewhat sheltered from the fierce coastal winds by cliffs that reminded him of those into which he crept near Candida Casa when he would be alone with his God. Here, like there, he prayed, and he asked God to take him to the very ends of the earth with the

Gospel which had proved to be the light that could illuminate the deepest kinds of darkness in the world. Christ had commanded that this be done. Ninian was willing to obey. He knew that the ultimate point of Thule lay yet further beyond these headlands, and that the midsummer's light in this far northern world would be the best time to attempt such a journey. This was the moment when, if Christ's command were finally to be accomplished, it could be. Ninian was so near that place. Now, surely, was the time. But he was so weak that he had to ride on a horse while his fellows walked. Was this a sign that he had gone as far as he should?

A British prince who had given up all to follow Christ, had given up everything and everyone, found for the first time in his life that he was struggling against the Accuser of souls. The thought came into his mind that in the inner core of his being he harboured ambition for himself. He could abandon a throne, all earthly power. He could spurn riches. He could harden his heart to the love of Medana. He could accept a life of hardship. So much he had given for Christ, and that had seemed very noble. But now, near the edge of the world, he had to face the possibility that he was, indeed, seeking something for himself, and really for himself alone. This would be a crown like none other, a greater prize than all those he had abandoned. Was he, after all, seeking the ability to claim that he, Ninian of the Britons, he and none other, had taken the gospel to the ends of the earth? There was such wonder in it all, the pride in being the one man on earth to fulfil the very command of Christ, the command that had driven men on in obedience through all the years since the resurrection of the Lord. This would be an assurance of fame through all the ages to come. No one would ever forget Ninian, not ever, if he reached Ultima Thule for Christ.

On his face, in the cold sand of the far north of Britain, Ninian wept bitterly. He knew that his strength was failing. He knew that his pride was growing. He knew that he was unworthy. He heard the words of the Lord to Jeremiah, "Seekest thou great things for thyself? Seek them not!" He fell asleep.

That night, when he had crept back to the house that sheltered him and his men, Ninian waited for the moment when he could tell

292

them that they must return, the task unfinished. He had no idea how he could explain to them that it had been his pride driving them on, not the purest love of the Lord. The task must be finished by someone who would not taint it by his sinful human touch.

There was a rap at the door of the hut, and a couple entered into the circle of the fire. They wore rough clothing. Their faces were sweet, round, expressive ones. Their eyes were huge with fright. In strange accents, their words interpreted by a friendly local man, they explained their presence.

"Come, for God," the man implored.

Ninian looked at them quizzically. He asked the interpreter to ask what they meant.

"Come, for God," was repeated. Then the timid man looked fully into the face of Ninian, a haggard, tired, defeated face. "Dream. God come to us in book. Say you come to us."

Gradually the story became clear. There had been a dream, a shared dream, and the people of the islands beyond this point of land had known from this strange dream that God would come to them. Travellers from over the water would bring the words of God in a book, and when they heard the words, God Himself would be known to them. In their dreaming, the men who carried God's book wore hooded robes and walked, but one of them would ride on a horse. Word had just reached the islands that such men were here, with their books, one riding on a horse. Enough boats had crossed from the island to carry them all, including the horse, to the islands where the people waited for their coming.

TWENTY TWO: The Orcades
"Off the Orcadian Cape......are the Orcades,
about thirty in number..."
Ptolemy (circa A.D. 150)
quoted by W. J. Watson in "The Celtic Placenames of
Scotland"

"They gave thanks to merciful God
who had revealed his name in these remote islands,
sending to them a preacher of the truth,
a light for their salvation,
and calling those, who were not his people, his people,
those, who were not beloved, beloved,
and those, who had not found mercy, as having found mercy."
"Vita Niniani" by Ailred of Rievaulx
trans. by Winifred MacQueen

The sea crossing was a terrible one. A group of coracles and curraghs, bearing between them island dreamers, frightened monks, and an almost crazed horse, plunged time after time downhill into troughs that seemed to be aiming them for the floor of the ocean. In the bottoms of the troughs, they cried out to their God as loudly as any Jonah from the belly of a whale. Even more terrifying were the moments that followed when the same waters rolled upwards until they were perched on frothy peaks, balanced precariously somewhere between earth and the heavens. Then, again, they would roar downwards towards the threatening underworld spaces.

Eventually, exhausted by their fear, numbed by it, they crouched in misery, huddled against drenched, salty skins stretched over bowed frames of wooden branches, all that lay between them and a drowning. Even the horse ceased its struggling. The Orcadians who piloted the flimsy vessels with astonishing skill and absolute composure ignored the exhibitions of panic by their passengers. Every visitor to the islands was the same, they reflected. Even holy men.

Finally there was firm ground, and they piled out onto the sandy shore of a wonderfully peaceful island. Calm. Just a gentle breeze. Even the sea looked calm from this place. Had it been only a nightmare?

These islands were mapped and claimed by Rome long before their fathers had been born, but it was unlikely that any representative of the Empire had ever bothered to set foot on its pathways. Ninian and his fellow travellers began to wobble along, following their guides. The islands lay low in this northern sea like a giant's version of stepping stones across a river, just high enough to be out of the water, just flat enough to give a secure foothold, near enough to each other for easy strides from one to the next. These were mostly beautiful, flower-bedecked grassy pads of land surrounded by the vast blue oceans. One island to the west rose mountainous, all stony and forbidding-faced, but the others were gentler, richer in their terrain. They were peopled by gentle, round-faced, soft-eyed folk who were obviously kin of the dreamers. Their homes were snuggled curves of stone-formed walling, topped by very curious large, thin slabs of stone that seemed to lie loosely everywhere on the shores and under headlands, as if ready cut for their roofing use by the hand of a stepping stone giant. Two stone slabs of such a size would amply cover the roof of a dwelling. It must be God's provision for a place where trees were nowhere to be seen. Since there was no wood for framing habitations, and little material to roof any shelters, the Creator had thoughtfully provided ready-made stones for those who would make their lives in such a place.

Curious people gathered when the men from the Solway appeared. The bell was rung, the book was read, and a declaration was made about the coming of God's Son to earth, all the words of the visitors interpreted into the local dialect by one of the guides. The Ordadians courteously accepted the words as true, for within their hearts was the sense that they were, and truth must be honoured. In token of their agreement with the announcement of the claims of the Christ upon them, pebble stones were gathered from a nearby shore and placed solemnly on the ground of the meadowy summit where Ninian had stood when he explained the message of the faith. A cross of Christ now marked the southernmost island of the Orcades.

From island to island they passed, sometimes wading the short distance between at the lowest tides, sometimes ferried in a local coracle, sometimes swimming, the horse swimming with them. Ninian still rode the horse. He was not yet strong enough to walk a day's journey, and he felt foolish riding along while his fellows walked, sometimes beside him, some times in front, sometimes behind. The monks pulled the hoods of their robes far over their faces when the Orcadian winds blew fiercely on their skin. The strange procession drew curious folks along with it like a gathering wave, and crowds of listeners quickly formed at each settlement they visited.

In the centre of the largest island there was a soft, grassy waist of land between two stretches of the sea. Here they paused, and here they preached. The place was empty of all but a few fisher folk who lived beside a natural harbour. Yet, with so many who had followed them joining those who rushed from around the island at the news the wind gossiped to them, the largest crowd yet seen gathered in the central place. Ninian preached to them. His earnestness reached through their first mild sense of curiosity, probing their hearts, eventually provoking deep thought and visible emotion. Those who had dreamed of the men of God, hooded, one on a horse, bearing words in a book, knew that they were understanding God's voice, just as the dream had promised they would. Many believed.

Always, wherever the Gospel claimed followers for Christ at the preaching of the Word, Ninian left a marker in the place as in the first cross-pebbled meadow. Sometimes on a pencil slim pillar of stone, other times on a precious wooden post he left a sign, always the shape of a cross. Here, though, there were no suitable pebbles, no trees, and no slender stones. Ninian took his own staff, a rounded, well-worn slightly crooked one-time tree branch. He asked for another, from among the monks who travelled with him. He had seen the ropes that the people cleverly wove of flexible straw in this island, and he sought a piece of one of these from among the onlookers. He fashioned together, with their twine and the two staffs of the evangelists, a simple wooden cross. With great reverence he dug it in until it stood upright on the grassy bank. There it would remain, for no one would touch it.

As Christ had once taught His ways to people gathered in a green place above a lake, Ninian of the Britons taught the same ways of the same Christ to people who hungered to learn, on this so far distant green place overlooking the sheltering harbour of a wild northern sea. Many were baptised. Among them were the man and woman who had sought him out because they had dreamed a dream. A congregation of Christians was being formed in the Orcades.

This was a mysterious place. The soil was rich for agricultural purposes, and the surrounding seas plentiful providers of food. The islands were populated by settlements of contented people; it seemed a safe place and as if it had been so forever; but, still, the islands had an air of lostness, a haunting emptiness, as if something from a long-forgotten past still stirred among the breezes. There were enormous stone circles, and also great conical mounds reminiscent of pyramids in the deserts of Egypt. The Orcadians themselves did not understand the significance of the memorials. It was as if these ancient symbols and sites belonged to another, more exotic world, not this plain, still, soft green island; it was as if they had been designed by another, more powerful people, a kind of people who would not claim to be ancestors of such quiet, soft-mannered folk as those who now occupied the lands.

Winds had gathered loose shore sand into heaps, heaps grassing over time into dunes that now lay behind the sandy shores. Sometimes storms blasted at these dunes, ripping away their grassed tops. People would then discover that beneath the dunes had lain hidden the remains of curved stone houses, whole communities of them, still filled with the personal belongings of people who had lived here, beside the shore, long ago. The present islanders had no stories among the traditions of their fathers to explain these abandoned homes. There was nothing in their legends about who these people had been, where they had gone, or why they had left their houses and all their possessions behind them.

The visitors from Britain walked onwards through this landscape of beauty and mystery, of forgotten past and living present, guided by Orcadians who led them safely to the last islands of the group. They could not ford this water channel, nor swim it. Boats like those that had carried them to the first of the islands were gathered again so that they might cross this wider stretch of sea. There, the messengers of the gospel of Christ stood on tiny islets where only seals sang mournfully to them. Always, even in these places, they prayed to God for His blessing on the land itself and on any who would come to live there in the future.

Younger disciples grew restive. Surely they had gone far enough, and it was time to turn back. Preaching to people, wherever they might be found, was worthy of their efforts. It was worth even the unpleasantness of having suffered seasickness to get to the people. Crossing seas to spend time singing with seals and praying over empty ground was another matter. Even if there were some remote scraps of humanity not yet encountered in these incredibly far-flung places, surely those who had recently become Christians could carry on the work to reach them!

Ninian would not turn back. He grew even more urgent in his purpose as he approached the last of these islands. His joy in this task was increasing, for he knew now that the Lord had, indeed, entrusted a precious commission into his keeping. He would not fail, as long as his horse could walk or a coracle could stay afloat. "The farthest point," he insisted, "must hear the news of the Lord's coming. I care not if only gulls hear me, or seals are our only congregation. 'The ends of the earth shall rejoice........' They shall!"

There was a stone fortress on the furthest island. Only one family lived in a bare shelter it provided, on an island they occupied with only a community of seals for company. There was no softness, no comfort, no civilisation in this place. Stone, wind, sky and sea. And fish. The seals lived on the same fish as they did. There was nothing else. Without fish they would die.

Ninian patiently sat with them, his interpreter alongside repeating his words to them, their words to him. News was imparted, line by line, sometimes slowing to phrase by phrase, that the world had been graced with a Saviour. They were joyful. They were thankful. They could love and would obey the God who sent His Son. They were baptised.

Ninian told them of the first believers, almost 400 years ago, who had been persecuted for their faith. They had adopted a secret sign between them, the sign of a fish. The letters of the Greek word for fish, icthus, reminded the believers of Jesus the Christ, Son of God, Saviour. Ninian showed them the word, and explained the letter symbols. Latin Scriptures were no use to these new believers. They could not read, nor write, in any language. Even so, in their eagerness, they quickly learned the strange word icthus, tracing out its letters in the sand, with the stem of a grass. They drew the sign, the fish. Then they found one small slice of stone that had parted itself from a rocky slab and they carefully traced on it the cross, and the fish. They began to groove the design into the rock. This was their symbol, the mark of their new faith. They would remember.

Here, at the furthest point of the Orcades, the islands mapped by a Greek cartographer for Rome's notice, the gospel was marked with Greek symbolism. Christ had claimed hearts where Romans had only claimed land.

Ninian sat again in council with his followers and helpers. They had accomplished a great work, but another, longer sea journey lay before them and the very thought made them all feel ill. They could see a pinpoint island in the distance and knew, for they had been told, that it was only halfway to Thule, the place regarded as the very ends of the earth, their ultimate destination. Thule lay beyond the sight of their eyes, but they knew that it was there. They had seen the map. Men around them spoke confidently of journeys to the place. Whatever their fear, however pale their faces turned or how much their stomachs heaved at the thought of such a long journey in such a northerly sea, they could not turn back now. They must go on, to the very end. So must the horse.

"....and still further above these, the island of Thule."
Ptolemy (circa A.D. 150)
quoted by W. J. Watson in "The Celtic Placenames of
Scotland"

"So he instructed the kingdoms at the end of the earth with his
teaching....."
"The Miracles of Bishop Nynia"trans. by Winifred MacQueen

There was no real darkness during a midsummer night. To the praying men crouched within currachs bearing them toward the farthest island on earth, this was a mercy. Whenever the boats rose from the dark troughs of the sea to its foaming peaks, they could still catch sight of a tiny islet on the water's horizon, just a drop of land, but land nonetheless. From the Orcades they had not been able to see the great island of Thule, but they had seen this little mound, and they had kept their eager gaze glued to it as they sailed. When they finally came alongside that single bit of solid ground in the ocean that rolled and roared between the Orcades and Thule, they could just begin to see the greater island itself appearing, finally, the land of Thule just barely rising in the north.

It would be good to rest here, halfway. They drew into the embrace of a peaceful cove, and were directed by people gathered on the shore to pull their currachs into secluded nestling shapes in the grass. These seemed to be little safe shelters hollowed into the landscape for the boats of the islanders themselves, boats presumably away on fishing expeditions during the summer's constant daylight hours.

This was an amazing little dot in the world, so tiny, but so fair an island, so full of life. Small oval stone houses, ditched and walled portions of land, even some sturdy protective brochs, marked the presence of a settled population. The landscape was rainbowed in pinks, purples, blues and yellows of God-designed lilies growing within the rich grasses of the fields. The cliff boundings of the island where strange and beautiful seabirds nested were cacophanous as millions of winged creatures sang and shouted to each other about the glory of their life while they soared, wheeled, dived, danced in the air.

The horse clambered out, searching for sweet summer grass. The men stretched their cramped limbs, and rested near the boats. People from the island came forward, shyly, and offered them food and water. They must not be lured to stay long here, for the pull towards Thule was a powerful one, now that it was within their sight. There was also the worry, at the back of their minds, that the lovely day could unexpectedly turn into a stormy one and their further, final, long-awaited passage be made impossible. They only took time to explain their message simply, to lay out the shape of a cross in stones gathered from the beach, and to pray that salvation would come to the kindly souls on this tiny, beautiful resting place in the middle of the sea, a place lying in isolation between the edge of the known world and edge of that which was unknown.

The wind was in their favour, and they made good time as they flew toward Thule. It was night when they landed, but it was a night which still glowed with light at midsummer's point. The earth was solid and comforting under their feet, the sand on the shoreline warmed by the light of long day's sunshine. Everything seemed quiet in the curve of a dune that blocked the sound of the sea's crashing, and the winds that whipped the sea. An obliging little spring seeped sweet, fresh water into their cupped hands. It washed salt from their lips, their eyes, refreshing them. They were exhausted and snuggled into dips in the grassy dunes, wrapped in their cloaks, in their dreams still feeling the movement of the rocking motion of the sea.

The sun was high when the travellers began to awaken. Some fish had been caught by the curragh men, and were roasting on a blaze that crackled heathery stems. The hot fish, crumbles of oaty cakes that had been sent with them, with gulps of the spring water restored them to strength, and they began to look around them. There was a sense of awe in them all for, although the name of the island was universally known, few people on earth had actually ever seen this place. Thule was a word whispered in the darkest of legends, a sound that teased children into fright.   Each man crept off to some quiet spot nearby for the soul's morning communion with God. Then they gathered to pray together, and to speak of this mission. Ninian longed to walk, to feel the earth of Thule, especially, under his feet. They protested, and he knew that they were right. He was not yet restored to his usual strength, and he must protect what energy he possessed for the preaching he would do in this place. The grazing horse was bridled, a saddling blanket pad girdled into position, and Ninian was again hoisted aloft to be led along whatever paths might have been grooved across the island's terrain.

Unlike the clustered, separate islands that comprised the Orcades, Thule seemed to be mainly formed of one lean piece of land gathered up from the surrounding seabed into an earthen spine stretching northwards from this point. Along its length there were many settlements of people, obviously gleaning a harvest from the sea, both from its fish and its fowl, but also tending flocks of sheep for their wool and mutton, herding cattle that provided milk and leather as well as beef, and even producing some vegetables from little patches of fertile ground that were carefully sheltered away from the fiercest blasts of the winds. During the almost endless days of the short summertime, the people of Thule took time to hack fuel from the peated earth, drying chunks of it in the sun and wind. The dried sod would burn, to cook their food and warm their bodies during the almost endless nights of the long winter months.

This was a rocky, windy, somewhat eerie world, but in it lived men, women and children with the same lives of love and delight, of fears and tragedies, as those men, women and children who occupied the more lush, sun-warmed, and reputedly civilised parts of the earth. Mankind at the edge of the world was the same as mankind at the centre of the world. He had just as much inclination to do wrong, and just as much potential for good. What the Messiah had offered in the Holy Land, what He proved in the heart of Rome,

302

He could bring to the people of Thule, God's message of love and salvation, peace of heart, a promise of eternity.

Not far from the southern point of the land, on the western side of the island, there was a place of singular beauty. A small, almost circular green peninsula lay just off the shore, connected to the rest of the island by nothing but a thin strand of shell-formed beach the pale creamy colour of the stones of Jerusalem. Looking down onto this scene from higher ground, the almost-island looked like an emerald hanging from a band of gold, glowing as it lay nestled within the blueness of the sea. Ninian stared. He had never seen such a sight. The monks decided to investigate this wonder. They tethered the horse on the side of the mainland, and started to walk in the soft pale sand toward the islet. They took off their sandals, and their toes were tickled. The sun burst out from behind a cloud, and the world was flooded with light. They couldn't help themselves. They skipped. They laughed. They dashed about like puppies at play, digging their feet into the softness. Even Ninian. He held his arms straight out, shut his eyes, lifted his face to the warmth of the sun, and twirled. He was dizzy. He staggered. He uttered a shout of delight, and fell.

At the end of the beach, they clambered up onto the green shoulder of the island, and there they found a little welling spring with sweet, cold waters. They drank. They lay on the grass, soaking up the warmth. They dozed. Some walked away to explore around the edges of the place. Such incredible beauty, in such a place. They couldn't believe their eyes. Finally, they gathered and knelt to pray together. "Oh, Lord, bless this place with salvation, for you have obviously already shown that you love it, and own it, by blessing it with such beauty." The joined "Amen!" rang out like a bell.

Strangers were rare sights in Thule, so the people who lived there flocked to see the hooded men who processed through their land, one on a horse, each carrying a staff, one carrying a bell, one carrying a book carefully wrapped in waterproof hides. These men had crossed a sea, even bringing their horse with them, to visit them. Such a thing might never again happen in their lifetime.

The story of Christ was shared at brochs, in humble farmed settlements, at towns that clustered beside harbours, and even in the roughest of isolated dwellings, those belonging to isolated shepherding families who guarded their grazing animals in the harsh moorland wilderness. Men who knew the dialect of the islanders of Thule and also understood the language of the Britons served as channels for the words of each to the other.

The planting of the crosses on the furthest south, east, west and north points of islands had never been more significant than here. Among the people of Thule were those who gained the very wonderful understanding that the book the visiting men read from seemed to speak of them, themselves, and this very group of islands. They were in awe when Ninian read to them the words written many ages ago by prophets and sages from far distant lands. From the Psalter, Ninian sang,

"I shall give you the heathen for your inheritance,
And the uttermost parts of the earth for thy possession."

And the monks sang, "Hallelujah!"

Again, Ninian intoned,

"The Lord reigns;
Let the earth rejoice;
Let the many isles be glad thereof!"

And the monks shouted, "Amen!"

Full of joy, the monks moved from place to place as the weeks of the summer passed. It could be seen by all the people of Thule, even those who did not care to listen to the words that seemed so important to them, that these were good men. They had come in peace. They laid hands on any who were sick and prayed for them. They counselled those who were troubled or grief-stricken, and seemed to bring them comfort. They carried water, gathered heather branches, cut and stacked the peats, mended broken stone walls or damaged stone houses, tended the sheep, and milked the cows. Sometimes they even joined in the carding and spinning of wool while they spoke with the people at their firesides during the chill of evening hours.

Thule became Christian. It was a matter of hospitality to do so. It was politeness to agree with visitors and concede to their requests. So they agreed to baptism, all of them, one community after another, as the evangelists made their way towards the northern edge of the islands. In some hearts, but only some, the truth had dawned in reality, and would be honoured forever, never relinquished, regardless of what the next visitors to Thule requested of them.

Beyond the northern tip of the main island of Thule lay a further island. The channel between them was narrow enough to make an easy crossing. In the north part of that further island, the men from Candida Casa were welcomed by a colony of people who were, perhaps, more eager than others had been to understand the faith that was preached to them. Willing souls were instructed fully and entered diligently into the practice of the new faith as quickly as they learned it. They faithfully answered the summons of the bell to prayers every morning and evening. Even after the formality of their baptism had sealed them into God's kingdom, their enthusiasm did not abate. They continued to come, spiritual hunger causing them to clamour as one for more and more teaching. A circled space for communal public worship was marked out, a land area that would come to be, as in Roman Britain to the south, a gathering place for living worship and a sanctified resting place for those who died as Christians, awaiting together the promised resurrection.

There was yet another island lying in sight of this new church's land, just across yet another narrow channel of water. According to the congregation of Thule believers, this was the last of their islands, the terminus point of terra firma. They insisted that beyond this point lay only sea, endless sea. They pointed to a rock on that farther, final island, a rock of headland that could be seen from their place of worship. " That is edge of the world," they would say. Then the mists would descend, or storms would cloud the world, and that point would be hidden from view until the next time when the sun would shine through.

One fine, still day Ninian reached his goal, that point. There was no one living there, near the rock outcrop at the end of the known world. The ones who had the clearest vision scanned the horizon until their eyes hurt. They shook their heads. No one could see anything. It must be, as the people had said, the last of the land. They knelt together there, and they solemnly placed an inscribed cross in a cleft of the rock. His voice straining to rise above the constant booming of waves, the moan of the wind, and the cries of the birds that colonised the cliff faces, Ninian read the words of Christ to those assembled.

"You will be witnesses unto me both in Jerusalem, and in all Judea, and in Samaria,
and unto the uttermost part of the earth."

And, again,

"All authority is given unto me in heaven and on the earth.
Going out, therefore, disciple all the nations,
baptising them in the name of the Father and of the Son
and of the Holy Spirit,
teaching them to observe all things that I have taught you;
and see that it is true that I am with you all the days
until the end of the age."

"Lord God, we give you thanks. We give you praise. You have enabled us, this day, to plant the symbol of the cross of your Son on this place, at the end of the world. You have allowed us to hear the voices of the people who live nearest this place confess your name. Your kingdom has come. May your will be done, now, on earth as it is done in heaven. Yours is the glory and power forever. Amen."

The purpose of Ninian's life seemed to be complete, and he should have known great, deep peace in his heart. Yet, down in the depths of his being there nagged a quiet voice. "There may be other lands. There may be other souls."

Rome's explorers had discovered no other lands beyond these. Everyone knew of other islands to the west of the mainland island of Britain further to the south. These were occupied places, and the tribes living there were well known. Beyond those fringing islands in the more southern west, it was the same as here, looking northwards. No one from the British mainland or these furthest islands of Thule had ever sailed yet further north or west and then returned claiming that there were other places, other peopled lands beyond these. Some had sailed out for days, even weeks, wandering in endless, terrifying seas, and returned ever marked by the horror of their experience. Others had sailed into the same endless oceans and never returned. It was always presumed that these were lost within the sea. No strangers, either had arrived witnessing by their existence to other lands in the north and the west, either.

Even so, there were signs that beyond the known world there might be, somewhere out of sight and out of the experience of men, more lands yet to be discovered. Storms brought lumps of unusual wood from unknown trees to the western coasts of Britain. Dead birds, occasionally found trapped in branches of such drifting wood, displayed plumage and form never able to be identified by those who knew all the native birds of all the world from the Mediterranean to the north. Sometimes strange husk things appeared as debris from somewhere unknown to the shores, and other times alien plants took root and grew, from seeds which had come on the wind, or in the water, from a seemingly alien world. There was a haunting feeling about that watery horizon, that it might not lead, as was supposed, to an edge of the earth where there was nothing solid, only the ocean.

They went back the way they had come, confirming the faith in those who were bursting with curiosity and full of questions, as well as in those who were confused and bewildered by the newness of a life without familiar gods and familiar ways. As they travelled along any western shorelines, Ninian kept looking out. There was one little spot of an island, just one, well to the south, out to the west, and he kept asking about it. "No one there," would come the reply. "Just sometimes visited by fishermen, just for a while." It was, to Ninian, the ultimate place on Thule. He knew that he could not rest without knowing that if anyone ever stood there, they could find a cross planted on its soil.

They reached again the beautiful islet linked by its golden shell chain of a beach to the main island. The chieftain of the place, who had embraced the truth of the gospel with a willing heart, met Ninian as he approached, and knelt before him. Ninian frowned, raising the man to his feet. "For you," said the leader of one of the communities of Thule, gesturing toward the green gem of land. "For you. Ninian. Thanks to you. Thanks to God that you come."

Ninian beamed at him. He could return to Candida Casa as the proud possessor of a paradisal foothold on Thule, if he wished, but he had no desire to own an island, even one such as this. "Thank you," he said, warmly gripping the hand of the local ruler. "For God. God's island, not for Ninian."

The chieftain bowed, assenting. He turned to his people, gathered around to witness this gift. He pointed back to the little island and cried, "God's land!" They cheered. It was good. God's land, and Ninian's joy.

As Ninian stood there, looking out over God's land, he saw again that tiny unclaimed dot on the far horizon. His brows knitted. It would not do. He must go there. He was weary, though, and the boatmen of the place explained that the journey there, to an uninhabited piece of land that was the most western part of the Thule group, was a frightening one if storms arose. No one wanted him to go. He didn't even want to go. Two of the younger, fitter men offered themselves. They would go and take a stone cross that could be engraved here, one made of the softer type of stone so freely available on the island.

All the others waited behind, trying not to be nervous, praying, watching the sea. The little curragh disappeared quickly from their sight. Days passed. Winds began to quicken, and the days began to grow shorter. Finally, the curragh was sighted again. They all ran down to the shore as it drew into the land, and there were cheers when the two bronzed, weather-beaten young men clambered ashore. The heroes grinned as they rushed through their fellows to where Ninian waited. "No people," one said. "But the cross is there waiting for whoever comes to the island. For Christ is claimed the furthest point of earth. He has conquered." They had brought back a skin of water from a spring on the island. Ninian prayed for blessing on that distant place, its spring, and the cross that waited for those who would come. "The work is done," said the men who had planted a cross on tiny Ultima Thule.

Ninian was not so sure. Something still niggled, deep inside him. "My work, " he agreed, "mine, at least, is done."

TWENTY FOUR: *Disciple All Nations*
"All power is given unto me in heaven and in earth.
Go ye therefore, and teach all nations,
baptising them
in the name of the Father, and of the Son,
and of the Holy Ghost:
Teaching them to observe all things whatsoever I have
commanded you..."
The words of Jesus Christ to His disciples
as recorded in Matthew 28, verses 18 - 20

"Many of the nobles and freemen
entrusted the education of their sons in holy scripture
to the blessed bishop.
He instructed them in knowledge
and moulded their characters........"
"Vita Niniani" by Ailred of Rievaulx (trans. by Winifred
MacQueen)

"This man, the whole glory of his own people,
studied heavenly wisdom with a devoted mind
in a cave of horrible blackness.
He frequented the path of the teacher,
giving the gifts of salvation.
He was able to understand books in the learned tongues,
from which he preached,
powerful in his words, what he fulfilled in his deeds,
and all that he taught other men,
he first of all practised himself....
To all nations and peoples alike,
who were destined to be summoned to the heavenly kingdom,
the holy man revealed worthy teaching."
"The Miracles of Bishop Nynia"
translated by Winifred MacQueen

The hours of daylight diminished as the hours of darkness increased, and soon there was a feeling of autumn chilling the islands. Ninian and his companions set out for home. God quietened the seas for their sailing, and held back the rains to firm the ground for their walking. The birds flew along in choirs beside them, dipping and diving and whirling and calling out the praises of God. The people everywhere wept their goodbyes as the teaching, preaching, singing, praying men of God passed out of sight.

They made good time travelling from Thule, southwards through the Orcades, and across to the mainland of Britain. Thule would all have seemed like a dream to them, but there were the faces of men from that island among them, youth eager to begin studies in the lands of the Novantae, new students for Candida Casa's teachings, and these were proof that it had been no dream that they had reached the ends of the earth for the Lord.

As they trudged along the coastal paths in the north, they encountered those they had previously met, taught, and blessed. There was warmth in their embrace now, people who had been, until so recently, foreigners and strangers to them and to God. Now, they were family, familiar and loved. Open where they had been distant, honest where they had been deceitful, faithful where they had been treacherous, kind where they had been cruel, fearless where they had been frightened, and always singing, they were changed for good.

There were others, though, who scuttled away at their approach. Some of those in the throngs who had confessed their sins and been washed in baptismal new beginnings had already forsaken this faith and were as mired in their old ways as before. Not all seed that was scattered produced a good harvest. Some would grow up quickly, but wither away just as quickly as if it had never been, for there was no root to the growth. Jesus had said that this would be so. Those who had preached the Word and felt exultation over every soul won into the Kingdom of Christ still sorrowed over every single failure in every single person thus lost to the fold, and prayers were made for them as they walked along, prayers mingled with tears, that these would return.

All through the land, it was the same as they passed. So many hailed them with joy and with sincere affection. This was the world outside Rome, a place that was pagan, barbarian, a place from which destroying waves of marauders had plagued the civilised world behind the shelter of Rome's walls, generation after generation. No longer so, it seemed. Even the chieftains who would delight in war and plunder found that they had no armies to command. Their people would rather sing hymns than utter battle cries, plough fields than carry swords, and raise sons to serve God than soldiers to bring them glory. It was a new world in which to breathe, and live, and work. For some, it was glorious; for others it was deeply frustrating. The latter group, those who would rather pursue the old paths, could only hope the new faith would quickly die away.

Gathering more willing scholars as they walked, the monks moved on. When Roman roads were again under their feet, they marched. The songs of Ambrose made the miles pass quickly. Leaves were golden, and rusted, and began to drop from the trees.

Like the triumphal processions in a Roman victory, the return to Candida Casa was full of celebration. People ran out along the way to meet them, cheering, calling to them, leaping and dancing. The new slaves of Christ, willing slaves of love, were not in chains so they could sing and dance with all the rest.

The nights were elongating into winter's world, but they were home safe. A great work was finished, but another would begin. Caranoc, the young prince who had followed the work from the Antonine Wall into the north and all the way back again, one of those who had gone to the farthest island off Thule, found that he could not rest. He knew the island of the Scotti, to the west of Britain, lay at the farthest point on that side of the known world. He had become convinced that for the mission of Ninian to be completed, they must be certain that the cross was planted there, and souls won from the Hibernian nation. He believed that he, one who had refused to go into battle against those people, must be the one to go to them with the gospel.

He approached Ninian with his request. The lands he coveted

for his mission could be seen from near the cave of Ninian's solitude on a clear day. They were as much within reach as the islands of the Orcades and Thule had been. Others would go with him. Ninian gave them leave, with his heartfelt blessing. He would have gone himself, if he could, but he was still too weak, and there was so much to do in overseeing the work here in his own neglected monastery.

With Bibles, staffs and a bell for calling the Scotti to prayer, Caranoc and his companions set out, quickly sailed from sight beyond the farther promontory of Tudwal's kingdom.

Much, so much, had happened in Britain and in the wider world during the short years of the missionary journeyings. Nothing seemed the same. For many days Ninian and the others were engrossed in conference with those who could tell them of all that had happened during their absence. There were letters from other parts of Britain, and from Rome, all waiting to be read and giving them much to consider.

Coel had increased his powers, like a river bursting its banks and flooding all the countryside around. It was if a peaceful river had become a devouring lake, filling all the space where it did not naturally belong, seizing and drowning what it overcame. Coel had seized all he wanted for himself and his followers, destroying everything that stood in his way. Anwn had been already humiliated by his advances, wiped out in the north, all Ninian's own family south of the wall of Hadrian forced to abandon terrain and strongholds, finally relocated to safer lands further south and west. Coel had done this in the pretence of providing greater protection for the people. Coel's son-in-law, good king Cunedda along with most of his family of fine princes, had finally been persuaded to abandon the lands against the border that touched Pictland to another area of the southwestern lands of the Britons, near Anwn's people. He had been told that he was needed there to hold the shores against more dangerous invaders.

With Anwn destroyed and other princes like Peibio and Ninian himself outwith the circles of power, the more southwestern Britons' hopes for warrior leadership had turned to Armorica, across

312

the Channel. The family established there from Conan's line had long awaited their chance to lead the nation. The most distinguished of the present generation of young royals there, Aldrien, declined the request that he assume the title of Briton's king. His younger brother, though, Constantine, had readily agreed to answer the call to the high kingship of Britain, the land of his fathers. With this power, for the sake of its security of claim, had already come his arranged marriage to Macsen's younger daughter, Severa. The Macsen and Elen line had merged with Conan's, and the joining of these powerful houses created a new and unchallengeable royal succession. Conan's line brought with it the claim of descent from the Lord's own family. Whispered rumours of divine blood mingling with the remembered claims of imperial blood made the blue blood seem bluer than ever.

Constantine the Third, seemingly proving God's favour upon the choice of him, quickly subdued the enemies of the Britons. King Niall of the Nine Hostages having earlier reached the end of his terrifying rule, the seas immediately grew calmer around the coastlines. Picts also went quiet, their ancient king spinning out his dying years, and many of his now Christian people content to live at peace with those they had tormented for so long.

While Britain seemed to settle and increase in confidence, Gaul was tormented and terrified. It was a deep, cold winter, and the Rhenus River froze solid. The great natural barrier between civilisation and the barbarian world turned into a highway of ice, broader than any ever built by Rome, and was crossed by thousands upon thousands of invaders. Nothing could stop them.

The memory of Macsen's rule over the western half of the very Roman Empire began to be recited in the ears of his son-in-law, Severa's husband. Young King Constantine III, seduced by the challenge to do what his father-in-law had done, crossed over to the Continent with all the Roman troops left in British lands, virtually every last one of them. His dream was to save Gaul and win the Empire's crowns again, to better Macsen. Queen Severa, daughter of the late Queen Elena, sister of Peibio the monk, was left to rule Britain alone.

As the months went by, more and more students arrived at Candida Casa begging to be taught by the master himself. Princes were sent by their fathers. A thorough education would make them better kings when their time came. Others came of their own volition, drawn by longings to learn to read, to understand the mysteries of God, to be trained in practical ways that would help their people.

The very same was happening, meantime, across the sea in the island of Hibernia. Caranoc and his companions had established a small branch monastery there, and the young came to them for learning. Travelling outwards through that land, sometimes opposed and sometimes welcomed, he met others who needed the message he brought. One young man, one day, was found feeding the pigs of his master. He was a Briton, rustic in his speech and ways but claiming that his had been a noble background. Carefully, patiently, Caranoc talked with the young man, teasing out of him the strange and tragic tale that he could hardly bear to share.

Succat had, indeed, been of a distinguished Romano/British heritage, but he had ignored the teachings of the faith and been rebellious against its claims during a misspent youth. He had not studied as he should, and his education was faulty. When he was sixteen, he had been kidnapped during one of Niall's raids along the coast of Briton and he had been forced to serve here as a slave for six years. Full of despair, reduced to a state of animal existence among the animals he must care for, the youth had prayed with all his heart, with all his strength, month after month. He had prayed for forgiveness. He had prayed in acknowledgement of all the claims of God he had previously ignored. He had prayed for salvation, both for his eternal soul and from his desperate plight. He had prayed morning, noon, and night, and all the times in between. Finally, peace had come to his soul, and he had begun to know the presence and guidance of God in that far off place. He blamed himself for his present suffering, for he had foolishly sinned, a grave sin, a year before his capture. God had brought him here so that he might finally come to his senses, and find his faith. Caranoc assured him that he was, indeed, forgiven, and baptised him there.

Caranoc returned to Candida Casa, full of praise to God. Ninian shared his joy. Between them they had touched all the points of all the islands they knew that lay on the outermost fringes of the world, both to the west and to the north.

For a while, all was well, secure, and dangers seemed to recede. There were gains for Rome and Constantine theThird, husband of Severa. He was recognised by the grateful Emperor Honorius as his fellow, the crown jewels sent to him in token of the fact. The peace was an illusion, and it did not last for long.

Rome was sacked. Rome was destroyed. The whole world reeled in horror at the news. The old sense of order vanished as if it had never been, in a single day. All confidence in any kind of future vanished with it. The proudest citizens of the world clutched their garments around them and fled, taking what they could, if they had time to grab anything, but grateful even to have escaped with nothing if only their lives were spared. The entire Mediterranean was seething, and distant shores were swamped by boats of refugees. Some Romans fled to Africa; some made their way, sobbing in terror, as far as the more distant Holy Land. People who for centuries had seized and milked other countries in order to feed their own increasing expectations for a sumptuous life now fled to the places they had stripped, seeking refuge in them.

Constantine the Third was killed. Britain, from which he had taken all soldiers of Rome, rebelled against his widow, Queen Severa, proud daughter of Macsen. Taking power to themselves, they raised a succession of new leaders, one after the other, rulers appointed, deposed, replaced, endlessly during a period of chaos. There seemed to be no one who could truly command rule and restore order in the island. There was no one who had the grip.

At the same time, ancient KingTalorg of the Picts died, his passing adding to the sense of turmoil everywhere. His successor was Drust, the man who had long been itching to fight —— anyone, anywhere. Drust had not converted to the new faith. He was no man of peace, and had no desire to be one. Drust had bided his time, and when he finally clambered up into the throne of the Pictish high king, he began to call on the tribes of the north to join him for war. There were wonderful possibilities open to those who now possessed the courage and vision to charge down into the lands of the dispirited Britons to conquer and plunder their riches. Britain was all like an orchard overripe. Footsteps on the grass would bring apples tumbling to their feet. The younger brother, Nechtan, too earnest a Christian, was entirely disapproving of Drust's intentions. He gathered support from others like him in spirit. Drust sent Nechtan away to distant kin who had married into the royal houses of the Scotti, hoping that they would make something of a warrior of him. Soft Nechtan was no use to the Picts as he was.

As the times grew more and more troubled, Ninian worked with increasing conviction that only in Christ was there an answer for the world's confusions and sorrows. He was focused on the preaching of the Word, the ministering of the sacraments to the people in the area surrounding Candida Casa and, even more, on the training of his students, the ordaining of priests and deacons, the consecration of bishops, the guardianship of women students too, all who were destined, in his understanding, to minister among their own peoples.

The future leaders of the land, both the young men and young women who came from influential families within all the tribal groups, must first become fluent in Latin to be of any use at all in the work of Christ. He believed that, in order to unify the land and its differing peoples, there must be a common language. Everyone must learn Latin until they were as fluent in the language of their learning and of diplomacy as they were with their own native tongues. Latin. Always Latin. Spoken Latin, written Latin, sung Latin, and recited Latin. He seemed obsessed in his insistence that his students become fluent, absolutely fluent, in the language. They called him, as they had called him in his youth, Latinus, more often than they called him Ninian.

For another, even greater, reason, the students must be fluent in Latin. It had long been decided that this language must be regarded as the universal language of worship. This had become more important than the fact that it was a universal language of government. Those Romans, or educated Britons, who ruled foreign language speakers could learn a few foreign phrases and quite adequately deal with their non-Latin speaking subjects. They did not need a whole language for that. A man could be ordered to stop, to bow, to pay his taxes, in his own tongue, quite simply, with few words, even with only gestures.

The discipleship of the Christians of the world was a different matter. The Scriptures, for a start, were large books, not just a few key phrases. No congregation could become well established in their faith if they did not have access to the whole of the Scriptures, the whole counsel of God, never mind knowledge of the prayers, the hymns, and the creeds that were employed in worship. It was a simpler task and a more efficient one to teach people of all the languages and dialects to read and speak one universal language for worship, that language obviously being Latin, than it would be to employ people for necessary lifetimes in translating all the Christian writings into all the dialects, many of which had no letters to express their sounds in written form anyway. Even if letters were invented for their linguistic sounds, all the people of all the tribes would have to learn to read them. That task was too enormous for anyone to undertake. Teaching Latin, with all the riches of learning already at the disposal of any who could study in that language, to those who would teach others, even if they translated as they taught into other languages, was a far more realistic goal.

Ninian drilled them. He was merciless. Time was of the essence. The world was changing so very, very fast, and the ends of the earth had already heard the first claims of the Gospel. Christ might return at any moment. The harvest must be secured. Learn! Learn! Latin! Perfect Latin! For some, this was a delight. They were hungry for it, and understood the need for it. For others, it was like a kind of slavery, and they chaffed as they were rebuked, found their heads aching as they strained to read and write and speak what their eyes and hands and tongues stumbled over by the light of flickering candles on long winter nights.

Troubles increased in the land. Britons turned against Britons while Rome's unifying governance receded into more distant memory. When foreigners invaded, or threatened to, there was no one to appeal to for help. Christians called out to God, but wondered if He had forgotten His world. Pagans cried out to the sun, to their rocks, to those who might hear from the bottoms of the wells or from the heights of the mountains.

There was an eclipse of the sun. The very light of the world seemed, in minutes of terrifying blackness, to have been blotted out forever. People screamed in terror, everywhere, wondering if the world would end. Some vowed to leave their lands and hastily buried golden treasures behind them as they fled, praying to old gods and the new God, all in one breath, to restore them one day to their lands and hidden hoards.

At Candida Casa, Ninian prayed his heart out. Alone in his cave on the rocky shore that looked out to a world so ravaged by so many changes, a world reeling from so many fears, it seemed to him that the Devil was challenging and overturning the whole triumph wrought in the name of Christ. Darkness, with a sickening cold dread, a wave of ugliness that caused deep, black grief, was overcoming the light that had seemed so glorious and had brought so much joy to so many believers. A fight was on in the heavenlies.

Ninian's pain was increased by the remembrance, suddenly renewed in his advancing age, that he was a prince of the Britons. It would have been expected, even as a younger son of his family, that he would have been ready to rise from obscurity to defend his people if they were ever in a time of jeopardy such as this. Though his royal birth seemed to be now forgotten by those who had once known, he knew who he was. He remembered his birthright, and its traditional responsibilities. He remembered that he had walked away from all this, to serve Christ. Such joys he had known in that service! ..... But what comfort should that be to a man who knew that he was a born leader, a leader who lived in an apparently leaderless land? Should he be huddled alone in a cave on a shore so far removed from the pain of the world of his people?

"Oh, Lord, have I done wrong?" The darkness that covered the earth covered his heart as he cried out, and waited for an answer. Slowly, but steadily, the light of the sun began to return to the Solway shore, to gleam and dance on the waves of the water, to burn its heat into the stones on the beach, and to probe its glory into the far recesses of the dark and lonely cave. Light overcame darkness. Such light as that of Christ would overcome any darkness, every darkness. All would be well, as it was well with his soul.

Caranoc was astonished and delighted one day when the British youth he had baptised in Hibernia appeared at Candida Casa. His story was an amazing one. After his baptism, prompted by voices that had urged him to leave, he had finally made his escape. In a long and terrifying ordeal, he had made his way to a coastline a great distance from where he had been held captive. Eventually managing to persuade a ship's crew to take him on board with them, he had sailed away from the place of his slavery. To his dismay, he discovered that the ship had taken him even further away from his homeland than he had been before. After disembarking, and nearly starving to death in a foreign country, he had found sanctuary in a monastery. His faith found surer footing, and he grew stronger. Finally, proving that God was with him each step of the way, even in times of further danger, he eventually found his way home to his people, a changed man.

Strangely, the conviction came to him after all this time that he must return to the land of the Scotti and tell the benighted people there, the very ones who had enslaved him, that they, themselves, were enslaved in spirit and needed the salvation of his Christ. At first he had not been able to believe that he was hearing what he was hearing from his heart. He fought against the call. When he confided to his family what he felt he was being asked to do, they pleaded with him not to go. Having suffered the grief of losing him for so long, they could not bear to lose him again. They tore at his heart with their protesting.

The voice became so strong and insistent that he knew he must follow its bidding. He had thus come to Candida Casa to learn what he must learn to work as an evangelist. He could read Latin, quite well already, he declared. He wrote less well. He needed Scriptures if he would go across the sea to share the gospel. That was why he had come here.

Caranoc had listened to the story, his heart strangely moved.

He, himself, had begun a work in that Hibernian land, and he wanted very much to return there. Now, this rough, uncouth, half terrified young man of lesser breeding than he was, one he himself had baptised, seemed to have been chosen to receive a divine call to serve God there, a call that Caranoc himself coveted. He bowed his head, and his heart, in the presence of his Lord. "Thy will be done," he prayed, and he began to prepare the young man named Succat for the work

Though his intentions had been firmly fixed, the young former slave was too impatient to study for long. His Latin was nothing like perfect yet when he declared one day that he had learned enough. His precious copied transcripts of Jerome's translations were finished and he made preparations to leave. He asked for no one's blessing, believing it was to God alone that he must answer. Caranoc could not bear to let him go, unless he could go with him. Ninian was not wholehearted in his approval, but gave the prince who had followed him a reluctant blessing as he now left Ninian to follow a student. Caranoc and Succat sailed off to the west, having agreed to divide the work of evangelism in the western island between them.

Many students came and went in the following years. Some left deeper impressions than others. A few loved the sweet spirituality of the quiet peninsula so dearly that they could not bear to leave at all, ever. Men students settled either among the monks with Ninian, in their simple huts nearer the Ket, or amongst the families in houses that had been built near the church. Women students who eventually refused to return to their families, some determined to avoid the marriages that had been arranged for them in their childhood, were given refuge in the community that had gathered with Medana a few miles to the south and west of the town.

All these, men, women, and families, met together on the Lord's Day at the church for the sharing of the Eucharist. They delighted in all the elements of all the services held there on Sundays, at morning and evening prayers, or on special occasions. The public readings from the Word of God, the repetition of creeds that established their understanding of basic truths, and the singing of hymns and psalms all blessed their souls. Visitors who heard of this place and travelled there to witness the life and work and fellowship of it were amazed and moved by the sense of God working among His people in this shining white church of the Britons.

From all throughout the north of the island, and the islands that lay offshore, as well as from the island of Hibernia in which Caranoc was gathering his own group of disciples, even from the tribes south of the wall of Hadrian as far down as the monastery established by Peibio, students had come to learn from Ninian. To these same places, accomplished ministers of the gospel had returned, in time, to work in the pattern that he had begun.

Congregations of believers met in smaller churches throughout the district, or even in open air enclosures marked as sanctuaries by the sign of the cross. The disciples of Ninian read to them from the Scriptures, taught them to sing, led them in prayer, broke for them the bread and shared the wine in memory of their Christ. They preached the gospel, prayed for the sick, rebuked those who erred from the straight paths, and pled with those who did not care if they fell away. Through their witness, many more came to believe, and some of their sons and daughters, another and younger generation, found their way to Candida Casa by the Solway waters to learn more of their faith so that they, too, might minister to yet others. The students from Candida Casa were marked by their devotion to God and their dedication to the service of others. Their Latin was usually, but not always, wonderfully fluent.

Fifth Part: Good and Faithful Servants

"....... and, lo, I am with you alway,
even unto the end of the world."
Amen
The words of Jesus Christ to His disciples
as recorded in Matthew 28, verse 20

Ninian:

For months I had lingered in Whithorn to learn the story of the great Ninian. Medana had told the tale with such eagerness, so vividly, hour after hour, week after week, and I had begun to feel that I was living alongside her memory in another time, in other places. I had never seen her friend, her teacher, her pastor, her dearly beloved Ninian, but in the light that shone from her eyes I began to feel that I could see something of his reflection. I felt that I would have known him immediately if he had walked up to join us. I would have known his face. I would have recognised his voice. I would have been familiar with his words.

Yet now, something changed in her. She began to falter. She was tired, I realised; but it was more than that. I sensed that she was becoming reluctant, as she neared the ending of the story, to revisit Ninian's death in her memory. I, too, was finding it hard to think of hearing about it. I would rather, I thought, remember the life of the man, as she had already so vividly described it to me, a life so full of brilliance and glory. Could we leave it there? Must I hear any more? Must she speak any more? Wasn't it enough, without the death?

She must have realised exactly what I was thinking. She stopped speaking, and looked squarely at me, a bit harshly. "We... must... walk... to... the... end," she said, in a stilted way, with strangely paced out words. "There was God's grace in his suffering.

322

Not a drop must fall to the ground. Every minute, every breath was precious." That was enough for that day.

On another day then, a day of utter stillness, when even the birds seemed to be hushed, Medana took her accustomed seat and I waited, dreading. "You would think," she began quietly, "that such a man would have drifted away in his sleep, wafted easily into heaven, blessed with an easy death by God because of all he had done, wouldn't you?"

I nodded, dumbly.

"No, " she sighed, and shook her head. Her eyes filled with tears, the kind that sting and burn and leave a face reddened. Pained crying, not pretty. "First there was trouble from Eira, " she said. "The people had determined that they would have young Succat as the leader of the churches, their bishop. They love him there, you know," she said, looking at me with a kind of background of argument in her tone. "He had forgiven them for so much. They had treated him badly when they captured him, but he came back with love to them. This showed them the truth of Christ's love for them." Her words had come out in a tumble. Then she spoke more slowly, "But Caranoc, poor dear man! His pride was so blasted by this choice of his own pupil over him. After all, he was a prince in Briton, a disciple of the famed Ninian, and he was even related to some of the royals of that land, never mind this land. He had powerful connections. Succat had none of these advantages, and the youth couldn't even write Latin properly. He had never completed his education."

"There was so much concern within Caranoc that he brought Succat back with him for a conference with the others about what to do. What a terrible thing it was. Caranoc knew of something Succat had done when he was scarcely more than a child. He had assured Succat that this matter, confessed and forgiven, was nothing to concern him any more, but in the light of potential elevation to power in the church in Eira, it suddenly seemed important to Caranoc again. Forgiven or not, he told the brothers here about Succat's sin."

"I don't know what it was, but I saw the results of the telling of the secret plainly enough. It was a terrible day. Succat was beside himself with shame. Caranoc was equally distressed by his own betrayal of the young man's confidence, and Ninian was trying desperately to do the right thing by both of them. He was stunned, I know, by the revelation. He seemed of the opinion that Succat, in spite of the long time that had passed between the sin and the present day, should show that he was truly penitent by accepting rebuke and submitting himself to punishment. Perhaps he thought that then Caranoc would be able to get past the deed, and that Succat would have proved his penitence was sincere. I don't know. There was so much confusion because Succat fled before they could approach him."

"He took a boat, without permission. It wasn't properly sea worthy, and everyone thought that he would drown. He left word that the sin was forgiven, that he would not be faced with it again, that God had forgiven him and so must they, that the people of Eira wanted him as bishop and bishop he would be, consecrated or not. And he was gone."

"Finally we heard that he had arrived safely there, that he had begun his work, and that the people of Eira were rejoicing in his work. Even if he took his authority in defiance, God was blessing him and there was a great harvest of souls. Ninian accepted this. Caranoc, though, was utterly distraught. He said that he was disturbed at the thought of having tried to block the work of God in another because of his own jealousy. He had betrayed his own protégé. He longed to return to work with Succat again. He didn't believe that this would be possible, that he could ever be forgiven for what he had done."

"We were all so concerned that no one noticed the decline in Ninian for what it was. Our dear bishop, abbot, our friend, began to fail in health and we were too preoccupied to see. We thought at first that he was merely saddened, as we were, or showing signs of advancing age. Then we realised that he was in pain. His body began to waste away in front of our eyes. Every day he looked worse than the day before. He tried to hide his discomfort, but in the end he couldn't. We were distressed."

"Ninian had prayed for so many people, and there had been so many answers to his prayers. Blind people could see again; deaf people could hear again; the crippled walked again; skin was made new. Why should Ninian, then, suffer like this? We couldn't understand it. We couldn't bear it."

"Some of us who loved him so dearly went to him together. We begged him to pray for himself as powerfully as he had prayed for others. We had prayed, ourselves, all of us, for him, desperately prayed, and yet he worsened. Surely if he, with his great faith, prayed for himself, he would be healed. Surely God would listen to him, if He would not hear us!"

Medana could not speak, then, for a time. She sobbed, terrible sobs. Then she was quiet for a long while.

"He said to us that all must suffer at some time, and he was no exception. This was his time, and he would bear what God would send. 'God is just, and God is good,' he said, so calmly. Once when we were alone and I was weeping, he said to me, 'Medana, I long to go to Christ.' "

"But I would not let him go," she whimpered, brokenly. "I could not release him. I was clinging on, begging God to restore him to us, just for a while longer. We all needed him. I needed him. We could not spare him. And, so, my dear Ninian suffered on, and on...... waiting for the day when we would give him our blessing to depart this life. How he suffered." She cried more, bitterly. She walked away from her stone seat and stood facing the sea. I could see how deeply she was breathing, trying to regain her composure. It was pitiful to watch her, but she needed to tell me the rest as much as I now needed to understand the ending.

"One morning," she said at last, "I found him radiant. 'Medana,' he said, 'I sensed the Lord Himself with me last night. He spoke to my heart.' "

"What did He say to you?" I asked, fearing to know. "He said, 'Come away, my dove, my friend. Come away to Me, for love's sake.'"

"I just stared at him." She stopped speaking again, and then finally went on. "I stared at him, and I waited for what else he had heard from the Lord. He said, 'I protested, Medana, but only a little. I said that my friends, my dear, loved friends, my dearest Medana among them,'" and her eyes flooded again with tears, her lips quivered, and her voice trembled, "..... ' "my dearest Medana too....... they will find it hard without me. They plead that I should stay, Lord." ' And Medana, do you know what He said to me?' I shook my head," she murmured on, speaking now through gentle sobs. "Ninian said that the Lord had told him that it was time for him to be cut away from earth's sorrows and engrafted into the glories of heaven. I put my hand on his, and I said, 'Go, my loved friend; go to Him.' He closed his eyes, and he was gone. My Ninian is with Christ," she said, and her story was done.

Medana:

When the telling of the tale was finally complete, I gathered the pages of my writings, and I made the long journey home. My family had wondered if I would ever return. My old parents and my young children were ecstatic when they saw me, but my wife was cool. To be truthful, she had reason to be. I had neglected my work and my care for my family during all the months that I had been so far away from them, even away from them in my thoughts. My wife bitterly accused me of neglect. It took some time, a great deal of explaining, and making up to her in every way that I could before she calmed down. Eventually, though, she became as absorbed by the story of Ninian as I had been, and in the end it was she who kept me at this task.

In fact, it was my wife who suggested that a copy of the completed work should be made for presentation to Medana. Carefully, so carefully, I wrote the words a second time. The pages were bound in the finest piece of hide that we could find. The precious book was wrapped, and wrapped again, to preserve it during the journey.

Just a little more than four years from the time of my first journey to Whithorn, I reached the outskirts of the place again, the place on the road where one could first glimpse, in the distance, the shape of the stone church that Ninian had built. It was suddenly like walking into a dream, for I realised that other people were gathering, walking with me along the road, silently and sadly. More appeared, walking across the fields from every side, approaching the town with me to the accompanying sound of a slowly tolling bell. This was not the Lord's Day, nor the morning or evening hours of prayer at Candida Casa, and I could not understand. There were tears on the faces of these people.

I became terrified that something supernatural had occurred, that I had stepped back into the time of my previous visit, that this moment was not the now I believed it to be, but the then, all over again. I asked a man who walked beside me, "What has happened?"

"Medana has died," was all that he could say, and he walked on, weeping aloud.

Grief overwhelmed me. I, too, began to weep, and I stumbled as I walked on, no longer steady on my feet. This time I was a mourner with all who mourned. I was no stranger. I was a son returning home to pay my respects to a dear mother.

Medana had carried on the work of her father in Christ, her best beloved friend Ninian, during these four years. One morning, she had not awakened at her usual early hour before dawn. One of her maiden companions had thought she was sleeping very sweetly, very late, but Medana did not waken. As peacefully as that, she had slipped the bonds of earthly existence. No one who knew her doubted that she was kneeling beside her Ninian, now and for eternity, in the presence of the Risen Lord whom together they had adored.

I gave my book into the hands of Caranoc. He had been summoned home to fill the shoes of his master, and of Medana. He had come unwillingly, grumpily, but with an air of resignation. His heart remained in Eira where he would rather be, alongside his own beloved pupil, Succat, preaching the gospel message. That neighbouring island, like the extreme northern and western islands of Britain, was another boundary on the edge of the known world, a place not yet fully claimed for Christ's eternal kingdom.

I went to pray at the grave of the great Ninian, and then again at the new grave of my friend Medana. Such lives, lived to the glory of God, must never be forgotten. I had done what I could, as best as I could, and I asked for God's blessing on the work of my pen.

My task fulfilled, I walked northwards on the road that led from Whithorn. A stonemason was chipping an inscription into a large block of whinstone. He was being watched at his work and instructed by Caranoc and by Barovadus, the son of Morvad, the heiress wife of Tudwal.

Throughout the world of the Roman Empire, an empire now vanishing from the earth, such stones were carved in memory of individual lives, numbering the years from birth to death. In the Pictish world, though, carved memorial stones commemorated only the years a king ruled his kingdom. The rest of the years of his life were not counted; they were buried with him in obscurity.

This stone, wrenched from the soil of the kingdom of the Novantae, a place where the two worlds of Pict and Roman met, was being inscribed with Roman lettering. It would pay tribute to the man who came from Rome to found a great church, and to his daughter in the faith who had briefly succeeded him in his work. In this place, between them, they had made a sanctuary for the people of God. His work, his rule, at Candida Casa was counted as one of thirty five years in duration and hers, as his successor, for four. No one must ever forget.

"Te Dominus Laudamus"

We praise you, Lord.

Postscript: Possibly.....

Macsen:

Historians tell us that before Constantine the Great became the Roman Emperor, he was married to, or had as concubine, a woman named Minervina. Constantine and Minervina produced a son named Gaius Flavius Julius Crispus. When he became emperor, Constantine set aside this relationship to marry a more suitably royal wife, the younger Fausta, daughter of his imperial rival Maximian.

Crispus, the set-aside son, was educated in Gaul under the skilled guidance of a worthy man, Lactanius. During the time when the children of Fausta were still very young, the young man Crispus was put to work by his father, and he excelled at all he did. As a soldier, a leader among men, a devout Christian (described as God-beloved by Eusebius) and a greatly loved charismatic figure generally, he was soon accepted by many as the natural heir to his father. There were coins struck in his honour. Crispus married, and a son was born to him.

Something strange happened then, and history cannot be clear about what that was for a very obvious reason. Crispus was executed by his father, Constantine. His wife and son disappeared entirely from public view because he was declared 'damnatio memoriae', his name and face by law to be removed from all memory and historical reference for all time. It is said that the Empress Fausta had claimed that Crispus, her stepson, had raped her.

About a year later, though she was Constantine's wife and the mother of his three young sons and his daughters, Fausta was locked into a steam bath where she died a horrible death. She, too, was declared 'damnatio memoriae'. It was rumoured by some that she had been discovered to have been lying, that she and Crispus had been involved in a consensual affair. Other voices said that she had made up the story altogether, that Crispus had been innocent of any involvement with her. She had made her claims in order to remove her popular stepson as a potential rival to her sons Constantine II, Constans, and Constantinus II. Neither her name nor that of Crispus was ever restored to favour, and the questions of guilt or innocence were never resolved publicly.

The three sons of Fausta jointly ruled their father's empire after Constantine's death, succeeded by Julian (the Apostate). After the death of Julian, the family of Constantine passed from power as a succession of soldiers were elected to be emperors by Imperial Council.

There are vague stories that the year-old son of Crispus had been removed from Gaul to a place of safety in Hispania by a trusted Hispanic knight at the time of his father's execution in 326 A.D.. This child, adopted into a Hispanic family, would thus have been regarded throughout his life as a Spaniard with 'no family'. History notes just such a Spaniard, a brilliant and charismatic soldier who eventually married the heir to the British High King's throne: Magnus Clemens Maximus, or Macsen Wledig.

Maximus, or Macsen, who is by some reckonings given a birth date coinciding with the period of the birth of the son of Crispus, must have been roughly the same age as a brilliant Roman general, a Spaniard, Theodosius the Elder. No mention can be found of the involvement of the Theodosian family with the raising of the young disowned grandson of Constantine, only that there was a "family connection" between Maximus and that family. Under the command of Theodosius the Elder, his friend and superior in rank, and the younger Theodosius, son of the General, Macsen is on record as having served some of Rome's most notable causes in Gaul, in Britain, and in Africa, establishing a considerable reputation for his effectiveness as a leader. He settled in Britain and became Britain's king by right of his marriage to Elen, daughter of the great over-king Eudaf. In the meantime, the famed Theodosius the Elder was executed, seemingly quite inexplicably, on the orders of the Eastern Emperor Valens.

Gratian, the son of the co-Emperor with Valens, Valentinian, succeeded to his father's throne of the Western Empire but did not manage to hold his entire half of the empire. He was forced by an action of the army to share his throne with his half-brother Valentinian II, just a small child.

When his uncle Valens, the Eastern Emperor died, Gratian was in a position to appoint his successor. He made Theodosius the Younger the Eastern Emperor. It seems to have been the elevation of his younger friend that created within Macsen some unexpected sense of injustice, prompting his own moves to acquire an imperial throne.

Britons began to say that Macsen's claim of right to rule was far superior to that of Theodosius (East), and even to that of the young rulers Gratian (Gaul) and Valentian II (Italy and Africa). They boasted that Macsen was the grandson of Constantine, of the gens Julia.

That this Macsen became a Western Emperor is a fact of history. His adopted British nation supported his claims and swept him to imperial power. He ruled from Trier. Though Gratian was murdered by one of Macsen's supporters, Macsen was accepted and acknowledged as Western Emperor by Eastern Emperor Theodosius, his former colleague in Rome's military machine.

Macsen had older sons by his first wife. By this time, during the years of 385 to 388 A.D., these sons would have been about the same age as Theodosius. They were named as Macsen's successors. His sons with Elen ferch Eudaf, who were younger, were granted kingship of lands in various parts of Britain. His two daughters were married into powerful royal families, one in Britain and the other to a descendant of the royal house of Conan's new sub-kingdom of Britanny.

Macsen over-reached himself in his ambitions and eventually had to be removed by Theodosius who had him killed in 388 A.D. Elen, his Empress, had been converted by the ministry of Martin of Tours when Martin had visited the Emperor Macsen in Trier during his unsuccessful appeal for the lives of heretics. After the death of her husband, Elen and her newly-devout son Prince Peibio returned to the part of Britain that is now Wales. They each established monasteries in that region and are remembered more as saints than as royals in history.

No reputable historians seem to have voiced the question of whether the famed Macsen Wledig might have been, in fact, a grandson of Constantine the Great.

I wonder.

These, then, are some of the facts, rumours and speculations that can be read about the most powerful character in Britain who lived during the generation of Ninian's father, if Ninian lived in the times of traditional memory about him.

Custennin:

Saint Ninian, Scotland's first recognised saint and missionary, was long reputed to have been born about 360 A.D. In researching the times of his traditional life, I looked for the names of men and women who would have been contemporaries of his father, probably those born in the years from about 320 to 345. I looked, also, for those who would have been the contemporaries of Ninian among those on record, any who were reputedly born between the years of 350 to 375. As I examined lists of British rulers and their families whose dates fell within those periods of time, the thought occurred to me that it was remotely possible that Ninian, himself, might appear there, somewhere, even under another name. There were so many variants of names in that period, the Celtic British forms and the Roman names all interchangeable and causing inevitable confusion. An example of this is the two names for Macsen Wledig, being his British designation, while his original name of Magnus Clemens Maximus always appeared when he was referred to in any Roman connotation.

Macsen's family provide further examples of this:

His elder son by Elen was Anwn Dynod among the British, but was also known by the Roman names of Antonius Donatus Gregorius.

His second son by Elen bore the Roman name of Constantine with the British form of Custennin. This son is reckoned to share the birth year of Ninian, 360 A.D.

The third brother of the family was St. Peibio, or Publicus, born about 362 A.D.

The two older sons of Macsen (Emperor Maximus) by his first marriage disappeared to the continent with their father and never returned, one at least having died there in battle. The younger family by Elen all settled in Britain.

Anwn was the king of the region around Carlisle as well as areas in Wales. He was pushed out of his northern kingdom by the more powerful Coel, and was eventually killed.

Peibio or Pebio gave up his claims to royalty and lived as a monk in a monastery of his establishment near the settlement that became Caernarvon.

Gratianna, the elder of two daughters, married Welsh King Tudwal.

Severa, the younger, was married to a Constantine of Conan's line from Britanny who, like Macsen, took the throne in Britain with his wife, then usurped the imperial western throne for a short time. He died in battle there. The widowed Severa was forced to marry Vortigern later in life, helping to establish the credibility of his rule.

Of all Macsen's sons and daughters, the only one about whom history is uncertain is Custennin, the one who is said to have been born in the same year as that of Saint Ninian's traditional birth. Custennin seems to have disappeared into oblivion. Yet, strangely, for all that there is nothing clearly remembered about his life, he bears the title of Saint Custennin the Great in Welsh annals.

Saint Ninian was regarded as a truly great saint in the centuries immediately following his own lifetime, and he was honoured for many more centuries afterwards.

As explained in the prologue to this work, it is always assumed now that the surviving accounts of Ninian's life are full of poetic religious exaggeration. Thus, everything that has been written about him within the last few centuries has been extremely cautious about, if not downright dismissive of, the accuracy of description within the original writings and the earlier understandings about them.

Ninian's father had been described as a king, but that was reduced to 'a local chieftain.'

Ninian was said to have studied in Rome with the finest of teachers under the personal patronage of the Bishop of Rome himself. The implications of that claim were ignored and now are usually dismissed out of hand. Some say that Ninian never went to Rome at all.

Ninian was described as having been deeply bonded in understanding with Martin of Tours, his greatest mentor. That relationship, too, has been dismissed. It is said that our Ninian never met the man.

Ninian was said to have preached the gospel to those at the ends of the earth. In modern times no academics seem to be able to believe that he went much further north than Stirling, in Scotland's central belt. The more northern place names that feature him are explained away as being of much later designation, even though they mark the sites of very early settlements and lie exactly along the line of the Roman marching roads and camps.

I would like to suggest, with a swing of the pendulum of considered possibility, that perhaps, not only might the original writings have related the truth, after all, but, even further, that the truth of the original writings may have been muted, not exaggerated in their detail.

Perhaps Ninian's father was a king, truly a king. Perhaps he was even the greatest king of the age, over-king Macsen, the man who became the Western Emperor for a few short years. If Custennin, the missing son of Macsen, might even possibly have been the same man who is remembered as the famed founder of Candida Casa, then a number of rather puzzling things about the seemingly obscure life of Ninian immediately become clearer to the understanding. The early stories gain, for the first time, a sense of consistency.

How could it have been believed that the son of a mere 'petty chieftain' in Northern Britain was so feted in Rome, even taken under the wing of a powerful and influence-loving pope like Damasus? If Ninian, however, were a son of Macsen, the British over-king and later the occupier of the throne of the Western Empire (during the last years of the life of Damasus), it would be easy to understand how such a pope would seek only the best teachers for such a prince who had arrived in his city on a high and holy mission. Even though that prince had disavowed all claims to royal title and estate in his determination to become a priest and eventually a missionary, he would still be accorded the significant respect due to his birth rank.

Not long after the death of Damasus, early during the papal reign of Siricius, Macsen was besieging and taking Rome itself. During that particular period, in fact, Ninian has been placed by some speculations in Bethlehem, not Rome, where he would be busily acquiring copies of Scripture and studying under Jerome. In one of Jerome's most famous letters to Marcella, a Christian lady friend in Rome, he tells her how many people from many countries are in the Holy Land to benefit from all that can be gleaned in visiting the actual sites connected with the events of the life of the Lord. He says, "Even the Briton is here... "The letter is dated 386, the very time when Macsen was expanding his part of the Western Empire and threatening to march on Rome.

In terms of practical reality, if Ninian were the son of Macsen, even if he were living in anonymity, it would have been far safer for him to have absented himself from the city while Rome was under siege by his own father. Macsen was despised by many, commonly referred to as a usurper from Britain even though he claimed to be a grandson of Constantine. Ninian, whether he was Macsen's son or not, and whether Macsen was Constantine's grandson or not, was a Briton, just as Macsen himself was described as being. During that particular time, besieged Romans would be less than kindly disposed toward any other Britons living in their midst.

As has been noted, the third son of Macsen with Elen, historically, was Publicus, or Peibio. This is the very name of 'the brother of Ninian' described in the "Miraculi." Ninyaw and Peibyaw were legendary brothers in the Welsh Triads. St. Peibio is well known in Welsh history. As has been related already, he and his mother, Elen, daughter of Eudaf, widow of Macsen, returned to Wales and both established monasteries there after Macsen's death. They had been converted under the influence of the famed Martin of Tours while Macsen ruled in Trier. Elen is recorded in the contemporary biography of Martin by Sulpicius Severus as having brought humiliation and rebuke upon herself by donning the garb of a servant and serving food to Martin herself out of respect to him.

If the mother and brother of Ninian had been converted under the influence of Martin while in Trier, and Ninian knew this, it makes profoundly clear the purpose of the detour he made to visit this great bishop before he returned to Britain. He would have owed Martin a great debt of gratitude for the Christianising influence upon the family he had been forced to abandon in order to follow Christ himself.

Further, the mention of Peibio, Peibyaw or Plebia in Ailred's 'Vita' is by many considered as significant with regard to Ninian's life and work. He is seen as an important figure in the story which describes him as 'one of the brethren' or 'the brother'. It is always assumed that this describes a brother monk. Is it not possible that this obviously distinguished holy man was, not only Ninian's brother monk, but an actual sibling?

Another child of Macsen was a daughter Gratianna. She married a British King named Tudwal, believed by some to be the very Tudwal who opposed Saint Ninian's work at the beginning of his ministry. This Tudwal would have been the same generation of Ninian. He was the brother-in-law of the 'shadowy' Custennin.

Another historically identifiable Tudwal of the period, the next generation down, was the son of Anwn (Antonius Donatus), the older brother of Gratianna. If this younger Tudwal were born twenty years after Ninian (and/or Custennin), he may have been twenty years old, according to the traditional timing, when Ninian established his work at Whithorn (when Ninian was aged approximately 35 years).

The stories of the encounter between the king named Tudwal and the saint, of the blindness of Tudwal, of his appeal to Ninian through a younger man, of his healing by the prayers of Ninian, and of his later faithful support of the work of Ninian, come alive when it is considered that the relationship between the saint and this king might have been, in actual fact, that of brothers-in-law, or of uncle and nephew.

This long chain of 'supposes', how ever neatly they fit and wonderfully they might enhance an understanding of the life and times of Ninian, will most likely be firmly discounted by any who would ask the naturally logical question, "Why, if this were true, would Ninian never be identified as Custennin, even after his lifetime?   Surely someone would have known the truth and mentioned it in a historical account."

There is a possible explanation for this. When people were cast out from their family, or when they abdicated from positions of responsibility and authority, there was a serious finality about the action they had taken, with a rigorous observance of its consequences. They gave up forever any ability to claim relationship with or benefit from their birthright. As was proved in the dramatic case of the son of Constantine's favoured son Crispus, dammed in memory, even the wife and children of such a person could be erased from history for all time, intentionally.

The biographer of Ninian made space for this possibility when he wrote the words he placed in Ninian's mouth : "...... I must betake me, that, going forth from my land, and from my kinsfolk, and from the house of my father, I may be deemed meet in the land of vision to behold the fair beauty of the Lord, and to visit His temple. The false prosperity of the age smileth on me, the vanity of the world allureth me, the love of earthly relationship softeneth my soul, toil and the weariness of the flesh deter me, but the Lord hath said, 'He that loveth father or mother more than me is unworthy of me, and he that taketh not up his cross and followeth me is unworthy of me.' **I have learnt, moreover, that they who despise the royal court shall attain to the heavenly kingdom.**"

I cannot prove that 'my Ninian' was Custennin, the son of Macsen Wledig, but I wonder if anyone can prove that he was not. I cannot prove that Macsen Wledig was the lost grandson of Constantine, but I wonder if anyone can prove otherwise.

There are very rich implications hidden within these possibilities. Constantine the Great established Christianity throughout his empire, endowing the often previously persecuted religion with power, riches, and security. In spite of the warning words of Christ that His Kingdom was 'not of this world', Constantine sought to make it so. With all his power and authority, he worked to establish the faith of Christ throughout the greatest empire the world had known. He is remembered for this.

Ninian, whether he was the son of an insignificant local tribal chieftain or the forgotten great grandson of Constantine, worked within an understanding that was the complete opposite to that of the famed Emperor's. Before the time of the coming of Christ to earth, the prophet Zechariah had stipulated the better way of accomplishing God's work of witness upon earth,
" 'Not by might, nor by power, but by My Spirit, says the Lord.'"

Ninian abandoned his birthright place of authority, whatever that was, within an earthly kingdom, wherever that was. He did this in order that he might personally seek to fulfil the command given by Jesus Christ that the good news of His 'otherworld' kingdom should be preached to all people, right to "the ends of the earth."

Ninian has been largely forgotten in this modern world. This is sad, for Ninian, (whoever he was), and Ninian alone, can be credited with having been the inspiration behind the preaching of the gospel message to the ends of the earth as they were marked on the Roman maps of his time. The "ends of the earth" in Roman understanding bore the name of Thule, a mysterious far northern place beyond the island of Britain, commonly believed to have been either the Shetland Isles or Iceland. In the lifetime of Ninian, no one seems to have lived in Iceland. Known groups of people did inhabit the Shetland Islands, though, and their most ancient church sites bore the name of Saint Ninian.

The Characters:

All references to well-known historical figures, places and events connected with the Roman and Romano-British worlds, Christian and pre-Christian religious history, and the Biblical/Holy Land or French narratives are bedded in commonly-accepted historical understandings. The journey of Jerome with Paula, for instance, is fully recorded in his letters. (Jerome's "Letter to Eustochium.")

The identification of Succat (Patrick) as the youth described in the 'Vita' who fled with a bishop's staff to Ireland is born of my own assumption that the tale as related by Ailred might be another perspective of an incident recounted in Patrick's own 'Confession'.

1) Historically based characters:

Ambrose = (born Aurelius Ambrosius) Bishop of Mediolanum (Milan) died 396

Anwn = son of Macsen & Elen, ruler of Solway and Welsh regions

Augustine = (born Aurelius Augustine) Bishop of Hippo in Africa, died 430

Barovadus = (named on the Latinus stone, Scotland's earliest Christian memorial) admittedly daringly speculative in regard to the given explanation of his family relationship

Brioc = the Briton, successor of Martin of Tours

Casa Community at Treves (Trier)

Coel = King of the Brigantes, husband of Ystradwal

Conan = nephew of Eudaf, king of Brittany

Cunedda = son-in-law of Coel, ruler of Lothian, Forth region, moved with his people to Wales

Damasus = Bishop of Rome, died 384

Drust and Nechtan = brothers, Kings of Picts

Elen = daughter of Eudaf, wife of Macsen, empress and saint

Eudaf = ancient High King of the Britons under Rome

Jerome = (Eusebius Hieronymus), Doctor of the Church, died 420 in Bethlehem

Jewish communities in Treves (Trier) and Rome

Macsen Wledig = British name of Magnus Clemens Maximus, Spanish soldier, British king, usurper, claimant of descent from Constantine the Great, a Julian, died 388.

Marcellina = sister of Bishop Ambrose and Satyrus

Martin of Tours = died 397; also, Brioc

Ninian = traditionally, died 431/2

Paula with her daughters Blesilla and Eustochium,

Peibio = son of Macsen and Elen, brother of Anwn, Custennin, Gratianna and Severa, monk and saint

Pelagius = influential 4th/5th British theologian accused of heresy.

Siricius = Bishop of Rome in succession to Damasus, died 399

Succat = Saint Patrick of Ireland, bishop from 431, died 461?

Symmachus = (Quintus Aurelius Symmachus), champion of paganism in the Senate, died 410

Emperor Theodosius = son of famed Spanish General Theodosius

Tudwal, King of Dumnonia (S.W. England, Wales), husband of Gratianna, brother of Ystradwal

Tudwal, son of Anwn, nephew of Peibio, Gratiana, Severa and Custennin; his wife Morfud (Morvad), princess of Garth Madryn; their son, Tudrig (and ? Barovadus)

?? and Medana

2) *Fictional characters:*
Devorah

Lugo and his family

The old priest in Britain and Rome, and the young priest in Britain

Incidental unnamed characters, such as the vegetable seller in Trier, the youthful Alpine guide, and unnamed converts of Ninian's mission

and Medana???

Glossary of terms and geographical names:

In general, Latin names and terms have been used throughout the book. Examples of exceptions are the deliberate anachronistic use of "Solway" (estuary), "Whithorn"(town), and "Ket" (burn). Roman terms for some places were either too unwieldy, confusing, unfamiliar or uncertain to be acceptable in creating for a reader the sense of the place as it is now. Apologies to purists.

Abus Fluvius = Humber River

Albion or Britannia = Island of Britain

Armorica = Britanny, extreme northwest corner of Gaul (France)

The Alpes = The Alps

Attacotti = One of the northern British tribes beyond the Roman boundary walls

Barbarians = people outwith the boundaries of the Roman Empire, implying uncivilised

Bodotria = Fort, Estuary and River

Candida Casa = The religious foundation established in Galloway, southwest Scotland, by Ninian

Cluith = Clyde River, Scotland

Coracle/Curragh = Celtic hide boats; coracles for up to three people, curraghs for more

Dubris = Dover

Dumbritton = Dumbarton on the Clyde River

Eboracum = York

Eamontum = Eamont River, Cumberland

Eren River = River Earn

Galil = the Galilee area of the Holy Land

Gaul = Roman Province between the Rhine and Spain, all of France, Belgium, Luxembourg, etc.

Gentiles = according to the Jewish religion, all people of the world who are not Jews

gens = Roman family name

Hibernia or Era = Ireland

Hispania = Spain as a Roman Province

Icena = Cree River

Ituna = Eden River (also the estuary, but the modern designation of Solway is used in the book)

Leucophibia = probably Whithorn (modern name used)

Levant = the whole area of the Eastern Mediterranean, including the Holy Land

Liger = River Loire

Lindum = Lincoln

Locociacum = Liguge (secret river = The Clain)

Londinium = London

Luguvalium = Carlisle

Lugodunum = Lyons

Mediolanum = Milan

Manavia = Isle of Man (also Anglesey)

Mosella = the Moselle River

Natzaret = Hebrew version of Nazareth

Novius = (Nouius) Nith River

Oppidum = a defined area/settlement used by Romans for trading with native peoples

Padus = Po River

Pax Romana = The Roman Peace from 27 B.C. to 180 A.D.

Pictavia = (Roman Lemonum) Poitiers

Picti/Picts = people of modern day Scotland, mostly north of the Antonine Wall

Pontifex Maximus = supreme figure of authority over all religion in pagan Rome; later, supreme authority over Christianity in the Christianised Roman world

Rhenus = the Rhine River and valley

Santones = Saintes in France

Scotti = people of Ireland

Sepphoris = Zippori, Herod's Galilean capital city

Shavuot = Jewish festival better known in Christendom as Pentecost

Shofar = Jewish trumpet, used in ceremonial worship or in battle

Tamesis = Thames River

Tava = (Taua) Tay River

Tavor = Mount Tabor in the Galilee

tel = mound formed over the abandoned remains of an ancient settlement or habitation

342

<u>Treves</u> = (Roman Augusta Treverorum) Trier, Germany

<u>Tueda</u> = Tweed River

<u>Turones</u>/ Turonensis = Tours

<u>Valentia</u> = a buffer state established in northern Britain in the time of the Emperor Valentian

<u>Vannetais</u> = (Roman Darioritum) Vannes in Britanny, France

<u>wadi</u> = desert country river course and bed, dry except in rainy seasons

<u>Yeshua</u> = Hebrew name of Jesus (Messiah = Ha Mashiach, Hebrew word for Christ, anointed one)

Bibliography:

The Holy Bible (various translations: including Authorised Version, Interlinear Greek-English New Testament, Complete Jewish Bible, NIV)
"St. Ninian: A Preliminary Study of Sources"
by Mrs. N.K. Chadwick (D&G.N.H.&A.S. Vol.xxvii.)
"St. Nynia" by John MacQueen +**"A Translation of 'The Miracles of Bishop Nynia'"**
by Winifred MacQueen (Polygon, 1990 and Birlinn, 2005)
"St. Ninian, Apostle of the Britons and the Picts"
by Archibald B. Scott
"Archaeological Light on the Early Christianizing of Scotland"
by G. A Frank Knight (James Clarke & Co. Ltd, 1933)
"Whithorn & St. Ninian: The Excavation of a Monastic Town 1984 - 91" by Peter Hill (Whithorn Trust, 1997)
"Wild Men and Holy Places" by Daphne Brooke
(Canongate, 1994)
"Candida Casa" by Rev. William Cumming Skinner
(David Winter & Sons, 1931)
"Two Celtic Saints:
"The Life of St. Ninian"by Ailred, and
"The Life of St. Kentigern" by Joceline
(Llanerch Enterprises, 1989)
"The Early Church"; (Pelican History of the Church, Part 1) by Henry Chadwick ; Penguin, 1967
"The Story of the Church" by A.M. Renwick (Inter-Varsity Fellowship, 1958)
"Eusebius — The History of the Church from Christ to Constantine" trans. G.A Williamson (Penguin, 1989)
"St. Jerome: Select Works and Letters":
"The Nicene and Post-Nicene Fathers of the Christian Church," 2nd Series, Vol. VI;
Ed. Philip Schaff, D.D., LL.D. & Henry Wace, D.D. (T. & T. Clark, Edinburgh, 1966)

"Jerome, His Life, Writings and Controversies" by J.N.D. Kelly (Harper & Row, 1975)

"Rome of the Pilgrims and Martyrs" by Ethel Ross Barker (Methuen & Co. Ltd, 1913)

"The Oxford Dictionary of Saints"; Second Edition by David Hugh Farmer (Oxford University Press, 1988)

"The Pelican History of the Church" by Henry Chadwick (Penguin Books, 1967)

"History of the Decline and Fall of the Roman Empire" by Edward Gibbons (on-line)

"The First Man in Rome" by Colleen McCullough (Avon Books, 1990)

"City Guide: Rome" (Blue Guide) by Alta Macadam (A & C Black, 2000)

"Historical Atlas of Ancient Rome" by Chris Scarre (Penguin, 1995)

"Vies des Bienheureux et des Saints de Bretagne" by M. de Garaby (J.-M. Williamson, Nantes)

"Martin of Tours" by Christopher Donaldson (Canterbury Press, 1997)

"Menhirs and Dolmens; Megalithic Monuments of Brittany" by Pierre Roland Giot (Editions Jos, 1990)

"The Oxford History of Britain" edited by Kenneth O. Morgan (Oxford University Press, 1988)

"Britannia, A History of Roman Britain" by Sheppard Frere (Routledge & Kegan Paul Ltd., 1967)

"Roman Britain and the English Settlements" by Collingwood & Myres; Second Edition (Oxford University Press, 1945)

"Hadrian's Wall" by David J. Breeze and Brian Dobson (Penguin Books, 1991)

"The Antonine Wall" by Anne S. Robertson (Glasgow Archaeological Society, 1968)

"Notes on Brampton Old Church" by John Robinson, B.Arch, A.R.I.B.A (Transactions of the Cumberland & Westmorland Antiquarian & Archaeological Society, Volume LXXXII, 1982)

"**Gildas, The Ruin of Britain and other works**"
ed. & trans. by Michael Winterbottom;
"History from the Sources" series (Phillimore & Co., 1978)
"**Bede; A History of the English Church and People**" trans.
by Leo Sherley-Price (Penguin, 1968)
"**The Anglo-Saxon Chronicle**" trans. by G.N. Garmonsway
(Everyman's Library, 1962)
"**The Church of Scotland, Past and Present**",
Edited by Robert Herbert Story, D.D.. F.S.A.
(William McKenzie, 1890)
"**The Early Chronicles Relating to Scotland**"
by Sir Herbert Maxwell (James Maclehose & Sons, 1912)
"**The Celtic Placenames of Scotland**" by William J. Watson
(Birlinn, 1993)
"**The Druids**" by Nora K. Chadwick
(University of Wales Press, 1965)
"**Celtic Britain**" by Charles Thomas (Thames & Hudson, 1997)
"**The Pictish Nation, Its People & Its Church**"
by Archibald B. Scott (T.N. Foulis, 1918)
"**Exploring Scotland's Heritage; Fife and Tayside**"
by Bruce Walker and Graham Ritchie
(Royal Commission on the Ancient and Historical Monuments of
Scotland, 1987)
"**Sources for the Early History of Ireland, An Introduction
and Guide**"
(Vol I, Ecclesiastical) by James F. Kenney, Ph.D.
(Columbia University Press, N.Y., 1929)
"**Patrick, The Pilgrim Apostle of Ireland**"
by Maire B. de Paor PBVM (Veritas, 1998)
On-line studies:
http://www.newadvent.org/cathen/ on-line Encyclopaedia
http://www.smithcreekmusic.com/Hymnology/
Latin.Hymnody/Ambrose.html —A hymn of Ambrose, chapter
14: From the Liturgia Horarum. Translation: Poet Laureate Robert
Bridges (1844-1930), Yattendon Hymnal (1899).
http://www.abbamoses.com/months/september.html (Orthodox
calendar of saints)

http://pomog.org/default.html?psalter/k2.htm (from Psalm 24, Orthodox Psalter; Holy Transfiguration Monastery's translation of the Septuagint, made available by Protection of the Mother of God Church, Rochester NY.)

http://www.celticorthodoxy.org/warren007.shtml (Celtic Orthodoxy: "The Liturgy & Ritual of the Celtic Church" by F.E. Warren)

http://www.stevebulman.f9.co.uk/cumbria/diocese_ferguson2.html ("Diocesan Histories: Carlisle" by Richard S. Ferguson , Chancellor of Carlisle)

http://www.kessler-web.co.uk/History/KingListsBritain

http://www.britannia.com/bios/ebk/ (work of David Nash Ford)

http://freepages.genealogy.rootsweb.com/~jamesdow (genealogies of early British kings)

http://www.hatii.arts.gla.ac.uk/MultimediaStudentProjects/98-99/9808220d/pro/roman/anton/anton1.htm

http://www.romanmap.com/htm/ptolemy/ptol.htm (Roman sites in Scotland)

http://penelope.uchicago.edu/Thayer/E/Roman/Texts/Strabo/3B*.html (Strabo: Latin rights/ Celts)

http://www.mimas.ac.uk/~zzalsaw2/pictish.html (The Pictish Chronicle)

http://www.nls.uk/digitallibrary/map/early/blaeu/index.html

http://www.st-andrews.ac.uk/institutes/sassi/spns/rnames.htm (Roman place names)

Personal Acknowledgements:

I wish to warmly acknowledge and sincerely thank:

Forrest, my companion in all the journeying,
for his whole-hearted support in this search for Ninian,

Kaye and Christy, for the cover,

Ina Munro for strengthening encouragement during the first
stages of writing,

Jean Smithson for her careful reading of the completed work,
and the blessing of her heartening words,

Patrick Bealey, a Quaker friend, for the sharing of incomparable
insights,

Janet Butterworth and the Whithorn Trust: Candida Casa,

Dr. Jane Murray (Prehistory in Galloway),

Brother John Hugh Parker (4th Century Rome),

Mr. T. C. McCreath (Scotland's agricultural landscape),

Mrs. Margaret Sheriffs of Innermessan Farm,

Elizabeth Macleod at the Iron Age House, Bosta,
Isle of Great Bernera, Lewis,

My publisher, Beverley Chadband, a true godsend,
and her editorial right hand, Sue Liddon

and all the other greatly appreciated people who have kindly assisted
along the way.

MAP 2

North Britain
The Mission of Ninian